Christopher Wood was born in Lambeth, South London in 1935. He was educated at Kings College School, Wimbledon and Peterhouse, Cambridge where at times of epidemic he occasionally played rugby for the university. He did his National Service in the Royal Artillery and was a Second Lieutenant in Cyprus during the EOKA troubles. His experiences encouraged him to write his second novel *Terrible Hard Says Alice*. After university he was one of those recruited by the Colonial Office to help organize a plebiscite in the then British protectorate of the Southern Cameroons in West Africa. Material gathered on this trip formed the basis of his first novel *Make It Happen to Me*.

At various times Christopher Wood has been a mason's mate, postman, waiter, ice-cream salesman, goods porter, warehouseman and advertising executive. He has written a number of books and the screenplays for seven films including the last two James Bond epics *The Spy Who Loved Me* and *Moonraker*. He has also written for television and radio. Christopher Wood is married with three children and has homes in Italy and France.

Singapore,

18 April 1983

Christopher Wood

Fire Mountain

Futura Publications Limited

A Futura/Jade Book

First published in Great Britain by
Michael Joseph Limited in 1979

First Futura Publications edition 1979

Copyright © Christopher Wood 1979

TO MY FRIENDS AT THE
PORT MORESBY SQUASH CLUB

ISBN 0 7088 1465 4
Printed by
William Collins Sons & Co Ltd
Glasgow

Futura Publications Limited
110 Warner Road, Camberwell
London SE5

To my friends at the
Port Moresby Squash Club

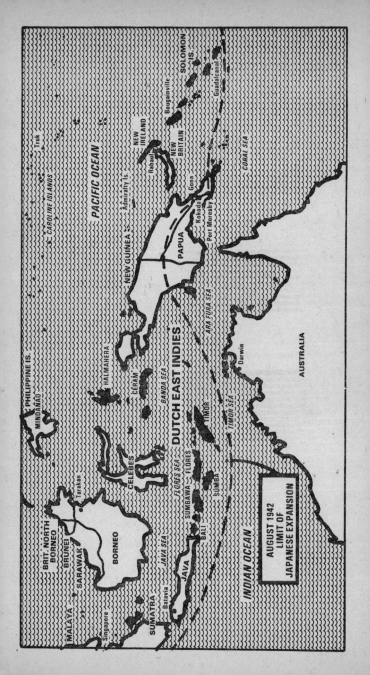

The year has gone
And also many friends
The lost, the uncounted,
The dead

*General Isoruku Yamamoto, architect
and presiding genius of the Japanese
attack on Pearl Harbor, wrote this poem
to commemorate its first anniversary*

Prologue

The footsteps echoed hollowly down the long marble corridor. It was ten past one and most of the outer offices were empty. Only the occasional secretary, enslaved by urgent business, pecked resentfully at her typewriter. The others were at lunch. The doors of the inner offices were usually closed, although some occupants could be seen sitting at their desks with chin cupped in hand or gazing pensively at wall maps. Certain people found the lunch hour a good time to put plans together.

'Mr Knox.'

Frank Knox looked up from his desk which bore a card carrying his name and the legend 'US Navy Secretary'.

'Hello, Tom.' He took the buff folder from the cipher clerk and glanced at the Decoding Department classification. A green tag—it was not considered top priority.

'Interesting?'

Tom Miles wobbled his head from side to side equivocally. He showed no sign of going away so Knox opened the file and read the sheet of paper that it contained.

> *Radio Interception Post, Dutch Harbour, Aleutians. Signal Intercepted 0840 hours, 14 April 1943. From Flagship Musashi, Truk. To Commanders Japanese Garrisons Rabaul and Bougainville. Admiral Yamamoto accompanied by Chief of Staff and seven general officers leaves Truk for troop inspections 0800 hours 15 April stop arrive Rabaul 1630 hours stop leave 1400 hours 18 April stop arrive Bougainville 1745 hours stop ultra secret document not to be copied or filed stop to be destroyed after implementation stop.*

Knox closed the file and looked up at Miles. 'He flits around, doesn't he?' he said. 'I guess he's boosting the troops' morale.'

'I'd like to boost his morale,' said Miles vehemently. 'Boost it right up his little yellow ass.'

'Sure, Tom,' said Knox patiently. He threw the file into the middle of the three trays in front of him.

'You know, in the old days that man wouldn't still be alive,' said Miles.

Knox turned over a page of the report he was reading and hoped that Miles would get the message. Some people never seemed to have a lunch to go to. 'What do you mean, Tom?'

'Well, they used to have single combat, didn't they? The commanders went out and fought each other in front of their men.'

'We don't do that any more,' said Knox.

'I don't know why not,' said Miles. 'I can think of two thousand men who'd like to have a crack at Yamamoto. They're lying dead at the bottom of Pearl Harbor. The fact that he's still alive is an insult to their memory.'

'That's right,' said Knox. He returned to his report and then, his mind triggered by something Miles had said, reached out and retrieved the buff folder.

'I'll be getting back,' said Miles. He paused at the door. 'You ought to eat something once in a while.' His footsteps started to echo away down the corridor.

'So ought you,' said Knox belatedly, his mind on other things.

He reread the times on the signal with growing excitement. *Arrive Bougainville 1745 hours.* Allowing for the time change, there was over twenty-four hours before Admiral Yamamoto arrived at Kahili airstrip on the island of Bougainville. Yamamoto was renowned for his punctuality.

Knox crossed to the wall map and sought the nearest US air base to Bougainville. Henderson Field on the island of Guadalcanal, approximately four hundred miles away. Knox frowned. He asked the operator for a number and tapped his fingers impatiently while he waited. The telephone rang and a hard, flinty voice sounded on the end of the line.

'Charles Lindbergh.'

Lindbergh, the first pilot to conquer the Atlantic solo, was adviser to the US Air Force on long-distance flying.

'Frank Knox here, Chuck. I need your advice. It's urgent. Would a P-38 flying out of Henderson Field carry enough fuel to make an interception over Bougainville and get back to base?'

'Hang on.' There was the sound of papers being shifted. Knox could imagine Lindbergh hurriedly making calculations on whatever surface was available to him. 'No. Not without extra fuel tanks.'

'How long would it take to fit them?'

Another pause. 'If you had the tanks it would take about ten hours. What did you have in mind, Frank?'

Frank Knox took a deep breath and found that he had underlined 'Bougainville' so hard that his pen had gone through the paper.

'I'm calling it Operation Vengeance,' he said. 'We're going to go after Yamamoto.'

I

Hudson screwed up his tired eyes and peered into the darkness. The sea was running high before a strong south-westerly, and the waves thumped in against the beach like body blows. Behind them was the heavy gunfire of the surf breaking over the reef. Black whirls and eddies ran like rumour through a lynch mob and the great weight of water stirred menacingly in the trough between shore and unseen coral. There was no peace or pity in the sea tonight, rather a mean, hungry spirit that roamed the shoreline restless for mischief.

Hudson looked at the dimly glowing numerals of his watch. Sixteen minutes past midnight. The submarine was sixteen minutes late. He began to recite a list of reasons for delay assembled from previous operations: engine trouble, inaccurate charts, difficult currents, Japanese patrol boat in area, submarine attacked en route to rendezvous point, submarine sunk. If only, just once, there could be an answering stab of light in reply to the first signal.

Hudson rose to his feet and held the flashlight above his head. There was a danger that with such a high sea running his signals were not being seen above the swell. He adjusted the red glass shield and switched on the light. One—two—three—four—five—off. He waited for as many seconds, his stomach tensing with anticipation. A flying fox exploded from a palm far above his head and the sound of the sea continued to drown the muted rustlings of the jungle. Before him—nothing. No answering flash. If the wind got up much more it was going to be impossible to use the inflatable dinghies. He sank to his haunches and looked down the line of palms tilting unevenly over the shelving beach. There was no sign of Joe, who he had posted to give warning of approaching Japanese patrols. His nostrils were spiked with the scent of rotting vegetation that even the stiff breeze off the sea could not banish, and the sickly smell carried with it premonitions of death, to which he was not accustomed. He had always thought about the job, never the consequences. Now he was thinking about both. Maybe it was a sign of getting old. You were supposed to get wiser as you got older, and not many additional years were needed to work out the odds against making eight secret landings on Japanese-held islands without something going wrong. Seriously wrong.

As if ripped with a knife, a narrow slit appeared in the clouds and the moon shone through, revealing the two horns of jungled headland that enclosed the bay. Tongue-licks of spent waves gleamed against the wet sand, and, fifty yards away, sprayed fingers of fresh water showed where the wasted, dry-season river now trickled listlessly into the ocean. The beach seemed empty but with the same intimation of impending action as a darkened stage. Hudson looked at the shadows and felt uneasy. Dried palm fronds slithered in the breeze and an orchestra of insects tuned up for a concert always pre-empted by the coming of daylight. The vent in the sky closed and it was dark again.

Hudson had chosen the bay because the river bed afforded a passable route into the razor-back mountains of the interior. The island was fifteen miles wide here, and two listening posts could be established on the northern and southern shores sending back information on Japanese shipping movements and the aircraft that passed overhead. Now they had been told to pull out—those that were left of them. Why? What was happening on the wider front of the Pacific war to prompt their recall?

Hudson looked at his watch again. Twenty-five minutes past the hour for rendezvous. He stood up and, keeping in the shadow of the palms, exposed the red light for five seconds. God help them if there was a Japanese vessel out there relaying the position of the strange red light to a shore patrol.

'*Tabauda*!'

Hudson was starting to turn as Joe called to him from the shadows. His ears, tuned by months of existing in the jungle were almost the equal of his native scout and sensitive to any unusual sound or movement. Hudson was not an easy man to creep up on.

13

'Jap-pan.' Joe's finger was pressed against his broad, flat nose and his head turned down the beach towards the river.

'Me smellim Japan, close-to.'

Hudson did not pause to ask questions. Joe was a human bloodhound who could pause on a jungle track and say how long since a Japanese patrol had passed down it. 'Bring Mr John, one time.'

Joe disappeared amongst the palms and Hudson tried to stay cool. It was not unusual for the Japs to send a patrol along the beach. They knew that coast-watchers were operating on the island and that they were taken off by submarine. It was just bad luck that they had chosen this particular stretch of coast on this particular night—or was it? Maybe his signals had been seen or perhaps the natives had discovered the hidden raft and alerted the Japs. If the latter, why hadn't the Japs been waiting in ambush?

'Yes, Skip?'

Hudson did not turn. His worried eyes were trying to break through the darkness to the north. 'Is the wireless hidden?'

'Yep.'

'Stay here with me. Don't open fire unless I do. We'll let them go past.' He turned to Joe. 'You savvy?' Joe nodded.

'Supposing they got dogs?'

Hudson lied for his own comfort. 'We'd have heard them.'

Two coast-watchers on a nearby island had recently been tracked down by dogs, tortured and executed. He took the wireless operator's sleeve and pulled him back towards the shallow trench made where a coconut palm had been uprooted. At least they were all together. If it came to a shoot-out they wouldn't be firing at each other. He had seen it happen too many times in night operations. He stepped back carefully into the trench and placed the flashlight at his feet. The others settled in beside him. All were equipped with American carbines, lighter than the bulky Lee-Enfield 303 and carrying more rounds. Hudson unbuttoned the restraining strap on his Colt 45 and waited. He was feeling better now. The sense of impending danger buoyed him up.

Beside him, Joe waited in the darkness. Joe would have been a giant in any company. He stood a shade beneath six and a half feet and was a Tolai from near Rabaul on the island of New Britain—three hundred miles from the east coast of New Guinea and where the Japs were amassing men and armaments for what appeared to be the inevitable assault on Australia via the stepping stone of New Guinea. The flesh across his shoulders appeared to be mounted on a girder and the slabs of muscle on his chest lunged forward like the gleaming, hand-beaten steel of a suit of armour. His not-so-distant forbears had been inveterate warriors and cannibals, and few missionaries or survivors of shipwrecks had taken one step ashore without finding the second leading them into a cooking pot. Whatever violent tendencies he had inherited from his ancestors—and there were many—were amply catered for on Hudson's coast-watching forays into the islands that overlooked the shipping approaches to Rabaul. Hudson watched Joe sliding his long fingers along the barrel of his beloved carbine and willed them to stay away from the trigger.

Leading Wireless Operator John 'Jeremiah' Johnson was the youngest member of the party and a survivor of the Australian garrison over-run when the Japs had taken Rabaul. He had escaped into the jungle, been captured and escaped again. It was something he chose not to talk about although sometimes he slept badly and mumbled incoherently in his sleep. Now he was very much awake, his head cocked for the first sound of approaching footsteps.

Hudson looked up through the swaying coconut palms and frowned. The cloud cover was beginning to break up, and a growing luminosity meant that the moon would appear at any moment. He strained his eyes into the darkness and nudged Joe, tapping his nose. Joe nodded vigorously. They were coming. How many would there be? Four? Five? Not more. The whole Japanese garrison on the island could not be in excess of thirty men. With any luck they would file past and head for the native village two miles away. Most probably they were after rice or women—or both.

There was a chink of metal from the beach. As if alerted by it the moon came out, splashing light through the gaps between the trees. Hudson shrunk down and saw the head and shoulders of the first Jap. His forage cap was pulled low over his eyes and he was carrying a rifle with bayonet fixed. He was also looking about him intently.

Hudson's fear of betrayal or discovery increased. The Jap was keyed up, as if walking through a minefield. Hudson felt Joe stiffen beside him. They were all like cats tensing as a mouse emerges from the wainscoting. Hudson placed a restraining hand on Joe's shoulder as a second Jap appeared, no less wary than the first. They were moving slowly along the very fringe of the beach, ducking under the leaning palms and passing within twenty feet of Hudson's position. A pause, then a third Jap appeared. Hudson tried to remember when he had last seen three of the enemy. You found their tracks, sometimes you heard them, but in the jungle you seldom saw them.

The Japs began to move on and Joe's hand closed about his bush knife. He turned and looked up into Hudson's face with an expression of pleading that was simple to read: 'We are three and the odds are equal. Let us wipe them out. We can cut them down silently within seconds.'

Hudson shook his head. It was too risky. One shot could bring more Japs and scare off the waiting submarine—if it was waiting. He frowned and prepared to send Joe to track the patrol until it was safely beyond the headland. Then he paused. Another Jap had appeared. The patrol had been split into two. It certainly looked as if they were expecting trouble. The fourth Jap was carrying a rifle and bayonet; and the fifth and sixth, a wireless set and a machine gun respectively. Six men. That made a radical difference to the odds. Hudson breathed deeply and tried to stay calm.

Johnson turned to look at him inquiringly, but he made no gesture.

As if left behind and hurrying to catch up, a seventh Jap appeared upon the scene. An officer carrying a sword, he made angry, clucking noises that arrested the rest of the party. He appeared agitated and spoke urgently, jabbing with his sword for emphasis. His voice, though soft, was thick and guttural, and vibrated like a bone stuck at the back of his throat. Whatever he was saying made his men look around them anxiously, and Hudson wondered whether they were being asked to remember the position of the hidden raft. Perhaps the natives had indeed found it and reported back to their new master. This party might well have been sent out to locate the raft and mount an ambush around it. The Japs would believe, rightly, that Hudson and his party had pushed on into the interior, planning to return to their boat when the mission was completed. If they got there first . . .

Hudson shrunk back involuntarily as the Jap with the sword suddenly pointed his weapon towards their position. It was if he knew exactly where they were and was urging his men forward. Joe started to raise his carbine with an audible noise before the officer turned in the opposite direction and gestured down the beach. He was hectoring his men, no doubt as to the position of the raft, which was, in fact, within fifty yards of where they crouched. Hudson felt Johnson's eyes boring into him and wondered what was the best thing to do. Gathered together with ten feet separating them, the Japs made a perfect target. At any minute they might fan out into the jungle, and engagement would become inevitable. Why not strike now whilst the element of surprise was in their favour? Hudson wondered why he was hesitating. Could it only be his fear of driving off the submarine that had come to pick them up? A strange paralysis gripped him. His mind refused to function with its customary incision. It was almost as if he was—

A bright yellow light stabbed from the seaward darkness and was immediately seen by the Japanese. It must be the submarine. Why the hell had it suddenly signalled, after making no reply? Hudson did not allow himself time to think. He rose to his feet and levelled his automatic carbine at the back of the machine gunner. A short burst and the man fell forward. The officer spun round screaming, '*Banz*—' The second syllable never left his lips as Hudson's bullets hit him in the chest. He swayed and dropped forward onto his knees, still clutching his sword.

Two more Japs went down as the others opened fire, and a third launched himself forward bravely, taking up his leader's war cry, '*Banzai*!' He charged towards the trench, seemingly supported by the bullets that were thumping into him. Only at

17

the last second did he falter and fling out his arms, throwing his rifle clumsily like a heavy lance. The bayonet stuck in the sand beside Hudson, and the Jap buckled at the knees and fell on top of him. He stank of stale sweat and urine, and his body trembled like that of a dying bird. Hudson shrugged him aside and tried to get a sight of the remaining Japs. One was being chased through the palms by Joe. The other? A bullet passed within inches of Hudson's nose. He spun round to find himself under fire from a dune thirty yards away. Two more streaks of flame and Johnson swore and clutched his upper arm. Blood welled through his fingers.

'Keep him busy. I'll work round the side.'

Johnson nodded and threw himself forward against the sand, sliding out his rifle with his good hand. Hudson started to slither out of the back of the trench, climbing over the still-moving body of the dying Jap. His mouth was open in the rictus of death, displaying metal teeth. Hudson crawled over the rim and quickly behind the fallen palm. Johnson unleashed a couple of shots and then there was a sudden silence, broken only by the moans of one of the wounded Japs. Hudson looked about him. No sign of Joe. He would be after the man who had fled into the trees. If he got back to camp the rest of the Japs would arrive in force.

A sudden burst of machine-gun fire exploded in Hudson's ears. For a moment he thought that more Japs had appeared upon the scene. He braced himself and then realized that the burst was coming from directly in front of him. He raised his head and saw that the Jap officer had managed to manoeuvre the machine gun across the body of his dead comrade. He was clinging to the trigger doggedly and unleashing one continuous burst that was kicking up a sandstorm around Johnson's position. There was no question of aiming, rather a last-gasp determination to carry on the fight with every resource available. Even as Hudson watched, the nose of the machine gun tilted forward and it fired into the sand inches before the muzzle. The sound became muffled and then died out altogether, along with the man responsible for it. His legs stretched out and he pushed the machine gun forward into the sand, as if thrusting it into the bodies of his enemies.

Silence. Save for the wind and the sea and the moans. No ugly jagger of automatic fire. Hudson's nostrils were filled with the sweet smell of some unseen jungle flower. Not for the first time he marvelled at how the presence of death can excite and sharpen the senses. With blindness one's powers of hearing grow, but with the threat of total extinction all feelings magnify and throb like a visual heart-beat. All is terrifyingly identifiable. The stench of the dying Jap was his stench. An amalgam of fear and foul linen. They were all the same here. When you saw a man dying you saw yourself.

Hudson cleared his mind and edged forward. A shot from the right told him that the Jap behind the dune was still in position. Johnson replied with two shots. Hudson continued to move warily. The Jap must know what was going to happen. He was pinned down and out-numbered. His only hope was that reinforcements arrived before somebody got behind him. A bullet struck splinters from a palm in front of Hudson. It was too far away to be aimed specifically at him. The Jap was trying to discourage anybody working round his flank.

It was as Hudson had imagined. War was chess played on a bloody board and the opening gambits were mechanical. He tilted his head and raised it slowly, until one eye was above the level of the grass-spiked sand. The dune swelled minimally but there was no sign of the Jap. Was he still there or had he made a dash for the jungle? Impossible. There would have been a burst of fire from Johnson.

Hudson looked up at the sky. A bank of cloud was approaching the moon. Within thirty seconds the beach would be in darkness. It would be his chance to get in behind the Jap. He would move round another twenty feet behind the cover of the palms and try and line up his exact position. There was a danger of being caught if Johnson opened fire, but this was not likely. Johnson would not waste ammunition. There was too little of it left.

Hudson held his rifle in his two hands and edged forward, his chin against the sand. Something alive moved across his fingers and scuttled away. Probably a land crab. He paused and listened for a moment before continuing.

The wind was now tearing at the palms, and they were bucking and rearing like frightened animals, the shades of their branches pawing at the beach. Hudson measured the distance to the next palm and wriggled forward again. What had they called this at the training camp? Bloody leopard crawl?—or something equally stupid. God help all middle-aged leopards who had to do it.

He reached the tree and peered down towards the beach. Now he could see a shadow behind the dune. Fifty feet away, no more. How long would it take him to get out there? Three seconds with fear on his heels. The man would not have time to swing his rifle round. One burst and it would be over. Hudson looked back at the sky. The first insubstantial veil of cloud was drawing across the moon. Ten seconds and the black mass would blot it out. Before him, the shadow on the beach stirred.

Hudson waited. Five—four—three—two—one. The beach went dark as if a light had been turned off. Hudson pulled himself up and started to run half a dozen steps and, suddenly, a figure almost collided with him. It was the Jap running for the shelter of the jungle. Hudson fired and missed and the Jap flailed at him with his bayonet, the point catching him across the back of the hand. Hudson felt the instant release of blood and parried blindly. His feet sank into the sand and the Jap lunged again. His weapon must have jammed or he had run out of ammunition. The two men were too close to fire. Locked together in the darkness, Hudson swung the butt of his rifle and felt it smash into the Jap's cheek bone. The man cried out in pain and reeled sideways. Hudson struck again, missing, and then found his target driving in two blows that stretched the Jap out on the sand. He raised the butt of his rifle and brought it down hard three times until the man's bloody, broken head was almost buried in the sand.

'Skip?' Johnson was calling softly across the sand.

'Yep.' Hudson was trying to get his breathing back to normal. His hand was awash with blood. The Jap's legs twitched against his. Hudson moved away from the body like a man walking away from a bad motor accident. Johnson loomed up beside him, his arm dangling by his side. 'Where's Joe?'

'Tidying up.'

The moon came out again and Joe was revealed bending over one of the Japs who had fallen near the trench. None of them was moving.

'Did he get the last one?'

Johnson shook his head.

Hudson swore under his breath and looked out towards the open sea. 'Can you move your arm?'

'It'll go everywhere I do.'

Hudson suppressed a smile. 'Good. Is there enough juice in those batteries to raise the sub?'

'I doubt it. Not in this weather.'

'Then we'll go out to meet them.'

'If they're still there.'

Hudson said nothing but started up the beach to collect the raft and tell Joe to throw the Jap's weapons into the sea. He would have liked to have taken them, but with this sea running it would be difficult enough to launch the raft. The wireless set could stay where it was.

Hudson dropped into the trench and found that the body of the falling Jap had smashed the flash light. Not for the first time he wondered if his luck was running out. A search of the dead Japs revealed that the officer was carrying a small torch with a red filter. This would have to do for signalling to the submarine.

Joe had stripped the Japs of all their personal belongings and was using the bloody knife with which he had cut their throats to remove their uniform insignia.

Johnson was dragging the raft towards the angry sea.

Hudson looked at the waves and wondered if they stood a better chance by staying and fighting it out with the Japs. At least they would take a few of them with them. In these conditions they would be lucky to get across the reef without foundering.

Joe stood up and stowed the small bag of insignia beneath his *lap-lap*—the ankle-length twist of cotton material around his waist. He looked at Hudson expectantly.

'Now we get to the difficult part,' said Hudson.

On the first two attempts at launching, the raft was torn from their grasp and bowled up the beach like a rubber toy. Johnson was nearly lost in the surf and a bitter south-westerly monsoon rain began to lash the beach. Hudson's spirits fell. The submarine would never expect them to launch in this. It would either withdraw or submerge; probably the former, so that it could recharge its batteries. He resolved to make one more attempt at launching and then, if necessary, they'd hide up on the headland.

'Joe, get 'em foreside. Johnson, throw yourself forward when we hit the first wave. You're better off as ballast.'

'What about if I pulled?'

'You couldn't pull a Boy Scout off his sister.'

Johnson's right arm hung like a piece of game outside a butcher. Bloody and useless.

'And stay forward.'

Joe was checking to see that the paddles were still securely strapped.

'Come on! The Japs are going to be here at any moment.'

Hudson positioned himself at the stern of the raft and felt the sea break about his legs. Being a coast-watcher was one prolonged act of suicide.

'Now!'

Joe drove forward through the wash of the wave carrying the raft like a battering ram. The surf smacked against its bottom. A wall of black water reared up in front, and Johnson threw himself untidily across the prow of the raft, slipping backwards as the wave broke across him. Hudson clung to the cord at the back of the raft and felt the icy water rush over him. For a second he thought they were on the beach again, and then his head broke the surface and he saw Joe scrambling over the side and tearing at a paddle. He launched himself forward and began bailing frenetically as the raft floundered in the trough. They slopped over another wave and suddenly the beach had disappeared and there was just the slanting rain pitting the surface of the vicious, swirling water.

Joe attacked with his paddle, and Hudson fought to keep the raft head-on to the raging seas. The rudder groaned in its mooring and Hudson wondered if it would hold. The sea was worse than he had expected, and they were still on the fair-weather side of the reef.

In the bottom of the boat, Johnson began to retch. Soon Joe did the same. At times it seemed that they were buried in the sea and that the raft was sure to founder.

Water rose above their waists and the sea surrounded them on all sides like a wall. Then they would be picked up and for a moment would find themselves on the crest of a wave before sliding down into the black trough. A stroke of the paddle could avoid all contact with the water or be submerged by it. In the terrifying darkness there was only the pounding of the sea to tell them where they were.

Hudson hooked his arm round the rudder and thrust his toes under the swollen sides of the raft. His whole body was aching, and the cold was beginning to numb his fingers. The rudder dug into his flesh, seeming to be scraping against unprotected bone.

A huge wave broke over them and the vessel nearly broached. Joe's giant body was submerged by surf, and Hudson thought he had been swept away. He lent his shoulder against the protesting rudder and brought the raft head-on to the next wave. The nose flicked up and Joe reappeared from the swirling wash to dig angrily at the attacking sea.

Above the howl of the wind and the rain squalls came a persistent angry roar. They were approaching the reef. The raft was flung upwards, and Hudson glimpsed a mountain of white water fifty yards ahead. If they got through that it would be a miracle. He had no idea where he was or where the openings could be.

They had to go forward. To steer sideways would be to broach. Each wave threatened to destroy them, as it was.

A plume of spray rose a hundred feet as a breaker thundered against the coral. Hudson felt awe in equal measure with fear. Was that a passage through the reef? A waterfall of silver running like molten steel from a furnace as the two levels of sea rose and fell, sucked and spat through the jagged coral. If they entered the channel on the ebb, could they pull themselves through before the next mad water dashed them against the coral?

Hudson shouted at Joe to keep paddling and concentrated on holding the raft steady. The wind was now little short of gale force, and the rain, grey tracer bullets.

Johnson was lying on the bottom of the raft, attempting to bale. He had voided the contents of his stomach and was now dry retching.

Spray from a breaking wave blinded them. Hudson glimpsed white as they skirted an isolated outcrop of coral. There was a gap here, but the sea rose and fell thirty feet as it rushed through it. On either side a seemingly endless comber of angry surf stretching away into the darkness.

Joe turned round and shook his head. Hudson swore at him and told him to keep paddling. He did not need to be reminded that he was asking men to perform the impossible.

Now the coral gleamed all about them. Joe called out as his paddle scraped against it. A wave broke almost on top of them and the raft lifted and shook itself like a soaked dog before rasping against the reef with a terrifying screech of tortured rubber.

Hudson waited for the raft to disintegrate and felt the rudder buckling against the force of water pouring through the channel. For several seconds they were battered against the jagged wave-washed coral and then the pressure relaxed. The raft slithered down into a trough, and Hudson and Joe paddled like madmen to escape the boiling water. Before them the sea was like a mountainous landscape, and below, a treacherous undertow tried to suck them back onto the reef.

Hudson shouted at Johnson to hold the rudder. It was as if a hand was gripping the boat. No matter how furiously they paddled there was no forward motion. The raft remained poised at the raging, white water mouth of the opening and the men's strength diminished as the pounding of their hearts became more urgent. Only as the raft edged sideways along the reef did it become possible to pull slowly away from the submerged wall of death.

Hudson took over the tiller again and wondered how much more they could take. He was mentally and physically exhausted, and he had not been violently and continuously sick like the others. They were coming apart as surely as the rudder was separating from its mooring. If that went—*when* that went—they would be done for; driven back onto the reef or capsized the moment they broached. They had only one hope: that the submarine was standing by and not too far away.

He could sense his strength ebbing. His will to survive flickered like the flame of a spent candle.

Hudson rode down the helter-skelter of a storm-whipped wave and drew out the torch he had taken from the dead Jap officer. It seemed so puny as to invite ridicule. A single glow-worm in the black forest of the night. He checked that it was working and held it above his head. The pitch and fall of the sea could not be less than twenty feet so that the moments of visibility were minimal. A few seconds at the crest of each wave. Like striking a match in a gale. The tiller nearly tore from his grasp and he lowered his tired arm, knocking the torch into the bottom of the raft. The sea swept over it, and Johnson searched blindly, before clutching it and handing it back. It was still working.

Hudson felt a surge of rage and bitterness against all the elements that confronted them: the sea, the wind, the rain, the currents, the undertow. Every devious trick of nature compounded to destroy them. Almost as a gesture of defiance he rose precariously and, gripping the rudder between his knees, jabbed the torch skywards with an oath. The wind screamed derision and then there came a long answering flash of yellow light.

Hudson heard Johnson and Joe whoop before he believed his eyes. God be praised! Could it be them?

Immediately, the tiredness fell away and new hope was rekindled. The sea seemed less awesome, the fears and despair of a few seconds before became almost unworthy. The yellow light vanished as they plunged into the trough of a wave and had disappeared when they resurfaced.

'It was there, wasn't it?' Hudson was not asking for a specific position. Rather, a confirmation of existence.

'Yes, Skip.'

'Then let's find the beauty.'

The paddles dug into the water with new vigour. Hudson tried to steer a course that would bring them towards the position of the yellow light.

The rain had stopped but a south-westerly gale was still snatching away the crest of the waves. Ten minutes. Twenty minutes. Fears began to return. Strength ebbed. Only the sea maintained its relentless spirit-breaking pressure.

Had the submarine really seen them? Were they on course towards it or were they being carried away by one of the treacherous currents that ran between the islands? Had the signal come, in fact, from the submarine or was it the Japs trying to lure them onto the rocks? Probably not the latter because there had been only one flash. The Japs would not have been so reticent.

Hudson also feared for the rudder. It could not stand much more buffeting.

He strained his eyes into the darkness and changed the torch from one tired hand to the other. 'Like the bloody Statue of Liberty' Johnson had described him.

'*Tabauda!*' The urgency in Joe's voice made him stare eagerly into the pitch black. 'Torch 'e buggered-up finish.'

It was true. The torch had gone out. That was it. The torch was well nigh useless in this sea, but it was a symbol. Hudson felt as if something inside him had been turned off. He lowered his arm and pressed the switch a couple of times. Nothing. Joe stretched out his hand.

'*Tabauda!*' Like an island, the great black bulk of the submarine loomed before them. Johnson and Joe let out a cheer and began shouting. Hudson closed his eyes and opened them again. The submarine was still there.

'Captain Hudson?' The American voice came through a loudhailer with the hint of a question in it.

'Yes, Commander.'

'Good to see you. Prepare to come aboard.'

Hudson fought a desire to laugh out loud. 'Prepare to come aboard.' Shades of bosuns' whistles and men in tricorn hats and knee-breeches. Hardly the world they had been surviving in for the last two hours.

The submarine was rising and falling through twenty-five feet of water. If they got too close the raft could be sucked beneath it.

A rope snaked out from the bridge and missed. Hudson swung the tiller desperately as the stern of the submarine smashed down against the water. The faces on the bridge were now level with his. The submarine disappeared into the trough and threw itself upwards in a cloud of spray like a harpooned whale. Rivulets of water cascaded from the gleaming hull and the raft danced uneasy attendance, trembling on the brink of the undertow.

The rope sailed out again, just missing Joe's stretching finger-tips. Hudson shouted at him to stay in the bottom of the raft. It did not need much to flip them over in this sea.

The rope was thrown for a third time and again it missed. If anything, the gale seemed to be getting worse. Hudson took the raft in as close as he dared and the rope fell squarely to be grasped by Joe. They made it fast to the prow and were almost immediately pulled beneath the hull of the rearing submarine. Only frenzied shouts persuaded the crew to slacken off and let the raft pull away to safety.

'We need another rope,' gasped Johnson.

'There's no time. We'll have to jump. You first.'

Hudson knew that the submarine commander could not go on risking his vessel in this weather. He probably had no clear idea how far off reef or rocks they were. He also knew that the rudder would part at any moment.

'Jump as she comes out of the trough.'

Johnson positioned his gaunt, exhausted frame at the edge of the raft and reeled as a wave broke over him. He steadied himself, rose with the motion of the swell and launched himself forward. Hands reached out to save him, but he fell short as the submarine reared, and landed sprawled against the edge of the sea-washed deck. For a second he did not move and then he began to slip backwards into the pit. His hand snatched at the rope. He clung long enough for a crew member to lunge forward and grasp his shirt. Other hands arrived and he was hauled upwards and deposited through an open hatch like an item of unwieldy cargo.

Hudson felt his heart lift and shouted at Joe to jump. The submarine crew were now playing the raft like a fish. Letting out rope as they sunk into a trough and hauling in on the rise. Joe chose his moment and leapt, clearing the small gap with ease. The raft fell back, grazing the side of the submarine and the bulging metal seemed about to collapse on them. Hudson broke his paddle trying to shove clear and another ton of water raked the craft from nose to stern. When it shook itself clear, Joe had disappeared through the hatch and it was Hudson's turn. He fought to hold the raft steady. With every man that left it had become more difficult to manoeuvre. The nose was tilting skywards and the contact with the surface was that of spit on a hot griddle. Without warning the rudder slipped out of its loosened mooring and was torn from his grasp. Now the raft was skidding across the surface of the water like a piece of wood towed behind a speedboat.

Hudson clung to the stern painter and watched the prow rise like a kite. The whole raft was vibrating and threatening to tilt back on him. There was no chance of jumping. It was all he could do to hang on.

Suddenly, a beam of light probed the darkness thirty feet to starboard. For a second, he related it to the submarine and then realized the probable truth. It would have to be a Jap patrol boat mounted with a searchlight. Now the submarine commander would have to run to save his ship. Compared to the lives of a hundred men Hudson was expendable. Above the roar of the sea he heard a voice calling from the bridge.

'Hold on. We'll pull you in.'

The submarine wallowed in the trough and Hudson felt himself being sucked down with it. This was it. The icy water closed above his head. His face was forced against the wooden slats at the bottom of the raft. He waited for the iron monster to roll over and crush him and felt water breaching his nostrils. Panic engulfed him. Trapped in the undertow he could not move. He was drowning. His head was going to explode.

Then he was rising. Fast. A dizzy sensation like the upwards sweep of a swing boat. He broke from the water and soared above the bar of yellow light balanced on the wave tops. Hands dug into his flesh like hooks. Voices shouted. His head struck something in a blaze of light. The noise of the sea dimmed and was replaced by a drumming sound and the high-pitched shriek of a siren. He was passed downwards through half a dozen pairs of willing hands and came to rest before a bank of instruments. It was warm. He looked about him and believed for the first time that he was inside the submarine. It was the sensation of awaking from a crowded nightmare in a strange room. Men were running past him to take up their stations. The alarm siren still shrieked.

His head began to clear and a twinge of pain drew his eye to the back of his hand. It was open like a thin, smiling mouth and he could see the white tooth of bone. The harsh vibration had softened into a rhythmic, nervous shudder. Hudson knew that they were accelerating to top surface speed.

'Enemy craft five hundred yards.' The calm, disembodied voice arrived via the public address system.

The faces of the men standing or sitting at the control were tense. When they glanced at Hudson there was a wariness in their eyes that at first he took for resentment. Then he looked across to Johnson, slumped against the wall with an orderly, and realized. 'Jeremiah' Johnson was the age of most of the young men about him but he looked ten years older. His skin was malarial yellow and stretched across his bones like paper on the framework of a model aeroplane. His legs were covered in ulcerous, weeping sores. His eyes were black holes that might have been burned with a poker. Even after being scrubbed by the sea he stunk like a goat. He was different. Different from the young crew members with their pink cheeks and bland expression. In comparison they seemed like plump babies lined up for a show. The expression in their eyes was a kind of disenchanted awe.

'Enemy craft one thousand yards.'

The atmosphere lightened. Men turned to each other and shrugged and winked. They shared relief whilst they had hoarded fear.

'Fifteen hundred yards.'

The submarine commander came over to Hudson. 'They'll never be able to stay with us in this weather.' He shook his head, 'I sure am glad to have you men aboard. I'd given you up.'

'So had I,' said Hudson. 'Did you see our shore signals?'

'We didn't see anything. Reckoned the sea must be running too high. Came in as close as we dared to the reef and gave you a flash in case you were there.'

Hudson smiled grimly. 'And you heard we were.'

The smile was returned. 'Yes, sir. When the shooting started we thought they were aiming at us. Then we got wise, pulled off and waited for you.'

'Thanks,' said Hudson.

It was, he reflected, a very small word to use to a man who had risked his ship and his crew to save their lives.

An orderly arrived with a tumbler and two miniature bottles.

The commander poured them both into the glass. 'I guess you could do with a drink. I've taken the liberty of breaking out the medicinal brandy.' He pushed the glass into Hudson's hand expectantly.

'Thank you, Commander.'

Hudson raised the glass in a toasting gesture and brought it to his lips. The rich, opulent scent nauseated him after so many weeks of deprivation. He hesitated. The Commander and crew were watching. He smiled and drained the glass in one gulp.

'Thank you.'

The fire curdled in his stomach and he nodded and turned away to find the heads. He knew that within thirty seconds he was going to be violently sick.

2

The slope fell steeply at first and then swelled into a gentle rise, climaxed by a knoll. This stubby, brown peak tilted forward jauntily to oversee a sharp descent that surged upwards into a second slope at a pinched right-angle. The two curves that followed were shaped like a cupid's bow with the arrow point pricking into a sharp depression and culminating in an isolated thicket rearing up precipitous and unexpected from its bare surroundings.

The woman followed the sweep of Carter's eyes with drowsy interest.

'What are you looking at?' she asked.

Carter raised his glance from her body. 'Your pussy,' he said.

The woman smiled and drew up her knees. She slowly parted her legs and let her head drop back against the pillow.

'Look a little closer,' she invited.

Carter smiled a conciliatory smile and changed his position so that his left arm restrained her across the breasts and his nose nudged her cheek. The scarlet poinsettia outside the window stood out clearly as if in a picture frame. It tapped admonishingly against the grill honeycombed with dead insects and made him wish he was outside this tacky Port Moresby bedroom with a woman who did not even have the tact to put her husband's photograph in a drawer when she invited home a lover.

'I must be going soon,' he said.

'I thought you said you had the whole afternoon?'

'I just remembered something.' It sounded like a lie but he did not care.

'You're a mean son of a bitch, aren't you?'

'If you like.'

'I don't like.' There was a pause while she reared up so he

could see the red leather of her upper chest suddenly melt ridiculously into her floppy white breasts.

'Don't get me wrong. I don't want you to tell me you love me or any of that rubbish. I just don't want to be treated like a piece of dirt.'

Carter sighed. 'I'm sorry. But I have got to get back to camp. A bathing detail. I said I'd stand in for one of the other guys. They need an officer to go down to the beach.'

He made it up as he went along.

'Believe me.'

He kissed her on the wrist and she slumped down beside him, half-forgiving.

'Can't they go by themselves?'

'Yeh, but they start brawling and whoring. You know what soldiers are like.'

'Especially Yanks.' Her right hand moved between his thighs hopefully.

'Yeh, they're the worst. You know why they call them that, don't you?'

His fingers entwined themselves in her wet pubic hair. She giggled in nervous anticipation.

'Because they—?'

'That's right.'

He began to tug at the tight curls and drew himself up on one elbow, leaving a sweat patch on the pillow where his head had been. Grudgingly, his own body began to respond to his pulling and kneading of the flesh beneath it. It was a kind of once-removed masturbation. The woman thought he was growing because she was working him with her slippery fingers. He knew it was his own memories of other women and other times. Times when there was something new and exciting about it.

The woman opened her mouth to be kissed, and he looked at the fillings along the line of her receding gums and pressed his face down against the pillow. He felt a sense of irritation and despair. Why were they doing this? What were they looking for that either had the power to give? They should have known better. He opened his eyes and saw a mole, like a pendant of flesh, dangling from the scrawny neck. It made him feel sick.

32

Like her smell. Not a body smell but a smell of false, sickly sweetness. Like his mother's toilet when there were guests coming to dinner. Christ! Why was he so depressed? The first post-orgasmic blues should be twenty minutes dead by now.

'Don't you want to?' Her voice was puzzled and sad.

'Sure.'

Poor cow. She was probably not having a very good time either. The difference was that she was trying. She knew that the only face-saving exit for both of them was the one he had already entered. He scrambled across her body and pushed himself forward, feeling nothing.

'That's good,' she said.

He had a shower before he left but by the time he was twenty-five yards from the bungalow the sweat had soaked through his shirt beneath the armpits. The heat had an almost tangible quality. It seemed to be packed into every hole in the body like oven-baked cotton wool. You could never forget it was there. Every sulky movement of the air brought it against you as if the door of a blast furnace had been opened. The glare hurt your eyes. A fine layer of dust infiltrated your nostrils and layered your tongue. Even the needle-sharp chirping of the insects in the *kurukuru* grass seemed like some demonically orchestrated accompaniment to the shimmering heat.

The bungalow lay between the town and the airfield in what was once a residential area but was now mainly abandoned or destroyed by Japanese bombing and army and civilian looting. Gardens were reverting to jungle. Bougainvillea, hibiscus and oleander throttled by vines. Gutted shells of scorched weatherboard and fibroplaster seemingly held up by the greenery that overran them. Smashed crockery, broken shelves, a doll with its stuffing hanging out. A smell of decay in the air.

Far to the north were the mountains, blue-black, with their peaks lost in cloud like white fleece snagged on a fence top. They stretched from left to right as far as the eye could see, menacing and aloof. The Owen Stanley range, rising to over twelve thousand feet where troops of the 2nd Australian Force and Japs trying to push their way down to Port Moresby from the north were locked in mortal combat. If Moresby fell, the Japs had secured their last stepping-stone to Australia. . . .

Carter looked across to the airfield carved out of a valley amongst low hills covered with four-to-seven-foot-high sun-browned *kurukuru* grass and irregular clumps of gum trees, their leaves limp and thick with dust. Gun emplacements were notched into the hills, and areas of ground were burned black where fires had been started by bombs or crashing aircraft. The burned-out shell of a Mitsubishi 97 stood apart from a detritus of allied aircraft that had been hit on the ground and bull-dozed to the side of the runway. A Wirraway, a Hudson bomber and a P-40 Kittyhawk, all damaged beyond repair. On the runway itself three American B-25 bombers were waiting to take off. Sandbag-protected pits concealed scattered fuel dumps and the men who flew and serviced the planes. There was an all-pervading smell of gasoline and a fine cloud of grey dust that never had time to settle.

As Carter watched, a battered Lockheed Electra taxied to a halt outside a corrugated iron shack, and three men and the pilot got out. One was a native, wearing a *lap-lap*, and one of the white men had his arm in a sling. The other was tall and gnarled, with baggy shorts that flapped about his knees as he walked. His peaked officer's hat seemed to have settled on to his head like the roof of a long-abandoned house. Somebody saluted him. He returned the gesture awkwardly and several paces later, as if it was an afterthought. He gave the impression that where he came from there was not a lot of saluting.

The jeep was where Carter had left it, nose pressed into a clump of gum trees beside the strip. He could hear his driver slapping at mosquitoes when he was twenty yards away.

'Did you pick up the mail?'

There was an enforced briskness in his voice to conceal various feelings of guilt.

'Sure did.' Jones rose lazily from behind the jeep, dusting down his uniform. 'Did you get what you were looking for, sir?'

To Carter's ear, the 'sir' came in a beat late. Jones was studying him with an expression that was almost lascivious, as if trying to get a vicarious thrill from proximity to someone who had recently got himself laid.

34

'Yes, thank you.'

'Did you have a good time?'

'Same answer, Jones.'

'What was she like?'

Carter paused for a moment. 'She was like your mother.' He let the remark sink in. 'Now, do you want to hang around here and watch the hospital planes come in or can we get back to camp?'

Jones gave an unruffled shrug. 'I'd like to show you something before we do, Lieutenant. It's kinda amusing. I wish I had a camera with me. I found it while I was waiting. Some kind of old Chinese grave-yard.'

He led the way towards where the brown grass was pressing against the gums. Almost overgrown was a small circle of grave stones.

'Look at this one.'

Carter looked down. Almost illegible were the neatly carved words, 'No Good'.

'I guess his Chinese name was 'No' and he thought he'd give it a local flavour,' said Jones.

'It must have worked,' said Carter. 'Nobody's written "son of a bitch" underneath it.'

Jones thought for a moment. 'That's very good. "No good son of a bitch."'

'Thank you,' said Carter. 'Now can we get back to the camp?'

He climbed into the jeep and nearly sat on a crudely carved wooden sculpture of a male figure with a grotesquely large penis rearing out of its loins.

'What the hell's this?'

Jones reclaimed his possession and laid it on the back seat almost reverentially.

'Native art. That's going to look real nice when I get it home.'

'You bought it?'

'There's a Limey on the strip who can get them. Do you want one?'

'No, thanks—and don't call them Limeys. They don't like it. They're Australians.'

Jones shrugged. 'What's the difference? They worship the

same King, don't they?' He jerked his head towards the back seat. 'I like it. It'll make a cute conversation piece. I mean, there's nothing unartistic about that, you know. That's the way they really carve them. With the big tits and the big cocks. The fertility thing is the whole basis of their culture.'

Carter nodded but did not say anything. The sculpture was badly carved with the stain hardly dry on it. It almost certainly came from one of the 'factories' set up by business-minded locals who knew that you could never go broke underestimating the American appetite for junk. Natives in the army hospitals were turning out objects like that for a pittance and, in some cases, being held back from a return to the front if their work found special favour. Meanwhile, in the jungle, men died and rotted from bullet, bayonet, malaria, typhus, leprosy, hookworm, yaws, grille, pneumonia, pleurisy, dysentery, beriberi, dengue fever, tropical ulcers and a variety of skin diseases that reduced flesh to rancid butter.

Carter shielded his mouth and nose against the dust and looked at the face of Jones beside him. Three weeks in New Guinea. Nineteen years in the world. Bland, unformed, more innocent than he could ever realize, his skin only just beginning to turn yellow from the anti-malaria tablets, his cheeks hardly pitted with insect bites. He had it all to come.

Carter's spirits rose with sight of the sea. It was a shimmering cobalt blue laced with green, and ran away like an enormous playing field to be bounded by the thin white line of the reef. When you were born and bred in the mid-west the sea meant something. Any sea. Inshore the water was shallow and transparent and he could see patches of wood and stony outcrops. The sand was a dirty brown, turned up as if by a plough and littered with gnarls of driftwood looking from a distance like droppings on the bottom of a parrot's cage. Two old black women were wading in the water, looking for anything that the war would bring them, and they were the only people on the beach. Behind the sand a long line of stately casuarina trees stretched down towards the bluff, and on the other side of the road were coconut plantations and a few large houses, mostly abandoned.

It was before one of these houses that Jones slowed down

whilst a sentry in a slouch hat surveyed the vehicle from the shade of the trees. A sign beside the double gates said 'REHABILITATION CENTRE, Quiet Please'. The building did not look like a hospital and was protected by a double row of barbed-wire fencing rising to a height of twelve feet. Such locals who took any interest in the place believed it to be a centre for treating allied servicemen who had suffered nervous breakdowns and other mental disturbances while on active service. This explained the large number of seemingly able-bodied Americans, Australians, New Zealanders, Dutch, British, Filipinos, Indonesians and island natives who passed through the gates seldom to return again.

In fact, the building was the New Guinea Headquarters of the Allied Intelligence Unit, and its prime function was the recruitment and supply of units working behind enemy lines, plus the digestion and implementation of the information they sent or brought back.

The small township of tents behind the house was divided between members of the American and Australian forces, sometimes working together but mainly concentrating on projects within their own spheres of influence.

Carter acknowledged the sentry as the gates swung open and the jeep passed through and behind an avenue of frangipani trees. Here, amongst the coconut palms, began orderly lines of khaki tents with a dried-up stream bed to divide the Australian and American lines. It was noticeable that the Australian side of the camp had smartened up considerably since the arrival of the Americans and that a keen undercurrent of rivalry existed between the two groups of men.

Carter saw an Aussie cleaning a hurricane lamp outside his tent and remembered the saga of the lighting. The morning after the last American tent had been erected, four trucks had assembled at the end of the first line. Truck number one had towed a post-hole digger and systematically bored forty holes. Truck number two had followed and inserted and secured forty poles. Truck number three had strung wire from the poles, and truck number four had attached the fittings, bulbs and shields. By nightfall, the Americans had electric lighting in their tents.

The Australians on their side of the creek had watched with initial derision that slowly changed to resentful awe. They had reminded him of the old boys at Lake Springs leaning against the rail and watching the dudes from St Paul check into the new motel. Looking at the chrome on the automobiles and the fancy luggage. Thinking what they could do if they had some of that money.

Carter dismissed Jones and went to his tent wondering whether it was worth taking another shower. His shirt was sticking to him, and he had a headache which might just be the first symptom of some kind of fever. There was a message on his bed. 'Report to me immediately. Dallas.' 'Immediately' was underlined twice. Carter sighed. That was the way to make something happen; go out and fuck somebody. The note was written in Dallas's handwriting so no doubt the major had delivered it personally. What could be that urgent?—or perhaps Dallas liked striding around camp seeing what everybody was up to and who was not where he ought to be. Dallas was the only man who strode in this heat. They said his shadow got tired trying to keep up with him.

'Major S. T. Dallas, USAMC' was typed with visiting-card precision on the centre of a rectangle of crisp white cardboard pinned to the door of an office on the second floor of the building looking out across the reef. Above it was another sign saying 'Task Force 19'. Carter could not remember having seen the second sign before. He knocked once and went in.

The room was dominated by a large wall map of Papua and New Guinea and the offshore islands spilling out to north and east. It included Cairns and Townsville on the Queensland coast of Australia. There was a fan hanging down from the ceiling like an aeroplane propeller but it was not working. Instead a small fan droned in a listless semi-circle agitating the corners of the papers strewn across the desk. The two windows were covered by a fine metal grill to keep out insects and further obscured by luminous green blinds plunging the room into semi-darkness. It looked cool but it felt hot and stuffy.

Major Dallas stood up impatiently as Carter came in. Sweat gleamed on his strained face.

'Where the hell have you been?'

'I went to pick up the mail.'

'The mail?' Was it Carter's imagination or did Dallas lay a mocking stress on the second word? 'It occurs to me that your talents are rather under-employed as a mail boy.'

'I'm sorry. There didn't seem to be any other demand for them at the time.'

'Not on the base.'

'Not on the base,' repeated Carter evenly.

His activities with Jean must be more widely known than he had suspected. Jones shooting his mouth off, most probably.

'May I remind you that you officially need my permission before you go off base. Not to mention the question of basic courtesy. Discipline is lax enough in this outfit as it is.'

Carter could agree there. He sometimes wondered why his secondment to the AIU from his old unit had arrived like a bad 25th-birthday present. He guessed it was an unflattering judgement by his ex-commanding officer on both his own capabilities and those of the unit he was now serving. There was a body of opinion in the US command that regarded the AIU as paying lip service to what was in reality an unworkable concept of Australian–American unity. Behind the scenes, each ally pursued his own projects in secret. Carter felt like a second-rater in a second-rate organization.

'I'm sorry,' he repeated.

He was beginning to feel disagreeable again. First the bad sex, now Dallas needling him. It was a lousy afternoon.

Dallas took a deep breath and walked to the wall map. He spun dramatically and jabbed his finger at it.

'What do you know about Rabaul?'

'I know what I read in the coast-watchers' reports—'

'Exactly!' Now the finger jabbed at Carter. 'You know it's five hundred miles from Moresby on the north-east coast of the island of New Britain. You presumably know that it has a deep-water harbour, that it is surrounded by extinct volcanoes and that there are sixty thousand Japs dug in there. Japs who over-ran the island in January '42 and have been building up ever since.'

'I knew that,' said Carter.

He sometimes wondered if Dallas had been an advertising executive in civilian life. He had a habit of leading off any address with a recital of established facts so that you would accept them as a co-relation of any statement that came subsequently.

'From Rabaul the Japs have landed troops along the north coast of the island, and they're bombing shit out of us here. Every day they bring more men and material into Rabaul. Why? So they can stamp on our faces when they step across to Australia.'

Dallas looked at Carter accusingly, as if he suspected that his face would be pushed forward suppliantly to receive the first Japanese boot. Carter waited for him to get to the point.

'And what are we doing? We're lobbing thousands of tons of bombs on the little yellow sons of bitches and we're getting nowhere. They're dug into those pumice-stone cliffs deeper than ticks on a sheep's back. We're singeing the wool but we're not getting down to the ticks.'

Carter nodded, as much in respect of Dallas's metaphor as of any new truth that it contained.

Dallas retired behind his desk and sat down, gesturing that Carter should do the same.

'You struck on a sore point when you mentioned coast-watchers, Will.'

Carter's voice showed genuine concern. 'Why, have we lost somebody else?'

Dallas replied with a curt shake of the head. 'No. But there's a feeling that we're relying on them too much.'

'I don't know what you mean. They know the country . . . they know the natives. You were just talking about Rabaul. What information we can get is eighty percent from coast-watchers. Shipping movements, planes taking off—'

He stopped as he realized that he was beginning to sound like Dallas.

'Yes, but that places us in a subsidiary role, Will. Whatever anyone else likes or doesn't like, we are in charge out here. The war in the Pacific is US responsibility.'

'Nobody's ever worried about that in relation to coast-watchers before.'

Dallas placed both his hands flat on the table. 'Somebody is, now.' He raised his eyes towards the ceiling.

Carter thought for a moment. 'MacArthur?'

'We are to take, and I quote, "a more dynamic initiative".'

Carter nodded. 'That must be MacArthur.'

'"American prestige is at stake in this theatre of war." I'm quoting again. Our general, as you know, has a low opinion of the Australian fighting man.'

'Has he ever seen one?'

'He was here in November.'

'I understand he spent an hour at the beginning of the Kokoda trail. The nearest fighting was thirty miles away. I remember because my mother sent me a newspaper cutting from the States. It said that General MacArthur was staying in a bungalow near the front line so he could be close to his men. You know what that bungalow was ? Government House.'

'The General is not responsible for his public relations releases.'

'You amaze me.'

Dallas sat back in his chair and frowned. 'Listen, Carter. I don't want you coming in here and bad-mouthing the General. He issues the orders.'

'Right,' said Carter. 'What's he issued that affects me?'

'He wants a more pronounced American influence on all those activities currently undertaken by coast-watchers. He wants the people back home to know that we're playing a positive role and not just sitting around here on our butts or screwing dames. He wants us to get ashore on New Britain and find out what's happening in Rabaul. He wants commando raids on Jap-held islands—'

'He wants headlines saying "MacArthur's wonderful raiders do it again." That's the trouble with generals. They always have to be seen to be doing something.'

'Don't look at everything on the basis of one personality. We need a morale boost right now. The British did the same thing when they were pushed out of France. They started making raids

41

across the English channel.'

'And lost a lot of good men.'

'That's not the point, Carter. We're losing a lot of good men anyway. The General wants to try something different and assert American leadership in this theatre of war.'

'You forgot to say "and I quote",' said Carter. 'OK. Where do I come in?'

'You're going on a special training course to prepare you for your new assignment. You and a bunch of—' Dallas paused to choose his words carefully, '—hand-picked guys.'

'Americans?'

'Americans, Australians, natives. This is a joint operation. There'll be some coast-watchers, too. At least, initially. I can introduce you to one of them.'

He picked up a telephone without waiting for a reply. 'Hi, Major Dallas here. Can you come down for a moment? I've got Lieutenant Carter with me.'

He replaced the receiver and, for the first time in the interview, smiled at Carter. 'Exciting, huh?' His voice struck the false note of the high school football coach reminding the team that there were thirty points to make up in the last quarter.

'There's one thing I don't understand,' said Carter. 'This outfit is crawling with special details sneaking out all over the place. What's going to be different about us?'

Dallas's smile broadened. 'You're going to be held in reserve for any special scheme that the General warms to. You're MacArthur's own.' He let the news sink in. 'I knew that would appeal to you.'

There was a knock at the door and Dallas rose to his feet.

'Come right on in, Captain. This is Lieutenant Will Carter. Lieutenant Carter—Captain Andrew Hudson.'

3

Hudson sat on the beach and looked at the two men swimming a hundred yards from shore. The sea lifted and they disappeared into a trough. Only the black speck that was the forty-four gallon oil-drum further out was still clearly visible bobbing on the crest of a wave.

'What do you think of this caper, Skip?'

'It's too early to say,' said Hudson.

He was lying. Being assigned to Dallas's cryptically-named Task Force 19 had made him feel that his worst fears about himself were being shared by others. Nobody knew what they were really supposed to be doing, and the unit comprised callow, young, American officers drawn from a variety of units and old-stager nationals like himself, whose continuing presence behind enemy lines was presumably thought to be a liability. Hudson sighed. Maybe he was just feeling the aftermath of one of his recurrent bouts of malaria. Whatever happened, he did not like what he had got himself into. He looked at Johnson's yellow-brown frame beside him and started to fill his pipe. The scar on Johnson's arm was healed and so were most of the leg ulcers. He had started to fill out, too. The food was crook but at least it put some weight on you.

'What do you make of the Yanks?'

Hudson sucked at his pipe. 'Too early to say. They're friendly enough. They haven't had the experience, that's all.'

Johnson brushed a fly from one of his sores. 'I feel I'm wasting my bloody time. I mean, swimming out to stick limpet mines on an oil-drum. Is that what we're going to do when we get back?'

The pipe started to draw and a thin wisp of smoke drifted across the beach like smoke from a distant stack.

'What do you mean "get back"? We don't know where we're

43

going, do we?

'Is it true that we're up for something special?'

'I don't know any more than you do.'

Hudson leant back and pulled his hat over his eyes to show that the interview was over. He could hear the heavy murmur of the sea and the occasional pounding and retreating hiss of a wave. There was a ventilation hole in his jungle hat and he could see through it like a peep-hole to palm fronds above. They moved backwards and forwards across each other like myriad pairs of scissors, fuzzy and out of focus. The effect was soporific and he closed his eyes and thought back to the thriving plantations he had been forced to abandon on the island of New Ireland. Twenty-five years' hard work going to waste.

He remembered the small trading post he had started with. The dirt track leading down to the wooden school with the open lattice-work sides against the heat. The truant eyes of the children rolling sideways as he rode past. The tulip tree in early summer. Eighty feet high and looking as if it had burst into flames. Candelabra of fiery red flowers at every branch tip. The giant pods lodged in the branches like nesting birds. And the soft water-filled buds, prized by the children because they could be used like miniature water-pistols. He thought of the careful acquisitions of land, the extensions to the store, the house he had built by the beach with its crisp white nameplate: 'Trade Winds'; the boys who had helped him work the plantation—Nambu, Bosko, Kita—and the other settlers who had arrived—Jeff Sculley, 'Ginger' Saunders, Ray and Doris White. All dead now, killed by the Japs.

Men fight wars for many reasons. Hudson was fighting to get his home back. Any Jap who stood in his way was going to die.

'I don't ever want to see Rabaul again.' Johnson's voice came unprompted and unexpected, like a wireless set suddenly bursting into action.

Hudson pulled his hat from his face and sat up. The boy was staring out to sea but not seeing the horizon. His mind was somewhere else. Somewhere that caused a nervous twitch to run across the back of his hand. Fear lurked behind his eyes and plucked at the corner of his mouth.

Hudson took his arm and shook it as gently as he would have done if the boy was having a nightmare.

'Do you want to talk about it?'

Johnson shook his head vehemently. 'No, I don't even want to think about it.'

'But you can't help it, can you? We all think about things we want to forget.' He saw the Japs throwing Ray White through the window into his burning house. 'Anyway—' he patted his arm, '—anytime you want to give it a burl.'

'Thanks.' The boy remained silent but still looking out across the Coral Sea.

Hudson was grateful for the silence. He did not want to talk. Words could never express what you felt. Not his words, anyway.

You made a gesture and that was it. You repeated things that people had said to you and you listened. That usually made people feel better. Doctors were great listeners; they could listen the breath right out of your body.

'Don't worry,' said Hudson. 'There's no talk about us trying to get to Rabaul.'

'It doesn't really matter,' said Johnson. He snapped back his head and nodded out towards the swimming figures. 'Is that joker ever going to get out to that drum?'

Hudson frowned. 'They shouldn't even be trying. This is shark water.'

Carter turned on his side and swam with his arm resting against the small float that supported the limpet mine. The drum was much further away than it looked from the shore, and the sea rougher. There must be a current, too, because the slowness of his progress could not be only due to the swell that was running. The water buoyed him up so that he could see the drum twenty yards away, then he fell back into the trough. He hated those moments when the tops of the palm trees disappeared and he was buried in a hole in the sea. He felt he was never going to come up again, that the water would enclose his head. The thought made him panic momentarily and strike forward in a flurry of legs. His foot touched something. What was that!? His mouth filled with water and he choked and gasped for air.

'Get it together, Lieutenant. You're the slowest of the bunch.'

The instructor was swimming beside him. A lazy crawl probably perfected in some Pasadena pool. His mouth was an ever-open museum in which his perfect white teeth were the prize exhibit, and his stomach hard and flat like the lid of a biscuit tin. Carter had taken an instant dislike to him that was now deepening into hatred. He cleared his nostrils and dog-paddled whilst he got his breathing working. A green mass of water surged past him and he found himself looking at the beach. A sprinkling of men watching from the shade of the palms. It was an evens bet that the old Australian with the baggy shorts and the pipe had his eye on him. He did not miss much, that one. And his wireless operator who seldom smiled and only seemed to speak in monosyllables. Strange guys. Still, they must know their jobs. It was up to him to prove that he knew his.

'Do you think you can make it?' The voice was mocking, not sympathetic.

Carter bit back the impulse to say 'Go fuck yourself!' 'Sure.'

'Let's go then, Lieutenant.'

The instructor flipped forward onto his stomach and flaunted the stirred honey of his shoulder muscles as he carved a passage towards the forty-four gallon drum. Carter looked at it apprehensively. It was straining against its weed-covered mooring and flopping through the water like a slowly turning top. It was not going to be easy to attach the limpet mine to either of the ends. One was almost below the surface, the other tilted in the air. And the mine was primed. Primed and packed with PLA, the newly developed plastic explosive that exploded on contact with water and came with each unit packed in a heavy-duty polymeric protective bag.

Carter rested both hands against the back of the float and kicked out with his legs. When it came down to it, the sea was something to be watched admiringly from the shade of the casuarinas on Ela Beach. Close to, he was frightened of it and of what he could not see below its always-changing surface. Something else brushed against his leg and he grit his teeth, half-expecting to feel the searing stab of pain that would tell him that it was a sea wasp or some other kind of jellyfish with a sting capable of causing death. He lunged forward and ordered himself to stay calm. He had enough problems with the mine without letting his imagination escape.

He rose to the crest of a wave and looked ahead. The drum was now less than fifty feet away, and the instructor had circled it and was coming back. Carter sunk into the trough and came up again. The instructor had disappeared. Carter waited for him to surface and wondered what the crazy bastard was up to. Was he playing some kind of dumb game? Swimming under water so he could grab Carter's leg and scare the shit out of him? Then the blood hit Carter. He saw it coming towards him down the wave like it was running down a gutter. Then the instructor rose out of the water screaming so you could see all the beautiful white teeth and halfway down his throat. A white pointer shark had him round the thigh and the blood was washing back over one of its glassy eyeballs.

Carter clung to the float and drew his knees up in silent terror. He could almost feel the rows of teeth sawing and ripping through his own flesh and muscle. Man and shark fell back into the sea, and a torrent of mad, bloody water bore past Carter and towards the shore, as if escaping from the scene of a murder.

Carter abandoned the float and struck out blindly, trying to turn every stroke into a blow aimed at beating off attack. Behind him, the instructor was still screaming. Carter heard a thumping noise and saw that the man was trying to scramble across the drum with the shark still coming at him. As he half-hauled himself from the water it could be seen that his left leg had been nearly taken off at the thigh. It dangled obscenely, blood squirting from severed arteries, the firm brown flesh burst apart like a bale slashed with a bush knife. Carter choked as he saw white bone, and he trod water, trapped by a feeling that he ought to try and help. But how, in God's name? The shark turned in a whirlpool of water and came in again like a robot. Its head broke the surface, and Carter glimpsed the teeth before they closed about the man and began to worry him. The tail thrashed and the drum spun slowly, unwinding its screaming burden into the bloody, churning water. Carter did not wait but struck out for the shore.

With every stroke he expected the shark's teeth to tear into him. Fear was like an electric dynamo propelling him through the water. He could hear shouts from the men on the shore and caught a glimpse of palm as he fought to the crest of a wave. There was no feeling of exhaustion now. Only fear. Fear that greased tired limbs and buoyed his body towards the safety of the beach. How many other sharks would the blood attract? Dozens of them, already fanning out from the spouting carcass, their killer instincts primed to rip at anything that moved through the water.

Carter lashed out with renewed frenzy and, in his panic, took in another mouthful of water that brought him to a choking halt. Desperately, he trod water and tried to draw some air into his blocked lungs. A wave washed over him and spun him sideways, forcing him to look back towards the drum. It rose above the trough and then slipped back again. There was no sign of the instructor. Nor of the shark. Then, without warning, something moved past him below the surface. A white shape, like a bolt of light. Carter twisted round, spluttering and kicking, trying to keep a watch on all sides. Seconds passed. He dared not swim because that meant he could not see what was coming up behind him. He was paralysed with fear and uncertainty, circling in the water. A dorsal fin cut the water twenty feet away and then disappeared. Carter drew up his legs almost to the surface and waited, watching every fleck and turbulence. Something white glinted in the corner of his eye, and he spun round as it closed with him. The float carrying the limpet mine. Carter felt sick.

The float skipped daintily over the crest of a wave and slid into the trough. It was ten feet away when the fin broke the surface beyond it. Carter could see it clearly and the twenty-foot shape of the shark beneath as it pointed back up a wave. Then it started to come in, the fin slicing through the water like a razor blade.

Carter could hear himself shouting at the top of his voice. He clenched his impotent fists and started to thrash the water. Pray God it would be quick. And then the shark veered to one side and he saw its mean pig-eye stare unblinkingly above its rows of swept-back teeth. He saw it lunge through the water and the jaw close about the bobbing float as if attempting to swallow it whole. There was a blinding flash and something stung his face. Then darkness.

4

When Carter opened his eyes he thought he was looking at grey sky and one of the wind pumps that brought up the water on his father's farm in Wisconsin. But it was a sun-faded blind and a slowly turning fan in a hospital ward crowded with men and flies. He began to remember what had happened and feel his limbs to see if they were all there.

'Hi. How are you?'

The nurse was pert but not pretty. Her uniform was damp under her armpits.

'I was hoping you were going to tell me.'

The girl nodded reassuringly and pulled at the sheet which covered his body.

'You're going to be fine. You swallowed a lot of sea water and you were concussed. You haven't got a problem compared to most of the guys around here.'

Carter looked at the surrounding beds and agreed with her. Even the strong smell of disinfectant could not disguise the stench of mortified flesh.

'When can I get out?'

'Depends on what the doctor says. Tomorrow. Today, maybe.'

Carter continued to stare at the girl's face. There was something unusual about it. He was used to the yellow complexion that resulted from taking the anti-malarial drug, Atebrin, but this was different.

The girl noticed his interest. 'It's my lipstick,' she said. 'Compliments of Uncle Sam's cosmeticians back home. Specially designed to go with yellow. Does it raise your morale?'

'My temperature's going up already,' said Carter politely.

The girl laughed and patted his wrist. 'I'll get you a drink. You must have a sore throat after swallowing all that sea water.'

She came back with a glass of lemon squash and a letter.

'This came for you.' She lowered her voice to the level of a stage whisper. 'I believe it was left by a lady.'

'You don't say.'

Carter took the letter. He could only think of one woman in New Guinea who would want to write to him.

Somebody started dying noisily three beds away and the nurse left to help. Carter opened the letter.

As he had expected, it was from Jean. 'Dear Will, I was very sorry to hear about your accident. I hope you will soon be recovered. I would like to come and see you but I don't think it would be a good idea with so many wagging tongues about. I had my own bit of sadness today when I heard that Jack has been killed—that's my husband. I don't know if I ever told you his name. We were never very close but we had some good times together. It makes me think that I will pack up the house and go south. As you know, I should have gone with the others anyway. Now that Jack is gone there is even less point in staying here—apart from you, of course, and you could be sent away at any time. I will stay with my sister in Sydney and see what works out. She is on her own now, except for the children, and will be glad of the company. When something like this happens it makes me glad that I don't have any children. It makes things better if you can think how they could have been worse, if you know what I mean. Sorry this isn't a more cheerful letter but you can understand how I feel. Perhaps there will be the chance for us to get together before I go. Much love, Jean xx.'

Carter read the letter through again and crumpled it up. It was no doubt a self-indictment but his prime emotion was one of relief. He did not want to see Jean again and this way it was going to be much easier. She seemed to acknowledge the fact herself—'Perhaps there will be the chance for us to get together before I go.' Hardly symptomatic of great passion.

And what of Jack? Poor Jack. 'His number had come up.' 'His luck had run out.' He had 'bought it', 'got his', 'stopped one', and half a dozen other expressions to avoid the indecency of the word death. And did Carter care? If he was honest with himself the answer was no. Not a great deal. Poor Jack was just another statistic thrown up by the war, and it might so easily have been him.

'And now you have a visitor.'

The nurse's tone was that of a mother trying to make a child appreciate the Christmas presents he was receiving.

Carter looked up to see Hudson approaching the bed. He appeared diffident, almost uncomfortable, holding his unlit pipe in his hand like a talisman. He glanced at the dying man and ducked warily as he approached the fan.

'Good day, Will.'

'Andrew. Good to see you. Pull up a chair.'

Despite the exchange of christian names the tension between the two men had not relaxed. Hudson perched his tall, spindly frame on the edge of a chair and looked about him uneasily.

'If this was a regular hospital I could offer you a grape,' said Carter.

'Do you need some fruit?' Hudson sounded serious.

'No, I was just referring to how when you're in hospital people come and eat all your fruit. You can't do that because there isn't any.'

'Oh, I see.' Hudson's expression lost some of its sternness. 'You're looking much better than I thought you would. You were blown out of the water, you know.'

'Like the shark.'

'Yes, but not in so many pieces. It was falling on the beach.'

'I was lucky.'

'You sure as hell were.'

Hudson studied Carter as if the reason for his good fortune was written across his face.

'Who got me out?'

'Corporal Johnson got to you first. Buy him a beer some time. The others went off down the beach for the boat. Stalled the bastard, straight off. Beaut operation.' His face split into a broad smile at the recollection. 'Mind you, it was a crazy idea in the first place. I should have put my foot down. People do things in a war that would get them killed in peace-time.' He smiled again. 'You know what I mean. Because there's a war, people start taking crazy risks.'

'You mean, like us.'

Hudson's face clouded. 'I didn't mean that. Anyway, I don't know what we're supposed to be doing yet. I can't comment. We're not a suicide squad, are we?' He laughed. 'Don't worry, I'm told that training is officially over.'

'They must have got scared they were going to kill us all before they could send us anywhere.' Carter took a deep breath. 'Listen, Andrew. I may be American but I don't know any more than you do. I know the General wants a closer involvement in your kind of coast-watching operation and I know he wants to find a way of striking at Rabaul. He's worried about the build up of men and materials and our failure to do anything about it. Shit! He's a right to be worried. One of these days they're going to come streaming out of there like wasps.'

'We may have to wait until they come,' said Hudson, seriously. 'We haven't got a force that can take Rabaul. They've got a network of tunnels that goes back miles into the hills. They have hospitals there, workshops, munition dumps, fuel dumps—and all underground. No bomb can touch them.'

'Have you been there?'

'Before the war, yes. Many times. My home was on New Ireland, to the north. I know the place like I know, say, Moresby.'

'So you think MacArthur is wasting his time?'

Hudson paused before answering. 'I think he may be inclined to underestimate the terrain. You don't walk in this country—you climb or you crawl. Most of the time you're fighting the climate rather than the Japs. Your finger can rot off before it gets the chance to pull a trigger. I mean, look around you. How many men in this ward are suffering from bullet wounds? Three out of ten? What about the rest? Bacillary dysentery, malaria and pneumonia, as a guess. Hell, I'm not saying that MacArthur doesn't know what he's doing. He did a good job in the Philippines by all accounts and that's not the easiest country in the world. I just think that Rabaul is something else. To get the Nips out of those tunnels is going to be like getting maggots out of a cheese.'

'So what do we do?'

'More or less what we're doing at the moment. Try and

53

contain them. Keep listening posts open to report all air and sea movements so that we can hit them when they do come out in the open. Wait until *we* can stockpile enough men and supplies to go in and attack.'

'Hoping that they don't do it first.'

Hudson shrugged. 'You always hope that, don't you?' He tapped the stem of his pipe against his teeth as if eager to start smoking it. 'Anyway, all this talk about Rabaul reminds me what I really came here for. Wasn't just to see how you were. The Yanks—' he broke off and held up a self-admonishing hand, 'an American PT boat picked up a Chinaman drifting in a dug-out canoe in the Solomon Sea. He apparently escaped from Rabaul after killing a Jap. I came along to see if he could tell us anything.'

'He's here, in the hospital?'

'Somewhere. Apparently he's in pretty bad shape.'

'Do you mind if I come along?'

'Not if you can make it.'

Carter swung his feet off the bed and winced as pain zig-zagged through his back. It felt as if he had been beaten by rubber truncheons.

'Can you manage?'

'Sure, I'm just bruised, I guess.'

He rose unsteadily to his feet and fended off the nurse's objections with a promise of speedy return. 'That lipstick is really growing on me,' he said. Halfway down the ward, the man who had been dying now had a sheet over his face. Dark patches of sweat showed through it and a wet circle which announced the position of the mouth. As Carter looked, a fly landed in the middle of it.

The ward was one of many that branched off bungalow-style from a covered corridor opening on to a pleasant garden in which mangoes, red ginger and angel's trumpet predominated. The hospital had been barely large enough in peace-time and was now surrounded by a hinterland of hastily assembled tents and inadequate walkways of coconut matting which would be washed apart in the first downpour of the rainy season. The contented murmur of insects did not come only from the blossom on the trees.

Hudson patiently showed a piece of paper to three black orderlies in turn and was eventually directed to a row of tents set apart from the rest and guarded by two Australian soldiers in slouch hats armed with heavy Lee-Enfield rifles. One of them saluted grudgingly and led the way to the last tent in the line. He pulled back the flap and gestured inside.

'There he is, poor bastard.'

At first sight, the man lying on the camp-bed appeared to be dead. He was pitifully thin and his arms lay on the sheets like sticks. They were a fiery red. So was his face, which had eyelids swollen like partridge eggs, as if the skin had been scooped from his hollow temples and packed into his eye sockets. His nose was also swollen and the scarlet skin about it split like that of a fried tomato.

A large water blister puckered his chin. Such was the grotesque rearrangement of his features that Carter wondered if this was the Chinaman. There was nothing about the face on the pillow that looked Chinese.

'He must have been in that canoe for days,' said Hudson. 'The sun's nearly finished him.'

Carter picked up the medical report card at the end of the bed. Clipped to it was a piece of paper torn from a log book and covered in neat writing.

'Hey, listen to this. "0500| hours. 8 March 1943. This man was found drifting in a dug-out canoe west of Bella Lavella Island—"'

Hudson whistled through his teeth. 'Poor devil was drifting the wrong way if he was hoping to get to New Guinea. Bella Lavella is south-east of Bougainville.'

Hudson continued reading. '"When taken aboard he was semi-conscious and badly sunburnt but recovered sufficiently to say that he had escaped from internment at Rabaul after killing a Japanese guard who had murdered his wife while raping her. All his personal effects accompany him when placed in care of Captain Henderson, RAAF. Signed this day, Lieutenant John F. Kennedy, US Navy. Commander PT 109."'

'They do a good job, those PT boats,' said Hudson. 'Got me

out of a few tight spots in my time.' He turned back to the figure in the bed and spoke softly. 'Can you hear me?'

There was no reply. Carter looked down at the small, emaciated body and wondered how it could have found the strength to kill a Jap guard. Then he thought of the man's wife being raped and murdered before his eyes and knew.

'Maybe we'd better find a doctor,' he said.

Hudson did not reply but levered himself awkwardly to his knees and placed his lips beside the man's ear. 'Can you hear me? You're at Port Moresby. You're safe.'

Again there was no reply and Carter began to wonder seriously if the man was dead. Then the swollen eyes opened slightly and the mouth peeled apart slowly as if the lips were held together by a zip fastener.

'Do you want some water?' Carter asked.

The man nodded.

'Easy with it,' said Hudson. He watched as Carter guided a beaker to the man's lips. 'We work for Allied Intelligence. If you feel up to it we'd like to ask you some questions.'

The man moved his head in what was clearly meant to be a gesture of acquiescence. Carter removed the beaker and dabbed at the two small rivulets of water that ran from the corners of the man's mouth. He winced at each touch.

Hudson spoke. 'You escaped from the internment camp at Rabaul, right?'

The man nodded.

'How many internees are there? Two hundred? Three hundred?'

The lips came apart, still joined by hinges of congealed saliva. 'Four hundred.' The voice was parched but showed little trace of accent.

'Many Australians and Americans?'

The head shook from side to side.

Hudson frowned and turned to Carter. 'Most of the prisoners the Japs captured went down with the *Montevideo Maru* when it was taking them back to Japan.'

Carter grit his teeth. By one of the ironies of war the *Montevideo Maru* had been torpedoed by an American submarine off the

56

Philippines. There had been hardly any survivors.

'Is our bombing doing much damage?' asked Carter.

Again, a shake of the head. 'Japs in tunnels.'

Hudson looked at Carter. 'Just as we thought.'

The Chinaman had managed to raise his head from the pillow and was looking round the tent as if searching for something.

'What do you want?' asked Carter.

The head fell back against the pillow and a scrawny arm pointed towards a bag lying on the floor in one corner. It was a *bilum*, a woven string bag used by the natives to carry their belongings. Carter picked up the bag and noticed that it had attracted a column of small red ants. He removed a pair of worn sandals, a tattered khaki shirt and a pair of frayed drill shorts. All the articles of clothing stank. The Chinaman gestured at the shirt. Carter quickly went through the pockets and found nothing. The Chinaman feebly moved his hand towards the shirt and raised himself on one elbow, his face contorting with pain. The liquid in his blister moved as if in a plastic container. He inserted a skeletal hand into one of the breast pockets to pry open the pleat. From this hiding place he withdrew a small white object and flopped back against the pillow, leaving it on his open hand. Hudson took it and found that it was a twist of paper that had become sodden and then dried under the sun until it was brittle. He began carefully to force it open. There was something written on the paper.

'Where did you get this?' asked Carter.

The Chinaman spoke, every word an effort. 'I was in a cell . . . chained with another man . . . slid my hands from the manacles . . . escaped. He gave me this.'

Carter looked at the twig-like wrists and believed that they could slip any handcuff. Hudson looked at the piece of paper he had unfolded and whistled. He handed the paper to Carter. It contained a crude, pencil scrawl. Immersion in sea water had almost obliterated the lettering. 'HAVE VITAL INFO THAT COULD DESTROY JAPS. MAKE CONTACT, HARRY GREEN.'

'Old Greeny. I thought he was dead,' said Hudson. He turned back to the Chinaman and spoke with a hard edge to his voice.

'Harry Green is in the prison camp at Rabaul?'

The man nodded.

'He gave you this?'

Another nod.

'What was he doing in the cells?'

The Chinaman raised his shoulders slightly in a gesture reminiscent of a shrug.

'Always in the cells.'

Hudson gave a short laugh. 'I can believe that.' He rose to his feet and carefully folded the piece of paper. 'Right, sport. Thanks for the information. When you're a bit stronger we'll be back to ask you to draw us some maps. Look after yourself.'

He nodded and jerked his head at Carter to say that it was time to leave.

The Chinaman said nothing but closed his eyes and turned his head slightly towards one of the walls.

'Do you know this guy Green?' Carter asked as they came out into the droning heat.

Hudson pulled out his pipe and started to stab at the crust of used tobacco with a penknife.

'I used to bump into him sometimes. Before the war. He was what you might call a character. Must be about fifty now, I suppose. Came out here for the Edie Creek gold rush but never struck it rich. Worked for the administration for a while—he was a nicely spoken fella—then he got a job recruiting native labour. I think he picked up an arrow somewhere. Anyway, he didn't stick it for long. Then he came out to New Britain. Tried his hand at the copra business. He was making a fair disaster of that when the war came.'

'Do you think it could be a trap?'

'I don't see why the Japs would bother. If we were actually on the island it might be different. I'd be suspicious of somebody handing me a note saying "Come down to the prison camp." From this distance?'

He shrugged. 'I can't see the Japs priming our Chinese friend to fry himself to death in an open boat just so they can trap a couple of coast-watchers.'

'So what do you think he means?'

'I dunno. Maybe he's gone crazy. He always liked a drop of the—' Hudson tilted his pipe to his lips as if it was a bottle. 'But on the other hand, I think it's probably dinkum. When it came down to it, Greeny was a straight shooter. I think we ought to go and take a look.'

'Are you serious?'

Hudson was trying to light his pipe and didn't answer immediately.

'Sorry about this thing. I can't smoke on an operation so I try and fit in as much as I can when I'm back at base. The boys say I ought to take it with me. A couple of whiffs and we'd clean the Japs off any island.'

He puffed enthusiastically before realizing that he had not answered Carter's question.

'Yes, sure I'm serious. If we keep the numbers down to the minimum we should get ashore without too much problem. I don't believe the Japs will think of us landing so near Rabaul. They're funny like that. We can get the Chinaman to clue us in on the exact position of the camp—it can't be too far from the sea from what he said. What I most like about the idea is that it's a good test operation for our set-up—what are we called, "MacArthur's Own"?'

'That's unofficial,' said Carter.

'Well, it doesn't matter what it is. Sooner or later we've got to cut our teeth, and this is a good exercise to get the logistics sorted out. Submarine drop, dinghy to shore, hide dinghy, trek to prison camp, talk to Green, back to the shore, pick up. We could be in and out overnight.'

'You make it sound simple.'

'I want to. Everything is based on making things simple. And good team work.' He looked at Carter levelly. 'I don't want to sound rude, Will, but I've already got a team. If I take you or any other American I'm working with an unknown quantity.'

Carter grit his teeth. 'Are you thinking about what happened when I was swimming out to the drum? Do you think I'm going to crack up?' He was aware that it was his own fear that was putting him on the defensive. His voice grew louder. 'I guess you think we're all milk-fed mothers' boys. OK with the hardware but lousy in the jungle?'

Hudson's eyes blazed. 'I don't think of Americans as being different to anyone else. If you were a Kiwi or a Pom I hadn't worked with I'd be talking to you in exactly the same way. All I'm saying is that I want to make sure that we can walk before we run. Because, sure as hell, one day we're going to have to run.'

He held Carter's gaze, his face grim, and then turned on his heel and walked away down the line of tents. He was a big man when he moved, and his head jutted forward angrily as if it was going to butt the sun to pieces. Carter followed him.

5

'Five minutes.'

The First Officer looked at Hudson. He nodded to show that he had heard.

'Can I fix you more coffee?'

'No, thanks.' Hudson felt he had been drinking coffee ever since he came aboard the submarine. He looked at the clockmaker's window of dials along the hull and then to Joe who was sitting with his back to a bulkhead, polishing the firing mechanism of his newly-issued Mills gun. Like a child with a new toy he had been taking it to pieces and reassembling it ever since he got it, polishing each segment until Hudson feared that he would take off a precious thickness of metal and render it unfireable.

'Ready, Joe?'

'One time, massa.'

Carter, too, was checking his weapons and the fastenings on his dark green combat uniform. He offered a piece of gum to Johnson and caught Hudson's eye as he was about to slip the tell-tale pack back into a pocket of his uniform. Carter nodded sadly and threw the gum into a trash can. Hudson said nothing. He had been at pains not to give any impression of riding the American, and Carter was making it easier for him. Relations between the two men had not deteriorated since the flare-up at Port Moresby Hospital. There was a wariness on both sides but no more. Johnson clipped the waterproof cover over his dry battery, an ATR4A wireless transmitter, and slid his arms through the two straps that held it to his back. His face was thoughtful but there was no sign of strain. He had made no comment when he had been told that their mission was on New Britain, and Hudson had not pressed the matter.

Every item of equipment that was going ashore had been checked and rechecked. The rubber dinghy had been inflated and deflated, and disembarkation drill had been carried out with the submarine on the surface. Hudson needed no reminder of the problems of coming alongside a pitching submarine at night in a choppy sea. He also wanted to make sure that Carter knew as much as possible about every problem that might arise. This desire was not only dictated by an obsession with procedural efficiency but, Hudson had to admit, by the resolve not to lose face before the American if some detail went wrong. Hudson was aware that there had been strong American pressure at Allied Intelligence to make the first leader of a joint landing-party an American. He did not want any slip-ups.

Hudson finished rubbing black anti-glare cream on his cheeks and pulled down the infra-red goggles that had been resting on his forehead. Through the sun-glass effect he could see the other members of the party doing the same. Wearing the goggles would ensure that they could see perfectly when coming out on deck at night.

'Nineteen-thirty hours.'

'Dinghy ready for launching, sir.'

'Right. Synchronize watches.'

Heads bent over wrists as Hudson gave the countdown. He could see Joe looking at his blackened face in silent amusement. Good on you, Joe. You deserve a laugh. Joe hated 'the steel fish', as the boys called it, but never complained.

He had sweated patiently through the day as the submarine moved up and down the coast making periscope sightings and looking for Japanese positions. Any sign of new building at the outskirts of a village was immediately suspicious. It might be a watch-tower or a 'house iron', a corrugated-iron strong-post enclosing a Nambu 7.7mm machine gun. By midday a landing spot had been chosen. It could be approached through a gap in the reef and was not near the cluster of native villages surrounding Rabaul. Occasional sightings had been taken through the day but there was no sign of movement in the jungle or on the narrow strip of beach. Joe had been certain that the nearest inland village was over two miles away.

As he came on deck, Hudson filled his nostrils with the hot, sweet smell that wafted off the shore a mile away and listened to the slap-slap of the water against the submarine's hull. He immediately felt a sense of identity with his surroundings that was lacking in the brightly lit interior of the submarine. There it was like being inside the mechanism of a giant watch. A phosphorescent fish slid by in the dark water and the shriek of a night bird told them where the shore was. The night was black and there were no stars.

Two ratings were securing the dinghy against the sloping side of the sub, ready to lower it into the water. Hudson approached the looming outline of the conning tower.

'Thank you, Commander.'

'Good luck. We'll be waiting for you.'

Hudson gave the order and the dinghy slid into the water and chafed against the hull. For just a second, Hudson thought of the hot, sweet, black coffee and the comfortable bunk he was leaving behind. Then he joined Carter in their predetermined positions in the prow of the dinghy and both men unstrapped their paddles. Joe and Johnson followed. The mooring lines were thrown aboard.

Four swift digs on the paddles and the submarine had melted into the night. There was just the whisper of the trade winds and the distant hollow drumming of the surf. Hudson studied the luminous face of his prismatic compass and gave orders that would keep them on their bearing for the shore. There was a swell of about fifteen feet running and a strong current pulling them off course.

Carter listened to Joe's rhythmic grunts behind him and tried to probe the darkness ahead. The sea seemed alarmingly choppy but there was no hint of anxiety amongst his companions. He dug down with both arms and felt the muscle-stretching satisfaction of his paddle moving a solid weight of water. Thank God to be doing something physical after two days poring over charts, checking equipment and establishing signalling procedures.

'This cow of a current is taking us to starboard, Skipper,' Johnson spat angrily into the sea.

'I don't think it matters. The tide's running high enough for us to shoot the reef. Keep pulling.'

Minutes passed and breathing grew heavier. There was a black outline before them, darker even than the night, and the sound of the surf was like native drums. Carter tried to control his fear as he thought of capsizing on the reef. The coral would cut them to pieces and their blood would bring the sharks in like iron filings drawn to the tip of a magnet.

Suddenly there was white water ahead.

'Right, you jokers, dig in. We're going straight through.'

Hudson dropped his shoulders and braced his knees against the side of the raft. He could feel it straining and trembling like a frightened animal as the mighty mass of swirling water thudded against the rubber, trying to force a way in. Four backs bent and the paddles flexed as the tide snatched at them. The dinghy surged forward and met wild water with the coral inches below. A wave threw them forward again and they seemed to be sliding in the centre of a white plate. There was a hideous rasping sound and the dinghy lurched sideways as if about to pitch them into the surf. A wave washed over them and then carried them clear into the lagoon.

'Jesus Christ!' The words exploded from Carter's lips as he looked back at the white water rushing over the coral.

'Wait till we have to get out,' said Johnson comfortingly.

'Shut up and keep paddling,' said Hudson.

The sea inside the reef was calmer, and within five minutes they could see the outline of the shore clearly. The once angry water was now sucking docilely at the bottom of the dinghy. They paddled until they reached shallow water and then slipped over the side and guided the dinghy to the beach. Carter felt the firm sand underneath his feet and looked back towards the sea. Nothing but darkness. He helped carry the dinghy up the beach and went back with Joe to brush out their footprints. When he returned, Hudson and Johnson were dragging the raft into the twisted mass of roots of a giant callophyllum tree and covering it with foliage.

'We're about four hundred yards off course,' said Hudson. 'Nothing serious. We'll check the wireless and then get going.' He turned to Joe. 'Go for bush. Savvy if Japan 'e come.'

Joe nodded and disappeared without a word.

Johnson slid the wireless from his shoulders and unclipped the waterproof case. He deftly manipulated the controls to the operating frequency and slipped on the headset.

'Alpha Bravo to Charlie Foxtrot . . . Alpha Bravo to Charlie Foxtrot. Report Signal Strength. Over.'

Carter listened to the static and counted the seconds. Hudson knelt beside Johnson and looked at him inquiringly. He was opening his mouth to speak when there was a sudden breakthrough in the static.

'Charlie Foxtrot to Alpha Bravo. Signal Strength Four. Over.'

'Little beaut,' said Johnson approvingly.

Hudson took the speaker. 'Alpha Bravo to Charlie Foxtrot. Thank you. Goodnight. Out.'

He stood up and jerked his head towards the bush.

'OK, let's go. We've got four hours' march ahead of us.'

Johnson started to pack up the wireless.

Carter unsheathed his bush knife.

'Don't use that until you have to,' said Hudson. 'Nothing shows up easier than the marks of somebody hacking their way through undergrowth.'

He delivered a high bird-like whistle and Joe glided from the trees. He reported that he had found a track and that there were footprints showing a heavy tread on the sole. These were almost certainly Japanese. The prints were not recent. Carter felt relieved that their own boots bore a specially moulded sole which was the replica of a native's bare foot.

Joe led the way through palm trees and bamboo thickets to a narrow path unrecognizable to anyone but a native. Once away from the open beach each member of the party switched on a small torch with a treated red glass that provided just enough light to reveal the immediate surroundings and could be mistaken for a glowing insect by anybody seeing it from a distance.

Carter walked third in line behind Joe and Hudson. He soon felt his face burning with sandfly bites. Tall grass closed in about them and the track began to twist upwards over ground broken by tree roots that looked like snakes or giant lizards in the feeble glow of the torch.

There was much to challenge the imagination on that march. The nervous, anticipatory chirping of insects. A sudden explosion of sound as some unseen creature ran or slithered through the undergrowth. The touch of wet moss on a tree trunk, giving like rotting flesh. A prickly vine tearing at the sleeve. Sharp razor nicks from cutting grass. Carter could see how the jungle could destroy, without any help from the enemy. He felt a sharp pain at ankle level and reached down to touch something soft. Disgusted, he stopped and shone the torch. Clamped to his ankle between gaiter and boot were the repulsive, shiny black swellings of three leeches.

Johnson stopped behind him. 'Don't touch them. When they're full they'll drop off. Start messing about with them and you've got a poisoned sore, then you've got an ulcer, then you've got a problem.' He paused. 'I know.'

Carter said nothing. The glow of Hudson's torch in front of him had disappeared. He hurried forward, nearly falling over a root. There were bigger problems ahead than the leeches.

They had been walking for nearly an hour when there was a strong smell of human excrement and a dog started to bark. Joe held up his hand. They were approaching a native village. The people were known to him and he did not trust them. 'Bloody monkeys—master belong Japan' was how he put it. It was agreed to skirt the village. Soon they came upon fences of bamboo, enclosing gardens of yam, sugar cane and sweet potatoes. On occasions there were the shadowy outlines of thatched huts and once the embers of a still-smoking fire. Eventually, they came to an open space and Joe paused.

'You savvy this fella place good, Joe?' asked Hudson.

Joe nodded and pointed to what seemed like impenetrable jungle. ''E got road.'

'You savvy him good?' asked Johnson.

''E no good long dis fella half, master, behind time 'e good fella.'

'It's a cow to start with but it gets better,' translated Hudson.

'OK. Let's take the bastard. This is Joe's back yard. He ought to know what he's doing.'

Joe led the way and they turned off the track and seemed to walk straight into the jungle.

'Leave it ten yards and we'll start cutting,' said Hudson.

He pulled out his bush knife and dug his shoulder into the undergrowth. Carter felt something sting his cheek and touched slug-like slime and softness. The leeches must be dropping from the branches above their heads. A sense of terrible isolation was now combining with one of fear. It seemed impossible that anybody could find their way in this jungle in pitch darkness and with seemingly no track to follow.

'Andrew,' he called out softly. 'Does this man really know where he's taking us?'

'He's jake,' said Hudson. 'These fellers have got a lot of tracks like this they use for hunting possum. They can tell the way by the feel of the earth under their feet. Grit your teeth. We're going to start climbing soon.'

He strode on, the pattern of his breathing hardly changed since he was on the submarine. Carter touched his cheek. Where the leech had been there was now a smudge of blood.

Hudson was right. The track suddenly made a sharp upward turn and lost its way amongst steep outcrops of rock and *pit-pit* grass. Sometimes it was necessary to claw their way upwards, as if climbing a mountain. Mostly it was just a case of feeling the thigh muscles ache as the knee came up before the face and another vertical foot was achieved. There was no relief from the insect bites. Carter felt the backs of his hands and they were an uneven mass of stinging lumps.

'When we get to the top we'll be able to see Rabaul. After that it's downhill,' informed Hudson.

Carter wanted to ask how much further they had to go but his pride wouldn't let him. The fact that they were scheduled to make the return journey in a few hours was something he tried not to think about.

Approaching eleven o'clock, the moon came out and Carter could see the jungle stretching away on all sides, as if growing in the bowl of an auditorium. There was no sign of the path they had taken. No glimpse of a gap between the interweaving trees and creepers. Only the sea, thousands of feet below, now looking no more menacing than a piece of black velvet. Carter grit his teeth and heard his sinews creak as he forced his legs forward and upwards.

Twenty minutes later he was at the summit. Rivulets of sweat were running down beneath his armpits. His flesh was stinging from cuts and insect bites, and his sodden uniform chafed his raw skin. He felt that he was being eaten alive.

Joe approached him solicitously and gestured towards the direction they were to take.

'Walkabout, 'e good fella now.'

Carter snorted. 'I'll believe it when I see it.'

He drank greedily from his water-bottle and crossed to Hudson who was looking through a gap in the trees.

'You can't see the town from here but that's one of the volcanoes, Matupi. It's on the far side overlooking the airstrip.' He pointed to the outline of a stunted pyramid, barely visible against the dark sky. 'The harbour was formed thousands of years ago when another volcano blew up. The sea rushed in to fill up the hole. Must be one of the deepest harbours in the world. How are you doing?'

'I'll be OK,' said Carter.

'I hope we all will,' said Hudson. 'From now on we can expect Japanese patrols or gun posts at any time. Don't fire unless you have to. Even if somebody opens up they may be shooting at shadows. Don't give yourself away. We've got a river at the bottom, so watch it.'

He called to Joe and waved him on impatiently.

'We should be there within an hour,' said Johnson, answering the unasked question, 'provided the river isn't a problem.'

'Why should it be?'

'Do you hear that noise?'

Carter listened hard and heard a noise like distant artillery fire. 'What is it?'

'There's a storm in the mountains. Sometimes the water comes down like a flash flood. The river level can rise several feet in seconds.' He nodded after Joe and Hudson. 'Better stretch it out.'

Carter drove his legs forward and the moon sulked behind a

bank of clouds. The descent was even steeper than the way they had come but Joe moved lightly from rock to rock, avoiding causing the small landslides of earth and stones that the others set in motion. Occasionally he would stop to listen and sniff the air and Carter would wait apprehensively during the long seconds before Joe's thick gleaming black arm beckoned them on. The only thing Carter knew for certain was the fact that the path was going downhill.

Another twenty minutes and the track broadened and led to a cluster of ragged huts thatched with sago-palm fronds. They stood amongst overgrown gardens and seemed to be deserted. There was no sound or sign of life. Joe led the way through almost on tiptoe. The moon appeared again and beams of light broke through the branches of a giant ficus-tree to paint ghostly patterns on the walls of the huts.

Carter began to feel that he was being watched; that somewhere beyond the dark shadowy doorways a machine gun was mounted on a tripod and a Jap was waiting with small, moist fingers, ready to feed the ammunition band through the chattering breech. The image was so potent that it dulled all physical sensations. He was entering a nightmare. He could see the doorway and the spot fifty yards on where they would be mown down defenceless in the middle of the clearing. With every step he became more convinced that he was walking to his death. So strong was the feeling that he wanted to call out to the others. To tell them to dive for cover. But he was in the grip of the nightmare and could say nothing. He walked on, counting the paces as brilliant moonlight flooded the clearing. Forty-seven, forty-eight, forty-nine—he spun round and faced the doorway, his heart pounding, his carbine standing out before him.

There was a crashing noise like a table being overturned and a pig ran squealing from the hut and into the bush. Carter released the first pressure on his trigger and stood where he was, the tension slowly ebbing out of his body in time with the drooping muzzle of the carbine.

Johnson shook his head admiringly. 'You got good ears, sir,' he said.

It was the first time that Carter could remember Johnson

addressing him as 'sir'.

After the settlement, the pathway became a track and the going was much easier. Vegetation thinned out and cultivated gardens were more frequent. They were approaching the bottom of the valley. Soon after passing a thick grove of bamboo they heard the sound of rushing water and came to the edge of what appeared like a wide, boulder-strewn ravine with a stream running down the middle of it.

Joe cocked his head upstream and listened intently. 'Water 'e come,' he said solemnly.

Carter could hear nothing.

'How soon?'

'One time.'

'Come on!'

Without waiting for a reply, Hudson started to slither down the side of the ravine and pick his way through the boulders.

Johnson nudged Carter. 'Step on it. The water's on its way. You don't want to get caught in the middle.'

He pulled at the straps of his wireless and launched himself forward into what Carter now realized was a broad river bed. Carter followed him and fell awkwardly, striking the stock of his carbine against a granite boulder. The pain ricocheted through his arm and he fell back against more sharp, wet stones. The river was not only the course in the middle but spread out to percolate almost invisibly through the surrounding rocks. Carter hurried forward and stumbled in a pot-hole. The boulders about him had been worn smooth by the passage of water and some were taller than a man. It was like picking a way through a maze of rocks. With every clumsy pace he strained his ears for a sound of the approaching waters. If he was caught here he would be dashed to pieces. His fear of the Japs had completely disappeared.

Johnson was waiting, cursing quietly, by the central torrent. He was soaked to the skin and his arm was bleeding.

'I slipped trying to ford the bastard,' he explained. 'I think I might have buggered up the wireless.'

Carter did not reply. Above the noise of rushing water could be heard a distant rumbling sound which came from upstream.

like the hum of a generator.

'We're very close now,' whispered Hudson. 'You two stay here. Joe and I are going to have a look.'

The two men disappeared into the bush and Carter sank to one knee beside Johnson, his ears straining into the darkness.

Five minutes later, Joe materialized beside him as if sprung through a trap-door in the ground. There was no sound to announce his arrival. Carter felt grateful that he was not a Japanese sentry.

Joe touched his arm. 'Come.'

Carter followed close on Joe's heels and found Hudson lying beside a clump of *kunai* grass.

'There it is,' Hudson said. 'Up there on the rise. It's the old prison. I've been here before.' He smiled. 'Strictly as a visitor.'

Carter settled down beside Hudson and peered in the direction indicated. A broad swathe of jungle had been cleared, and in the centre of it were upwards of fifty thatched huts surrounded by barbed wire. Outside the barbed wire was a weatherboard bungalow and a corrugated iron hut that gleamed in the darkness like a tin box. A dirt track led past the hut to the wire. The only light visible came through cracks in the walls of the hut. There was a strong smell of excrement and decay.

Hudson sniffed. 'The Japs will be in that hut. They always do their business on the doorstep. Pity about the light. I hoped they'd all be asleep. How do you reckon this lines up with our Chinese friend's plan of the place?'

'Seems accurate enough. Green should be in one of the middle huts.'

'Right. Let's pay him a visit. Joe, you stay here. Give a signal if there's any movement from the hut—and keep your itchy black finger off that trigger!'

Joe's teeth showed white in the darkness as he grinned. 'Yes, *tabauda*.'

Hudson rose to a semi-crouch and moved swiftly from the *kunai* grass to the shelter of the jungle. Carter followed him and the two men skirted the trees until there was an open space of twenty yards between them and the barbed wire.

'Now we crawl,' whispered Hudson. 'Hope there isn't a death

adder crawling the other way.'

He threw himself down and started to edge forward, his head barely off the ground. Carter waited to take a last look round and followed, holding his weapon in front of him with two hands. Somebody inside one of the huts was moaning in pain but there was no other sound.

Hudson approached the wire and tested it with his hand. The strands were about five inches apart with the lowest almost at ground level. They were stretched tight and there was virtually no give. Hudson said nothing but turned on his back and unbuttoned a pocket at his thigh. He withdrew a slim system of metal rods little longer than a fountain-pen and pressed it between the two bottom wires. Carter did the same. There were now two uprights of metal a shoulder's width apart. Taking their knives, both men activated a spike set in the middle of the handle and inserted it into the centre of the metal rods. As the knives turned so the two end-pieces of metal were forced apart like the operation of a miniature car-jack, taking the wires with them. Eventually there was an opening wide enough for a man to crawl through and one of the strands had been broken. Carter replaced his knife. MacArthur's special training programme had not been a complete waste of time.

Hudson motioned him through and wondered whether to dismantle the system once they were inside. The Chinaman had told them that there were no regular system of sentry patrols but that the Japs would walk round the perimeter wire when the mood took them. Inspections of the wire itself were infrequent and always took place during daytime. Hudson decided to leave the rods in position. If a guard did make a sortie he would be unlikely to look down and see that anything had been tampered with. It would be more risky to take time to set up the system again from the inside of the fence. He wriggled through the hole and pulled grass against the wire before joining Carter who had doubled to the shelter of the nearest hut and was standing with his back flat against the wall and his weapon across his chest. The moaning had stopped and there was now only the sound of snores and people stirring in their sleep.

Carter jerked his head over his shoulder. 'What do we do now?

74

Go and rout him out?'

Hudson held up a restraining hand and listened. From a nearby hut came a creaking sound and the noise of unsteady footsteps dragging across a rough palm wood floor. Hudson beckoned Carter to follow.

The man emerged from the hut and opened his mouth in amazement as he saw Hudson standing in front of him. Before he could say anything Carter's hand closed over his mouth from behind and forced him against the wall. The whites of the man's eyes widened in terror as Hudson came close to his haggard, unshaven face.

'I'm sorry to frighten you. We're looking for Harry Green. Is he here?'

The man nodded vigorously and Carter decided that it was safe to remove his hand.

'Where?'

'In there.' The man indicated the hut behind him.

'Tell him some friends have come to see him—just him!'

The man looked inquiringly from one face to the other and then decided that he did not have any questions. He retreated into the hut. Carter remained with his finger on the trigger and watched the shadows. A large rat moved unconcernedly from behind the next hut and began to climb the bamboo wall to the thatch of *nipa* leaves. There was a mumble of voices behind them and a figure appeared in the doorway. It was that of a man wearing a tattered pair of shorts and a torn shirt that finished short of his waist. Perhaps the shorts had once fitted, but now they were barely able to make contact with the hip bones. The man's shoulders were stooped and he was wasted by disease and malnutrition. He was also shivering, due, Carter felt, to a bout of malaria rather than the cold. It was difficult to tell his age but he was certainly over fifty. He looked old.

The man's eyes lit up when he saw Hudson, and he seized his hand and held it tight. Then, looking round to see that no one was watching, he drew him along the row of huts without saying a word. Carter followed until they came to a roofless, *kunai* grass structure that his nostrils told him could only have one use. Hudson was led inside and Carter, unwillingly, went after him.

'Andrew Hudson. By God, it's good to see you.' The man's eyes blazed with excitement and fever. 'Sorry to have to bring you here, but it's amazing what people will do for a few extra grains of rice from our nippon overlords.' He turned to Carter whose hand was over his mouth. 'I envy you, young man. I can't smell it any more. If I smelt a pretty woman I'd probably throw up.'

'Harry, this is Lieutenant Carter of the United States Army. He's working for Allied Intelligence with me.'

Carter stuck out his hand. 'Will Carter. Glad to know you, Harry.'

'An American,' said Green with real interest in his voice. 'Do you know a chap called Flynn? I had words with him once.'

Carter looked quickly at Hudson before replying. 'No, I don't think I do.'

'You must do. Errol Flynn. He's a famous Hollywood actor. Used to loaf around out here like me. Been rather more successful though. I knocked him out once. Of course, I was in better shape then, weighed a bit more, too.'

'Harry.' Hudson's voice was patient but firm. 'We didn't come all this way to listen to your life history.'

Green's voice immediately became contrite. 'No, by God. Forgive me. I imagine you're here because you got my message? Amazing. I never thought our little Hong Kong friend would get through.'

'He nearly didn't,' said Carter. 'He was picked up by a PT boat after God knows how many days in an open canoe.'

Green whistled through his teeth. 'Poor devil. I hate to think what the Nips would have done to him if he hadn't slipped those cuffs. He escaped through a hole I wouldn't have bet on a cat getting through. Bloody little buggers took it out on me.'

'What were you in for?' asked Hudson.

Green screwed up his eyes. 'Damned if I can remember. Vindictive little sods seem to think I owe them some kind of respect. Out of the question.'

Carter found himself admiring the spirit of the bent little man. 'There are about four hundred internees?'

'Probably less than that now. They brought in a lot of Indians

76

after the fall of Singapore. They're digging the tunnels and dying like flies, poor devils. The rest are mainly Chinese and a few civilian Aussies. They make us work in the docks.'

'Is there much stuff coming in?'

'A hell of a lot after dark. Spare parts for planes, mortars, machine guns—even light tanks. A lot of men, too.'

'So they're building up?'

'Definitely. Our rations are suffering because of it. Hardly any rice. Salt stopped months ago.'

'And our bombing?'

Green laughed hollowly. 'It feeds the little buggers. After every raid they come out of the tunnels and collect all the dead fish floating in the harbour.'

Hudson swore under his breath. 'Bloody marvellous.' He took a deep breath and expelled it through pursed lips. 'OK, Greeny, what have you got to tell us?'

There was a long pause as Harry Green opened and closed his fleshless fingers nervously.

'By God. I hope I haven't brought you fellows here for nothing. I was so positive, but now, faced with saying it . . .' His voice tailed away uncertainly.

'What is it, Harry? We've got five hours to get back to the sub.'

Green raised his head and pulled back his shoulders. 'What do the years 1874 and 1937 mean to you, Andrew?'

Hudson thought for a moment and shrugged. 'My wife died in 1937. 1874 doesn't mean anything.'

Green took a quick breath. 'In both those years, Rabaul was destroyed by a volcanic eruption.' He searched their faces for reaction to the news. 'In 1937 I was here. I saw it.'

'Go on, Harry.'

'By God, Andrew. I think it could happen again.' There was a slight tear in Green's voice.

Carter tried to digest the implications of what Green was saying.

Hudson leaned forward intently. 'What makes you think so?'

The fervour in Green's eyes rekindled. 'So many of the signs are the same. There have been more tremors lately.'

'There have always been tremors at Rabaul,' said Hudson.

'I've never known them so persistent or so strong. I remember suddenly thinking, "This is exactly like '37." And then there's the dead fish in the harbour.'

'Killed by our bombing,' said Carter. 'You just told us.'

Green shook his head vehemently. 'No! These fish weren't stunned. I saw them when I was working in the docks. The flesh had been boiled off the bones! It was pulp. The same thing happened in '37. The sea was boiling near Vulvam Island before the eruption.'

'What else?' said Hudson.

'I talked to a fisherman who'd been round near Matupi. He said there was a great yellow stain in the water and that the fish were dying. You know what that is, don't you? Sulphur. Something's stirring down there at the bottom of that volcano. It's beginning to get angry.'

Hudson tried to control his excitement. 'Is that all?'

'No. I talked to a Tolai who'd been hunting up the other side of Matupi. He said he'd come across a stream running boiling sulphur. You understand what all this could mean, don't you? If we had another major eruption the harbour would be choked with pumice and the Japs would be running back up their tunnels with the lava scorching their backsides. In '37, the boats in the harbour were buried up to their smokestacks and half the town was destroyed. You couldn't move. I think that this time, everything points to an even bigger explosion. I know the positions of the Jap tunnels and I could guarantee that two-thirds of them would be sealed, perhaps even completely penetrated. You couldn't devise a better method of getting at them if you tried. And it's here, waiting right on the doorstep.'

'Waiting for Nature to press the button,' said Carter.

Green looked at them levelly. 'Perhaps nature needs a little nudge,' he said calmly.

'What do you mean?' asked Hudson.

'I've been thinking about this ever since the idea came to me,' said Green. 'I'm certain that everything is primed for an eruption but I can't be absolutely positive that it's going to happen. Yet, what an opportunity lost if it doesn't.'

'I agree with you,' said Hudson. 'What do you suggest we do?'

Green paused and swallowed hard. 'Force Matupi to erupt.'

'Start a volcanic explosion?' said Carter incredulously.

'Not start, trigger off,' said Green. 'There's a great yellow boil throbbing up there. What we've got to do is lance it.'

'How?' said Hudson. 'Bombing?'

Green shook his head. 'I don't think you could ever guarantee the accuracy. Also, the run in that gives you most chance of lobbing something into the crater takes you straight over the airfield. The strip is plastered with anti-aircraft batteries. Coming in low, which you'd have to do, you'd be shot out of the sky. I have another idea.'

He paused, waiting for the inevitable request to continue.

'Go on,' said Hudson.

'I got to know Matupi pretty well when I was searching for butterflies—'

'Butterflies?' queried Hudson.

Green looked slightly shame-faced. 'One of my little wheezes. I was going to mount them in glass boxes and sell them to dealers in New York and London. Bloody war put the kibosh on that, of course. Anyway, when I was up there swishing my net about, I came upon a tunnel going into the side of the mountain. Must have been an ancient blow-out, I suppose. I went down it a few yards and turned back. Didn't have a torch, of course, and it was full of bats. The tunnel seemed to go on though. You see what I'm getting at?'

'Putting a charge inside the volcano,' said Carter.

'Exactly,' said Green. 'I don't know how much explosive you'd need but I expect somebody could work it out.'

'Is this tunnel easy to find?' asked Carter.

'No,' said Green. 'I literally stumbled into it. There was a Grass Yellow on a vine. I took a swing at it, slipped, and went straight through the vine. Must have fallen about ten feet. Terrifying experience. When I looked back it was if I had penetrated a bead curtain.'

'So you can't see it from the outside?'

'Not a hope. I bet you the local *kanakas* don't know it exists.'

'Could you draw us a map of how to get there?'

Green shook his head. 'Couldn't guarantee you'd ever find it.

The backside of Matupi is thick bush going nearly to the rim of the crater. It's criss-crossed with hunters' trails. You'd lose your way in no time. I'd have to show you where it is.'

Hudson looked at the frail, stooped figure before him and tried to remember the well-covered six-footer he used to know.

'Harry, you're not in shape to walk to an ambulance.'

Green pushed a matchstick arm against Hudson's chest. 'Don't you believe it, old boy. You catch me at a bad moment. Twinge of malaria. Always suffered from it. I'll be A1 when you next see me. I guarantee you I won't let you down. One thing about this place I've kicked the booze.' He laughed, a reedy treble that ended in a burst of coughing.

Hudson patted him on the shoulder. 'Harry, you're incredible.'

Green's eyes glinted. 'And what's more, I've got a motivation worthy of an Englishman—well, I suppose you'd better call me an Islander now.'

'Patriotism?' asked Carter.

'Greed,' said Green. 'Patriotism isn't enough.' He gave another cackling laugh. 'It's worth a hundred thousand quid for me to get out of here.'

'Come with us now,' said Hudson.

Green shook his head. 'Daren't do it, old boy. If I'm missing at roll call tomorrow morning they'll kill every woman and child in the camp. They said so after the Chinese fellow went.'

'So how the hell would you ever be able to get out to lead anyone to the tunnel?'

'Have to do it in the course of a night,' said Green. 'Last roll call is at six. Then they leave us alone until eight in the morning—unless we're Asian women. You'd have to spring me and bring me back.' He turned to Carter. 'That's the expression, isn't it? Don't you spring people from jail?'

'That's the expression,' said Carter.

Hudson looked seriously at Green. 'Harry, do you really think you're capable of walking from here to Matupi in a night? And what's going to happen to the people here if it goes off?'

'*When* it goes off. Let's have positive thinking. The people here will be all right. They'll be protected by the hill. Just a few boulders flying about, and some ash and smoke. They'll be cheering so loudly their lungs will burst.'

He coughed again and turned it into the noise of someone clearing their throat.

Hudson's expression was grim. 'But what about you, Harry? It's not just your health I'm concerned about. If you pack up we could lose a lot of lives.'

'I know that,' said Green. 'And I repeat what I've said before. I know my capabilities. You've got to be pretty tough to survive in this place.' He held out his wrists to reveal the festering sores left by manacles. 'I may look like a wreck. I may be a wreck. But I won't let you down.'

'I'm not promising anything,' said Hudson. 'It's an incredible idea, but back at HQ they may not think it's worth the risk.'

'Don't let them waffle,' urged Green. 'They'll talk, they'll make reports, they'll weigh up the pros and cons. In the end they'll decide to let Nature take her course and nothing will happen. You know it's worth the risk. The prize is fantastic.'

Hudson took Green's arm soothingly. 'Stay ready and keep out of trouble. Our wireless is crook so we've got to get back before we can put anyone in the picture—' There was a shrill three-note bird call from the entrance to the camp. Both Hudson and Carter recognized Joe's warning signal. Hudson quickly moved to the latrine entrance and looked beyond the wire. He beckoned to Green.

'Somebody's coming. Get back to your hut. See that clump of rattan over there?'

'Yes.'

'When we're coming for you, two of the stems will be broken across each other. We probably won't be able to give you much warning.'

'Got it.'

Green quickly shook the two men's hands and hurried away.

Carter was surprised by the strength of the grip and the ungainly speed with which he covered ground. Maybe he really was tougher than he looked.

A minute passed and there was silence save for the sound of scavenger beetles rummaging amongst the excrement. Then

Carter felt Hudson's fingers tighten on his arm. A guard was approaching outside the perimeter wire. His forage cap was pulled low over his eyes and his rifle with fixed bayonet was slung over his shoulder. He was a small, fat man, meandering close to the fence. Too close, thought Carter. He approached the spot where they had entered and stopped. Carter listened to his heart thumping and looked at Hudson. His gaze was unflinching. Only his hand moved slowly down the barrel of his Mills gun to ease off the safety catch. The Jap unslung his rifle and leaned it against the wire. Carter felt certain he must have seen something. Then the guard pulled open the front of his baggy trousers and began to urinate noisily. Carter breathed more easily. The guard finished, reslung his rifle and moved on his way. He reached the corner and performed a small dance step as if thinking of happier times and another place.

Carter found himself almost liking the man and then wondering if he was one of the Japs who had raped and murdered the Chinaman's wife. Did he really know himself, he pondered. He could so easily identify with the harmless failings of a fellow human being and yet feel totally alienated by the baseness.

Could he, Will Carter from Wisconsin, given the right—or the wrong—circumstances commit rape and murder?

The Jap moved out of sight and Carter looked at Hudson who shook his head and cupped his hand to his ear. 'Wait here till we get the signal from Joe,' he was saying.

Twenty minutes passed accompanied by the hoarse, ratchet-like croaking of tree frogs and then came the reassuring bird call from Joe. This time, two notes signalling the all-clear. Hudson said nothing but moved immediately and swiftly to the entrance hole in the fence via the cover of the huts. Away from the open sewer of the latrine, Carter filled his lungs and breathed in the heavy scent of a jungle gardenia. He felt tired but this was submerged by a sense of excitement and anticipation. This time he would know the route they were taking. He had a goal to look forward to. Even the eternal presence of marauding insects seemed less important.

Hudson slithered through the gap and waited. Carter followed, cutting his forearm on the wire but hardly noticing it.

Together, the two men dismantled the miniature steel jacks and pressed the undergrowth back into place. Satisfied that they had covered their tracks, they retraced their route along the trees and were joined by Joe. There was now no light showing from the corrugated-iron hut. Hudson took a last long careful look at the camp and then led the way back to the river bank.

Johnson was waiting with his finger on the trigger of his carbine. He rose from the ground almost at their feet. He asked no questions but jerked his head over his shoulder.

'The river hasn't gone down a lot, Skip. I reckon we'll have to cross *kanaka* style. I rescued a couple of logs.'

'Good man.' Hudson looked at his watch. 'Four hours to go so we've got to move a leg.' He turned to Carter. 'I don't think we covered this one on the course so Jerry and I will go first to show you the hang of it. You bringam Mr Will, Joe.'

Joe nodded. 'Yes, *tabauda*.'

Johnson led the way to the water's edge where two gleaming twelve-foot trunks had been half-hauled onto the bank. Quickly checking that all their equipment was securely fastened, he and Hudson took one trunk and their weapons under their left arms and stood poised at a point where the bank sloped gently into the fast flowing water.

Hudson looked over his shoulder. 'Right?'

'Right!'

Immediately Johnson had spoken, the two men ran down the bank into the water and began to strike out strongly with their right arms. The current snatched them away but it was clear that they were heading diagonally towards the far bank.

Joe stationed himself at the head of the second log and Carter obediently took up a position behind him. The water looked dark and menacing. Long strips of snake-like liana drifted by and Carter decided that it would be as well not to get mixed up with them. While he was thinking about these and other sinister shapes, Joe started forward without a word and the log was nearly wrenched from his grasp. He caught up just before Joe entered the water and was amazed how soon he felt nothing below his feet.

The rise in the level of the river had been phenomenal. Two

strokes and the bank had disappeared. His cheek scraped against the log and he struggled to keep the breech of his carbine out of the water as he dug frenziedly with his right arm. It was easy to see why Joe had positioned himself at the head of the log. With every thrust of his powerful arm he seemed to jerk it a foot sideways. Carter looked out for the far bank and was relieved to see foliage reaching out over his head. His foot struck something and for a split second he saw the mangled leg of the instructor dangling by its ligaments as the man tried to claw himself onto the bobbing drum. Fear drove his arm to thrash like a paddle wheel. Within seconds the bank loomed up and he felt shingle below his feet. He released the log and floundered towards the shore, pausing only when he felt himself safe from the current. Hudson splashed through the shallows towards him as he sucked in mouthfuls of air.

'OK?'

'Fine.'

'Right. Let's go.'

He strode off, talking softly to Joe. Carter decided that first impressions could be misleading. Hudson might wear baggy shorts and look like an arthritic basket ball coach wondering where the next win was coming from, but he was definitely worth having on his side during a war.

Joe found a track that would take them back to their approach road and the next hour passed with hardly a word being spoken. Insects glowed, crawled, chirped, whirred, hummed, droned, buzzed, and stung. By the time they reached the summit of the hills overlooking Rabaul, Carter felt numb with fatigue. The blisters had rubbed off his swollen feet and his toes were stuck together with a mixture of blood and sweat. His ankles ached as if a tourniquet had been applied to them. He looked down at the dark, stunted mass of Matupi visible through the trees and felt no rekindling of his earlier excitement.

The volcano looked long dead. There was no soft, crucible glow at its crown to indicate that a ticking time-bomb lay inside. Could there by anything in what Green had said or was he just a cranky old man, his imagination inflamed by recurrent bouts of fever?

Fifty yards ahead, the trees started to rustle as if shaken by a violent wind. There was the sharp crack of a branch breaking and the ground beneath Carter's feet started to shake. A tree beside him trembled and then rocked as if about to fall. A boulder groaned and there was a swift flurry of falling stones. Carter braced himself as the tremor became more severe and tried to understand what was happening. Then, as suddenly as it had come, the shaking died away and there was only the sound of a stone bounding away down the path.

Carter stood still, listening to the silence, not certain whether it was safe to move. Hudson came down the track towards him.

'That was a tremor, in case you didn't know. What our friend down there was talking about. I've never experienced one like it at this height.' He looked down towards Matupi and put his hand on Carter's shoulder. 'You know, I think old Greeny might really be on to something.'

6

At three o'clock it started to rain. A continuous heavy downpour that drummed against the leaves and turned the track into a miniature waterfall. Burdened by his wireless set, Johnson fell heavily and there was a delay of thirty minutes while the party searched for his torch. It was vital that nothing was left to be found by the Japs.

Soaked to the skin, Carter scrambled in the mud on his hands and knees, with the undergrowth tearing at his exposed arms and face. He could see the leeches glistening on his flesh and briefly wondered if mosquitoes fed on leeches as, despite the icy rains, they seemed to be greedily sucking blood from the rest of his body. Eventually the torch was found and the party slithered on for another half-hour through a steady downpour before Hudson called a halt.

'We're not going to make it,' he said. 'To get to the beach on time for the sub we'd have to skirt the village, and there's a risk that some of the women will be out in the gardens by the time we get there. We'll take a long way round and lie up till nightfall. We'll be in better shape then, anyway.'

He started to repeat the change of plan to Joe in pidgin.

Carter felt both relieved and disappointed. He was eager to get away but aware that he was becoming dangerously tired. It was not so much a question of physical strength; he would be capable of putting one foot in front of the other for hours, but now he had a diminishing sense of awareness, fatal for survival in the jungle. He was becoming clumsier, stumbling more often. His senses, once attuned to every sound and movement in the bush, were becoming blunted to the point of indifference. He walked like an automaton. Landmarks he had carefully notched in his mind repeated themselves or disappeared altogether. Distances between remembered points shrank or magnified without reason. At times he wondered if he was walking in his sleep.

By five o'clock the rain had stopped and the going was flatter. Hudson called a fifteen-minute halt and the party huddled together under a clump of lop-sided tamarind trees.

Carter listened to the rain drops dripping from the leaves with the regular beat of a metronome and closed his eyes. When he opened them it was to find himself being shaken awake by Johnson.

'OK, Lieutenant. We're on our way.'

Carter struggled to his feet, his sodden clothing working itself into knots against his flesh. His eyes were gummed together and their lids swollen with insect bites. The inside of his mouth tasted like charcoal. Every limb ached as if the sinew had shrunk, pulling the bones out of their sockets. He took his place behind a silent Hudson and willed himself to keep his wits about him.

As they walked on, the sky began to lighten and the cold give way to the thick, clammy heat of day. Pockets of mist hung above their heads and the vegetation steamed. Parrots called shrilly from the tops of trees, and the paths became infested with large black slugs, some of them almost a foot in length. Joe led the way through a variety of pathways and tracks and frequently told the others to wait whilst he went ahead to scout. After one such expedition he hurried back looking worried.

'*Tabauda*, you come! Me lookim leg belong Japan.'

He led the way to a track running across the one they were travelling on. Clearly imprinted in the soft earth was the pattern of a Japanese boot.

'How long?' asked Hudson.

Joe looked warily down the track. 'Japan 'e come small time.'

Fear woke Carter with a start. The Japanese had passed down this track recently? It was barely daybreak.

'Which side 'e go?' asked Johnson.

''e go for place belong *kanaka*,' said Joe.

'The village,' said Hudson.

'Are they after us?' asked Carter.

'Very unlikely,' said Hudson. 'We can't take any chances though. How long for beach, Joe?'

Joe pointed down the track with the Japanese footprint on it. '*Lik-lik, tabauda*.'

Hudson looked serious. 'In that case, we'd better go long-long.'

'What the hell's going on, Skip?' asked Johnson.

'I don't know,' said Hudson. 'Maybe the *kanakas* found the boat and tipped off the Nips.'

'Bastards,' said Johnson.

'If they did, they'll be waiting for us. We'll make a wide detour and take a look at the beach.'

He began to gabble pidgin to Joe.

Carter looked about him with renewed apprehension of the Jap presence. The jungle itself was a full-time adversary. Sometimes it was possible to forget that there was another enemy.

Joe led the way and the party moved forward slowly and warily. Every fifty yards Joe scouted ahead and returned to give the all-clear. The sun was climbing in the sky, visible only as a pattern of rhinestones against the dense foliage above their heads. Even in daylight the jungle was a dark and sombre place, illuminated by unexpected flashes of colour as some plant or creeper burst into grotesque life.

After an hour's snail-like progress, the jungle ended abruptly at the edge of an overgrown coconut plantation and Carter could see blue sky through the trees. Joe left his weapon and sauntered forward, as though a native looking for a good tree to climb. He reached the far side of the grove unchallenged and disappeared for a few seconds before standing up in a half-crouched position and giving the signal for the others to move forward. Carter followed Hudson, anticipating with almost child-like relish his first sight of the sea.

'Holy shit!'

Bemused, Carter sunk to his knees behind Joe. Four hundred yards from where they crouched, a motorized barge was riding at anchor, a large Japanese flag flopping loosely at its stern. Carter recognized the barge from aerial photographs. It was one of a fleet used for ferrying troops along the coast and for unloading vessels that weighed anchor outside Rabaul harbour at night. Half a dozen Jap soldiers were visible on board, the same number on shore. They had been ferried by a small tender which was pulled up on the beach. Some smoke from further up the beach suggested that they had lit a fire. Within a hundred yards of the moored tug was the callophyllum tree where the rubber dinghy was hidden.

'Bastard!' said Johnson. 'What the hell's going on?'

'I hope they're just beating the drum through the villages,' said Hudson. 'They've probably sent a party ashore to tell the headman that the rising sun shines out of the emperor's whatsit.'

He wondered what the commander of the sub would be thinking as he watched the scene through his periscope. If only the wireless was working.

'They'd better not find the boat,' said Carter.

As he spoke, a Jap appeared from the direction of the callophyllum tree, carrying an armful of dry palm fronds.

Johnson whistled through his teeth. 'If they start poking around for firewood, we're up the creek.'

As if some malicious fate had overheard his words, two more Japs began sauntering along the beach looking for driftwood, slowly but surely closing in on the callophyllum tree. Hudson and the rest watched, alarmed and powerless, as a desultory gabble of Japanese floated towards them. The dinghy was concealed below a few layers of palm fronds and would be immediately sought out by anyone entering the tangled root structure in search of firewood. The first fuel collector rejoined his comrades and, after a few moments spent rearranging one of their loads, stepped under the archway of roots.

A shrill cry rang out.

For a moment, Carter thought that it signalled discovery of the boat, and then a large party of men began to emerge from the jungle. Half a dozen Japs and upwards of a hundred natives, men, women and children. Most of the natives moved forward like prisoners under guard, cowering and frightened, but there was a separate group wearing khaki *lap-laps* and armbands who strutted along carrying long spears. Carter recognized the armbands from descriptions in intelligence reports. They were those of the Kempei Tai, a native police force recruited by the Japs and predictably brutal in their methods.

The arrival of the party of the Japs on the beach was galvanizing. Firewood was dropped and weapons sought at the double. More Japs appeared from the shelter of the trees and NCOs barked orders. Clearly responsible for the display of activity was the Jap at the head of the arriving party. Both by his uniform and the deference with which he was treated, it was obvious that he was an officer of high rank. He carried a long, curved ceremonial sword and was followed by a soldier bearing a Japanese flag scarcely smaller than that on the motorized barge. His breeches were of riding-school quality and his green cap more precise than the crumpled khaki forage caps of the ordinary soldiers with their neck flaps to protect against the sun.

'What rank is he?' hissed Hudson.

'I think he's a lieutenant-general,' said Carter. 'Could be Koji, commander of the Rabaul Garrison.'

Hudson shook his head in puzzlement. 'What's he doing here? It must be more than flag-waving.'

'Looks as if we're going to get the chance to find out,' said Johnson grimly.

Down the beech, the General flourished his sword arm towards the coconut plantation and the natives fell over each other to stumble forward like a herd of frightened sheep. Eager to implement his superior officer's order, a lieutenant lashed at them with a stick while the common soldiery chivvied with boot and rifle butt, ably assisted by the Kempei Tai. Carter winced as a spear was thrust into a man's haunches so that its oval tip disappeared into flesh. He eased back the safety-catch on his carbine, determined to kill the spearman with his second shot. The first would be for the General. Hudson sunk down nearer to the ground, raising and lowering his palm in a 'keep calm' gesture.

Fifty feet from their position, the lieutenant snapped out an order. The natives stopped and stood still. A child started to cry and was immediately shaken into silence by its terrified mother. The General stationed himself before them. His standard-bearer stood close behind him so that the flag brushed against the General's shoulder. Seen from close to, he was a spruce man of about fifty wearing round, rimless spectacles. His face was cadaverously thin and he sported a Hitlerian moustache. The soldiers fell in menacingly close to the natives, and the General began to speak, waiting after each sentence for one of the Kempei Tai to translate. Carter looked at Hudson inquiringly until he relayed Joe's translation in a whisper.

'The *kanakas* are a lot of lazy so-and-sos. . . . They were ordered to build a watch-tower on the beach for the Emperor so he could help defend them against the corrupt Americans and Australians and they have done nothing. . . . The Emperor is very angry. . . . He says that they must be punished and made to realize that this is "time belong hearim talk"—time to do what they're told.'

As the General's address reached its end, his voice became more and more angry and shrill and was only exceeded in intensity by that of his translator, who drove the helm of his spear into the sand to emphasize each point.

The atmosphere was one of brooding fear that communicated far beyond the huddle of natives, and Carter felt a nagging sense of impotence that amounted almost to connivance. Something terrible was going to happen but any intervention was out of the question if they were going to survive and get back with the information to Moresby. He had to lie here and watch.

The General finished speaking and saluted the Japanese flag and then snapped out an order to the Kempei Tai. Like dogs that had been waiting for the order to retrieve, they sprang into the crowd and dragged out five men who were thrown to the ground at the General's feet. One pathetically tried to rise to his knees and deliver a salute but was knocked half-senseless by a blow of sickening force from a spear haft. The men's arms were secured behind their backs and they lay still, like chickens trussed for the market. There was about them a chilling refusal to offer resistance. Not one of them struggled or cried out. It was as if they had no hope and were totally reconciled to what was going to happen to them.

Another actor arrived upon the scene, a middle-aged Jap soldier with the build of a sumo wrestler. He waddled down the beach carrying something wrapped in a silk cloth that rested on his hands like a sacrificial offering. He, too, saluted the General and the flag and then began to unroll the silk cloth, revealing the gleaming blade of a *katanga*, or samurai sword, its edge shining viciously in the bright sunlight. The cloth was handed to a soldier, who folded it carefully, and the squat man took some practice swings, making the sword hiss through the still air. He wore no shirt, and the sweat dripped off his fleshy shoulders and glistened in the rolls of fat round his waist. Satisfied that he was ready, he nodded to the Kempei Tai, who fell upon the prisoners and set them up on their knees like a row of targets, facing the band of silent natives. A child began to whimper unrestrainedly. Like a snail tentatively leaving its shell, the first man put his head forward.

Carter felt sick and lowered his head to the ground. If he could have taken his hands from his weapon and covered his ears he would have done so. He closed his eyes. There was something about the way the man had meekly extended his head for the sword that made him want to throw up. Five times he heard the dreadful swish of the falling blade and the gentle 'chunk' noise that told of a head being separated from its neck. Five times, the dead-weight fall of a body toppling over like a sack of flour.

When he looked, the heads were scattered almost to the General's feet, the necks pouring dark blood into the sand. Unable to control their blood lust, the Kempei Tai sprang forward and began to plunge their spears into the corpses. Carter grunted and drew up his weapon. There was a level beyond which he could stand no more. Seeing the look in his eye, Hudson threw himself sideways and pinned him to the ground while Johnson clung to his weapon. He looked like an epileptic in a fit and then the spasm passed and his arms went limp. Slowly the others released him and he lay still, his face against the ground, breathing steadily through his half-open mouth.

Suddenly, from the beach, came the sound of a girl screaming. A terrifying wail full of fear, anguish and hate. The sound of an avenging fury. Running from the jungle came a long-limbed girl, her black hair streaming behind her, her feet kicking up sand. She ran with head rolling, as if there was a race to be run or she was being pursued by a wild beast. She wore an old European dress that finished at her thigh but she was clearly Melanesian. With a sobbing shriek she threw herself amongst the severed heads, thrusting her head against the sand so she could look into each face. On hands and knees she scrambled from one to the other until a piteous scream told that she had found what she was seeking. She plucked the head up and crushed it to her breasts, wrapping her arms round it until they were sticky with blood and sand. A Kempei Tai attempted to seize her but she shrugged him aside and snapped at his hands as if she was a dog. Furious, he struck her with the shaft of his spear and the girl slumped sideways, unconscious, still clutching the head to her bosom.

Spurred by the girl's example an angry murmur at last broke from the throats of the herded natives but this was silenced almost immediately by a combined rush of the Kempei Tai and the Japs who broke ranks and presented their weapons. A few clubs and kicks and any threat of resistance was banished. On the ground the girl stirred and was seized by one of the Kempei Tai, who twisted her arm viciously behind her back and held her, head pressed into the sand.

When all was under control, the General continued his peroration, and Hudson let out an audible groan.

'They've got to build a watch-tower by nightfall or the Emperor is really going to fall upon them.' He looked to Joe for a further translation. 'A watch-tower capable of holding a "big glass". Jesus! That's a searchlight. How the hell are we going to get to the boat with a searchlight playing all over the beach?'

'*Tabauda*! Go for bush! *Kanaka* come cuttim bamboo.'

Joe started to wriggle away like a snake and the others followed. A volley of guttural bellows from the beach suggested that the natives were being unleashed to make up for their dilatoriness, and hardly had the party reached the comparative safety of the thick jungle than a jumble of natives poured into the coconut grove and headed for an adjacent clump of bamboo. Bush knives and stone axes were produced, and the grove began to melt away as hefty canes were dragged back towards the beach. Four Japs appeared to supervise the operation but they soon became bored and moved away leaving the field to the Kempei Tai, who lashed out indiscriminately at anyone in sight until they too became tired and squatted under the coconut palms. There was no sign of the girl.

Hudson left Joe on watch and retired deeper into the jungle with Carter and Johnson.

'Right,' he said, when they had found a hiding place amongst a clump of sago palm. 'Let's examine the situation. The sub will be lying offshore until midnight tonight. They might push off after what they've seen but I don't think so. Our wireless is crook and any other form of signal is out of the question at the moment. Without the searchlight there's a faint chance we might be able to get to the boat and launch it further down the coast. With the searchlight we're buggered. We'll never get near it.'

'If it hasn't been found by then,' said Johnson.

'Thanks, Jerry,' said Hudson. 'I knew I could rely on you for a word of cheer. Now, forget walking.'

'Sure thing,' said Johnson, grimly.

Carter glanced at the man's face. It had turned ashen grey beneath the blotchy tan. The eyes were haunted and the corner of the mouth twitched as if nerves were suddenly stretched to breaking-point.

Johnson saw Carter looking at him. 'I walked from Rabaul in '42,' he said simply. 'That's when the Japs got me.'

Hudson moved on rapidly. 'As I see it we have two alternatives. First, we can move down coast, build a raft and hope there's an opening in the reef we can get through.'

'Then find the sub,' said Johnson.

'I already prefer the second alternative,' said Carter. 'What is it?'

'Wipe out the searchlight post and retrieve the boat.'

Hudson watched them digesting the idea.

'I know it puts the kibosh on the Japs not knowing we've been here, but if we don't get back nobody's going to know about Matupi either.'

'That's jake, Skipper,' said Johnson. 'It's going to put them on their guard though, isn't it?'

'They're on their guard already if they're bothering to put searchlight posts along the coast,' said Carter.

Johnson laughed bitterly. 'What bloody luck! They must have looked at this place and thought just what we did. A nice quiet place to make a landing.'

'You talk about wiping out the post like it's as easy as going to the john,' said Carter. 'Have you any idea how we're going to do it?'

'Depends how many Japs there are,' said Hudson. 'My guess is they'll leave a section to set up the searchlight and show the Kempei Tai how to use it. Maybe they'll man it themselves. I reckon on about four Japs and the same number of Kempei Tai. Best thing we can do is rest up now and take another look when everything quietens down.'

He pulled open a pouch and took out a neatly folded square of mosquito netting. 'Jerry, show Joe where we are and take the first watch. Wake me in an hour.'

He settled back against a stump and draped the netting over his head and shoulder so that he looked like a beekeeper about to take a nap. His eyes were closed before his chin touched his chest.

Carter envied the man his ability to fall asleep so easily. His own mind was still in turmoil after what he had seen on the beach. The ritualistic brutality of the Japs. The unfettered savagery of the Kempei Tai towards their own people. Above all, he thought of the girl. Her beauty had moved him as much as her courage. What had happened to her?

Johnson was drawing himself to his feet to move off.

Carter touched his leg. 'I'll take the first watch, Jerry.' Johnson looked towards the sleeping Hudson as if worried by the change of plan.

'It doesn't make any difference, does it?' added Carter.

'I guess not. I'm pretty tuckered.' Johnson settled down opposite Hudson with his carbine across his lap and his finger on the trigger guard.

Carter picked his way carefully to Joe's position and guided him back to the sago palms.

'I'm going to take a quick look at the beach,' he said.

Joe looked unhappy. 'Me go you,' he said.

Carter tried not to show his irritation at Joe's protectiveness. 'No. You stay here.'

Carter did not wait for a reply but moved back towards the coconut grove, all senses primed. Shafts of harsh sunlight broke amongst the trees, and the clump of bamboos was decimated and deserted save for the insects greedily clustered on the sap that ran from the severed shoots. Carter rested on one knee and looked and listened. From the beach he could hear the hollow thumping of axe against bamboo and then, suddenly and unexpectedly, the long, continuous blah of a siren. He hesitated for a moment and then guessed that it was the barge preparing to leave.

Hoping that all eyes would be directed seawards, he crept swiftly through the palms towards a point where the ground began to rise and reunite itself with the jungle. Near the beach, a tall rain tree elbowed itself out from the undergrowth, its branches craning over the sand. Carter tore himself free from a prickly vine and saw the blood running down in fork marks on his arms as he pulled himself up into its lower branches. He rested for a moment and then propped his carbine among the foliage and worked his way out laterally, hearing the tan-coloured pods that hung from the branches rattling like miniature castanets. Suddenly his head poked out into the dazzling sun and the wood beneath his fingers was almost too hot to touch. He looked sideways and could see along the beach.

Close to the spot where they had first lain hidden, the structure of the watch-tower was taking shape: a bamboo framework lashed together with liana. Beyond, the barge was pulling away from the shore, the Japanese flag beginning to flow out as it gathered speed and left a V in the placid waters of the lagoon. The tender bobbed obediently behind, like a duckling fearing separation from its mother. Five Japs on the shore waved to their departing comrades and called out across the water.

Carter noted the number of the enemy that had been left behind and also the searchlight and generator which had been unpacked and were standing among the crowd of sweating natives labouring on the tower. Nearby, the corpses of the slain men lay where they had fallen, their flesh now glistening under a moving mantle of flies. Their heads had been mounted on Kempei Tai spears and faced the labourers as a grim reminder that it would be unwise to slacken their efforts. The message appeared to have been taken.

Carter looked for the girl and felt relief that she was not lying amongst the dead men on the beach as he had feared. He searched amongst the men and women trimming and lashing lengths of bamboo but there was no sign of her. Perhaps she had come to and been able to slip away into the jungle. It was strange but he felt sad that he would never see her again.

The Japs started to move up the beach and Carter studied their weapons. One Nambu 7.7mm machine gun carried by two men, one of whom was swathed in ammunition belts, and four rifles. Two of the men had canister grenades hanging from their belts. They were not lightly armed.

Carter checked that the Japs were on course for the shade at the top of the beach and then began to wriggle back down the branch. He felt mildly pleased with himself. He would enjoy the small personal triumph of reporting back to the others on what he had seen. Complacency gave way to fear as he looked back and saw what was dangling from a horizontal branch above the one he was on. A bright yellow snake nearly a metre in length. Its head swayed towards him inquiringly and he froze. Common sense told him that it was probably a small tree python and incapable of giving a poisonous bite, but a deep-rooted fear of all reptiles made him unwilling to put the theory to the test. He stayed where he was and watched the bulging grey eye with its bisecting pupil play steadily on him. He shook a foot menacingly and the snake merely dropped onto the same branch as if attracted by the movement. Christ! Perhaps it was a poisonous tree snake and he had succeeded in arousing it. Carter tried to remember the illustrations on a leaflet giving details of his life expectancy after being bitten by various varieties of New Guinea snake. Only one general picture had lingered in his mind. All snakes were dangerous. Steer clear of them. That was not going to be so easy in this case.

Suddenly, from the beach, came the sound of Jap voices raised in anger. A guttural scream of rage that sounded like a bronchitic throat being cleared. And the shouts did not stay on the beach. They came nearer.

Faced with a choice, Carter quickly decided that he feared Japs more than snakes. He was barely twenty feet from the ground and easily visible to anyone looking up into the branches. He needed more protection. Gritting his teeth he continued wriggling back towards the trunk. The snake twisted towards him, hissed a warning, and then dropped to the ground, its tail flicking his leg. Hardly had it slithered away than there was the sound of someone running through the undergrowth. Carter pressed himself flat against the branch and peered down through the fork, his heart pumping.

The girl ran into the small clearing. One eye was almost closed and her hands were tied behind her back. A length of liana secured to one ankle suggested that she had either shaken free of her bonds or escaped when they were undone. She looked about her, desperate for somewhere to hide, and then up into the tree. Her eyes met Carter's and she started back in alarm. Carter opened his mouth to speak and then said nothing.

Two Japs crashed through the undergrowth and the girl tried to flee. She had taken two steps before her foot caught a root and she fell heavily. The two Japs threw themselves on her triumphantly. She bit one, making him scream out in pain and hit her hard in the face, and was then bundled over with her face in the dust and a Jap sitting between her shoulder blades. Her legs drummed and then lay still.

The second soldier squatted beside his companion like a monkey and for a few seconds their heavy breathing was the only sound to be heard. Then three more soldiers arrived, talking excitedly. Carter prayed that nothing would make them look up.

He need not have worried. They only had eyes for the girl. They squatted round her and one pulled back the remnants of her skirt and inserted his hand between her legs. The others laughed derisively as she struggled and kicked. Carter felt powerless and humiliated to a degree that almot surpassed his fear. A set of dice was produced and as each man cast and reacted to his fortune, Carter realized what they were throwing for: the order in which they would have the girl. If only he had Hudson's Mills gun in his hands. None of the Japs was carrying a weapon and they could have been mowed down in two bursts. Cramp was beginning to make his limbs ache painfully, but the mental agony was far worse.

The Japs were filthy, and there was one who did not bother to brush the flies from his face. Their stench rose into the tree and made him feel sick. The shrill flow of the men's chatter reached a climax and the girl was dragged to her feet, still trying to bite the hands that seized her and lashing out with her long legs. A cruel blow to the jaw half stunned her, and she was stripped and hurled down on her back directly below Carter's hiding-place. A Jap sank down beside her with a bayonet and for a second it seemed that her throat was to be cut. Then the bayonet was placed with its point inside the girl's nostril. If she moved or struggled, her nose would be split open. A second Jap took off his belt and pulled open the front of his trousers, letting them slide towards his knees as he sank down and edged forward between her brown thighs.

The girl opened her eyes and looked up at Carter. There was no expression in them. No reproach, no call for help. Just a blank, unfeeling stare that told nothing to the animals who were gloating over her, eager for the signs of fear and pain that would feed their lusts. The Jap mounted her and his haunches began to quiver. The girl closed her eyes.

Carter felt a sense of revulsion that made him press his open mouth against the bark to choke back the sobs. He had never realized that the act of rape was so bestial, so demeaning. He felt as if he was personally involved, one of the men waiting to void himself in the girl's thighs. She could have betrayed him to give herself a chance of escape but she had said nothing. Now his silence betrayed her. He had justified himself once. Could he do it again? Was he doing nothing because he dare not put the operation at risk or because he was afraid?

The first man achieved satisfaction and changed places with the Jap holding the knife. The girl opened her eyes again. They were now wet with tears. Carter hoped that the tears in his own eyes would be seen and build some bond of sympathy between them. What he was watching was the murder of human dignity, something he knew that men had practised on women since the beginning of time. Something so common that it was almost treated as a joke. Nothing that he had ever seen had made him despise himself so much.

The second Jap was followed by the third, and the others clustered round, smoking a shared cigarette and making jokes. Not once did they raise their eyes a few feet from what was happening on the ground. The girl began to cry, and they kicked her. It was impossible to understand what they were saying but it sounded as if they were reminding her that this was a punishment. Perhaps even they felt some need to justify what they were doing.

Eventually, the last Jap was finished. He clamped his belt round his waist and pulled his sweat-rimed cap on to his head. After a final hefty kick, the girl's wrists were freed. She lay slumped on the ground as the Japs walked away, justice done.

Carter waited until all was silent and quickly dragged his cramped limbs down from the tree. The girl turned her head swiftly as he approached and shrank away. Perhaps it was hardly surprising that she should expect him to be searching for the same gratification as the Japs. He laid his rifle down beside her and sank to his knees.

'I'm sorry,' he said. 'I surely am sorry.' The tears were running down his cheeks and he began to sob. 'Sorry,' he repeated.

He took one of her hands and squeezed it. She looked at him in astonishment and then began to cry. He put his arms round her shoulders and hugged her to him like a child that had just woken up after a nightmare. For nearly a minute they clung together and then the girl drew away and looked up at him.

'You Australian?'

'American. You speak English?'

The girl pulled her long wavy hair forward over her shoulders and smoothed it over her naked breasts.

'A little. I was a children's nurse at Rabaul before the Japs come. You are pilot? Your plane is shot down?'

Carter looked into the swollen but still beautiful face before him and wondered what to say. There seemed to be no alternative.

'Yes.' He was used to lying to women but this time it hurt a little. 'What's your name?'

'Sula.'

Carter pointed a finger at his chest. 'Will.'

'We-e-el.' She repeated the name with difficulty. 'You are the only man left when plane crash?'

'No. I have friends close by—' He paused as Sula suddenly

seized his arm.

'Men come!'

She snatched up the tattered remnants of her dress and pulled him by the hand. Carter could hear nothing but did not doubt her for an instant. He snatched up his rifle and followed her long, loping stride.

Thirty seconds later, the first of the Kempei Tai burst into the clearing, his spear raised expectantly. The Japanese masters had told them that they could do as they wished with the girl and they shouted angrily in frustration when they found that she was no longer there.

7

By six o'clock in the evening the tower was finished. Forty feet high, with the searchlight mounted on a platform at the top and the machine gun on its own platform a few feet below. Thirty feet from the jungle and fifty from the high-water mark, giving an uninterrupted view along the beach and out to the reef. The tropical sun sank fast behind the jungle like a leaking balloon and a chorus of insects began to chirp its requiem.

No sooner had darkness fallen than the generator was started and the searchlight switched on to startle the flying foxes returning from their evening run on the village gardens. The light cut swathes along the beach and swept out like an admonishing finger to point at the opening in the reef. The faces of the watching villagers borrowed a little of its light to show their fear and awe. Only the fly-blown eyes of the severed heads failed to observe the splendid edifice their deaths had contributed to.

'*Raus!*' This was one word of German-borrowed pidgin that the Japs had learned. To accompany it, the searchlight was tilted downwards so that it shone directly in the faces of the watching natives. They scattered before the dazzling light and ran into the jungle, pursued by the beam until it shattered into fragments against the closely packed trees. The Japs laughed at the savages and began to eat the roast pig and yams they had requisitioned, throwing their left-overs down towards the swollen corpses still humming with insect-life. More sensitive nostrils would have found the stench insupportable, but these were men who had been at war in the Pacific for nearly two years and were well used to the sight and smell of rotting flesh. Besides, the bodies served as a reminder that the Emperor's word was to be obeyed; they would stay there until the first high tide hissed amongst the bleached bones.

Corporal Toyoda had already decided that he would pack one of the heads in wet sand and take it back to Rabaul with him when he was relieved. He would bury it until the flesh and brains had putrefied and then put it out in the sun to whiten. Perhaps if he boiled it in his helmet the process could be speeded up. It would be amusing to show a human skull to his friends when he returned to Nagasaki. They would be impressed. He could use it as a paperweight and keep his writing brushes in the eye sockets. Perhaps not the latter. That would not be respectful, and his mother would be offended.

The light was cut and he leaned against the bamboo balustrade and looked along the beach. Without the searchlight it was difficult to see more than thirty paces and the darkness began to play tricks; the bundles of unused bamboo seemed like attackers crawling towards the tower and even the corpses looked as if they were stirring.

He gave the order and the light was switched on again, to play against the twisted roots of the grotesquely shaped tree half-way down the beach. As the light began to move on, something caught his eye and he ordered it to be swung back. He had seen something glinting among the roots and wondered if it was an animal. He peered down the beam and frowned. It was difficult to see through the roots but there appeared to be some ind of thatched, oblong structure with something bright gleaming on its side. What could it be? Some kind of trap set by the natives? But for what? It was too high to be a fish trap, and wild pigs were unlikely to come down to the beach. He debated with himself and decided to go and look immediately. It was going to be a long night cooped up on top of the tower and already the insects were beginning to bite. He heard the ammunition belts stirring on the floor below and the sliding noise as the gunner tested the traverse of the machine gun on its tripod.

The wireless set crackled and the signaller from Rabaul came up asking if there was anything to report. Situation reports were to be made every hour with an immediate call if anything unusual was seen or heard. The call was answered with the minimum of words and the set switched off. At beach level, the generator started to hum.

Temporarily distracted from the object amongst the roots, Toyoda searched for the flashlight and prepared to detail two men to accompany him. Hardly had he found it than there was the sound of a voice from the edge of the jungle. The searchlight swung round, momentarily dazzling him, and the machine gun moved with it so that it was pointing down the centre of the beam. A lone figure was picked out, framed by two trees. Toyoda blinked and rubbed his eyes. It looked like the crazy girl they had amused themselves with earlier. She stepped out of the trees, talking the native language and gesticulating towards the bodies.

'She is mad that one,' said Private Tishoro. 'What does she want?'

'She wants to buy the men we executed,' said Toyoda.

'If we shoot her that will save her the trouble,' said a voice from the platform below. The men laughed.

'Shall I shoot her?' said the machine gunner.

'Not yet,' said another voice. 'I think I could use her again.'

'If I shoot her in the right place, you *can* use her again,' said the machine gunner.

'Shoot her in many places so we can all use her,' said another voice.

There was more laughter and the girl continued to talk and wave towards the bodies.

'*Raus!*' shouted Toyoda. He had a stomach-ache after eating too much undercooked pork, and he did not want to fuck the woman again. Neither did he want to let the machine gunner waste ammunition. Let the native police have her for the cooking pot.

Suddenly, the girl stopped gabbling and ran towards the jungle, with the searchlight following her as if she was making a fast exit from a darkened stage. Toyoda was surprised by the swiftness of her withdrawal. She must have taken fright before their shouts.

'Tishoro, Kobi.'

He called the names of the men he wished to accompany him and moved towards the rough bamboo ladder. Strange. Was it the shadows playing tricks or had a figure just run into the jungle on the opposite side from the girl? He looked down and let out a shout of alarm.

A small red flame was burning at the foot of the tower. A small red flame that moved.

Toyoda threw his leg over the side of the guard-rail just as there was a blinding yellow flash and a violent explosion that blasted his eardrums and lifted him into the air like a handful of feathers. One corner of the tower was blown away and the whole structure keeled over and toppled towards the jungle. Fragments of bamboo penetrated Toyoda's stomach and spleen like shrapnel and he felt the ghastly sensation of clutching at nothing and hurtling downwards. He hit the sand with sickening force and bounced almost into the jungle. Behind him, the machine gun lay on its side with one of the buckled legs of the tripod holding off a roof of collapsed bamboo. One man was dead beneath the gun; the others screamed in pain and in an attempt to instil courage into themselves as they struggled to find their weapons. They never did.

Four figures burst from the jungle, and a volley of automatic fire crashed into the shattered framework of the tower, making it reel. Splinters of bamboo flew like chaff, and the four Japs were mown down, trapped in a cage. Toyoda saw the angry streaks of light and heard the ruthless gabble of the Mills gun paring the cries to silence. Instinctively his hand had gone to his wound, but now he withdrew the warm, sticky fingers and tried to crawl to the jungle a few feet away. A spasm of pain shot through his stomach as if a knife had been plunged into it but he bit into the sand and struggled on. He realized now that the girl had been a decoy. Whilst they occupied themselves with her, someone had stolen up to place a charge against the tower. He, Corporal Ito Toyoda of the 38th Division Infantry Group of the Imperial Japanese Army, had been guilty of negligence and stupidity. He knew that he was shortly going to die but before that happened he must make amends to the Emperor he had failed. He felt something dragging against the sand and slid his hand under his belly. It was his own intestines beginning to leak out. The news comforted rather than alarmed him. It was if some divine agency had performed the hara-kiri with which he would have sought the propitiation of the spirits for his incompetence.

He wriggled on, sheltered by a slight dip, and dragged his body behind a sparse scrub of mangrove. Turning sideways, he lay on his shoulder and struggled to unhook the grenade at his waist. The pain was now almost unbearable and he bit another mouthful of sand and swallowed it. At the third try, the clip on his belt released and the grenade dropped from his fingers. He pulled himself up, hearing a bubbling sound from his stomach, and peered towards the beach. The enemy were searching the bodies of his comrades and cutting the insignia from their uniforms. One man was pulling apart the shattered framework as if looking for something. He turned and spoke urgently to the others in English. At his words all the men stopped what they were doing and looked inquiringly towards the jungle. They must have discovered that he was not amongst the wreckage. Well, they would soon know where he was. Toyoda rubbed one of his bloody hands in the sand and grasped the grenade securely. He prised up the firing device and put his finger in the loop. One last effort and his life could end with some honour still attached to it. His finger tightened against the metal and something appeared before his throat. It was a knife. He looked up and saw the girl. Most of all he saw her bared teeth. He was still looking at them as the knife started to slit his throat.

8

'Well?' said Carter.

Major Dallas walked across the room and paused before tossing his hat onto the desk. He rubbed a finger up and down the side of his nose, arched in his swivel chair and spun it round before leaning forward importantly and clasping his hands.

Ask a simple question and you get an academy award performance, thought Carter.

'The Colonel is not overtly enamoured of the concept,' said Dallas. 'He wants the opinion of a second vulcanologist.'

'Christ!' Carter looked across to Hudson who withdrew his pipe and blew an angry puff of smoke at the ceiling. 'You know how long it took to find the first guy. And what did he say? He thought it was probably possible to blow up a volcano if it was ripe, but he wasn't certain how much explosive without seeing the volcano and where it was going to be placed. I thought we were going to have to take him back with us.'

'You're never going to get a definite answer,' chipped in Hudson. 'The most important thing is that this joker thinks it can be done. I'd be worried if he said it was plain bloody stupid.'

'Why don't we go straight to MacArthur?' said Carter. 'He'd think it was worth a try.'

'The Colonel doesn't want to put any proposal forward unless he thinks it has at least a fifty percent chance of success,' said Dallas. 'Don't knock it, Will. It's your goddamned hide he's thinking about. We can't rely on beautiful native girls to get you out of trouble on every mission.'

Carter shook his head wearily. 'I've told you. We had to bring her back with us.'

'We couldn't leave her,' added Hudson. 'It was odds on the Japs would find out that she'd helped us. They'd already beheaded her father. I don't like to think what they'd have done to her.'

'I'm not blaming you,' said Dallas with mock sincerity. 'Like I said, she's a beautiful girl.'

'I think so,' said Carter simply. 'She saved my life.'

'She saved all our lives,' said Hudson. He emptied his pipe into an ashtray. 'Now, can we get back to the plan? I have the feeling that nobody is very enthusiastic about it. It's nearly a week since we got back and everybody is looking around for another in-tray to dump it in.'

'Yes, what about the "dynamic initiative", Major?' Carter asked.

'MacArthur is the dynamic initiative and he's in Pearl Harbor at the moment,' said Dallas. 'You've got to go through the Colonel to get to him. I'm sorry it's taking so long but it's totally outside the scope of anything that's been tried before.'

'I expect that's what they said when somebody discovered gunpowder,' said Carter.

Dallas gave him a smile which had no warmth in it. 'Very smart, Lieutenant. Is that the great plan, nestling there on your lap? Why don't you give me the twice-nightly version. You're going to need me on your side as well, you know.'

Carter looked at Hudson, shrugged, and opened the buff file.

'Ok, but don't take everything I say as gospel. We're still working on a few things. First of all, some basics. I've checked it out and the most effective explosive for us to use would be PLA. The engineers tell me that a thousand pounds of that placed internally would blow the top off a small mountain.'

Dallas whistled. 'A thousand pounds! Jeeze. How are you going to get it there—in a truck?'

'I'll come to that,' said Carter. 'Second basic. The Japs have gun emplacements and searchlights all round the entrance to Rabaul harbour and Matupi Bay. Sula tells me that a curfew has recently been introduced and that this includes movement by water. Any native canoe moving about after dark is liable to be blown out of the water. Apparently, the Japs are very jumpy about night attacks, and our little bust-up isn't going to make them feel any more relaxed.'

Dallas said nothing.

'Third basic. We have to get Green out of the prison camp after six o'clock in the evening and return him before eight a.m.'

'Otherwise he turns into a pumpkin,' said Dallas sarcastically. 'Honestly, I don't know why you guys are puzzled by a lack of enthusiasm. You've got to be a super optimist or a madman to see two bits change out of this plan.'

Carter bit his lip. He was finding it increasingly difficult to control his mounting anger. For the first time in his military career he had been feeling enthusiastic about an assignment and confident of his own importance to it. Now Dallas was undermining everything, making him feel that the mission to Rabaul and all the careful planning he had done with Hudson had been a waste of time.

Hudson sensed the danger and began to talk calmly. 'It seemed to us that we were faced with two alternatives,' he said. 'Either to get ashore a safe distance from Rabaul and manhandle a thousand pounds of explosive through the jungle, or devise a means of getting as close to Matupi as possible. If we choose the first alternative and get ashore without being seen, it's virtually impossible to avoid bumping into some native on the way to the volcano. Once we do that the word will be all round the peninsula and the Japs will be onto us. It's impossible for us to give them the slip weighed down with all that explosive.'

'You'd have to find some bearers to carry the explosive,' said Dallas. 'That's going to tip the Japs off, too.'

'Right,' said Carter. 'The average weight a bearer carries is fifty pounds. A strong man can carry double that over a short distance. If we can land near Matupi we'd only need ten bearers compared with twenty further away. The shorter distance to cover would also obviously lessen the risk of discovery.'

'Except that the whole of the shoreline is going to be crawling with Japs,' said Dallas. 'How are you going to get past the searchlights and the gun positions?'

'The searchlights are going to be no problem because we'll be landing by daylight,' said Carter.

Dallas looked at him and shook his head slowly from side to side. 'You're loco,' he said. 'It's impossible to land in daylight.'

'It depends what you're landing in,' said Hudson.

Carter flicked through his file until he found an aerial photograph, which he then placed on the blotter in front of Dallas. A section of the photograph was circled in blue chinagraph.

'That's a tiny little beach below Matupi,' he said. 'It's tucked away behind the Japanese gun emplacement at the mouth of the bay. The Japs can see out to sea and across the bay but they can't see back to the beach.'

'I can see that,' said Dallas shortly.

'Do you see what's lined up on the beach?' asked Hudson.

Dallas picked up a magnifying glass and layed it on the photograph. 'Looks like native canoes,' he said.

Carter nodded. 'That's right. Native outriggers. They belong to the local fishermen. That's what we intend to use.'

Dallas looked from one face to the other and tapped his finger on the desk. 'How?'

'I'll give you the plan,' said Carter. 'Zero day minus two. A submarine drops Joe down-coast from Rabaul. He knows a bay with deep water right up to the reef. Joe swims ashore and makes his way round to Matupi, avoiding all villages. Now we get lucky.'

'I was wondering when we were going to,' said Dallas drily.

Carter ignored the interruption. 'Joe's home village is near Matupi. He will spend a day checking out the land and recruiting local bearers. That will take us up to the morning of zero day. Immediately after first light, when the curfew is lifted he will paddle out to sea with two outriggers, as if he and another native were going fishing.'

'Just before dawn, a submarine will have dropped us with the explosives at a point off the main shipping lanes outside the harbour,' continued Hudson. 'We'll rendezvous with the canoes and return to Matupi Bay. The Japs will think it's the same fishing canoes returning.'

'Surely they're going to notice the extra people?' queried Dallas.

'Not if they're lying in the bottom of the canoe covered with brushwood,' said Hudson.

'And the explosive,' said Dallas. 'You're not going to tell me you can store a thousand pounds of explosive in two pencil-thin dugout canoes? What kind of volume are we talking about?'

'Approximately five cubic feet,' said Carter. 'We're aware of the problem and we're working on it.'

'I'm real glad to hear that,' said Dallas sarcastically. 'Because you haven't forgotten that you've chosen an explosive that's liable to detonate on contact with water?'

'I'm hardly likely to forget it,' said Carter, remembering the whiplash sting of the shark's guts hitting his back as the explosion blew them both out of the sea.

'We've thought about that and decided it's a risk we'd have to take,' said Hudson. 'No other explosive packs the same punch for such a low weight and volume. If we wanted to get the equivalent blasting force with a conventional explosive we'd need to carry twice as much.'

Dallas moved the fan so that what little air there was in the room became his own private property.

'I hope you guys aren't intending to finance this operation by issuing share options. On what you've told me so far you'd be pushed to raise the price of a life-jacket. Do you know how many submarines we have operational in the Pacific at the moment? Less than fifty. And they're stretched like a piece of chewing gum from here to Salt Lake City. I can't see Admiral Halsey giving you one to play with for several days.'

Hudson started to fill his pipe. 'Do you mind if I continue with the plan, Major?' he asked with only the slightest edge to his voice. 'Let's say we land in the little bay below Matupi at around eleven hundred hours. Joe will take a look around and if everything is clear we'll hide up there until nightfall. As soon as it gets dark, Will and Joe will go to the prison camp and get Harry Green. Jerry and me will stay with the bearers and start lugging the explosive round the backside of Matupi. We aim to rendezvous around ten o'clock.'

'Green leads us to the tunnel and we place the explosive,' continued Carter. 'We've left three hours for that as the going is apparently tough as hell and we're doing it at night. Green's memory might be getting a little rusty as well.'

Dallas nodded as if he felt that might be the least of their problems.

'Let's say we're through by two o'clock with the charges set to go off at eight. That leaves us four hours to get Green back before sun-up.' Carter sat back in his chair.

'Then what?' said Dallas.

'Then I hope we hear a bloody great bang and start breathing soot,' said Hudson. He gave a cracked laugh and pushed the stem of his pipe between his teeth.

Dallas looked at the pipe unlovingly and pulled the fan nearer before turning to Carter. 'Well, Will?'

'We'll lie up during the day and head for a pick-up point at nightfall. Andrew has got two lined up. The choice depends on whether the bastard blows its top or not.'

'We don't want to have to wade through molten lava,' said Hudson. 'Our feet should be warm enough by then as it is.'

Dallas stood up and walked across to the window. He pulled aside the green shade and looked down to the frangipani trees and the stunted palms.

'Do you really think this plan has a hope of success?'

Hudson looked to Carter before replying. 'I don't think we can afford not to try it. Let's put it like that.'

Carter looked at the yellow, festering scratches on the back of his hands and turned them over. The lines that ran across his palms were now etched deep and black. One of them was his life line. Best not to know which one and start checking for a sudden rupture.

'It seems to me that there are so many things that could go wrong,' said Dallas.

'I don't get you,' said Carter. 'When you first called me in here you were talking about commando raids on Rabaul. About really shaking things up. Now we come up with a scheme and you start having second thoughts.'

'I'm trying to set the total risk involved against the chances of success,' said Dallas.

'In that case, tear up the report,' said Hudson. He took the file from Carter and tossed it onto the desk.

'I don't read you,' said Carter, bitterly. 'Are you worried about signing away a lot of expensive equipment and screwing up relations with the navy?'

'I'm not thinking of myself,' snapped Dallas defensively. 'Somebody has to see the broad picture. Put yourself in my position. Four guys are going to paddle into the middle of sixty thousand Japs, spring a guy from prison and blow up a volcano. It's kind of incredible, isn't it?'

'You've got it slightly wrong,' said Carter. 'Four guys and a girl—'

Dallas spun round. 'Now wait a minute—!'

Hudson held up a silencing hand. 'Why don't *you* wait a minute.' He turned to Carter. 'I think it would be easier if we showed Major Dallas exactly what we're talking about, don't you, Will?'

'Definitely,' said Carter.

Hudson stood up as if there was no need for further discussion.

'That way I can get to smoke my pipe without asphyxiating anybody.' He smiled at Dallas and extended a polite hand towards the door.

9

The freighter had been hit by bombs from two Mitsubishi 97s and now lay, a rusting hulk, at the entrance to Port Moresby harbour. The top deck sloped at an angle of 45° to the sea, and when a heavy sea broke over the reef it twitched and groaned like an old dog riding out troubled sleep.

Carter braced himself against a section of bomb-gouged deck plating and raised a loud-hailer to his lips.

'OK. Are you ready inside?'

'No!' A muffled shout came from the interior of the freighter.

Carter turned to Dallas who was propped up beside him and looking down at the choppy water uneasily. 'I figured if we could do it from this, it could hardly be more difficult with a sub.'

Dallas nodded. 'I agree. Provided you don't hit bad weather.'

'If we hit bad weather we're in trouble anyway,' said Carter. He reapplied his mouth to the hailer. 'Come on, you guys. Shake it up. You're keeping the Major waiting.'

There was an indistinguishable grumble from inside the hulk and then Hudson's voice. 'Right-o. Ready when you are.'

Carter carefully placed the loud-hailer at his feet and produced a stop-watch. Green weed swirled like drowned hair against the submerged bulkheads and from inside the wreck came the thwack of water slopping through its rusted metal guts.

'Go!'

As his finger went down on the stop-watch an inflated rubber dinghy attached to a line was tossed into the water from one of the deck housings. Following down the line came Johnson, dressed in a combat suit and with a Mills gun strapped across his shoulders. He let himself fall into the bottom of the boat and scrambled to his knees in time to unstrap a paddle and cover the few feet that separated him from a second inflatable rubber dinghy which had also been tossed into the sea. Joe slid down the second line and helped secure the two boats alongside each other by fastening their paddle straps. When this was done he scrambled into Johnson's boat and caught a third line. This was secured to the stern of the raft. No sooner had Joe's giant fingers fastened the knot than a plump plastic bag slid down the rope. This was attached via a hole punched in the three-inch overlap of plastic that surrounded the bag and through which the rope was threaded. Joe swiftly slit the plastic to release the bag and passed it to Johnson who stashed it in the bottom of the empty dinghy. Other bags arrived thick and fast, and these were passed to Johnson as quickly as he could handle them. The rubber boats rode on the swell and the sea slapped against their bottoms.

Carter glanced at his stop-watch and turned to Dallas to see how he was reacting.

He nodded approvingly. 'Not bad.'

'We know we're asking a lot, bringing a sub to the surface during daylight. That's why we want to ensure that it's a question of seconds rather than minutes before she can submerge again.'

The first dinghy was filling fast and Johnson began to unfurl a rubberized cover that could be zipped over its cargo.

'It works out good,' said Carter. 'Two hundred and fifty bags each boat.'

As he spoke, the cover was zipped and clipped over the first load, and a third dinghy was launched to be brought alongside the others. After it was secured, a loading rope was lashed to its stern. Bags slid down immediately and were packed tight along the floor of the boat. Both men worked feverishly and the sweat dripped off their faces and soaked their shirts. At last there were no more bags waiting on the line and all three ropes were cast off.

Carter snapped down his finger and glanced at the watch triumphantly. 'Well done, you guys. That's the fastest yet.' He turned to Dallas. 'The moment the last bag is off, the sub can submerge.'

Dallas looked sceptical. 'Leaving three rafts lashed together. Two of them stuffed to the gunwales with plastic explosive. Do you really believe you're going to be able to tow that ashore without the Japs seeing it?'

'No,' said Carter.

'I mean, even with the native canoes—' Dallas broke off in perplexity. 'What do you mean "no"?'

Hudson appeared, sweating, from the inside of the hulk and leaned back against the part of the sloping deck that was in the shade. 'We've been working on an idea.' He nodded towards the reef. 'Watch.'

Moving smoothly towards them with the blue horizon behind it was a slim outrigger canoe. A hollowed-out trunk with a framework of spars attached to a parallel log which gave extra stability. Paddling the canoe with practised skill was Sula, the muscles rippling in her graceful honey-brown arms. She did not wear a flower in her hair but in every other respect she responded to the picture postcard image of the beautiful South Sea maiden gliding up to do trade with a visiting merchantman. Her white teeth flashed up at Carter and her fine breasts swelled proudly beneath her loose-fitting cotton smock. She looked at him with undisguised affection.

'That's another thing,' said Dallas. 'The girl.' He pursed his lips disapprovingly.

'The only thing you can have against her is that she's a woman,' said Carter.

'Be realistic,' said Dallas. 'I know she played Pocahontas to your Captain John Smith but that doesn't make her suitable for what you're trying to do.'

'It doesn't rule her out either,' said Hudson. 'Look at the pluses—she's a native and she knows the area and speaks the language. As it stands at the moment, we're dividing into two parties, but we've only got Joe if we need an interpreter and somebody who knows their way around.'

'If we send her in with Joe, she can bring one of the canoes out,' added Carter. 'She swims like a fish, she's got more guts in her little finger than most guys I know have in their whole bodies and she's sharp as two tacks.'

'And being a woman could be a big advantage,' said Hudson. 'Once we get ashore she's going to fade into the background much more easily.'

'OK, OK.' Dallas held up his hands in a gesture of surrender. 'Now answer the sixty-four thousand dollar question. How does she spirit a thousand pounds of high explosive back to shore when there's a detachment of Japs within spitting distance?'

'She's only responsible for five hundred pounds,' said Carter. 'We're going to have two canoes, remember?' He extended a raised thumb towards the canoe. 'OK, Sula.'

Carter found himself watching with proprietorial interest as Sula made a few deft dabs with her paddle and the canoe swung in towards the rafts. Her mood had changed dramatically since their return to Moresby. She had stopped watching everyone like a cornered animal and smiled for the first time when Johnson slipped getting out of the Catalina flying-boat and nearly fell in the sea. Port Moresby she remembered, having been there with the family she had worked for as a nursemaid. She also recounted, not without pride, that she had visited Brisbane when her planter employer had returned there on leave. Finding somewhere for her to stay had been a problem because the native compound only catered for male natives and it was thought, not unreasonably, that the introduction of Sula might be a disruptive influence. Eventually she was billeted with the cook, a large black lady who stood no nonsense from anyone and boiled taro until it looked as if it had been put through a liquidizer. This arrangement worked well although she missed Carter.

Carter missed Sula, too. He found himself inventing military excuses so that he could be with her and ask questions about the Japanese defences around Rabaul. Sometimes he would look into her large brown eyes and forget to take notes, but it did not matter because he had nearly always asked the same questions before. What he found most difficult to analyse in his feelings was the degree of sex involved. It must be there, he thought, but partially disguised by what had happened under the rain tree. He had seen her mentally and physically exposed in a way that placed him almost too close to her. There could be no sexual mystery, no sense of 'first time' with this girl. When he touched her, they both would remember. He recalled the stag party in St Paul and the whore called from the motel. There had been five of them then, one after the other. It had been the same ritual even though they paid for it and made dumb jokes whilst the girl chewed gum and looked at the ceiling.

Sometimes, he found it difficult to look Sula in the eyes. He felt like one of the Japs. By being present he had taken part. By doing nothing he had collaborated. The ultimate violation. Had he a chance of ever having a complete relationship with this girl? Was this sense of participation why he had never mentioned the rape to the others? He had told them that he had found the girl running from the Japs. She had given no sign that she understood his lie or was grateful for it. Sometimes he wondered how much she did understand. More than the others suspected, he felt. Perhaps when living with the planter's family in Rabaul she had realized that the more people talk, the less they say. She observed everything and spoke infrequently.

It was strange, but when he thought about it she was the first woman that he had ever respected.

A young barracuda bullet-nosed through the clear water and Sula brought the canoe round so that the outrigger came within Joe's grasp. He clung to it while Johnson unstrapped one of the boats packed with explosive. Dallas watched, his impassivity barely distinguishable from boredom.

When the boat was floating free, Johnson pressed the air intake valve and there was a loud hissing noise. After a few seconds, the sides began to crinkle and the boat spread itself lower in the water like a deflating balloon. Dallas glanced at Carter questioningly but could not catch his eye. Johnson waited a few more seconds and took his hand from the valve. The swell was now washing over the side of the gunwales. Sula spread her long body across the spars that held the outrigger to the canoe and started to pull the near-submerged boat beneath her so that it was enclosed between the two parallel timbers. Joe climbed into the dug-out and began to untie some long bamboo poles that were lashed to its side. These he in turn fastened to the top of the raft while Johnson let out some more air. Like a grill, three canes pushed down on the raft and, when secured to the lower outrigger spars, held it securely just below the water, below hull and outrigger. No trace of the raft was now visible.

'That's neat,' said Dallas, grudgingly. 'Can you move it OK?'

'Sure,' said Carter.

He called down, and Joe and Sula began to paddle away from the two remaining rafts. The canoe moved more slowly through the water but there was still no sign of the raft.

Six miles away in the foothills there was the crump-crump of anti-aircraft fire, and puffs of smoke began to hang in the sky. Some Zeros must have sneaked in from Rabaul to strafe the air-field. Dallas was scrambling up the deck trying to find a higher vantage point.

'I think he's impressed,' murmured Hudson.

'Yes,' Carter grinned. 'Better not tell him it's the first time we got it right.'

He clambered after Dallas, trying to avoid touching the sun-baked metal with his bare flesh.

'I'm just trying to find a spot where I can see if it shows up under the water,' said Dallas. 'I must say it's good. It's damn good.' He realized he was in danger of indicating approval for something that might be vetoed by higher command. 'Of course, a rough sea is going to bitch you.'

'Sure,' said Carter, unworried that Dallas was repeating him-self and eager to pursue the line of optimism. 'This method of carrying the explosive is very effective when it comes to landing. We can bring the canoes right in, a few feet offshore in shallow water, and nobody is going to notice anything. Then we unload them at nightfull.'

Hudson watched Carter explaining the procedure to Dallas and smiled to himself. The boy was shaping up well. The idea of semi-deflating the dinghy and concealing it under the outrigger had been his. Hudson had been sceptical at first but after a period of trial and error it had begun to work. Now it was a ques-tion of seeing whether they would be permitted to use the tech-nique in a real life situation. Hudson felt for his pipe and pulled his slouch hat over his eyes.

The anti-aircraft guns were still blasting away at Six-Mile Field, and there was the sullen rumble of exploding bombs. The Zeros must have been escorting a squadron of Kate bombers. The poor bastards on the strip; they got it more often than a mug of tea.

Hudson turned his eyes away from the shore. It was funny how he unconsciously described Carter to himself as 'the boy'. If Marjory had ever been able to have a child he would have been about Carter's age now. The thought had never occurred to him before. He cupped his hands around the bowl of the pipe and sucked in the flame.

All along the line, things were turning out better than Hudson had expected on first acquaintance with Task Force 19. Dallas's manner set his teeth on edge but the man at least showed signs of being manoeuvrable. Carter was proving a quick learner. The initial scratchiness had disappeared and he was revealing that he could work as a member of a team. The trek to the prison camp had been tough and Hudson had seen the fear in the boy's eyes. Nevertheless, Carter had kept going. He would be better equipped next time.

And Sula? Hudson looked down at the slender figure standing in the prow of the canoe. She was certainly beautiful. Beautiful and unspoilt. Unusual for a native girl who had lived amongst white people, she appeared to have retained the best features of both races. He was confident that if they went for the volcano she would not let them down.

And Joe, sitting on the side of the canoe chewing betel nut. Joe was what he always had been and always would be—a black rock of Gibraltar. A staunch friend and implacable enemy who would walk through molten lava if he had to.

Only Johnson worried him. There was nothing he could point to specifically. It was just a feeling he had. There were occasional moments when he thought the man was going to crack. When the past was crowding in on him. A twitch of the mouth. A tremor in the voice. Things you only noticed if you had lived with a man when death was the sound of a snapped twig away. Maybe he should not come on this mission. But how do you tell a man that? What excuse do you give? And what would it be like in the jungle without 'Jerry' Johnson behind you? Like looking round and not seeing your shadow, maybe. Once you started breaking up the team you had to play a different game. Andrew Hudson was too old to change.

The banshee wail of an eleven hundred horsepower engine made him spin round and face the shore. Screaming out of the sun was a fighter. It took him a split second to recognize it as a Jap Zero. It levelled out feet above the sea and came streaking towards them. The pilot must have been heading for home after strafing the airfield and seen the cluster of boats round the wreck. Hudson shouted a warning and jumped.

Further up the sloping deck, Dallas felt as if he was pinned to the middle of a target. He slithered down the hot rust to a twisted deck housing and threw himself forward, hoping in mid-air that he was going to clear the submerged scuppers. The water closed over his head and he clawed his way to the surface, to find himself behind Johnson and the two dinghies. Instinctively he flung an arm over the side of the first dinghy before he realized that it was resting on five hundred pounds of high explosive. He let go of the side of the raft and then grabbed it again. Dallas could not swim.

Ahead, the Zero was coming in on a line straight towards him and so close to the sea that it seemed to be taxying on it. 20mm cannon shells hammered into the rusty deck plating behind him and a whiplash of machine gun bullets cut up the water like a squall of rain. He could see the line of bullets coming towards him and ducked down behind the dinghy waiting for the explosion that would spatter him over the deck of the freighter like an action painting. There was a bang loud enough to make itself heard above the screech of the Zero and the dinghies disappeared. Dallas found himself clinging to a piece of sinking fabric in a sea turned white by the contents of the ripped white bags. The Zero sped towards the horizon pursued by a P-40 Kittyhawk.

Dallas was so surprised to be alive that he nearly drowned. Carter swam to his side and pulled him to the outrigger. He clung gasping for several seconds before nodding to the bulky outline below the surface.

'What about that fucking explosive?'

'I thought you knew,' said Carter. 'We were using dummy bags.'

10

The convoy was small but impressive, and the two small pigs tusking by the side of the road butted each other back to the shelter of the gum trees. An armoured car was in front and a jeep with a rear-mounted 180° traverse machine gun behind. In the middle was a jeep carrying four helmeted and gaitered military policemen armed with sub-machine guns and an officer with a heavy filigree of oak-leaf cluster on the peak of his hat. He raised his arm in salute to a small boy who looked up at his mother inquiringly.

The convoy was moving fast, as it always did, and the vehicles huddled together as if joined by invisible couplings. The dirt road gave way to tarmac and the convoy emerged as if from a cloud. It was now entering a residential area in which beautiful tropical shrubs passed in on featureless houses like garlands round the necks of ugly tourists. A wireless crackled from the armoured car and further down the road a heavy iron gate started to swing open. Hardly slackening speed, the convoy passed through and stopped before a second gate covered by two concrete command posts. A sentry stepped forward and saluted smartly as he peered into the middle vehicle. He gave a signal and the second gate opened. The convoy passed through and continued up a long drive flanked by English-style lawns that had been allowed to turn brown so that they did not attract attention from the sky. The house was wide and low with many windows on the ground floor and a verandah that ran round three sides.

Outside the large front entrance, two military policemen came to attention. 'Here comes World War Three,' murmured one of them.

No sooner had the vehicles stopped in front of the house than the officer stepped down briskly, acknowledged the salutes of the guards and went into the house. He was met by an ADC who told him that there were no important messages and that the party had been waiting for an hour. The officer nodded, said that he wanted to go to the john and returned to be conducted to large double doors guarded by a military policeman. The door was opened and he passed through.

Carter had only seen General MacArthur on the newsreels. He was impressed by how the man looked in the flesh. Tall and rangy, with a Roman nose that made him look like a hunting eagle. The impression carried through to the all-seeing blue eyes and the lean, spare face. He could have been a Hollywood film star playing himself. Even the uniform seemed to have been specially tailored in a material not available to enlisted men, the creases put in by a conscientious wardrobe mistress seconds before he entered the room.

The ADC made the introductions. 'Gentlemen—I mean, lady and gentlemen—General MacArthur.'

The General jutted out his chin and nodded agreeably.

'Major Dallas, Captain Hudson, Lieutenant Carter, Corporal Johnson, Native Orderlies Korachi and Teosin.'

'I must apologize for keeping you waiting,' said the General. 'However, I don't have to remind you that there's a war on.'

There was a thin ripple of laughter led by Dallas. Sula looked puzzled.

'Let me offer you a drink and then I can quickly come to the point.' He nodded to an orderly who stepped forward and started taking orders. 'First of all I want to congratulate you—' he looked at Dallas as he spoke '—on the imagination and initiative shown in the development of this plan. It is exactly what I had in mind when I asked for your group to be formed.'

Dallas avoided looking the others in the eye. 'Thank you, sir.'

'Furthermore, I have studied your proposals and I think, given the right circumstances in regard to the volcano, they have an even chance of succeeding.' He broke off and turned to the ADC. 'Did we get those photographs of the inside of the crater?'

'No, sir. The cloud cover was too low.'

'Too bad.' The General frowned and then turned back to the

others. 'Well, you're going to know what it's like soon enough. I only have one comment in relation to your plan and that's to ask you if you think you're taking enough men.' He conquered Sula with a smile. 'No disrespect intended.'

'I think the only time we need more men is to get the explosive to the volcano,' said Hudson. 'And it's not worth taking them just to use as pack animals. There's a slight risk involved in using native bearers but five of us in the bush are less likely to be seen than fifteen. If this mission succeeds it will be because the Japs don't get wind of us until it's too late.'

The orderly took Carter's drink order and nodded disapprovingly towards Joe. 'What does he drink?'

'Human blood,' said Carter. 'Be nice to him.'

MacArthur nodded at Hudson. 'I accept what you say, Captain. I'm very aware of the work you've done in this area in the past. Aware and grateful. I speak for all American servicemen when I acknowledge the debt we owe to the coast-watchers.'

'Thank you, sir,' said Hudson.

MacArthur drew himself up and raised his glass. 'I wish you all the luck in the world and I look forward to welcoming you back here after a successful mission. I make no secret of my belief that with the recapture of Rabaul we push over the first in the line of dominoes that will fall back across the Pacific to crush Japan. When I see you standing here—Americans, Australians, Islanders—I have no doubt that you will succeed. Your brave action will light a candle of hope that will shine from Sydney to Washington.'

Carter looked at the crossed American flags behind the desk and swallowed a lump in his throat. Hudson looked at his feet. There was a tight, emotional silence, a few farewell words and then the party was shown out by the ADC.

MacArthur retired behind his desk and clipped open the despatch case. He had smoothed out the first piece of paper as the ADC returned.

'One thing, sir.'

'What is it?'

'It relates to the volcano operation, sir. The Major's report cites the need for an assault group to be in readiness to take advantage of the situation should the volcano erupt. We haven't lined anything up yet.'

MacArthur continued to smooth out the despatch without looking up.

'Newman,' he said, 'when you light a candle, you don't make plans to recover the melted wax.'

In the depths of his concrete bunker Lieutenant-General Mori Koji pushed the tray of decoded radio messages away and thoughtfully stroked the sides of his moustache. Watching him from across the dimly lit room, his adjutant, Major Yukichi, could tell that he was worried. He had served the General long enough to know the signs. At the same time he had served him long enough not to ask questions. He waited patiently for the moment when the General would choose to speak.

Despite the thickness of the walls, the sound of falling bombs revealed itself as an intermittent thumping noise, sometimes accompanied by the lights flickering and dust falling from the roof.

'How many tonight?' asked Koji.

'Forty bombers,' said Yukichi, 'and a fighter escort. We have shot down three fighters and the anti-aircraft batteries claimed two bombers.'

Koji said nothing for a moment but reread the piece of paper in his hand.

'Let them squander their resources. They can drop bombs till the end of our lives and we will still die of old age. My only hope is that they do not kill all the fish in the harbour.'

Yukichi smiled politely. It was true that the American attacks were building up but they did little damage. Only a floating crane that had been towed to Rabaul after the fall of Singapore and a couple of barges caught on a wharf provided visible evidence of success.

General Koji tapped the paper against his finger tips. 'I have some information here that gives me cause for alarm.'

'Yes, sir?' Yukichi kept his voice level.

'We are about to be visited.'

Yukichi inclined his head in a respectful gesture that could be construed as compliance with whatever statement came next. 'Yes, sir.'

'Admiral Yamamoto is making a tour of key battle stations. He will be with us for three days.'

'Admiral Yamamoto!' It was impossible to keep the excitement from Yukichi's voice. The architect of Japan's day of destiny: 7 December 1941, when the attack on Pearl Harbor had shattered the myth of American invincibility and initiated the most rapid territorial expansion in the history of the world.

'You have not met him?' asked Koji.

'I have seen him but I have not had the honour of exchanging words with him.'

'A remarkable man,' said Koji. 'A man of vision, too valuable to lose.'

Yukichi nodded. 'His presence here will do much to raise morale. The men are getting bored. Living like rats in the tunnels saps their spirits.'

'We have come far and we have come fast,' said Koji. 'It is wise to rest and build up our strength. Only a fool tries to outrun his feet.'

Yukichi acquiesced and waited for the General to continue. He had anticipated that Yamamoto was coming to Rabaul to direct an invasion of Port Moresby, something that he had often discussed with his commanding officer and which would provide the logical base for expansion into Australia.

But Koji said nothing and continued to draw his fingers down the thin paintbrush of his moustache.

Yukichi reflected and decided that in the circumstances it would not be impolite to ask a question. 'May I inquire the purpose of the esteemed Admiral's visit?'

'He wishes to obtain first-hand information on the state of the war and show himself to the troops.'

'There is nothing specific in terms of our position here at Rabaul?'

The moment that he had closed his mouth, Yukichi realized that his question had earned disfavour.

General Koji pressed his spectacle lenses closer to his eyes, something that he always did when he was displeased. 'I am not privy to every one of the Admiral's plans and if I was I would think twice before discussing them with you.'

The riposte was more severe than the question had invited and both men knew this.

Yukichi bowed his head to acknowledge culpability and show regret.

'Sir, you said that you had information that gave cause for alarm?'

General Koji stood up and walked to the map of the Pacific that had been painted on one wall of the bunker. 'I was referring to the Admiral's visit.' He saw Yukichi raise an eyebrow. 'Let me explain. Since Pearl Harbor the American attitude to the Admiral has been paranoid. There have been three attempts on his life: a bomb in Bougainville, a sniper at Brunei and an amphibious assault on his headquarters on Luzon—luckily he was not there.'

'I was not aware of this,' said Yukichi.

'The attacks have not been made general knowledge for obvious reasons,' said Koji. 'What is clear is that the Americans are determined to revenge themselves for what they choose to call "The Day of Infamy".'

'Is it infamous when a nation decides to die on its feet rather than live on its knees?' asked Yukichi, passionately. 'Their oil embargo forced us to fight.'

General Koji sniffed as if disapproving of the outburst. 'My immediate preoccupation is with Admiral Yamamoto's safety while he is with us.'

'Here?' said Yukichi. 'We now have sixty-five thousand men inside the most impenetrable stronghold on earth. The Admiral could not be safer in the middle of Tokyo.'

'You really think so?' said Koji levelly. 'Your complacency is alarming. What about the raid on the searchlight post?'

Yukichi said nothing.

'Five men wiped out by an American raiding party. I have a personal interest in the affair. I was standing on the beach five hours before they died. Very probably in the sights of an American carbine. If me, why not the Admiral?'

Yukichi folded his hands in his lap. 'Yes, sir. I see what you mean.'

'Good,' said General Koji.

He turned back to the wall map and with his finger drew a line round the area of the harbour and Matupi bay.

'I believe that if the Americans get wind of Admiral Yamamoto's presence here they could well put a party ashore to try and assassinate him. They could even be here now! We have no evidence that the group that destroyed the radar post did not retire into the jungle.'

'No, sir.'

General Koji struck a match and applied it to a corner of the message. He held it at arm's length, watching it burn.

'You and I, Major, are going to devise a plan that will guarantee the Admiral's safety while he is with us. It will cover every eventuality.'

He droppeed the message just before the flame reached his fingers and the two men watched it burn to ashes on the stone floor.

II

The night Sula left to fly to the submarine base, Carter called for her at the cook's house and Jones drove them to the airfield. It was a strange, sad occasion, a mixture of the social and the military which to Carter their relationship always was. She wore a khaki *lap-lap*—too large—and a WAC blouse—too small—which polarized the extreme of the ambiguity. She sat in the front of the jeep beside Jones and looked around with interest as they drove through the mainly abandoned suburbs of Port Moresby. Occasionally she turned to smile at Carter as if encouraging him to talk to her. He smiled back and started remembering her face in case he never saw it again.

Her nose was long and slightly arched. Her forehead was high. Her shimmering black hair could take many shapes and was now pulled back behind her ears to spring forward in bunches onto her shoulders. Her nostrils were wide and haughty, her eyes the brown of stirred chocolate, and her smile as guileless as the two dimples that parenthesized it. Beside her was a small *bilum* of coloured wool which contained all her belongings. Carter could see a grass skirt and small packets which contained salt and trade tobacco. The girl would have to live off the land. She carried no visible weapon. It had been decided that there was no time to instruct her in the proficient use of a firearm and that if she fell into the hands of the Japs her chances of survivial, and those of the arriving party, would be better safeguarded if she was carrying nothing to distinguish her.

Carter thought of what they were asking of the girl—and how eagerly he had canvassed her inclusion in the party—and felt guilty. She should have been a spectator in this war, not a participant. But could there be any spectators? Perhaps, high in the cloud-covered mountains, men looked down and wondered if the sound of falling bombs was distant thunder, but for the rest war was the marauding ogre destroying their gardens and raping their women. To survive you had to slay the ogre.

The girl could fight. The white teeth could bite to the bone. She had cut a man's throat as easily as one might slit open an envelope. Killing was in her people's blood. But then, as Carter ruefully reflected, on the evidence of the present war, killing was in all people's blood.

Dallas, Hudson, Johnson and Joe were waiting at the airstrip. A heap of blazing metal was being bulldozed off the runway.

'The ack-ack wallahs just got a Kate,' explained Johnson. 'Little bastard tried to crash it into the control tower.'

Carter shook hands with Joe and there were a few desultory words of farewell. Joe gave a smart and touching salute which Hudson replied to in his usual awkward fashion.

Carter took Sula's hand and squeezed it. She returned the pressure and he knew that anywhere else but in this fucking stupid war they would put their arms round each other just in case there was never another time. Then he released her hand, and she and Joe climbed into a Lockheed Tristar that already had its props turning. It dawdled down the runway, turned and took off over the dust-covered gum trees. Somebody waved from one of the windows.

On the way back to camp, Carter got Jones to drive him down the street where Jean had lived. The house was empty and boarded up against looters.

'Everybody moving out of town,' said Jones.

'Yes.'

Jones had been unusually quiet that evening. Carter had imagined it was out of respect for the mood of the occasion.

Jones kept looking in front of him and chewing gum. 'I'll probably be going soon. I've put in for a transfer to a combat division.' He gestured towards the overgrown gardens and the tired weatherboard houses with names like 'Dunrovin' and 'Shangri La'. 'This place is a dump.'

Carter thought of Jones getting his legs blown off on some distant Pacific atoll. 'They're all dumps,' he said.

*   *   *

Two nights later, Carter was lying on a bunk staring at the ceiling inches above his head and wondering how a fly got onto a submarine. Wondering also how it could stand the heat. The fan seemed to blow in hot air rather than take it out. He glanced at his watch for the third time in half an hour and was relieved when Hudson entered the cabin.

His face was grim. 'I've just been talking to the Commander. He's got the latest weather reports—high seas and near gale-force winds.'

Carter swore. 'And we haven't had a chance to practise the launching drill.'

'You can forget about it—if the weather doesn't improve, you can forget about the whole mission.'

Carter swore again. It seemed ridiculous being cramped up in this suffocating heat listening to the vibration of the engines when sixty feet above their heads a full-blooded storm was blowing.

'How much longer have we got?' asked Hudson.

Carter did not need to look at his watch. 'Approximately three and a half hours.'

'Let's hope it dies down. Do you want to sleep?'

Carter shook his head. 'I could hatch in this place but I can't sleep in it.'

Hudson smiled. 'Don't bet on it. When you come back after this mission, you'll go off like a baby.'

Carter nearly said 'if I come back', but he stopped himself. 'I guess you're right. I wonder how Joe and Sula are doing?'

'They know how to look after themselves,' said Hudson firmly.

'They've got one hell of an important role in this thing,' mused Carter. 'Rounding up the bearers, getting the canoes, finding us—'

'Let's run through the fall-back procedures,' said Hudson.

Carter smiled. 'To take my mind off it?'

'To take both our minds off it,' said Hudson.

At 0500 hours there was another weather report stating that the wind had dropped but that there was no knowing how long this would last. Bad weather was still forecast for the launch area.

'We'll just have to take a look when we get there,' said the Commander. 'I hope you can go because I as sure as hell can't wait to get that thousand pounds of explosive off my ship.'

At 0545 hours Hudson was called to the control room. Carter went with him. The change in engine noise told him that they were hove to, presumably just below the surface.

The Commander confirmed this. 'We're in the launch area,' he said. 'I'm just going to take a look.' He turned to the rating beside him. 'Stand by for observation. Up 'scope.'

With a pneumatic hiss, the periscope rose from the well and the rating snapped down the handles. The Commander dropped to his knees on the deck, seized the handles and pressed his eyes to the eyepiece. He rose to his feet with the ascending periscope.

Carter waited, feeling tense and excited. At last something was going to happen. He could stop worrying and start doing.

The Commander stepped back. His face was solemn. 'Take a look.'

Hudson advanced and stooped awkwardly over the periscope. He swung it through a hundred and eighty degrees as the Commander had done and stepped back.

'Apart from the fact that there's a heavy sea running, I can't see anything, sir.'

'Neither can I,' said the Commander. 'We've come up in the middle of a thick fog.'

Carter looked at Hudson disbelievingly. If this was a sample of their luck, they might as well give up and go home immediately.

'I know this coast, sir, and I think there's a good chance that it's localized,' said Hudson calmly. 'If we can move on a few thousand yards we may be out of it.'

The Commander nodded. 'Very well, Captain.' He slapped up the handles and the periscope hissed back into its well. 'Officer of the deck, come right north and tell manoeuvring to make turns for eleven knots.'

Hudson turned to Carter. 'It's a bastard but it's not the end of the world. Might even give us some cover from the Japs. I'm more worried about the sea.'

Ten minutes later the periscope went up again and the Commander shook his head. 'No change,' he said.

Carter pressed his face against the rubber surround of the eyepiece and experienced the unreal sensation of looking across the surface of the sea as if he was swimming in it. Not that there was so much a surface as a broken swirl of water fragmenting against the periscope glass and affording glimpses of deep troughs and swells enclosed in a stygian gloom that reduced visibility to a matter of yards.

'I'll take her up and you can have a look,' said the Commander. 'Stand to, the launch team.'

The order echoed through the tannoy system and the area around the bridge quickly filled with ratings wheeling trolleys containing the bags of explosive. The internal drill had been run through many times on the voyage from New Guinea and each member of the team knew his job once the hatches were opened.

The Commander turned to Hudson and Carter. 'Right, gentlemen. I would appreciate a quick decision when we surface.'

'You'll get it, sir,' said Hudson.

Carter stood at the bottom of the ladder leading to the bridge and felt a crippling sense of anticlimax closing in around him. Was it possible that after the slog through the jungle and all their training, planning and testing, the operation was going to be called off before it had even begun?

The sight that met his eyes when he got to the bridge was even more depressing. The submarine was wallowing like a breaching whale and waves were washing over the decks. The fog pressed in on all sides and seemed to be resting on their heads.

'Blast!' said Hudson. 'I was hoping to load the dinghies on deck and float them off when you submerged. That's cooked.' He turned to Carter, 'What do you think? You're the launching expert. Shall we give it a burl?'

There was an innate confidence beneath the surface cheerfulness of Hudson's words that got through to Carter. That the idea of launching the dinghies in these conditions could be seriously considered made him feel that, this hurdle surmounted, the rest of the operation would be virtually child's play.

'Why not?' he said.

'Does that mean you're going ahead?' asked the Commander.

'It does, sir', said Hudson.

Seconds later, the forward deck hatch opened and the first dinghy went over the side with Carter leaping into it. The sea threw it up nearly level with the deck and then troughed to almost swallow it. Hudson came with the second dinghy and the third arrived immediately so that the three lashed together would achieve a better platform in the water. Within seconds, Carter was soaked to the skin and abandoning the idea of using a paddle to reach Hudson. With the sea in this mood one had to bend to its whims. When Hudson came near enough, he would grab him.

Eventually the two rafts were thrown together and Carter lunged out to throw himself across the gap and cling to the side until Hudson had secured the straps. Now the two dinghies bounced on the waves and threatened to close like a cigar box while the crew played the third within their reach. Finally, it was hauled back on deck and released again almost on top of them. Hudson snatched at the rope and clung to it until Carter could secure the straps. The two-hinged structure buckled over the waves like a fairground carousel, and Carter felt nausea as the sea swept past before his eyes.

On the bridge, Johnson waited for his moment and drew back his arm to throw down a rope with a weighted end. It spiralled out and was caught by Hudson. He swiftly lashed it to the centre raft. As soon as it was in position the first bag slid down, barely clearing the grey-topped rollers that slapped against the hull of the sub. Hudson snatched at it with cold, pinched fingers and nearly dropped it.

'Try and hold us steady!'

He thrust a paddle into Carter's hands and sprawled across the gunwale to stow the first bag. On the submarine, the crew manning the ropes hunched their heads into their shoulders and watched through narrowed eyes as the bags began to hang from the ropes like seed pods.

'Not so fast!'

The rope suddenly dipped, and the platform of rafts swirled in towards the submarine. For a second it seemed that the explosive

134

would be ground between the hull and the side of the rafts. Then Carter worked his paddle through the rudder-mounting and took the full force of the swell on his blade. The boats quivered and swung away to a safe distance.

'Hold her there, for Christ's sake!'

Hudson worked feverously as the rope stretched taut and glistening bags began to cover the floor of one dinghy. Carter started to count them, knowing that at any second he could reach the unlucky number that blew them all to kingdom come: 'Sixty-five, sixty-six, sixty-seven—'

The mist still pressed in but the sea lost some of its fury. The spiteful, wind-whipped claws of waves were sheathed in a persistent glaucous swell with a rhythm that could at least be learned and tamed. Carter dug till his arms ached in their sockets and watched the dinghy fill: 'Two hundred and one, two hundred and two—'

'We're winning,' panted Hudson grimly. 'Just hold her steady.'

The first dinghy was filled and the cover unfurled. Then one of the zips stuck. Hudson swore as Carter had never heard him swear before but it refused to budge. From the bridge, Johnson and the submarine commander watched anxiously. With every second that passed they were challenging the moment when the fog lifted and the submarine became a sitting target on the surface.

'Leave it!' urged Carter. He noticed the ominous strain that was being placed on the securing straps but said nothing. Hudson changed sides and started to stow the bags. His face was grey with fatigue and tension. His knuckles white with cold. His fingers were beginning to fumble and he dropped the short-bladed knife with which he had been freeing the bags. It dropped blade downwards into the bottom of the dinghy. Carter closed his eyes. When he opened them, Hudson was retrieving the knife from the plastic overlap of one of the bags. He muttered something to himself that Carter could not hear.

Johnson was now holding up two hands from the bridge and starting to clamber down the outside ladder from the conning.

'Ten more!' shouted Carter as an encouragement to himself.

135

'Holy shit! I never thought we'd do it.'

Hudson said nothing but grit his teeth and reached out for the remaining bags like a man picking ripe peaches. The deck crew tightened their grip on the two ropes that held the dinghies and prepared to haul.

'Got you, you beaut!'

Hudson closed his hands round the last bag and triumphantly untied the loading rope. The deck party pulled the rafts nearer to the submarine and Johnson judged his moment and jumped into the waiting arms. Good luck messages were shouted from deck and bridge, and suddenly the hatch was slamming down and the bridge empty.

Carter looked up at the gaunt outline of the submarine and experienced a terrifying sensation of isolation. As the hull began to settle in the water he felt like a sailor watching his ship sinking. This was the point of no return—the moment when they were really on their own. The water swept over the foredeck and the stern tilted. The conning-tower made a bow wave of its own and then tilted forward, as if nodding a courteous farewell. It glided through the water, gathering speed and sinking fast until it slid below the surface in a small eruption of white bubbles. The waves rolled on and there was no sign that it had ever been there.

Alone.

Carter finished securing the cover of the second explosives dinghy and looked about him. The mist still closed in eerily without a break. The swell was running high. It was difficult not to feel afraid.

'Got you, you cow!'

Hudson freed the stubborn zip on the first explosive dinghy and locked it in the closed position. He slumped into the bottom of the dinghy, soaked and exhausted but with a look of triumph on his face.

'Right,' he said. 'I think this calls for a small celebration.' He felt in the breast pocket of his tunic and fumbled with cold fingers to produce three brandy miniatures. 'Captain's compliments. Keep you warm until the sun comes up.'

Johnson lost no time in opening his bottle and downing it at a gulp.

'I bet he's a happy old sod now we're gone.'

Carter drank his brandy gratefully. He needed some fire in his guts. 'Have you any idea where we are?'

Hudson had his compass in his hand. He jerked a thumb over his shoulder. 'If the Commander knows his business, that's Rabaul.'

'What shall we do?' asked Johnson. 'Take her in towards the shore?'

'Trouble is, we don't know our exact position,' said Hudson. 'If we go in and the mist suddenly lifts we could find ourselves staring at a beach full of Japs.'

'While if we stay here the current could take us out to sea or miles down the coast,' said Johnson.

'The weather's not getting any better,' said Carter.

He was right. The sea swirled around them as if stirred by a giant spoon and the water slapped mournfully against the stretched fabric of the rafts. Once again, Carter noticed that one of the straps was parting with its mooring.

'A bit of a squall could blow this bloody mist away,' said Hudson.

Suddenly there was a thumping noise, like a heartbeat, coming louder and nearer with every second.

'Christ! What's that?'

The three men looked at each other and Johnson felt for the Mills gun strapped across his shoulders. The thumping noise became a mad, mechanical judder hammering at their eardrums. It seemed to be coming from all around them. Then, like the head of an attacking shark, the bows of a destroyer broke through the mist and bore down on them. There was no time to do anything but see it and be terrified. Carter glimpsed the concave sweep of its prow towering above him and then the bow wave tossed them contemptuously aside and he was hurled into the water.

Down, down, down, until it seemed that his eardrums must burst and the water invade his lungs. His eyes closed tight in fear and panic. He kicked as if on a hangman's rope and felt at last that he was rising. Just when it seemed that he could hold his breath no longer, his head broke the surface and he sucked in mouthfuls of air. Relief was short-lived. Around him there was nothing but angry, churning sea and fog. No sign of the destroyer, nor of Hudson and Johnson. No sign of the rafts. The mist drifted above his head like smoke across a battlefield. He listened carefully but heard nothing. He called out and listened again. Nothing.

The destroyer must have been steaming out of Rabaul harbour and making about thirty knots. She would never have had time to see them, but it hardly seemed to matter. Not now.

He rose with the swell and called out again. Still no answer. What in God's name was he going to do? Had the rafts blown up? Were Hudson and Johnson drowned? If the explosives had gone up the destroyer would have gone with them, but there was no sign of wreckage. The others must be in the fog somewhere. Should he try and find them or use his remaining resources of strength and swim to shore? And where was the shore? He pulled at the compass that hung round his neck and trod water while he tried to read it. A wave swept over him, and he choked on a mouthful of water. His teeth were chattering and the Mills gun strapped across his back cut into his flesh painfully. He shouted again and heard the helpless echo of his voice across the water. At the back of his mind there was always one thought—sharks. In each swirl of water he saw a dark shape closing to take off his leg. Every wave-tip was a fin. The touch of something unseen beneath the surface made him start with terror. And then he saw it.

Fifty feet away. A dark outline in the mist. Terror instantly changed to hope. The rafts! He shouted and struck out desperately. The shape dipped into a trough and disappeared again.

Carter panicked. Was the current taking them away from him? His arms lashed at the water burning up his strength. If he did not catch up with them soon he would be done for. He raised his head and saw the bulky shape momentarily outlined on the crest of a wave. But no sign of Hudson and Johnson—they must have been swept overboard. He struggled on, expecting at each moment to feel banks of razor-sharp teeth paring his flesh to the bone. His arms were very tired, and the cold was numbing. He looked again and for a moment thought that his objective had disappeared. Then it bobbed up out of a trough thirty feet away and he saw that there was only one raft. As it tilted he recognized the cover of one of the explosives dinghies. The stress generated by the destroyer must have finally forced them apart.

The sight of temporary salvation within reach gave him new strength. He covered the distance in ten untidy strokes and clung to the rope that ran round the gunwale. For a few seconds he sucked in breath and then his fear of sharks made him attempt to haul himself from the water. His feet strayed under the raft, and it took several attempts before he could rest his elbow on the side and pull himself up and out, to sprawl across the hump of bags. He lay face down, with his heart pumping and the salt water stinging his face, and opened his legs and arms so that he had a better purchase on the raft. Five hundred pounds of plastic explosive. This was the sanctuary he had found for himself!

Carter was still drifting in fogbound open sea in the shipping lanes at the entrance to Rabaul harbour. He shouted as loud as he could and then listened intently. Perhaps it was his imagination but there seemed to be the sound of distant surf. He pulled out his compass and checked the direction of the noise. It was possible, but, if true, it meant that he was in a current moving along the face of the coast. He hoped that it was towards the pick-up area. Another shout and he sank down exhausted, his head resting on the side of the raft.

When he looked down into the water he saw something that sent fresh currents of fear churning through his stomach: an eye looking back at him. A small, beady eye set in the end of a hideous cylinder of flesh. A huge hammer-head shark was staring up at him. The hammer was four feet wide, the length of the shark nearer thirty than twenty feet. It overlapped the raft by the height of a man. As Carter watched, horrified, it gave a petulant flick of its tail and veered in to nudge the raft challengingly. Carter knew what would happen if the shark attacked. The V-shaped mouth below the hammer would slice through the rubberized material in seconds. If it bit into a bag of explosives he would die immediately. If it did not, death would take longer and be infinitely more horrible.

There was something about the two eyes on the end of their fleshy stalks that made it the ugliest creature he had ever seen. A refuge from some primaeval nightmare. A sudden light glowed in that small eye and it glowed with malice.

Carter lay still, lest any movement encourage the shark to attack. Should he ease off his gun and attempt to lodge a bullet in its tiny brain or would such a move run the risk of being botched and spark off an attack? Whatever happened, it would give his position away to anyone in the vicinity and would certainly produce enough blood to attract more sharks. Better, perhaps, to do nothing and hope that the shark would become bored and go away.

Carter stretched out his fingers to change his cramped position and suffered another unpleasant surprise. His fingers strayed into a small ruckle that had appeared along the side of the raft. As he pressed so the material wobbled like a flabby belly.

It was leaking. Was he imagining things? He felt another ruckle appear beside the first. Now there was no doubt about it. Slowly but surely the raft would collapse into the water. If the hammer-head was patient enough it would get him. He lay as still as the tossing sea would allow and felt a despair that was deathlike.

Suddenly, the atmosphere seemed lighter and a faint shadow fell on his hand. He looked up and saw blue sky through a gap in the fog. To the left, also, it was lifting. Drifting away to reveal a glimpse of distant, jungle-covered coastline with clouds and mountains in the background. He looked down and for a moment thought that the shark had disappeared. But it was only circling him. It glided up expectantly the moment he raised himself.

'Kal-o-o-o-o-o-o-o!' The call echoed across the water like the noise of a reed instrument. He paused and then tried to imitate the sound. It was repeated but this time from further away.

'Kal-o-o-o-o-o-o-o!'

The hammer-head move in and butted the raft. Time was running out.

Carter turned and let out an exclamation of surprise and relief. Coming towards him was a sight to make him momentarily forget hammer-head sharks and leaking rafts. A dug-out canoe skimmed down the waves, and kneeling in its stern was Sula. She called out triumphantly as she saw him and plied her paddle to come alongside.

'Mary, Mother of God,' said Carter.

Sula looked more like a Gauguin painting. She wore no covering on her upper body and her fine breasts stood forward, proud and firm. A single cowrie shell dangled between them and there was a pig's tusk bracelet curved round her upper arm. Her khaki *lap-lap* had been replaced by a grass skirt. To all intents and purposes she was a native girl out on a fishing expedition. A net heaped in the prow provided further evidence of this.

Carter looked upon her and thought that the English language was singularly lacking when it came to words for expressing gratitude.

'I look for you long time,' she called, almost apologetically.

'You'd better look out for this fellow, too,' said Carter indicating the hammer-head. 'Have you seen the others?'

She shook her head. 'Joe is looking. What happened?'

Carter quickly provided a run-down of events since they had left the submarine.

'What's happened with you?'

'The Japs are very excited. There are patrols and road blocks everywhere. Joe wonders if they have found out that we are coming.'

'They couldn't have,' said Carter, knowing that in fact everything was possible. It suddenly flashed across his mind that Green might have inadvertently blurted something that had got back to the Japs.

He indicated the raft.'How are we going to handle this?'

She pointed to the shark. 'First we get rid of him.'

Carter watched admiringly as she brought the outrigger firmly against the raft and then leaned out across the framework of spars so that the hammer-head was circling below her. Seconds passed and she positioned the paddle as if it was a billiard cue playing a high-angled shot. A swift, downwards jab and the blade of the paddle struck the hammer-head sharply in the eye. Its tail lifted to smack against the outrigger and then it dived and did not reappear.

'That's quite a trick,' said Carter.

'Sometimes,' said Sula. She smiled engagingly.

141

Carter thought that it would be best not to press her for an explanation of exactly what 'sometimes' meant.

The sea was calmer now and the mist had vanished. The clouds were breaking up fast and great rifts of blue appeared. Only on the distant mountains did the clouds still loom, as if guarding dark secrets. Carter looked about him but there was no sign of the others. Sula saw the worry in his eyes and knew what he was thinking.

'Strong current,' she said. 'Maybe they go further down coast.'

'Maybe.'

He started to let air out of the dinghy while keeping an eye open for the hammer-head or anything else that might appear. A school of moon jellyfish drifted past, their slimy milk-white bodies glistening like dirty plates, and he was grateful that he was not still in the water. The thousands of stinging tentacles descending into the depths could be up to twenty feet in length.

Carter worked his way onto the framework between the canoe and the outrigger and started to draw the semi-inflated dinghy underneath. He had left it a little fuller than during the tests to compensate for the leak. The canes were lashed in place to keep it steady and below the water-line, and he climbed into the dug-out facing Sula. The solid feel of sculpted wood was immediately reassuring and he unharnessed his Mills gun and checked that the waterproof bag had done its job.

Now that he was back on schedule he felt much better. Two hours had been lost but since they had intended to rest during the day this was not serious. His only worry, apart from Sula's report of increasing Jap activity, was the fate of Hudson and Johnson.

'Hungry?'

'Starving.'

Sula produced a paw-paw and half a bunch of bananas. Carter fell on them greedily.

'We go to the beach?'

He nodded, his mouth full, and reached for a paddle. The net he placed at his feet so that he could hide underneath it when they came within sight of land. At first they seemed to be making no impression on the distance, but slowly a line of beach separated from the trees and he could see the entrance to a bay. Rabaul and its harbour were round a point to port and invisible.

What soon detached itself from its surroundings was the huge, flat-topped mass of Matupi rising out of thick jungle to the right of the bay. Its summit gleamed back in the sunlight. It was a brooding, sinister presence, the dark shadows on its side showing where the jungle had poured in to fill subsidiary craters. To the right of the volcano, the ground levelled off swiftly to flat marshland that marked the delta of a large river flowing down from the mountains.

Carter's eyes absorbed the sunlight and he looked into the sky beyond the volcano. That was where the main airfield should be. As he watched, a biplane appeared, climbing to the left of the volcano. It turned lazily and started to fly over the jungle. A spotter plane! This was a complication they had not thought of. With a stab of fear, Carter wondered what would happen if the plane flew over them. They had never checked the visibility of the submerged dinghy from directly above. He watched anxiously as the plane came down low and started to fly along the shoreline.

Caution bred from the sight of the spotter plane made him consider that he might be visible from the shore to anyone with a pair of powerful binoculars. Hurriedly, he tried to explain to Sula and lay down on the bottom of the canoe, his shoulders chafing the sides, his Mills gun between his legs. He turned his head to talk to her and saw that she was wearing nothing beneath her grass skirt. She in turn saw his glance but made no effort to change her position. She had no cause to be ashamed. Nor need she be afraid. This man would not steal what she would gladly give.

The paddle drove in and a lattice-work of muscle flickered up Sula's arm. Small drops of water anointed her breasts and glistened like jewels around the aureoles of her nipples. Carter felt a sense of complicity rather than desire. For the first time in his life he could look upon a woman, almost naked and within reach of his arm, and enjoy her body because it existed rather than because he was possessing it.

'The plane.'

Sula shot a warning glance towards the shore and Carter quickly pulled the net over his head. Through the chinks one wary eye watched the sky. After a little while came an elderly buzzing sound and the biplane passed over fifty feet above their heads. Carter glimpsed the goggles of the observer as he looked down, and prayed that the dinghy would not be seen. Then the biplane passed out of his view.

He was beginning to breathe again when there was a change of engine note. The biplane was turning to make another sweep. Had they seen something? He pressed backwards, his shoulders scraping the sides. The engine note grew quickly into a roar. This time it passed within twenty feet and a Jap voice shouted something from the cockpit. What were they saying? 'Wait where you are?' Was a wireless message being flashed ashore to alert a patrol boat? The sound of the plane turned into a drone and then died away altogether. Carter pulled the netting away from his face. It smelt of fish but that was the least of his problems.

'What did he say?'

Sula paddled on, unperturbed. 'I think he like me.'

Carter smiled at the irony of it. The Jap had enjoyed looking at a pretty girl as he had done. For a few seconds they had both escaped from the cruel realities of war.

Carter pulled the net over his head and raised himself up to peer over the side of the canoe. The entrance to Matupi Bay was now less than four hundred yards away, and he could see the first line of the Jap defences—two large, concrete block-houses built in the water and providing uninterrupted fields of fire over the narrow strips of beach on either side. Their cold, impersonal hardness amongst the lush vegetation was frightening. Somewhere behind those narrow slits, interested eyes were watching. Carter quickly glanced towards the submerged dinghy and the spars and canes that held it in place. He saw nothing to alarm him. He sank back and tried to wriggle into a more comfortable position. Now came the worst part. Waiting.

Sula stretched out her legs until they were almost touching Carter's head and hunched forward to present a stooped and unappetizing apearance to those watching from the shore. If the Japs wanted a woman they would not let a few feet of water frustrate them. The canoe was now so close to the block houses that she could see the glint of a man's spectacles behind one of the slits. In the shallow water beside it, four naked Japs were washing, one of them still wearing his cap. They looked up as she passed and the man in the cap strummed his penis with his forefinger. The others laughed.

Further along the shore was the rusting hulk of a landing-barge knocked out by a direct hit from a mortar during the Jap invasion of '42. She could see a wireless aerial rising from the deck and could hear the intermittent gabble of the signalman inside. Stretching away from the beach, the ground rose unevenly amongst palm trees with their tops blown off by bombs, to sandbag emplacements which concealed the big guns. The area between was an untidy warren of trenches and fox-holes covered by barbed wire.

'*Tomare!*'

She knew that the word meant 'stop' and that it was directed at her but she kept paddling.

'*Tomare!*'

This time the voice was angry and accompanied by the sound of a rifle bolt sliding back. Sula continued to paddle. Bang! The shot splintered the top of the outrigger two feet above the explosive. A parakeet screamed in alarm and crashed away through the palms. Sula stopped paddling.

On the shore, half-hidden by a clump of mangrove, was a dug-out canoe. Two Japs hurried towards it, one of them shouldering his rifle. Sula saw the netting stir as Carter fumbled for his gun. One of the Japs climbed into the canoe and the other pushed it off and scrambled aboard. They started to paddle clumsily. Sula stood up and prepared to greet them. There was no movement from the netting. When they were half-way to the canoe, the man in the bow started to talk and gesticulate and her heart fell. The Japs wanted all the fish she had caught.

At all costs she knew that she must stop them searching the canoe. She dragged the net up and shook it, indicating with her head that she had caught nothing. At her feet, Carter lay exposed, as vulnerable as a baby in its cradle. The Japs kept coming. Either they did not understand or they did not believe her. They were pitifully thin, the skin stretched tight across their cheek bones and their sun-bleached uniforms hanging like cast-offs from larger men. They came in until the prow of their canoe was resting against the outrigger. If they looked down they must see the raft. But they were looking at her body. Not with admiration but as a hungry man looks at a piece of meat. Sula had seen that look before. The man in the prow reluctantly took his eyes from her breasts and craned forward to see what was in the canoe. He spoke to his companion and they started to paddle round the outrigger to take a closer look. Sula held her breath and slowly looked down to her feet. The netting twitched in anticipation. The first Jap stretched out his hand to seize the side of the canoe above Carter's head.

The wail of the siren pierced the silence and fell across the water. The Jap withdrew his hand and looked round. Approaching fast across the bay, its prow out of the water, was a small launch flying a Japanese flag. The two Japs looked at each other apprehensively and allowed Sula's canoe to drift a few feet from them. The launch swung round and stopped like a skate on ice, throwing out a wave that washed over both canoes and nearly capsized the Japs. Its engine raced and an angry froth of water bubbled from its stern. No less angry was the voice of the Major standing in the prow and surrounded by a Lieutenant and half a dozen men. He shouted at the two Japs in the dug-out and waved imperiously towards the shore.

Sula waited for someone to see the outline of the raft now clearly visible beneath the limpid blue water but all eyes were either on the Major or the miscreants. The Major's guttural gabble ended with a final retch of speech and the launch sped on towards the shore. The two Japs raised their heads from their chests and hurriedly paddled after it without a backward glance. Sula noticed that the bathing men had disappeared and that there was activity in the fox-holes. Men hurried into position and a soldier was speedily removing some articles of clothing that had been laid out to dry on the wire. It looked like a surprise inspection—more disturbing evidence that the Japs were expecting something to happen.

Sula settled down in the canoe and began to paddle. She dug a toe into the netting until she could feel Carter's head.

'They have gone. You can uncover your face.'

Carter pulled back the netting and looked up at the sky through stinging eyes. Sweat lathered his forehead and the hair stuck close to his head. He turned and kissed the sole of Sula's foot.

'Thank you. Tell me what happened.'

The canoe moved along the shore past a torrent of tropical greenery that tumbled down steep slopes to jostle at the water's edge. Unseen birds called from the tops of trees and there was the repeated shrill chatter of an angry monkey. Looming over all was the unstable mass of Matupi, looking menacing even in the sunshine. The jungle clung to its side like moss to a great boulder.

Sula looked down and saw a catfish swimming weakly, barely able to move below the surface. And then another, belly up and twitching. It was puzzling. There was no mark on them. Nothing to suggest that they had been attacked by another fish. She looked towards the end of the bay and then looked again, shading her eyes. No, she had not been mistaken. The water was stained with clouds of yellow. She veered towards it and within the space of twenty strokes was confronted by a thick yellow tide sprinkled with dead and dying fish. Even as she looked down she could see a stream of yellow bubbles rising to the surface. She sank to her knees and dipped her hand in the water. It was hot.

Carter turned his head anxiously. 'What is it?'

Sula shrugged. 'I do not know. The water is hot and yellow.'

Carter lowered his head and his expression relaxed. 'Good.'

As yet untouched by the yellow tide and recessed inland from the Japanese position was the small beach of black volcanic sand that had shown itself on the aerial photographs. Half a dozen dug-out canoes were drawn up on the sand, but there was no sign of the upright paddle wedged against the outrigger, which was the signal to say that the other party had arrived and landed safely.

Sula was more worried by the presence of several children splashing in the shallows. She was desperately aware that Carter needed to get ashore and rest but she knew also that it would be dangerous if the children saw him. They were of Joe's tribe, but the word would spread like wildfire if a white man was known to be in the area. Her presence had already excited comment amongst the villagers. She was known as 'Joe's woman', a title with an implication that added fresh lustre to Joe's already impressive reputation.

Sula waited until she was fifty yards from the beach and then started to beat the water with her paddle, shouting 'Shark!' The bathers fled for the beach and started to clamber over the surrounding rocks for a better sight of the mythical raider. Sula brought the canoe close in and wedged it against a shelving rock a few yards from shore which had been pre-selected for the purpose. The beach was empty and the children scrambling amongst the rocks.

'Wait.'

She slipped into the water and waded ashore, checking the sand for any sign of fresh bootprints. There seemed to be nobody about. The sun was high in the sky and the sand almost too hot beneath the feet. The natives would be in their huts and, hopefully, the Japs on the local post occupied with their visitor.

Sula waited at the edge of the beach for a few minutes to see if anyone appeared and then waded out to the canoe. She started to lift out the net and under its cover Carter slipped into the water and started to rub the feeling back into his cramped limbs. Sula returned to the beach to lay out the net on a framework of drying poles. Carter waited and then felt his way through shoals of minute fish apparently nibbling at the shore, to lie with his nose barely above the water and his chest pressed against the sand. Sula waited till the children's attention was occupied amongst the rocks and gave the word. Carter scrambled to his feet and ran stooped beneath the net to throw himself into the shelter of the bush. He lay panting and rubbed the sand from his elbows. Seconds later, Sula sauntered to his side and without pausing led him to the hide-out she had prepared with Joe.

At first glance this seemed like a clump of thick rattan, but when Sula picked her way carefully through the undergrowth to pull back the outside canoe, Carter could see that a narrow tunnel had been made and the centre of the clump hollowed out to make a cool, open chamber. The severed canes provided a rough floor. Carter unslung his weapon and withdrew it from its waterproof bag before stretching out. He felt exhausted but grateful—and a little surprised—to be alive. Sula looked down at him for a moment and then moved to take up a position at the mouth of the tunnel. When he looked next she had disappeared. He lay back and tried to find promise in the glimpse of sunlight breaking through the dark foliage far above his head. Then he closed his eyes and fell asleep.

12

When Carter awoke it was to a hand over his mouth and another pressing against his shoulder. He opened his eyes, not certain if he was having a nightmare, and saw a haggard Hudson looking down at him. Behind were Johnson and Joe. There was no sign of Sula.

'Thank God,' whispered Carter when the hand was removed. 'I thought I was going to have to blow up half a volcano. What happened to you guys?'

'Same as you, mate,' said Johnson. 'Bloody current took us half-way to New Ireland. I thought I was going to be in America before you.'

'I'm going to get Joe another medal for finding us,' said Hudson.

Joe's smile shone in the half-light.

'You can order one for Sula while you're at it,' said Carter. 'Where is she?'

'Keeping watch.'

Carter looked at his watch, relieved beyond measure that the others were alive and with him. He doubted if he would ever be able to master the jungle on his own. Half-past three. That meant that he had been asleep for over three hours. The others would hardly have time to close their eyes before getting ready for the night's operation. He looked at Hudson.

'Are you going to be in shape for tonight?'

Hudson looked slightly piqued by the question. 'Yes,' he said. 'I'd rather keep moving than stay here. The sooner we get that explosive out of the water, the better.'

'Too true,' said Johnson. 'Mind you, once or twice I thought it was going out of the water and taking us with it. We nearly lost our outrigger coming past the Japs. I was holding it on with a prayer.'

'Was there a launch there?' asked Carter.

'No,' said Johnson. 'They all seemed to be tidying the place up. Bloody amazing. You know what they're like. If you see a bloke shitting three yards from his fox-hole instead of two, you know he's the sanitary officer.'

'Tell me more about the launch,' said Hudson.

Carter gave an edited version of his journey ashore with emphasis on the spotter plane and the officious major.

Hudson frowned. 'It bears out what Joe has been telling us. Our little yellow friends are definitely on their toes.'

'Any idea why?'

Hudson shrugged. 'I think they're probably a bit mad about what we did to the searchlight post. It's a bloody shame we were forced to let them know we were there.' He looked at his watch. 'Right. Jerry and I will get our heads down for a couple of hours. Joe will make contact with his people. Will, wake me at sunset. I want us to have a scout round before it gets dark.'

He lay down and seemed to be asleep the moment the soles of his boots had moved from the horizontal to the vertical.

Johnson lay down opposite him. Joe saluted and went out. Carter wondered if he ever slept. He stripped and reassembled his Mills gun to make sure that it was in perfect working order and moved to the mouth of the tunnel. Through the rattan he had a partial view of the clearing and could see the overgrown pathway leading to the beach. There was no sign of Sula. He listened intently for several minutes and could detect only the usual sounds. Occasional bird cries and the constant background throbbing of insects. No human noise. He felt a familiar pricking sensation and stooped to find the first leech on his ankle. His arm was already red with unnoticed mosquito bites. He wondered if increasing exposure to the jungle was yielding him some kind of immunity to discomforts which, if initially revolting, caused a deeper offence to the eye than to the body.

He wondered, too, where Sula was. Not far away, probably. Ready to materialize, Joe-like, from the bush as he came near. He listened again and stepped forward from semi-darkness into the twilight of the forest. Nearby, a swallow-tailed Uranus Moth, with a wingspan as wide as his spread hand, paused on a jungle blossom and then shadowed away amongst the creepers. Stepping carefully so as to leave no trail of crushed vegetation to the rattan he joined the path and made his way warily back towards the beach expecting to see Sula with every step. He was surprised when he suddenly saw the black volcanic sand and that there was no sign of her. The children had disappeared and the beach was deserted. He looked across to the rock and saw that a second outrigger canoe had been moored against it. Several of the support spars were dangling in the water to bear out what Johnson had said about the damaged outrigger.

Carter turned his head and looked up towards Matupi. Its sliced top was just visible over the trees. As he tried to calculate how long it would take to reach the summit, a flight of planes appeared flying directly over the crater. Two Betty bombers escorted by six Zeke fighters. Carter was intrigued. The Zeke was the latest and more manoeuvrable version of the Zero, with tapering wings. Whoever was in the bombers must be important. The Betties peeled off to land and the Zekes began to circle protectively until they in turn came down one by one to disappear behind the trees.

Carter waited to see if he could hear or see anything else of interest and then withdrew from the fringe of the beach. He had taken about a dozen paces when he heard somebody approaching down the pat. There was no thick cover available so he ducked down behind a tree with jungle ferns up to his shoulders. A large yellow grasshopper struck him on the chest like a missile and he jerked back in surprise before pressing forward until he was peering through the whorls of lichen-covered liana that encircled the trunk. Although on his guard, his apprehension was tempered by the belief that he was going to see Sula. Quite unintentionally he had placed himself in a position to ambush her. It would be amusing to see the expression on her face when he stepped out from behind the tree.

But it was not Sula approaching down the path. Something was brushing through the undergrowth below waist-height. Before Carter could move, the ferns parted and he was face to face with a large and vicious-looking dog, its long pink tongue lolling from its mouth, slaver dripping from its teeth. The dog seemed about to spring at him and Carter stood up raising his Mills gun. Behind the dog loomed a near-naked native carrying a long hunting spear. At the sight of Carter he drew the spear back threateningly.

'No!' Carter thrust his weapon out in front of him and the native's arm froze. It was almost possible to see the decision being formed behind the wide, staring eyes: the white man's bullet could travel faster than his spear. The trigger would be pulled before his arm had advanced beyond the shoulder. Slowly, he lowered his arm and said something to the dog which drew back from the crouch position, its red eyes still on Carter's throat.

The native looked at Carter's gun with an undisguised loathing that he obviously felt for its owner. He had a grizzled beard, and urea and sweat had dried into hard, glue-like patches in the folds of his skin. His fingers moved surreptitiously against the shaft of his spear as if he was seeking a new grip to take advantage of any lapse of concentration on Carter's part. The two men faced each other, silent, as if discovered in the opening seconds of a duel.

The tension was broken by Sula, who appeared silently from the foliage on the other side of the track. She looked at Carter, seeking an explanation.

'Ask him what he's doing here,' said Carter.

Sula spoke swiftly in Tolai but the man shook his head. She resorted to pidgin.

'You makin whatname long dis fella half ground?'

The man paused for a moment and shifted uneasily before replying, 'Me lookim pig?'

Sula made a 'humf' noise which clearly expressed disbelief. 'You findim pig?'

The man again relapsed into a sullen silence and looked at his dog. Carter thrust the Mills gun forward a couple of inches to discourage any order to attack.

'Is he saying that he's hunting pig?'

Sula scowled. 'Yes. I do not believe him. I ask him if he had seen any.' She repeated her question. 'You findim pig?'

The man widened his mouth to show a causeway of broken teeth and it slowly dawned on Carter that he was smiling. A smile made doubly sinister by its patent lack of sincerity.

''E no got pig long dis fella half. You gammon!' Sula spat out the words and turned to Carter. 'He is lying. There are no pigs here.'

The man looked anxiously towards Carter, sensing what was being said. Carter agonized over what to do. The man did not speak the local language and was hunting pig where none existed. Carter knew enough about New Guinea to know that no man wishing to stay alive would hunt alone in another tribe's territory. He also knew that the Japs used native trackers and dogs to hunt down coast-watchers. Every indication was that the man before him was one of them. He had to weigh the success of the mission against the risk involved in letting this man live. Was it so difficult a decision? When the volcano erupted many innocent natives would die along with the Japs. Perhaps Green would not return and the inmates of the prison camp would be executed. What difference would one man's life make?

But to kill a man in cold blood—that was the difference. Something inside Carter revolted at the idea. The man was carrying a pig spear. Perhaps he was telling the truth. And he was so ugly. Like an insect that one wants to kill because its appearance frightens and disgusts. And if he had to be put to his death. How? A shot was out of the question with the Japs less than a mile away. Was he, Carter, capable of cutting the man's throat? The answer was simple. No. He would have to take him back to the others. Hudson could play Solomon.

Carter was about to speak when he saw Sula gliding up behind the man. Her hand moved to her thigh and parted her skirt to withdraw a slim dagger made of sharpened cassowary bone. She started to raise her hand and the muscles in her arm tightened.

'No!'

As Carter was commanding Sula, the man saw his chance. He shouted at the dog, which leapt on Carter, and spun round to try and disembowel Sula with his spear. She twisted away and the spear was hurled at Carter as he fed the dog his forearm rather than his troat. The spear thumped into the dog's back with sufficient force to transfix its body. The dog released its hold and fell kicking to the ground. The man ran.

Once again, Sula moved with greater speed and resolution than Carter. She took three pursuing steps and threw her dagger to lodge squarely in the middle of the man's back. He staggered but did not fall and in a few seconds was swallowed up by the bush.

Sula was furious. 'Why did you not let me kill him? Now he will tell the Japs.'

Carter looked at his arm. The dog's teeth had punched deep holes and he could see sinew. As he watched, the blood welled up and began to flow down his arm to his finger-tips and drip onto the ground. Flecks of foam appeared around the dog's mouth and the first blow-flies homed in gratefully.

'I'm sorry,' said Carter. He held his hand over the wound to stop the blood dripping. 'We must warn the others.'

When he burst through the rattan, Hudson's gun was pointing to the pit of his stomach. 'What's up?'

Carter quickly reported what had happened, and Hudson's face grew grim.

'What the hell you were doing out there in the first place we can discuss another time.' He nodded to Johnson. 'Bind his arm up.'

'What are we going to do?' said Johnson. 'Stay here and chance it?'

Hudson shook his head. 'If they've got dogs and native trackers they'll be here in no time. We'll have to go deeper into the bush.'

'What about the explosive?' asked Carter.

'We'll have to take a chance and leave it here. We can't move it now.'

Sula interrupted by pulling at Hudson's sleeve and placing her hand against her mouth. His head turned towards the wall of rattan. Carter listened and at first heard nothing. Then there was the sound of stealthy movement through the undergrowth. Johnson finished tightening the last knot on Carter's dressing and silently picked up his gun. Hudson made a 'fan out' gesture and faced the entrance corridor with his weapon at the ready. The noise grew louder. It was clearly made by more than one person. The ever-present ache of fear became more intense. Had the fleeing man run into a Japanese patrol?

As if at a signal, the noise suddenly stopped. Carter placed his finger inside the trigger guard and waited. His arm ached dully and a dark stain appeared through the bandage. A drop of sweat dripped from his forehead onto the breech of the Mills gun. The seconds passed. Ten. Twenty. Thirty.

Then there was a rustle of the rattan and Joe appeared. He had brought the bearers who were waiting nearby.

'Japan ' e come,' said Hudson. 'All fella *raus!*'

They came out of the rattan like a football team from a tunnel. But there was no cheering crowd. Only a cluster of frightened natives who melted away into the bush the moment that Joe had finished speaking to them. Hardly had they disappeared than there came the distant baying of dogs.

'Japan 'e kerose-up too much!' said Joe.

Hudson waved him down the track and started to run.

'Where are we heading?' asked Carter.

'The swamp,' said Hudson. 'It's the only place we'll lose those dogs.'

'We'll never make it,' panted Johnson.

'We will if we can stop them up the track,' said Hudson.

They ran hard for three hundred yards, tripping over roots, stumbling in pot-holes and slithering through mud patches until they came to a small clearing in the forest. That it had once been a garden was obvious but the grove of bananas and bread-fruit trees had been choked by vines and the sweet potatoes and yams were only visible as mounds amongst the invading *kunai* grass.

Hudson halted and unslung his weapon.

'Jerry, you and me behind the cedar. Will, take Sula and get in between those bamboos. Joe, over there behind the bananas. Fire when I do, then we'll get the hell out of here. I want to stop them, not fight a pitched battle. If there's just a couple of dogs—kill them first.'

He was moving towards cover before the last words were out of his mouth.

Carter shouldered his way into the bamboos, turned and dropped onto the mattress of rotting leaves and humus. Sula brushed past him and lay at his shoulder. He turned to glance at her but she avoided his eye and looked down the track.

Hudson checked his field of fire and wrapped the sling of his Mills gun round his forearm to steady his aim. Beside him, Johnson lay on his side with one hand extended to his crotch. In the hand was a grenade waiting to be thrown. The regular, warning-note tick of an unseen bird exploded into a raucous cackle and was swallowed up in a flutter of departing wings. Now, all that could be heard above the susurration of the insects was the distant baying of the dogs. It was getting louder.

Hudson narrowed his eyes and peered across the clearing, waiting for the first flicker of movement along the track. When it came he pressed back the safety-catch. Johnson sank from his elbow to his left shoulder and hooked his forefinger in the ring of the grenade.

First to appear were three *kanakas* with dogs on leashes. Behind them in single file were a party of Japanese marines wearing uniforms of dark-green cloth, close-fitting, camouflaged steel helmets and black canvas boots and gaiters. Each man carried a pack made of hide with the hair on the outside to keep out the rain, a rolled raincoat groundsheet, ammunition bandoliers and either a snub-nosed sub-machine gun or a bolt-action Mauser-type rifle. Normally the Japs would have been spread out at fifteen yard intervals and moving warily. Now they were pressing forward in continuous file with no thought of being attacked. The path seemed to be choked with them.

The first men came into the clearing and paused as the dogs broke up to follow the diverging scents. Hudson waited till there was a cluster of fifteen and then turned to Johnson and nodded.

Johnson drew the pin, and his arm rose straight like that of a siege gun. He had already ranged on the spot where he wanted the grenade to land and was reaching for his weapon a split-second after his throwing hand was empty. Hudson waited until the grenade was in mid-air and fired a long burst into the centre of the group of Japs. Three were going down as the grenade landed amongst the dogs. There was a flash and then a crump of metal fragments ripping through flesh. A dog was blown half-way across the clearing. Another lost a hind leg and turned its head, amazed and terrified to find that the limb had gone. The third dog survived because its companions had absorbed the main force of the explosion. Hudson shot it dead.

More Japs went down as Joe, Johnson and Carter opened fire, but there was no panic. Men who could move dived for the near-est cover, and those further down the track broke out fast to find as much space on the flanks as they could. These men were battle-hardened veterans who in less than six months had over-run half the Pacific, reducing two of the most powerful nations on earth to the status of punch-bags.

Within thirty seconds the clearing was empty save for the dead and the dying. The maimed dog nuzzled the spot where its leg had been and yelped pitiously. Men moaned, coughed, splut-tered, trembled, shook and bled. Two of the native guides were dead, the third one wounded. Hudson and Johnson withdrew, crawling for twenty yards, and then ran stooped along the path to be joined by Joe, Sula and Carter. Behind them, bullets started to rip into the position they had vacated. Hudson knew how the Japs would work. They would fan out sideways in a con-tinuing semi-circle, searching the target area before them with a moving arc of sub-machine gun fire. Once they had located the enemy fire-points it would only be a question of time before they outflanked each position and overran it.

The Japs were methodical but slow to change their tactics. Hudson calculated that it would be ten minutes before they started levelling the vegetation and realized that the enemy had withdrawn.

The path narrowed and twisted through a grove of bamboo, the entrance splashed with brilliant sunlight. As the others went through, Carter dropped to one knee and unclipped a grenade which had been wound with fine wire. He quickly unwound the wire and passed it round two palms at ankle level so that it was strung across the path and practically invisible to anyone emerg-ing from jungle darkness into dazzling sunshine. He adjusted a sliding hook on the wire and snapped it onto the firing-pin ring of the grenade, keeping the wire taut. The pressure of a man's ankle against the wire would pull the pin.

A hundred yards behind, bursts of automatic fire ripped through the foliage. Carter started to run after the others. Fifty yards ahead, Joe was waiting to direct him off the track and down a steep bank to where the ground was soft under foot and the vegetation smelling strongly of decay. The jungle closed in to form a roof overhead and the mosquitoes hung in swarms.

Carter slipped and slithered and splashed through patches of swamp where the mud sucked hungrily at his boots and small water-snakes wove like stitching through the stagnant water. The further they went, the worse the smell became and the more moribund the vegetation. Dead trees rotted in the water; others leaned against each other like drunks. Even the creepers hung listless and emaciated, trailing away leafless above the water. A ghostly, grey-green moss clung to everything, muffling noise and life.

Carter had caught up with the others when he heard the grenade go off. There was a scream that turned into a continuous, agonized wail, and sporadic bursts of automatic fire as the Japs took cover. Carter listened to the noise and felt a grim satisfaction that his booby-trap had worked.

Hudson was alarmed. The Japs had pressed forward much sooner than he had anticipated. They must have been able to tell there were not many men before them by the fire power that had been brought to bear and gambled on a withdrawal.

As the water got deeper and the jungle gave way to continuous swamp, the sky opened up and reed beds began to cluster round the rotting trees. Streams of bubbles rose from the water as if there were men below still trapped in a graveyard of wrecked ships whose gutted superstructures loomed menacingly above the surface. Narrow channels ran through the reed beds. Carter surmised that they were on the fringes of the river delta he had seen from the sea.

Johnson was looking about him anxiously. 'Keep your eyes open for crocs,' he said. 'Do you see him?'

Carter followed the pointed finger but only to see a widening ripple and a cloud of mud.

'Close up,' said Hudson. 'They won't have a go if we stick together.'

Carter looked down at the brackish water now rising nearly to his knees. It was thicker than Turkish coffee and as impenetrable to the eye. A crocodile could glide up to within inches without being seen. He stepped forward and nearly fell as his foot sank in the mud. The stinging sensation from his ankles told him that the leeches were at work. His eyelids were swelling with mosquito bites.

'Where are we heading?' he asked.

'There's a fishing village round here,' said Hudsonn. 'We'll get hold of a canoe and hide up in the reeds till they pull out.'

'And then what?' asked Johnson.

'Work back and see if we can pick up the explosive. We'll need twenty-four hours but Green isn't expecting us.'

'Let's hope the Japs aren't,' said Johnson anxiously. 'If some kids find it or one of Joe's boys blabs, that beach will be staked out waiting for us to come back.'

'Save your breath,' said Hudson.

He sounded worried and was looking about him as if for a landmark. He spoke to Joe, who gestured ahead through the lopsided screen of thinning vegetation towards what looked like a prairie of waving grass. There was no limit to it, no mountain range to say where it ended. It stretched to the horizon like the sea. In the foreground, where the last stunted trees of the forest emerged from the water like the piles of a rotting jetty, was a thickly thatched house built on thin, spindly stilts, looking like a warbler's nest amongst the reeds. A long, thin dug-out canoe was moored at the foot of a crude ladder.

Carter's heart lifted when he saw the canoe and he looked behind him warily. For five yards a thin line was traced through the green confetti. Then the surface knitted together as if they were towing a dipper and there was nothing to show that they had passed.

Hudson approached the canoe and swore softly. It was half-full of water, rotten and holed beneath the freeboard. How far it could carry five people was debatable. Carter heard a buzzing beside his ear and turned to find a diadem of flies clustered around a lump of human excrement which was smeared against one of the piles. As he looked up, a hideous face looked down and then withdrew. It could have been a man or woman—bald, toothless and depraved. The face of a hobgoblin.

Hudson turned to Sula. 'Give her some salt and tell her that we need the canoe. It can't be the only one they've got. It hasn't been used since God knows when.'

He pushed his finger into the hull as if it was putty.

Johnson started to pull the nose of the canoe from a bed of lilies, and there was a shrill, angry chatter from above. This time, the whole of what was apparently an old woman came into view. One envelope-flap breast had shrivelled to almost nothing, the other hung like a razor strop to her navel. Her whole body was patterned with a gridwork of grey, flaking scales that became scabs when they reached her crown. Carter reckoned it was a skin disease and selected grille. He swallowed hard and clenched his fist. The appearance of the woman was truly horrifying.

Sula gamely climbed the ladder and entered the hut. The angry gabble turned into what sounded like monosyllabic barks of refusal.

Johnson looked at Hudson plaintively. 'How much longer are we going to wait, Skip?'

The question was answered from another quarter. A burst of automatic fire kicked up water and exploded splinters from the piles beside Carter's head. He threw himself full-length and floundered behind a tussock of tall grass. At the outskirts of the forest, Japs were visible between the trees. They were not hanging back but advancing fearlessly, calling to each other and splashing forward with their weapons held across their chests. Carter selected a man more ambitious than the others and let him reach the cover of a liana-covered stump. He drew a bead on the stump and fired a short burst the moment that the man had taken two steps from it. The Jap stopped in his tracks as if struck by a thought rather than a bullet, paused, reached for the tree, clutched at a vine and fell backwards, still clinging to it. In the water he looked like a hooked fish. Carter fired another burst and looked round for the others.

Johnson was sprawled across the canoe and for a moment Carter thought he was dead. Then he pulled himself up, his hand on his side. It came away bloody. Then he sank down into the mud so that the patch of red at his waist disappeared below the water. He looked at Carter and there was no hope in his eyes. A second rattle of small-arms fire made Carter duck, thinking that the Japs had outflanked them, but it was Joe firing out on the left. His shoulders glinted behind a clump of sorghum. Above their heads the old woman was wailing as if this invasion of her world had tipped her into madness.

Bullets were coming from all directions. Hudson hauled at the prow of the canoe and the slime sucked greedily. Three paddles slapped down from the stilt house and Sula leapt after them, disappearing up to her waist in the mud. Her action prompted a long Jap burst which shivered the cane walls to sawdust. The wailing stopped abruptly. Hudson grunted, heaved and panted, and the canoe started to move. Johnson tried to push and then collapsed face downwards in the water. Carter heaved him over the side and turned to fire at two Japs who were less than twenty yards away. One went down, the other veered sideways to find cover and a firing position. A pulled stitch of bullets streaked past Carter's right side and he fired a haphazard burst in the direction of the shots.

The canoe was now manoeuvrable with Sula aboard and Hudson scrambling in. Johnson had pulled himself up and was trying to wield a paddle. Carter saw Joe splashing through the water and unhooked a grenade.

'Come. Quick!' It was Sula calling him.

The canoe was moving forward. Forward and away from him. The Japs were shouting and coming forward in clusters. Carter pulled the pin from the grenade and drew back his arm. One-two-three. His arm straightened and he threw himself flat so that the water closed over his head and his face was pressed into the mud. There was an instantaneous explosion and the mud shuddered with the force of the impact. Carter did not turn to look but rose and ran, expecting with every pace to feel the bullets shredding his flesh. He caught up with the canoe and slumped across it, not trying to get in for fear of capsizing it. Five strokes and they had cleared open water and entered a narrow channel between the reeds. Another five and they were totally enclosed.

13

Yukichi stayed within the shade of the tunnel mouth and looked across the road to the thin, sloping beach dropping away through the coconut palms to the sea. The water sparkled invitingly and the bulk of Matupi smiled benignly in the sunshine. Yukichi glanced at his watch. Two minutes to go. It would be interesting to see if the reputation for punctuality was maintained. He glanced sideways and saw General Koji mopping his brow. He was surrounded by a galaxy of officers from the Rabaul garrison, shifting uneasily in a manner that was not totally attributable to the heat.

In the distance, there was a hum of engines and a light 95-type tank appeared through the dust followed by two vehicles. A member of the crew stood in the turret with his goggles pressed up against his forehead and his hands resting on the stock of the 7.7mm machine gun. His eyes ranged the cliff face.

Yukichi concentrated on the second vehicle as it stopped outside the tunnel. Beside the driver sat a man wearing the white dress uniform of an admiral of the fleet in the Japanese navy. He wore a white-topped, short-peaked hat, white shoes, and a high-buttoned uniform carrying four rows of medal ribbons.

The man was approaching sixty but looked younger. His expression was benign and open, his mouth sensual and sensitive, his eyes watchful but not suspicious. It was an intelligent, feeling face that might have belonged to a university professor. In fact it belonged to Admiral Isoruku Yamamoto, Commander in Chief of the Japanese Combined Fleet.

Yamamoto waited for the door of his vehicle to be opened and then stepped out to exchange salutes with General Koji and the assembled party. It was noticeable that his salute was not a compromise gesture towards military etiquette. It was brisk and firm, with his stiff fingers quivering against the peak of his cap. There had been no relaxation of protocol since the first meeting at the airfield.

'You are a most honoured visitor,' said Koji. His salute was not inferior to that of Yamamoto.

'I have heard a great deal about what you have achieved here,' said Yamamoto, pleasantly. 'Six miles of tunnels, I believe?'

'Nearer seven at the moment,' said Koji. Japanese diffidence made him qualify this statement in case it sounded like presumptuous boasting. 'The pumice-stone lava is very easy to tunnel through.'

Yamamoto nodded. 'I will be most interested to see what you have done.' He cast an eye over the officers who had been assembled to receive him and moved into the mouth of the tunnel. He took half a dozen paces and came to a halt before a forty-foot barge incongruously mounted on a low trolley. He looked questioningly at Koji, who turned towards Yukichi. A mode of procedure for the visit had been established between commanding officer and adjutant shortly after it had been announced.

Yukichi spoke. 'We have found that the best method to resist enemy air attacks is to unload supply vessels at sea and maintain the barges in these tunnels. Disembarkation takes place at night and the barges can be swiftly winched to and from the tunnels.'

'You mean, across the road and down the beach?' said Yamamoto.

'Precisely, sir,' said Yukichi.

Yamamoto looked about him and then down to the narrow-gauge railway line on which the barge's trolley rested. 'And that?'

'If a barge is damaged or requires servicing we can move it to the workshops which are located further back in the tunnels. The track also facilitates movement of the barges within the tunnels. We normally berth a number of barges in each tunnel.'

Yamamoto nodded approvingly. 'I imagine materials can also be brought direct into the tunnels without going through the docks?'

'When necessary, yes, sir.'

Yamamoto moved deeper into the tunnel, past a second barge

and a group of men who were working on repairs to the rudder assembly. Yukichi told him that the barge had gone aground on a reef. Yamamoto had been allowing himself the unaccustomed luxury of looking forward to his next meal but now all thought of food had been brushed aside. He was genuinely intrigued by what he could see about him. The twenty-foot-high tunnel with its own lighting and ventilation system sloping away before him. With seven miles of such tunnels the scope for concealing men and armaments was enormous. It was impossible to imagine how the enemy could ever breach them. He paused again, faced with a structure like a small tank on rubber wheels.

'We use these for pulling loads around the tunnels,' explained Yukichi. 'They are battery-driven floats which are charged every night.' He bowed his head respectfully and ushered Yamamoto onto the protected metal platform backed by stacked truck batteries.

'There are no gasoline fumes to pollute the air.'

Yamamoto stepped onto the float and nodded approvingly. 'Very simple and effective,' he said.

General Koji and Yukichi stepped onto the platform beside him and the driver pressed the control lever. With a faint whirring noise the float began to glide forward. The other officers moved forward to climb aboard two other floats that were standing by. They felt honoured and relieved. The first stage of the visit appeared to be going satisfactorily.

Ten minutes later, Yukichi was grasping a wooden pointer and facing a wall-chart that showed the layout of the tunnels. In the place of honour among his audience in the large chamber hewn from solid rock sat an attentive Yamamoto with his hat on his lap.

Yukichi cleared his throat and began. 'As an introduction to your visit, Admiral, I would respectfully wish to show you the structure of the tunnels. You can see how the perimeter of the cliffs follows a semi-circle. We have tunnelled in from this at six points so that the tunnels are like the spokes of a wheel culminating at what might be termed the axis—where we are currently situated. Barges are berthed in the mouths of five of these tunnels and there are rail tracks leading back into the interior.'

He tapped the point where the tunnels met on the chart.

'In the central command area we have administration offices, armouries, interrogation cells, radio station and, of course, the briefing theatre where we are now sitting. All communication radiates from the centre. Between each tunnel we have constructed other joining tunnels like the cross-links of a spider's web.'

His pointer ranged the chart.

'In these are contained hospital facilities, ammunition and supply dumps, accommodation for the troops and extensive workshops. We can repair damaged equipment and also assemble material that is shipped in to us by our gallant brothers in the merchant marine.'

Yamamoto nodded approvingly. 'And there is no danger from air attack?'

Yukichi shook his head. 'None. We are scarcely aware that enemy bombers are overhead.'

'All disembarkation of supplies is done at night and that is the only time that our barges can be caught in the open,' added Koji. 'We have lost only four in the last six months.'

Yamamoto studied the chart closely. It was clear that he was impressed. 'And the dotted lines going inland from the junction point?'

'Tunnels under construction, sir,' said Yukichi.

'We are constantly enlarging the network, as you know,' said Koji. 'With the increasing build-up of men and materials we need more space. I also wish to initiate a system by which all fuel reserves can be stored within the tunnels. I intend to create a series of reservoirs so that oil and gasoline can be pumped ashore direct rather than brought in by the various methods we are forced to employ at the moment.'

Yamamoto listened with increasing pride and satisfaction. As long as this underground fortress maintained its impregnability it seemed impossible that the Americans and their allies could ever take Rabaul. The potential for another giant leap forward by the Imperial Army remained undiminished.

'Excellent,' he said. 'I would like to see the excavation that is being done at the moment.'

The party left the briefing theatre and emerged into the brightly lit area which formed the hollowed-out junction of the six tunnels slanting up to the cliff face. They passed General Koji's office and the radio station and moved on foot into a tunnel showing signs of recent excavation. A temporary lighting system had been erected and a concertina ventilation-pipe followed the wall like an endless worm. They passed a side tunnel revealing packing cases stacked to the ceiling and were met by two emaciated Indians pushing a barrow full of rubble. Their tightly stretched skin glistened with sweat and their legs were obscenely thin, the knees standing out like knots in a piece of cord. Behind them came a guard, his nostrils and mouth covered by a lint mask. He responded to Yamamoto as if brought face to face with a ghost and stood stiffly to attention before being told to go on his way.

Despite an attempt at ventilation, the air was difficult to breathe and laden with particles of dust. It was hot and humid and there was a stench of human excrement, suggesting that sanitary arrangements were a low priority as far as the men digging the tunnels were concerned.

Yukichi looked at the walls. There were indications that heavy boulders were mixed with the pumice. The excavation could not be easy at this point. Two hundred yards down the tunnel the heat became almost unbearable and the uneven floor strewn with rubble. A generator shuddered and there was a concentration of lights and the rattle of an electric drill.

The scene was like an impression of hell. Near-naked skeletons toiling in a crucible of heat. Dirt. Noise. The drill biting into the rock. Wasted men levering and jabbing with arms scarcely thicker than the picks they were wielding. Others straining their sinews to load rocks and rubble onto barrows. The guards with their dust-covered masks looking like plump larvae, giving the impression that they fed on the flesh of their emaciated prisoners.

Koji saw Yamamoto narrow his eyes as he looked upon the Indians.

'I am considering transferring all prisoners and internees to work in the tunnels,' he said. 'We have lost many of the men that we brought from Singapore.'

'I am not surprised,' said Yamamoto. He looked round the assembled officers who were mopping their brows. 'Who is responsible for these men?'

There was a moment's pause and a grizzled colonel stepped forward and bowed. He had lost an eye at Guadalcanal and was known to be a gallant soldier.

'I am, sir. Colonel Namura. 17th Army. My responsibilities include the prison camp.' He spoke the last six words with a slight but perceptible edge of distaste in his voice. It suggested that he did not believe that looking after prisoners was the work of a gallant soldier.

Yamamoto spoke calmly and without emotion. As he did so, he lowered his voice so that only those near him could hear what he was saying.

'If you cannot keep your prisoners alive, their work will have to be done by our own men. I am certain you share my belief that our soldiers' energies are best reserved for fighting the enemy. Please bear that in mind.'

Namura dropped his head to his chest in acknowledgement of the rebuke and the party retraced their footsteps down the tunnel. The two Indians were returning with the empty barrow and Yukichi looked upon them coldly. If they had fought to the death like honourable men they would not be here now. It did not seem fair that Namura should be criticized for his treatment of such creatures.

Koji, too, was annoyed by the Admiral's remarks. He had hoped that the short visit would be an unstinted success—now his satisfaction was diminished. It was difficult to know what to do about Namura. He was a soldier who itched for active service; he involved himself with his duties at the military police headquarters in the town but rarely visited the prison camp. To relieve him of his duties would be seen as a punishment and was too severe a solution. Perhaps he could arrange that Yukichi discreetly took over responsibility for the prison camp.

Koji looked towards his adjutant and saw he was being approached by a signalman who had emerged from the radio station. The man appeared highly agitated. Koji felt uneasy. Did one small setback preface another more serious? He saw Yukichi enter the radio station and turned to Yamamoto.

'I have prepared a room for you next to my office. Would you care to take some saki whilst we continue our discussions?'

'I would prefer some tea,' said Yamamoto.

He mounted a flight of stone steps and a door was slid open by an armed guard. The remaining officers bowed their heads and were dismissed.

Yamamoto had barely settled into a chair when there was an urgent tap on the door and Yukichi entered. Koji could see from the expression on his face that something was wrong.

'I am sorry to interrupt you,' he said, 'but we have received a rather disturbing report. A small party of the enemy have apparently come ashore in the Matupi area.'

'Matupi?' said Koji. 'But you visited our detachment there this morning.' His voice was scolding.

'That is correct, sir.'

Koji's real anger was not vented against Yukichi but against fate for having disrupted his plans. He controlled himself and turned to Yamamoto.

'I think that we must be prepared for the fact that this raiding party is a suicide squad put ashore to assassinate you. I have been expecting something like this.'

Yamamoto looked from Koji to Yukichi. 'In that case I am surprised that they were able to land.'

Koji and Yukichi bowed their heads in shame.

'I am sorry, sir,' said Koji. 'We have taken certain precautions but they have clearly failed. I accept full responsibility.'

'How many raiders are there?' asked Yamamoto.

'The report states three,' said Yukichi. 'Also, two natives, one of them a woman.'

'I think we can consider that as being five,' said Yamamoto drily. 'Where are they now?'

'One of our native trackers found them and alerted our marine detachment at Matupi Point. There was a skirmish, and the raiding party withdrew into the swamps. I understand that one of them is seriously wounded.'

Yamamoto pursed his lips disapprovingly.

'In other words, they escaped.'

Yukichi swallowed. 'Yes, sir.'

'Are they being pursued?'

Yukichi nodded emphatically. 'I have ordered a K-boat to proceed to the swamps immediately. I doubt if the raiders will be able to survive the night.'

Yamamoto smiled grimly. 'I hope you are right. Please keep me informed of all developments.'

'Of course, sir.'

Koji intervened deferentially. 'Despite the measures that are being taken, I think we should proceed with great caution in respect to the rest of your visit. May I suggest that a khaki uniform would make you less immediately identifiable?'

'The purpose of my visit *is* to be immediately identifiable,' said Yamamoto calmly. 'I will not let seventy thousand men see me hiding from five.' He turned towards the orderly who had arrived with the tea. 'Come gentlemen, we must not alarm ourselves. I have every confidence in your ability to rectify the situation. I have also seen the swamp.' He extended his hands to receive a bowl of tea and smiled grimly. 'I have confidence in that, too.'

14

The sun was sliding down the sky. In half an hour it would be
dark. Somewhere in the swamp a crocodile barked. Feather-
topped grasses, wild grains and ferns gave way to palisades
of eight-foot-high canegrass that crackled like a fire as the prow
of the canoe pushed them aside. The humidity was stifling.
Narrow passages were carpeted with pink-flowered water lilies
and blue nymphaeae. In open water-holes fish jumped and terrapins dived for the mud three feet below. Always there were birds.
Marsh eagles kite-diving above. Egrets, cranes, ducks and geese
on the lagoons. They turned in surprise as the canoe approached
and then lifted in their hundreds like massed sentinels.

Carter looked down at the water in the bottom of the canoe. It
was alive with darting water-fleas and stained red with
Johnson's blood. The canoe was sinking.

'Where are we heading?'

Carter tried to keep his voice calm. In reality the claustropho-
bia of their surroundings and the impending night terrified him.
It was a question of time before the rotten fibrous hull of the
canoe became totally waterlogged and slid below the surface.
Then they would face the darkness and the marauding crocodiles
up to their waists in a limitless swamp.

'Joe says there's a village round here somewhere. We'll be able
to get another canoe.'

Hudson's voice was terse and tired. He caught his paddle in a
knot of underwater tubers and the canoe lurched alarmingly.

Johnson swore and moved his hand from his side. The blood
that seeped through his shirt was already flecked white with
blow-fly eggs.

Carter grimaced in disgust. Their position looked hopeless.
They were paddling deeper into the swamp in order to find a

canoe that would take them back to Matupi. If they did not find the village they would be worse off than if they returned towards the jungle. But if they returned, the Japs would be waiting.

The canoe emerged into a small lagoon choked with lilies and surrounded by sedge. There was no onward passage visible. Something disturbed one of the lilies and a stir of mud washed over the leaves. Carter felt that just above the surface eyes were watching him. Waiting. Knowing that he would soon be down there in the water and totally vulnerable. The canoe scuffed across the lilies and nosed into the cane, which recoiled like a pontoon. The root systems had become so solidly enmeshed as to form a floating raft.

Joe pressed his paddle down flat amongst the cane and scrambled out of the canoe. The platform sank a few inches and a stream of foul-smelling bubbles rose to the surface. One by one, Hudson, Carter and Sula followed. Johnson sat where he was. He could not lie back because his head would have been below the water. He took his hand from his wound and looked at the fresh blood.

'Sodding mosquitoes are still biting me,' he said. 'Why don't they help themselves to this lot?'

'Just hang on,' said Hudson. 'We'll take a look at that when we get to the village.'

Normally, Johnson would have queried the 'when' but this time his face gave no indication that he had heard Hudson's remark. He looked like a man who had come to terms with something.

Dragging the canoe through the floating island of cane was like walking on a trampoline. The surface undulated and it was impossible to find any point of purchase. Sudden holes or a thinning of the root cover would cause men to stumble up to their waists. Joe hacked a path with a bush knife but the cane still chafed and the leaves often carried an edge like a razor blade. Worst of all were the tiny goads that drifted from the leaves of certain canes like a dust of silver needles to set up a violent, itching rash that infected the eye, armpit and groin.

Above their heads the sky turned grey and the light leaked away amongst the forest of canes. Battalions of frogs began to croak and an air-force of flying foxes flapped overhead towards their evening feeding grounds, like giant smuts drifting over the still-smouldering heat of the swamp.

Hudson looked up at the flying foxes.

'Could mean that there's a village fruit garden near here.'

His voice held out little hope and nobody diverted breath from the effort of pulling to answer.

Suddenly there was an explosion of wings from a point twenty yards to their left, and a flight of magpie geese took to the air. As they shrilled away, Joe's bush knife bit into the cane with renewed vigour and he hacked towards the spot where the geese had risen. As abruptly as it had begun, the sedge gave way to an open lagoon, patterned by a mosaic of water-weed and clumps of lilies with circular, tray-like leaves. Through the water-weed was a path of clear water that might have been made by a boat.

The canoe was launched. Carter watched the water begin to flood the bottom as if soaking through a sponge. He climbed gingerly in and Johnson slumped back against his knees. He could feel the man trembling and lent forward to touch his forehead. It was hot and feverish. They crossed the lagoon and were entering a narrow waterway when Joe pointed to a cage-like structure built across a narrow passageway into the reeds. It was a bamboo pen with a drop gate propped open just above the water. Any small crocodile or terrapin entering the cage would dislodge one of the supporting poles and be trapped.

'Thank Christ,' said Hudson. 'There must be people near here.'

Joe sniffed and touched his nose, nodding in agreement. He gestured ahead and indicated a wide channel going off to the right.

''E go for dis side, *tabauda*.'

Driven by new hope, Carter dug his paddle into the dark water. The canoe jerked forward, making the bilge slop against the sides. At the end of the reach the sedge drew back to form the borders of a small lake, and a low parcel of land was visible rising abruptly from the swamp, its centre crowned by a huddle of rose-wood and cedars interlaced with palms.

As the dusk deepened, the distance between canoe and land

narrowed, and the square outline of huts could be seen against the trees. A single fire flickered weakly, and human figures drifted amongst the shadows like wraiths. It was a gloomy place made welcome only by the sight of half a dozen canoes pulled up on the muddy strand.

Hudson let the canoe ground and stepped ashore warily. Normally, the arrival of a party of strangers would bring small children clustering round the canoe whilst young girls giggled behind their hands and even the most timid local watched from the doorway of his hut. Here, nobody came forward and Hudson advanced to an old man who was sitting by a meagre fire. His features were ravaged by leprosy, his nose two holes in the middle of his face. Carter tried to recognize the blackened bones that littered the area about the fire. He had not seen anything like them before. The old man did not look up and responded with a grunt to Hudson's words of greeting.

Carter recognized an identical feeling to that he had experienced in the settlement behind Rabaul. He felt that he was in the presence of a malignant spirit. That he was being watched. With a start of fear he wondered if the Japs could have got there before them. Figures were emerging from the shadows now. Old men, women, even children. They were painfully thin and covered in tropical ulcers that opened on their bodies like extra, dribbling mouths and showed bone instead of teeth. They stood back like attendants at a ceremony.

Carter cocked his weapon. He had suddenly realized that there were no young men in the village. No young men *visible* in the village. Were they hunting? Making war on a neighbouring tribe of marsh-men? Or lying in ambush?

Hudson called to Sula who was tending to Johnson in the canoe. She arrived bringing the salt and trade tobacco in her *bilum*. The old man hardly turned his head to look at the 'gift' as it was placed at his feet. It was wet, he said. His shoulders were scuffed with whorls of ringworm and the lobes of his ears frayed to tatters by the weight of ornaments that had torn free over the years. When he used his matchstick arms to make a contemptuous gesture, flakes of grille fluttered to the ground. He was coming apart before their eyes. The whole island was a charnal house.

Hudson said that the salt and tobacco would soon dry. The old man shrugged and muttered.

Carter turned quickly as a figure glided up behind him. It was a swollen-bellied young girl with one breast twice the size of the other. She was suckling a baby. The baby withdrew its head, squealed and spluttered milk. The baby was a pig. It rediscovered the teat and sucked greedily. The girl looked at Carter with empty, expressionless eyes. It was as if the pig was sucking the life out of her.

Hudson told the old man that they needed a canoe. He paused for a moment and then spat out a stream of betel juice as if hawking his own blood. There was no mistaking the meaning of the gesture. 'We're never going to get anywhere with these people,' said Hudson. 'We'll have to help ourselves.'

He had begun to address the old man again when there was a shout from the canoe. Johnson was wrestling with a native who had tried to snatch his weapon. Carter started to run and the man released his hold and fled like a shadow for the huts. Suddenly, the clearing was empty save for the old man. He spat more betel juice at Hudson's feet and gesticulated angrily as flakes of grille fell like scales from a decomposing fish.

'What is he saying?' asked Carter.

'He says that if we take one of his canoes, the monster that lives in the swamp will drag us below the surface and eat us,' said Hudson. 'I still think it's a better bet than staying here.'

He spoke again to the old man and pointed towards the darkening horizon. The old man ignored him and muttered into his fire.

Hudson started to walk away. 'I asked him if that was the way to the sea. I hope he'll think we're heading that way and tell the Japs. Did you see those bones?'

'What about them?'

'They were human.' Hudson did not wait for Carter's reaction. 'They are the cruellest people on earth. When they take a prisoner and they don't want to eat him right away, they cut his feet off so that he can't make a run. To stop him bleeding to death they hold the stumps in the fire to seal them. That way they can keep a man alive for days.'

Carter shuddered. 'Where are the warriors?'

Hudson looked worried. 'That's what I'm asking myself. I've got a feeling they're not too far away. I saw a fellow poling into the weeds as we approached.'

When they got to the canoe, Johnson was lying back with his head half-submerged in water. His face was crawling with insects that he was too weak to brush away. Sula and Joe lifted him into one of the canoes drawn up on the shore. Hudson and Carter faced the huts, weapons at the ready. Only the old man was visible in the gathering darkness. He had thrown the salt on the fire and his ravaged face showed up in the ghostly blue-green light like a warning skull. His lips moved ceaselessly. He was a magician muttering spells and incantations.

Johnson lay with his head in Sula's lap and Joe pushed the canoe out into the lagoon. Long after the outline of the island had disappeared the light of the fire winked and wavered like a will-o'-the-wisp.

Johnson began to groan and mutter like a man having a nightmare. It was as if he were the mouthpiece for the old man they had left behind. Quick flurries of incoherent speech punctuated by references to Japs and pursuit. His body twitched as he tried to urge it onwards away from the invisible enemy.

Hudson listened grimly. This was what he had feared. The demons of Rabaul had overtaken Johnson. 23 January 1942. The last resistance to the invasion had ended, and the Japs were masters of the town. Johnson and the shattered remnants of the 2/22 Australian Battalion had taken to the bush intending to follow the coast round until they could be taken off by boat and ferried back to New Guinea. But it was a Jap boat that came ashore and 180 exhausted men surrendered at the Tol Plantation on the south coast. They had read leaflets telling them that if they surrendered they would be treated honourably like prisoners of war. At first the leaflets seemed to tell the truth. They were given food and cigarettes and paraded for a roll-call. Then they were stripped of their identity discs and their hands tied behind their backs with fishing line.

The Australians were divided into eighteen parties of ten men.

The Japs fixed their bayonets. Men began to look at each other anxiously. One by one, files of prisoners were marched into the overgrown plantation. Johnson turned and saw that the Jap at the rear of his file was carrying a pick and shovel. They were going to be murdered. Men began to weep and curse and the Japs moved in with rifle butts. Some men made a run for it and were shot in the back or beaten back into line. Johnson saw his chance and dived into the bush. He heard shots and screams and the sounds of men being clubbed and bayoneted to death. Then the orderly sound of pick and shovel digging into earth. Then the noises of the jungle and the hum of flies.

When it was dark he had got up and gone past the shallow graves of his dead comrades, some of them barely covered by a couple of shovelfuls of contemptuous earth. His hands had been tied so tightly that it was impossible to free them. For days he had wandered in the jungle while the flies blew his open sores and the twine cut deeper into his wrists. Leeches, mosquitoes and flies had tortured him until he rubbed his flesh away against the trunks of trees. His excreta clung to him and he became semi-conscious with malaria. Nowhere could he find a sharp outcrop of rock against which to sever his bonds. When he tried to drink in a shallow, muddy rill he overbalanced and nearly drowned in a few inches of water. He had been kept alive by eating the soft green heads of ferns and burrowing for tapioca roots like a pig. At night the rain drenched him to the skin. Never was he free from the itching of the maggots eating their way nearer to his bones. He had been found by another party of his own men who could barely bring themselves to look at him as they cut his bonds.

It was this hell that Johnson was reliving and which had plagued his mind on isolated occasions in the past. Always simmering just below the surface, threatening to break out. Now there was another hell. Would any of them survive it?

Carter looked about him warily and kept his Mills gun propped against the side of the canoe so that he could snatch it up at half a second's notice. It was now dark. The reed beds formed sinister hedges on either side crackling with unseen creatures. A cloud of fireflies danced like golden rain and ghostly patches of luminosity hung in the water like the reflections of Chinese lanterns. Mosquitoes arrived in droves, greedily lighting on the hand that brushed them away from the face. The slime slurped and sucked at the paddles. On a mud-bank, three shapes loomed up. Two slid noiselessly into the water like ships being launched. The other was a log.

Joe shouted and pointed towards the reeds. There was a sound like that of a flimsy door being kicked open and a long, high-prowed canoe burst into the open. It was propelled by twelve men grunting in unison as their paddles bit into the water. The canoe was a hundred yards away and moving through the water like a whip snake. It was coming to intercept them.

Hudson looked about him. A narrow waterway to the left offered the natural escape route. He called to the others to steer for it and then changed his mind. The position of the channel was too fortuitous.

'Hold off! We'll go in further down!'

The canoe shuddered as the full weight of the paddles was thrown against the water and the bow came round. Immediately, there was an angry bellow from the reeds at the mouth of the channel and something sailed through the air to fall with a splash beside the canoe. It was a throwing spear. The sedge exploded with shouting men. Some charged into the water to hurl spears and insults. The arrival of the canoe had clearly been timed to drive them into an ambush.

'Bastards!' spat Hudson.

The canoe was closing fast and three men rose, holding spears. Their arms came back and Carter raked the prow with a burst of automatic fire which splintered wood and jerked one man into the water. One spear fell short, another thudded into the hull inches below the gunwale. The marauding canoe veered away, its crew screaming hate and defiance.

Hudson saw a spot where the outline of the reeds dipped against the sky and drove the canoe towards it. The dug-out clattered through a screen of canegrass and entered a narrow channel choked with hanging fronds, twisted tubers and festoons of creepers studded with orchids. Giant spiderwebs draped over them like dust-sheets and something like a mouse with eight furry legs raced up Carter's arm and across his face before darting into the sedge. Frogs and roosting birds scattered.

After several minutes' urgent paddling, Hudson gave the order to stop. Carter slumped forward and sucked in mouthfuls of hot, clammy air. His savaged arm was beginning to throb painfully and his lungs ached. Plops, splashes, crackles, rustles and squawks gave way to a steady chorus of frogs. There were no sounds of pursuit.

Hudson turned on his torch. Its thin beam probed the darkness ahead, attracting a feather-boa of moths, some so large that their wingbeats sounded like those of a bird. Tentacles of jungle reached out through the sedge or tried to straddle it. Garlands of closed flowers hung down to trail the water. Where the wild sugarcane met the slime, clusters of glow-worms formed chokers round the roots.

'Do you think they'll give us any more trouble?' asked Carter.

'You never know,' said Hudson. 'It depends if they can get ahead of us. They can find their way around this swamp blindfold.' He produced a prismatic compass and studied it. 'At least we're heading in the right direction. We'll press on as far as we can go and then rest up till daybreak.' He looked back at Johnson. 'How are you feeling, Jerry?'

At first there was no reply, and then the voice responded faintly but with increasing determination.

'I'm not going to walk. This time, I'm not going to walk.'

'Sure,' said Hudson gently.

Sula bathed Johnson's forehead and looked up at Hudson. She shook her head.

Johnson was going to die. His lower ribs had been shattered by automatic fire. Fragments of bone had penetrated his stomach. For the rest of the party it was better that he did die. They would never be able to carry him through the jungle. Nor would they be able to leave him behind. They would have to make the effort, and the effort would ensure that the Japs caught up with them. If Johnson died by daybreak they had a chance.

Joe's back muscles rippled and the canoe nosed its way deeper into the enclosing foliage. Carter brushed the wet creepers from

his face and listened to the flat, gutteral bark of a hunting crocodile. The swamps abounded with them but he had yet to see one
close up.

Ahead, the channel opened up into a dark waterscape of mud-
banks topped by thick clumps of cane and reed. A small red eye
gleamed jewel-bright fifty yards away in the centre of the stream.
Carter craned forward. It must be the eye of a crocodile; a large
one, because it seemed several inches above the surface. Carter
watched and the eye flew heavenwards.

'A croc-bird,' explained Hudson. 'They're bad news if you're
hunting. Look just like a croc at water level.'

'Did you hunt a lot?' asked Carter.

'When I was a young man, yes. Thought I was going to make
my fortune. Then it got so there were almost more hunters than
crocs.' He was silent for a moment. 'Amazing bloody thing, the
crocodile. It's so efficient that it's never changed over millions of
years. You know what else hasn't? The cockroach and the shark.'
He paused and laughed. 'Beauty isn't everything, eh?'

Carter held up his hand. 'Wait a minute!'

He had heard something. The soft putt-putt-putt of an out-
board engine. It was a long way away but getting nearer. Hudson
listened and swiftly hissed instructions to pull in to the bank. The
noise continued to come closer. Carter quietly laid his paddle at
his feet and picked up his Mills gun. Was it likely that the natives
had a motorboat? Hardly. It must be the Japs. The engine note
maintained a steady rhythm. Carter guessed that it must be travelling on a stretch of open waterway that lay beyond the mud-
banks. Perhaps one of the main tributaries of the delta. Johnson
smothered a groan and was comforted into silence by Sula.

There was a crashing noise from the sedge and the sound of
something slithering across the mud. Then the faintest splash.
One of Hudson's crocs, thought Carter. They must love this war.
Men were too busy killing each other to hunt them. Still, they
would understand—crocs ate each other as well. On an impulse,
Carter moved his hand from the side of the canoe and looked
down. Two close-set slit eyes glowed up at him like converging
tracer bullets. He looked around and there were three other pairs
standing off a respectful distance, like tugs around a liner.

Crocodiles, waiting quietly and patiently, no doubt attracted by the scent of blood. How long would their patience last? The canoe would not be difficult to capsize. The crocs would interpret their enforced immobility as defencelessness. Sooner or later there would be a lunge, the sweep of a powerful tail capable of knocking down a horse, and they would be struggling in the water. And then the nutcracker jaws would snap shut through bone and sinew and the victim borne down to the crocodile's larder in the mud.

Carter watched the eyes and wished more speed to the approaching motorboat. It must be close now. He darted a glance ahead but could see nothing. The engine note diminished in volume and a small wave ran as a ripple along the muddy banks and rustled through the reeds. The red eyes bobbed and the canoe rocked on the wasting swell. Carter was moving to pick up his paddle when a bright, dazzling light shone through the cane-grass like a falling sun. It turned from a fragmented circle into an oval and scythed through the reed beds with a flashing blade of light.

'Big glass,' breathed Joe.

They huddled low in the canoe as the searchlight swept over them again. It was fortunate that the Japs had not switched it on a few seconds earlier. Carter listened anxiously for any abrupt change in the engine noise which would denote discovery, but the boat moved on steadily until the searchlight was just a glow in the sky.

'What do you reckon?' whispered Carter.

'We'll give them a few minutes, in case they come back,' said Hudson. 'Then we'll push on.'

Carter settled back and rubbed his eyes. Apart from the insect bites, they were aching with tiredness. Danger. Tension. Fear. These were the stimulants that kept him awake. To relax for an instant was to become drowsy. He looked at the eyes glowing in the darkness and saw that they had been joined by two more pairs. Small red lights that warned against sleep. He moved the fingers of his bitten arm to stop them from seizing up.

Seconds turned into minutes and batteries of frogs opened up to drown all other sounds. Carter looked expectantly towards

Hudson. Surely it was safe to move now.

'*Tabauda?*' Joe's voice was low and urgent. 'Smellim fire.'

He was pointing back the way they had come.

Carter strained his nostrils and could smell nothing beyond the stench of slime and rotting vegetation. Then the merest whiff of something more pungent than the sweet smell of decay wafted from the grasses. Hudson sniffed and slowly stood up. The canoe wobbled and the semi-circle of red eyes closed in expectantly. Where the dark mass of the reeds met the grey of the sky a faint comber of light suffused the horizon. It might have been the first hint of dawn but this glow rose in the north. Hudson listened intently. Barely audible was a distant oven-like roar.

'They've fired the grass,' said Hudson. 'They're trying to flush us out so the Japs can get us.'

Carter sniffed again. This time there was no mistaking the acrid smell of burning vegetation. No mistaking either the sound of the motorboat returning. Their position was serious. The searchlight began to sweep through 360 degrees, and it was clear from the angle of descent that the boat was passing nearer to their position. They must be very close to the main channel. Carter ducked and smelled smoke willowing like a mist almost at water level. It stung his already smarting eyes and forced him to cough.

Thank God there were the small muddy islets in front of them to offer some protection from the full probing power of the searchlight. The light moved on and Carter looked towards its source to see the shadowy outline of the mast on which it was mounted. A cane-rat broke from the sedge, slid down the bank and started to swim strongly. Two pairs of red lights detached themselves from the pack and the cane-rat disappeared with a screech of fear and surprise. A wave slapped against the side of the canoe.

Now the sky behind them was red and curlicues of flame flared up like gas jets. An angry, crackling roar urged on the flames and clouds of sparks danced like fireflies before hissing into the water. Smoke billowed from the reeds. The fire was leap-frogging towards them at the pace of a running man. Johnson choked and gasped for breath, crying out in pain. A refugee army of snakes, frogs and birds began to burst from the undergrowth. The sky was now streaked with red, yellow and white—a vivid, dancing palette disturbed by brush-strokes of swirling smoke. The air was sucked away to feed the flames and it became painful to breathe. Smoke and hot ash swept over the canoe, burning through clothing to the flesh beneath. The transformation was swift and terrifying. Almost as if the reeds were soaked with some combustible fluid that needed the touch of a flame to become a blazing inferno.

Hudson shouted above the mounting roar and dug his paddle into the water. To stay where they were would be to die. The canoe lurched from the bank and found the middle of the channel in a rain of hot ash. Half a dozen feverish strokes and they could find air to breathe. There was a chance that they could survive here if they could build up enough distance between them and the heat and the suffocating smoke.

And then the searchlight found them. It swept across the waterscape and caught them in the crenellation between two islets. The light dazzled and numbed, arching past and then immediately jumping back. Carter could see the others before him, white on black, like an undeveloped negative. Within two seconds there was the yammer of automatic fire and the water about them turned into a boiling cauldron. Carter had anticipated the bullets and momentarily closed his eyes. Then they were behind a low mud-bank and the bullets churned up the mud. If they continued firing at this rate they would level the mud-bank to the water.

Suddenly, the firing stopped and there was only the noise of the advancing fire. An updraught of air had hoisted aloft a tornado of cinders which illuminated the scene like marker flares. The lighthouse beam of the searchlight splashed over their heads and wavered warily, darting to each extremity of the mud-bank in case they tried to slip away.

Carter turned and looked behind him. There was no islet nearby that was not within the searchlight's beam. They were pinned down and at the mercy of the Japs.

What would the Japs do now? Move straight in and mop them up? Put a party ashore to outflank them? Wait until daybreak? A pit-shelled turtle arrived to rest its flippers on the mud beside the canoe. It looked up to see Carter, quivered its bottle-top nose and disappeared in a small whirlpool. Carter wished that it could be so easy for him. The engine note of the motorboat and the position of the searchlight did not change. What were the Japs planning? From the left, a pall of smoke drifted across the water. Here, perhaps, was a chance. The Japs might find their ruse of firing the reeds rebounding on them. It might in fact provide a smokescreen.

And then an eerie whistling noise, building up into a screech and terminating in a violent explosion on the far side of the mudbank. The Japs must have a 70mm gun mounted on their boat.

They were using it in its upper trajectory as a mortar. A fountain of mud was hurled into the air and the waters raged.

'Scatter!' Hudson was over the side, his feet sinking knee-deep into the slime. Smoke rolled over their heads.

Carter clutched his weapon and scrambled from the rocking canoe, the mud swallowing him like a soft, greedy mouth. He struggled to move his legs while the death whistle gained in intensity above his head. It was a nightmare in which the pursued is incapable of flight.

Cromp! The blast flattened him like a skittle almost separating him from his legs. He lay still as the mud rained down on him and listened to the singing in his ears. What would he find when he came out of this paralysis of shock? An arm missing? A gaping hole in his side like Johnson? He staggered upright and began to blunder through the slime, seeking only to put some distance between himself and the next ranging shot of the mortar. With each step the mud tried to suck the boots from his feet and slurped and gurgled obscenely. As the searchlight bobbed and darted, he saw Joe and Sula dragging the canoe by its headline. Under cover of the smoke they were heading for a small islet further into the main channel. A burst of machine-gun fire came perilously close, and Carter threw himself down behind a tight-knit clump of reeds. Something bit, scraped or stung his leg from below the surface of the mud but he hardly noticed it. What was a little pain when death was so close?

Another 8½-pound shell plummeted into the mud nearby.

Water rushed in to fill the cavity. It was fortunate that the mud was absorbing most of the impact. On a harder surface they would have been mangled by shrapnel. Carter pulled himself upright again and suddenly felt his legs sinking as if he was dropping into a pit. In an instant the slime was above his waist and still rising. He spread his arms wide and released the Mills gun to give himself greater manoeuvrability. What breath he could steal from the smoke he held in an agony of fear. And then his feet touched something firm that gave only slightly in the mud. A log buried years before, perhaps. He waited until certain that he was no longer sinking and then tried to force himself upwards by pressure on his arms. His arms sunk into the mud. He looked about him for something to cling to and froze in fear. Emerging from the water was the head of a crocodile, two feet of interlocking teeth visible along its jaw. They gleamed evilly in a rapacious smile. The head turned to survey Carter. The small, bright, laser eye widened and gleamed and two huge, four-toed webbed feet slapped against the mud.

Carter looked desperately for his gun. It was out of reach. He stretched and nearly lost his foothold. The crocodile lumbered from the water, revealing that it was over twenty feet in length. An ancient denizen of the swamps, probably more than a hundred years old. It surveyed him with head cocked to one side, perhaps wondering what this strange creature was, so different from the fowls, fish, turtles and terrapins that made up most of its diet.

Carter lunged again, and the crocodile swung its tail to fall into line with the rest of its body. It skidded across the mud with a noise like a sword being unsheathed. The stench of the rotting flesh wedged between its teeth was stomach-turning. Carter fought panic and stretched out his arm again. This time his slimy fingers brushed against metal. The gun was settling into the slime. He transferred all his weight to one leg and pressed down. His foothold flinched and the mud slurped and sucked as it sought to keep hold of him. The crocodile opened its mouth a few inches and a fresh wave of foul, contaminated breath travelled across the twelve feet that separated them. Even with the mouth apart there was no gap between the two rows of teeth. They ranged like twisted, irregular bars of a prison. The crocodile tilted back its head to show the white underneath of its throat and delivered a short, vexed bark.

Carter reached out again and felt the slime oozing beneath his fingers. He could not feel the gun. The crocodile barked again and lowered its head to rest on the mud. Its orangey-red eyes gleamed, twin watch-towers of evil. Pressed flat against the bank, its position was that of a dog about to attack.

A mortar shell exploded behind, bringing down a fine rain of mud that splattered along its back. A sub-machine gun opened up fifty yards away. But nothing happened to disturb the crocodile's concentration. Carter sensed that at any second it was going to rush him. He pressed his hand deep into the mud and felt the tips of his fingers touch something. He found another inch and his fingers closed about the sling of his Mills gun. He pulled it towards him and the gun came free with an obscene swalching noise. As if alerted by the sound, the crocodile rose up on its four legs, arched its tail, and charged, its mouth opening like a portcullis.

Carter found the safety-catch and fired. A jagged lightning flash of yellow flame ripped from the barrel and into the open mouth. The crocodile lurched onto one leg and then turned its head sideways as if diverted by the force of the bullets.

Carter shot for the eye and saw the shape of the head change as hot lead chewed into it, throwing out a spray of blood and mucus. Under the impetus of its weight, the crocodile slid across the bank towards him, its head thrashing and its tail lashing the mud with a sound like whipcracks. The Mills gun emptied in mid-burst and Carter desperately thrust it forward to parry the snapping jaws. The crocodile slithered against him and lay still. The weight of its body was almost pinning him to the mud. The tail swung twice and then stopped in mid-swirl. The mouth stayed half-open. The stench was insupportable.

Carter could feel his heart thumping. He waited for some reflex action that would make the brute suddenly snap into a last flurry of death-dealing movement. Nothing happened. Around them, a red light danced in the sky and tongues of flame licked through the smoke. Burning grass drifted through the air to fire clumps of reed on the islets and a crackling roar echoed on all sides. The scene was like the aftermath of an air-raid.

Carter sensed that there was only one way for him to escape from the mud. He would have to pull himself out using the dead crocodile for purchase. Gingerly at first, he seized one of the forelegs, more than two handbreadths wide, and threw his arm over the carcass. A python slithered down the bank and into the water followed by a water-rat and a bandicoot. The grasses on the islet were burning. Carter hauled himself upwards and the crocodile lurched on the mud, as if it were still living. The foreleg moved slowly of its own accord in the first throes of rigor mortis, and Carter trembled. Not for the first time he wondered how much more he could take. Not just the physical suffering but those terrors that gnaw away at the will to survive.

The mud sucked and squelched, eager to restrain him, and small, unseen creatures writhed and wriggled against his flesh. With one determined effort he managed to drag his weight across the crocodile's back and paused to recover his breath before drawing up his legs. A slight updraught was carrying the smoke above his head so it was possible to breathe at water level. Another burst of automatic fire came from the direction of the centre of the channel. He guessed that it must be either Joe or Hudson trying to keep the Japs at bay. The searchlight was now only turned on intermittently and the boat's engines had been cut.

Carter wondered about Sula. Was she still alive? He searched the shadowy outlines of the mud-banks but could see nothing. He must try and find the others. The automatic had stopped and there was only the sound of the fire. He rolled sideways with one last look at the empty eye socket and slithered through the slime as if he had taken on the persona of the slaughtered saurian. He was terrified of standing up. Of feeling himself sinking into the bottomless pit again. He approached a clump of speargrass in order to have something to cling on to if necessary and rose unsteadily to his feet. The mud came no higher than his knees.

The searchlight stabbed again. He could tell that the boat had changed its position. It had either been poled or allowed to drift in the hopes of catching them unawares from a different angle.

The beam swept past him and rested on the dead crocodile and the churned-up mud. Carter lay flat with a cheek pressed into the slime and saw the teeth gleam in a mocking grin which seemed to say 'You will soon share my grave'.

A brief burst of fire splattered mud around the corpse. Then there was a swift gabble of Japanese and the light was cut. Carter rose and splashed through mud and waist-deep water to the next bank. Smoke swirled about him. He flinched as the water parted and a shape glided towards him, but it was a white-tailed rat, the size of a small cat. It chugged past him and scuttled up the bank and into the grass as the light came on again. It was like a crazy game. Throw yourself flat when the light comes on or you are dead. The beam jabbed angrily above his head and then splashed and dappled over the surrounding banks. There was a short burst from a Mills gun and the sound of bullets striking armoured plating. Carter tried to locate the sound.

Somebody was still alive. He moved again and saw a dark shape lying on a bank. Another crocodile? He approached warily. The shape spun round and levelled a Mills gun at him. It was Sula with Johnson's gun. She seemed to be trying to pull the trigger before she saw that he was not a Jap. Covered in mud from head to toe he must look like some monster from the swamp. He slumped down beside her, grateful that she was still alive. She touched his arm in a spontaneous gesture of warmth and then returned to scrutinizing the nearby banks.

'Are you all right?' asked Carter.

'Yes.'

'And the others?'

'I think Captain Hudson is over there.' She gestured towards an islet further from the reed beds. 'Joe, I do not know.'

Carter looked around him. 'Where's the canoe?'

'Johnson has taken it.'

'Taken it?'

Sula continued to look around her warily. 'When the bombs came, we pulled the canoe to a bank. I took Johnson's gun. When we look round he is paddling away.'

Carter let his head drop forward so that his cheek was resting against the mud. It might have been his grave. Any last vestige of hope drained from his body. With the canoe gone they had no chance of escaping from the swamp. They were marooned and at the mercy of the Japs. Johnson had done what he had been threatening to do. He had taken leave of his senses.

15

Johnson knew he was going to die. When he moved, it was as if his stomach was full of broken glass. Sharp needles of pain dug even deeper into his entrails, but the pain was good. It goaded him into action. He had awoken from a fitful sleep into a period of perfect clarity, as a man racked by fever can suddenly sit up and talk coherently to those who have waited by his bedside in a state of mounting despair. But there were going to be no words. He knew what he had to do. Nothing needed to be explained.

He dabbed with his paddle and felt the faintest tremble of a current against the side of the canoe. This must be one of the fingers of the delta reaching out to the sea. Above his head were stars. Before him, another wilderness of swamp registering as a black hedge of reeds silhouetted against the sky. The stars were the fragments of pain that danced in his body. Tiny lancet splinters of bone. He felt an affinity with them. Small, hot coals on black velvet fanned to glowing by the stagnant vapour that bubbled from the swamp in place of wind. Smoke swirled about him, patches of mist hung eerily above the water. The searchlight rippled out, laying bars of light like stepping-stones. The light was still probing amongst the banks and flats. He had paddled back and come out into the main channel where it began to curve sharply. He had been able to cross to the other side without falling into the path of the searchlight. Now he was drifting down in the lee of the far bank.

When the searchlight came on he could see his target clearly. A long, shallow, draught vessel with reinforcement above the water-line and a swept-back prow. The searchlight was mounted on a platform half-way up a stubby mast. No armament was visible, but flashes of light which accompanied random bursts of automatic fire suggested that the machine gun was mounted behind shields in the prow. Johnson moved his hand to his waist and closed slippery fingers around the clip that held the last grenade.

His fingers were jelly, barely capable of exerting pressure. He squeezed and the metal mouth parted and then snapped back again. Pain set fire to the inside of his stomach and a dangerous swoon of nausea swept over him. Whatever happened he must stay in command of his senses. He must use the pain to stay conscious. He pressed his hand against his side and felt the blood escaping through his fingers. The dressing was incapable of staunching the flow. He was weakening, despite his resolve. A shower of sparks hissed into the water and spillikins of burning grass dropped just short of the bank. If the fire jumped the channel they would surely see him.

He returned his fingers to the grenade clip and suddenly realized that he had let go of the paddle. It had slipped from his hand and was drifting away. He reached for it, forgetting the pain that any movement caused, and nearly capsized the canoe. Silently, he cursed himself. He was coming apart; like a marionette whose strings are being snipped one by one, he was losing the use of his limbs. His mind was shouting messages and his body not replying. There was another paddle in the canoe but he could not reach it. He grit his teeth and squeezed, making the pain prise the metal apart. The grenade fell into the bottom of the canoe.

Now everything was becoming fuzzy. The fog drifted across the mist and clouded his stinging eyes. Every object was framed in a penumbra of light, its definition suspect. Was it the smoke or was the sight ebbing out of his eyes? Could it be anything other than imagination that made the boat seem to loom up before him? He tried to concentrate and found himself slipping backwards until he was lying on his back with his head in three inches of water. Smoke drifted over his head but he could still see the stars. With a start of fear he realized that his stomach had stopped hurting.

The helmsman was the first to see the drifting canoe. He called out excitedly and the lieutenant peered through one of the slits in the armour-plated screens that protected the sides of the boat. Machine guns were brought to bear. The canoe appeared to be empty. It twisted in the water like a sycamore leaf, barely moving in the listless water. Smoke from the still-burning grass fire hung heavy over the upstream river. The lieutenant gave an order and the searchlight was swivelled to cut through the swathes of smoke. There were more excited cries.

A body was lying in the canoe, blood glistening from knee to shoulder, the head tilted to one side. The jungle green uniform and the Western features said clearly that it was one of the raiding party. The lieutenant smiled. Without the canoe there was no chance of the others escaping.

The lieutenant unstrapped his Luger and peered again through the slit. The man was nearly beneath him and he could see that his eyes were closed. He drew a bead on the head and then hesitated. If the man was still alive perhaps he should be taken back for interrogation. But the man could not be alive. He must have bled to death an hour before. The lieutenant rested his gun against the edge of the slit and took aim again. A bullet neatly between the eyes. An act of mercy if the man still lived and of personal gratification whether he lived or not. The canoe tapped softly against the side of the hull as if respectfully announcing its presence. The lieutenant started to pull the trigger and froze. Below him, the eyes had opened. With a ghastly smile, the man reached up and thrust something beneath the armoured screens and into the motorboat. The lieutenant looked down as the corporal's machine gun splayed the canoe. A hand-grenade was resting against his foot.

Carter heard two explosions almost simultaneously and looked up to see the motorboat blazing from prow to stern. The fuel tanks must have exploded. The screams of burning men were almost drowned by the exultant roar of the flames. The armour-plated sides of the boat had turned it into a casserole in which men were cooking. A blazing rag doll threw itself into the water and was followed by another. There was a flash and a third explosion and Carter ducked instinctively. One of the mortar shells had exploded. The flames licked even higher and the mast toppled over slowly as if melting, spilling the now extinguished searchlight into the water. Another explosion rocked the vessel and it began to settle. The flames fed hungrily and noisily, and the only human sounds came from the water. Pitiful moans and groans, distorted through burned mouths.

Carter watched the vessel founder and felt amazement that his emotions could change so quickly from hatred to compassion. He might have wished on them the fate that had befallen these men but he could not exult in it.

There was a splashing from the water and the funeral pyre glow thrown by the boat showed a man trying to swim towards him. He was swimming clumsily and crying out in pain through a burnt hole in his black and blistered face. He slapped at the water as if blind. His feet touched the bottom and then he rose clumsily to reveal that he was naked. Whatever uniform he had been wearing had been burnt from his body. The raw, welted flesh gleamed in the darkness. The man cried out for help and advanced unsteadily, arms pawing the air before him. Carter felt horror at the sight of this scorched and hairless apparition heading straight towards him. It was as if the man was seeking him out, saying 'You are my brother. You have done this to me. Help me.'

Carter glanced sideways at Sula. Her expression mirrored his own feelings. Apprehension. Distaste. Horror. She raised her gun and then lowered it again. The Jap came on so that in a few more paces he would emerge onto the mud-bank and stumble over them.

The burst of automatic fire from the right jarred Carter as if awakening him from a nightmare. The Jap was knocked sideways and sprawled dead in the shallow water. Hudson appeared with Joe behind him. He reslung his Mills gun and nodded towards the corpse.

'The best thing we could do for him,' he said.

Carter turned away from the small, still body.

'What the hell happened out there?'

'I think Jerry had more idea what was going on than we gave

him credit for,' said Hudson.

'Jerry?'

Hudson sank to one knee and peered towards the blazing boat. 'Yes, I saw a canoe drifting past on the far side. I think it was him.'

Carter shook his head. 'So that was why he took it. I wish I'd given him the benefit of the doubt.'

'I had plenty of doubts, too,' said Hudson. He looked as if he was going to continue and then turned away. 'We'd better find out if there's anything left of that canoe.' He started to wade into the water, calling out to Joe. 'Stick together. This is the best free feed the crocs will ever have had.'

Ash was falling like black, flakey rain as they entered the water. Creatures, some of them scorched and maimed by the fire, swam past in an irregular convoy. Occasional splashes and flurries suggested the activities of hunting crocodiles or the death struggles of badly wounded animals that could swim no further. All around, the fire was dying down, the risk of it leapfrogging to the far bank becoming less. Carter passed a second naked corpse lying half-submerged and face downwards in the water. The mud sucked treacherously at their feet and underwater tubers encircled their legs like restraining fingers.

Carter looked beyond the still-burning boat to see a pencil shape lying on the water. He called out to the others and pressed forward. The boat settled deeper into the mud and there was an angry hissing sound as red-hot metal sizzled like a branding iron into the water. A few paces revealed that the shape was the canoe but there was also the dark outline of something perching on it. A bird or a possum, thought Carter, until he came close enough to see that it was another Jap, the head barely above the capsized hull. He looked at his enemy with expressionless eyes and then released his hold and allowed himself to sink below the water. He did not reappear.

Nobody said anything. Joe and Sula quickly righted the canoe. As they did so, the body of Johnson materialized on the surface, as if he had been trapped beneath it. A stitchwork of bullets ran from his cheek to his thigh. The thick dug-out construction of the canoe had absorbed the blast without visible damage.

'Put him in the canoe,' said Hudson. 'We don't want to leave him here.'

They lifted Johnson into his original position in the canoe. Joe found a paddle. The flames from the motorboat had sunk to below the level of the hull. The night now glowed rather than blazed. Without another word they climbed into the canoe and steered towards the reeds.

16

It was ten o'clock in the morning and already the sun shone down on the corrugated-iron building behind Rabaul harbour like a blowtorch. The panels groaned before the onslaught, strained against their rivets and buckled in the heat. Geckoes scrabbled across the walls as if frightened of getting their feet burnt by resting in one place. An untidy queue of men curled away from the locked entrance and quickly found the shelter of the surrounding palm trees. The men were Japanese soldiers, officers and other ranks, all wearing uniform and all impatient. Two guards with the tips of their fixed-bayonets rising higher than their heads stood with their back almost against the door. There was the sound of bolts being drawn and the front of the queue pressed forward eagerly. Men who had been squatting in the shadow or climbing for coconuts hurried to take up their places. There were arguments and scuffles. Officers and NCOs exerted their authority and order prevailed, usually at the expense of those without rank.

The main door opened with a crack, as if it had expanded in the heat, and a small, round-shouldered Japanese girl was revealed. She wore a simple kimono, and her once elaborate hairstyle was now no more than contained on her head like a shored-up building. She looked very tired. She spoke a few words of greeting and bowed. The men at the front of the queue bowed in return, and those behind pressed forward. There were cries of anger and more scuffling. The guards held their rifles across their chests and pressed back those who attempted to slip inside the building. Any possibility of a riot was averted by the appearance of a second woman. She was plump and middle-aged and her hairstyle bore no concession to coquetry. Her voice had a hard edge to it, and when she talked it was at a level barely less than a shout. Her gestures made it obvious that if there was any more trouble the door would be shut—permanently. Her words were received in silence. When she had finished and retired inside the building, the first eight men in the queue entered without challenge from the others. Hardly had the door closed on them than the leaves of the palms began to shiver and the ground shake. A powerful tremor lasted for several seconds and the walls of the tin house trembled bringing down a cloud of dust. The men waiting outside cheered and made ribald remarks. The tremors were becoming ever more frequent in Rabaul, but this one was particularly well timed.

Across the dirt road from the House of Contentment and Love set up by His Majesty the Emperor of Nippon and serviced by the Daughters of the Rising Sun, Major Yukichi digested the scene and frowned. It was clearly necessary that the officers had a separate brothel. The interests of dignity and discipline could not be served when officers and men stood shoulder to shoulder in the same queue and emptied themselves into the same women. If there were not enough Japanese women available—and it was already rumoured that Rabaul was ill-served in this respect, compared to other garrisons of the Imperial Army—then the men would have to make do with native women. There were enough cases of rape reported to suggest that this should not prove too much of a hardship. Yukichi made a note to express his feelings on this matter to General Koji and ordered his driver to proceed to the morning briefing session.

When he arrived at the command bunker he was surprised to find two light tanks and a detachment of marines in attendance. The troops were dispersing amongst the trees and beginning to dig trenches. The morning briefing session had been cancelled and General Koji wished to see him alone. Yukichi stepped forward uneasily.

The General was alone as Yukichi entered the room. He barely acknowledged Yukichi's salute and promptly handed him a slip of paper. The messages had arrived from the radio station and was timed as having come in an hour before. It came from the spotter plane and was very much to the point.

'K-boat burned out west of Pari village. No sign of survivors or enemy. Am continuing search.'

'Burned out?' Yukichi repeated the words incredulously. 'But our last report stated that the enemy had been located and pinned down. That it was merely a matter of time.'

'That report was ten hours ago,' said Koji. 'Did you not experience any moments of anxiety during the ensuing silence?'

Yukichi said nothing. He preferred not to reveal his complacency. He had assumed that the five members of the raiding party had been wiped out without problem.

'The fire, sir,' he said eventually. 'Is it not possible that the fire destroyed everything? Perhaps the K-boat was engulfed? Perhaps the enemy were killed as well?'

'Perhaps,' said Koji. 'But we cannot assume that to be a fact. I will not be reassured until I see the bodies. To survive as long as they have done, the enemy have shown considerable initiative. If they have escaped again—and I do not consider this to be beyond the realms of possibility—then they constitute an even more serious threat to Admiral Yamamoto than I had feared. We must redouble our efforts to locate and destroy them.' He looked Yukichi squarely in the eyes and tapped back his spectacles. 'I am relieving you of all other duties so that you may concentrate on bringing this gang of assassins to heel.'

Yukichi bowed his head and hoped that his anticipated fear on hearing the words 'relieving you of all other duties' had not shown too clearly on his face. It was not unusual in such a situation that a scapegoat should be sought. Certainly, he considered ruefully, his new responsibilities made him an ideal candidate for the role.

'I am honoured by your choice, sir,' he said.

Koji nodded briskly. 'Take as many men as you need. You will have my sympathetic ear should any of your plans meet with opposition from other service commanders in the garrison. I suggest that you commence by reconsidering the contingency plans that we discussed and presenting me with your up-to-date recommendations. Never cease to remember that the protection of Admiral Yamamoto is our prime objective.'

'Yes, sir.'

'And use your initiative, Yukichi.' General Koji looked coldly upon his adjutant. 'I am relying upon you.'

Major Yukichi saluted and turned on his heel. The implication behind the last words was not lost on him. Failure would be measured by not finding the raiders. Disaster by anything happening to Yamamoto. The weight on his shoulders was heavier than when he had entered the room. He smiled grimly as he went through the door. It had clearly not been the moment to discuss the brothel arrangements for the troops.

Carter awoke and attempted to open his eyes. At first it seemed that there was an adhesive sticking them shut. Then they parted painfully, weighed down by swollen lids and gummed by mucus. A few inches from his nose, the thick jungle foliage pressed in, sombre in its perpetual gloaming. The mud on his limbs had dried and encased them like a plaster cast. He moved and it cracked. His arms and back ached and he felt feverish. His bitten forearm throbbed. He started to unwind the blood-soaked bandage and wriggling white maggots dropped to the ground. When he came to the wound, the teeth-marks were surrounded with yellow circles of pus. The flesh was soft and weeping. He touched it with his finger and it felt like sodden tissue-paper about to disintegrate. His other superficial flesh wounds were the same. Suppurating, separating, rotting. He flicked the last maggots from the fly-blown bandage and glanced at his watch before starting to rewind it.

One o'clock. He had been asleep for nearly seven hours. Sleep that had come upon him like death the moment they had staggered from the swamp and penetrated a few yards of protecting jungle. The escape through the swamp had been a hell that drained every last resource of mental and physical strength. Lagoons, creeks, channels, canegrass thick as a picket fence. An abundance of water or none at all except, below, a treacherous carpet of matted tubers and razor-sharp grasses. Patches of festering slime where the stench of nitrogenous wastes gagged the throat and only crocodiles could live. Places where the channel disappeared in an impenetrable convolution of jungle foliage, and it was necessary to retreat and try another route. Always the feeling that one was lost in a maze from which there was no escape.

With the dawn they had seen the jungle and the shadow of Matupi behind. At the same instant they had seen the black speck of the spotter plane against the eastern sky. Like a searching vulture it had begun its sweeps with a method and diligence that was typically Japanese. As the plane got nearer so the jungle became closer. Eventually they had been able to shelter between the spreading roots of a moss-strewn tree that rose from the water like a huge deformed spider. While they were here, the plane passed forty feet above their heads without seeing them. They had watched it lift over the jungle and then wheel to take up a different tack.

It was here, too, that they had left Johnson, sliding him into a watery coffin formed by a basket-work of submerged roots. Joe and Sula prayed out loud. Hudson closed his eyes and his lips moved. Carter said nothing and wished that he could feel more than respect for the man who had saved their lives. Life was easier if you could believe in something other than good fortune.

When the plane had gone they had picked their way through the water forest to the jungle proper, where the canoe had been hidden. The party then collapsed into sleep.

Carter stood up, fighting off a wave of giddiness, and looked about him. Hudson was asleep with his hat over his face. Joe was digging at a rotting stump with his bush knife. He prised deep into the soft, spongy wood and a handful of fat, white grubs fell to the ground. He popped three into his mouth like sweets and, instinctively sensing that he was being watched, turned to Carter.

'Dis foine chop,' he said. He held out the grubs with a friendly smile.

Carter shook his head. 'No thanks. I think I'm going to become a vegetarian.'

It was not altogether an attempt at humour. After what he had seen and experienced in the last few days, Carter doubted that he would ever eat meat again. With so many creatures living off him the thought of consuming flesh nauseated him.

Joe shrugged, ate the grubs, and returned to probing the

stump in search of more. Carter knew that he was being fastidious, but what indulgences did he have left? He saw a patch of wild tapioca and moved towards it, feeling the side of his boot drag. The stitching had rotted and the upper was beginning to separate from the sole. In this climate and terrain nothing survived for long, whether it was man or material. He dropped to his knees and excavated a root of tapioca. It was painful to eat because his lips were cracked and sore but he swallowed the stringy pap because he knew he was going to need every ounce of strength it could give him.

Joe stiffened and gestured to Carter to take cover. Seconds later he heard someone approaching through the undergrowth. There was only one other creature apart from man that made a noise when it moved through the jungle: the cassowary, a large emu-like bird protected in its blunderings by its ability to eviscerate a wild pig with one sweep of its razor-sharp claws. There was a double bird-call and Joe relaxed.

Sula appeared, moving easily through the undergrowth. Carter marvelled at her powers of recovery. There was no hint of weariness in her stride. She had obviously found somewhere to wash. Her flesh gleamed and her wet grass skirt clung revealingly to her thighs. She smiled at him and beckoned.

'Good bathing place close.'

She turned and he followed, almost unable to contemplate the luxury of clean water against his ravaged flesh. It seemed that he had never known anything else except stinging, itching, chafing pain every time he moved a limb. He was becoming inured to it.

Sula led the way through knee-high vegetation studded with tall trees and patches of swamp until they began to ascend a gentle slope bordered by the beginnings of a stream. This was scarcely wider than his shoulders and running through a channel worn in the soft earth to the depth of a hip bath. A fallen log had helped form a waterfall and it was to the small pool beneath that Sula pointed. A shaft of sunlight fell like a spotlight from the canopy of foliage above and splashed onto the brilliant scarlet flowers of the Flame-of-the-Forest climber which hung like a hundred-foot streamer from the forest top.

Carter waded into the pool and felt the bottom firm beneath

his feet. There was even a clump of moss that came to the water's edge. He placed his weapon on it and began to peel off his equipment and uniform. It was only when he was nearly naked that he thought about Sula. He turned and saw her watching him without apparent concern. She retired beneath some low-hanging branches as if keeping watch. Carter removed the last article of clothing and sat naked in the pool with his back against the log and a gentle cascade falling about his shoulders. The cool, clear water against his skin was the most tangible luxury that he could ever remember. Even the air seemed easier to breathe as if it had been miraculously transported from the upper reaches of the Mississippi where he had spent so many boyhood vacations on his grandfather's farm.

He closed his eyes and tried not to think about Johnson. Tried not to think about what lay ahead. Just for a few moments he wanted to escape. Above his head came the weird, wheezing cry of a hornbill. The bird flopped from the branches like a half-opened parachute and slowly flapped away, its head drooping as if unable to support the weight of its enormous, parrot-like beak. Carter closed his eyes again and lay back. The water was so cool. Even the insects kept their distance. He felt like a different person. The thought of getting back into his filthy, fetid uniform was like returning to a dirty cell after a period of parole. He stood up and started to rinse his foul-smelling tunic, seeing it quickly turn the clear water a muddy brown.

Through the jagged leaves, Sula watched. The broad shoulders tapering down to the narrow waist. The tight, flat buttocks. The slack promise of the heavy penis hanging down from its foliage of hairs. The thick bars of muscle in the swelling thighs. She felt an unashamed desire for sex on the bed of moss with her legs dangling in the water. She wanted this man inside her. Her feelings were as uncomplicated as the beacons of desire that excited them.

She knew that Carter found her attractive. She had felt his gaze in the outrigger canoe. She could sense his eyes seeking her out with the same affection that she bore for him. She wanted to walk to the edge of the pool and take off her skirt. Step into the water beside him and take the uniform from his hands. She hated the uniform. It was ugly. It disguised his natural shape which was beautiful and should be seen—by her, above all others, because she wished to place herself in a position in which she would have the most opportunity to see him.

She could live with this man. Make children with him. The danger that they were both in, the possibility that death might arrive at any moment, made it more difficult for her to conceal her feelings. To die leaving them unexpressed would be too sad. Yet at the same time she knew that the war must come first. His war. Her war. Their war. If they were to survive, all thought and effort must be concentrated on the mission. And survival was the only thing that mattered.

Carter forced his legs into his sodden trousers and felt the familiar chafing pains as the material rubbed against the scratches, insect bites and deepening sores. Vacation over. He pulled on his T-shirt and slipped his ID tag over his head. How good it had felt, just for once, to be completely naked! Free, even of the small pieces of metal that told him he belonged to the US Government, in the way that a dog carries its master's address round its neck.

He sat on the moss and pushed his swollen feet into his boots. What had once been tough leather was now like pulpy kid. They might last another day without falling apart. He tightened the laces warily and reached for the rolled bandage. His arm seemed to be stiffening up. He flexed his fingers and hoped that his imagination was making the situation worse. If the wound became gangrenous . . . he bit his sore lips. It was better not to think of it.

Sula emerged from the trees and came towards him. Her walk was that of a princess. Erect, high-shouldered. Feet drifting over the ground as if disdaining it. Her breasts lifted slightly with each pace. She waded into the pool and took the bandage from Carter's fingers. Dropping to her knees she held it under the small waterfall and then carefully began to encircle Carter's forearm. Her head tilted to look at his chest and her lips parted.

'Car-ter,' she read, laying an equal stress on each syllable.

Carter looked into her eyes. 'Sula,' he said.

She smiled as if somewhere deep inside her the word had lit a fire.

When they returned to the resting place, Joe had accumulated a small pile of edible roots and Hudson was awake and cleaning his weapon. He gestured to the ground before him and Sula knelt down gracefully. Carter sat cross-legged and began to strip his Mills gun. Joe hovered nearby.

'Right,' said Hudson. 'Don't know about the rest of you, but I am more determined to succeed than ever. Not just for us, but for Jerry.' He spread his hands flat. 'That's all I'm going to say about him. I'll leave the fancy words to someone with the gift of the gab.' He lowered his head as if honouring a few seconds' respectful silence. 'Now, we've got to put the last twenty-four hours behind us. Nothing has changed in relation to our plan. We're rested up and ready to go on Phase Two. But we now have two major problems. The recovery of the explosives and the fact that the Japs know we're here.'

Carter chewed on a root and spat out the stringy pith. 'Maybe they'll think we bought it in the fire.'

'Maybe. But they won't take it for granted. When they see us hanging up by our heels, that's the only thing that's going to persuade them that we're dead. Right now they'll be combing the bush for us.'

'But they do not know why we are here,' said Sula.

'Hudson nodded. 'I hope you're right. It depends whether they've found the explosives and are good at guessing. The whole future of the operation depends on the explosives. If we can recover it and get carriers, we'll go tonight. Exactly as planned, but twenty-four hours later.'

'And if they've found the explosives?' asked Carter.

'Then we're cooked,' said Hudson. 'We'll fall back on our withdrawal procedures.'

He punched his fist against the palm of his hand. 'But I'm not prepared to think about that at this stage. We must be positive. The mission is going to succeed.'

He paused. 'We've been through too bloody much for it not to.'

Carter slotted a full magazine into the breech. 'So what's the plan?'

Hudson beckoned to Joe. 'We'll work back to the beach to retrieve the explosive. Then we'll split up. Will and Joe to fetch

Green. Sula and me with carriers. Rendezvous at a spot to be agreed at twenty-two hundred hours.'

'Do you think it best I go with Joe or Sula?' asked Carter.

'Won't Joe be more good to you lugging those explosives?'

Hudson hesitated and Carter wondered if he thought there was some ulterior motive for him wanting Sula with him. He had taught her how to disassemble Johnson's Mills gun and she was now deftly putting it together again in a manner guaranteed to bring an approving glow to any sergeant major's heart.

'Maybe,' said Hudson, brusquely. 'We'll decide when we've recovered the explosive.

He was beginning to talk urgent pidgin when Joe placed his finger against his lips and pointed to the bush. He made a 'disperse' gesture and drove his clenched fist up and down to indicate haste. Weapons were snatched up and the party melted into the thick foliage. Seconds passed and Carter watched a large brown ant carrying an egg across a leaf before his face. While it went about its daily business he lived on the edge of death. But the ant was never very far from death. Was there any creature that was not? Far away he heard a twig crack. Then the sound of something brushing through the undergrowth. Perhaps it was a wild pig. A cockatoo yelped from the top of a tree, and for a second he thought that it was a dog barking and felt terrified. Then there was more rustling and the crackle of a wireless set. Japs.

Carter twisted his head and looked up. He was terrified of seeing something but even more frightened of being taken by surprise. He dared not move in case a sound gave his position away. If a Jap stumbled upon him it was a question of which of them would react the faster. All around him were leaves, shoots, tubers, roots, creepers, climbers. Different shapes, different greens. Some solid, some opaque, some translucent. Wrapped in their Medusan coils it was impossible to see someone standing three feet away.

The crackle dipped as another channel cut into the static and then continued to sizzle. There was no sound of voices. No wheezes, no sighs, no coughs. The silence was unnerving. He knew that the Jpas were listening, too. Waiting for the faintest unfamiliar sound.

A minute passed. Carter's limbs began to ache unbearably. Sweat dripped from his temples and fell in a steady trickle from his armpits. An ant found its way inside his trouser leg and stung him in the thigh. Other insects crawled all over him.

The crackle became marginally louder. Perhaps the man carrying the wireless set had turned his back. A few more seconds and the crackling became fainter, eventually to die away altogether. Carter stayed where he was and listened. There were no unfamiliar sounds. Insects, birds, a spasmodic belch of frog-talk from the swamp. He slowly eased his body-weight from one hip to the other and wondered if the Japs had withdrawn a few yards to take up cover and see if anyone moved. He felt alone and terribly debilitated by his loneliness. Soldiers were supposed to fight in platoons, companies, brigades, armies. They were never isolated except in death. This jungle was a living death, making him feel that he had been foresaken and abandoned by those who had once been his comrades and support. He was fighting loneliness, despair, a crucifying terrain and a pitiless enemy. With every hour that passed he felt the odds against him lengthening.

17

Yukichi squatted on the sand and dangled his fingers in the water. It was warm. Shoals of small minnows pressed in upon the shore. They stirred listlessly, barely interested in avoiding his fingers. Some floated on their backs, dead. A cloud of yellow suffused the water. Further out it was the colour of stale mustard. Yukichi wondered if it was always like this. Some volcanic leakage, most likely. Perhaps it was not merely the heat of the sun that made the shallow water so warm. The sulphurous smell was most disagreeable. He wrinkled his nostrils and stood up.

To the left was the marine detachment at Matupi Point that he had visited shortly before the raiders were sighted. Behind him was the spot where the native tracker had blundered into the enemy. Why had they landed here? Was it by accident or design? The post at the mouth of the bay had been bombed many times so the Americans must be well aware of its existence. They would hardly choose to put a party ashore near it. Most probably the strong currents had swept the inflatable dinghies away from their intended landing positions. They would have had to have come ashore by night, but even then it was a miracle that they had not been picked out by the searchlight.

Yukichi looked along the small bay to the five dug-out canoes pulled up on the beach. His brow furrowed. It did not make sense. The raiders could not have landed here. Yet they were discovered nearby and close to a heavily fortified defence post they must have known about. What were they doing here? Planning to attack the post? It hardly seemed likely. Yukichi began to pace backwards and forwards along the sand. He paused as a thought occurred to him.

Perhaps the raiders believed that Admiral Yamamoto was

going to visit the post and were preparing an ambush. He reconsidered the idea and his enthusiasm for it waned. To start with, there were no plans for the Admiral to make such a visit. If the Americans had learned of the trip to Rabaul they would know this. Secondly, the post was well fortified from the land as well as from the sea. Whether the Americans believed that the Admiral was going to visit the post or not, there could be no special advantage in choosing it as the site of an assassination attempt.

What else then? Yukichi looked about him thoughtfully. On his right the volcanic mass of Matupi thrust itself into the air, a thin column of smoke drifting from its muzzle. The steep, jungle-covered sides began to rise a quarter of a mile away and fell steeply on the side that overlooked the airfield. Yukichi paused in his walking and examined the sharply defined outline of the volcano. Suddenly he began to feel excitement. A possibility was starting to grow in his mind.

The fussy putt-putt-putt of a motorcycle made him look past the three marines with sub-machine guns who stood facing the jungle at the head of the beach. A despatch rider appeared, his face and goggles thick with dust. He spoke to one of the bodyguards and then slowly steered the heavy machine over the uneven sand. The suspension creaked. He stopped five feet from Yukichi, cut the engine and struggled to pull the bike onto its stand. This done, he removed a gauntlet, saluted, and opened one of the despatch boxes fastened on either side of the back wheel. He removed two sheets of paper and handed them to Yukichi.

They were both signals. One came from an amphibious party that had followed the trail taken by the K-boat. It reported that three white men and a black man and woman, all armed, had landed at Pari Village in a waterlogged canoe. One of the white men was injured and remained in the canoe. The spokesman for the party spoke good pidgin and was believed to be an Australian. He had demanded a canoe and when this was refused he had taken one at gunpoint. The villagers had given chase but had been beaten off. They had noted the direction that the invaders had followed and informed the K-boat when it arrived. In agreement with their masters they had fired the reed beds so that the invaders might be burned or driven into the hands of the Japanese. In the night they had heard much shooting and a series of explosions. In the morning they had paddled to the area and been surprised to find that the masters' boat was destroyed and the water littered with the corpses of burned men mauled by crocodiles and other predators. The report went on to say that the area of the incident had been visited and the natives' story substantiated. All of the bodies recovered appeared to be Japanese and there was no sign of the raiders.

Yukichi crumpled the piece of paper in his hand. It merely substantiated most of the facts he already knew. He started to read the second message and immediately his interest quickened. Returning after a series of unsuccessful sweeps over the swamp, the spotter plane had noted what appeared to be the body of a white man floating in the area between jungle and swamp. It was being drawn through the water by a crocodile. The pilot had made several dives and succeeded in frightening off the crocodile. It had also made contact with one of the patrols that Yukichi had sent to the area. They in turn had located the corpse and retrieved what remained of it. A swift examinaton had revealed wounds caused by sub-machine gun fire. Also, burns.

Yukichi began to feel better. One of the raiders was clearly dead. Now there were only four. He looked at the map reference on the message and hurried up the beach. The despatch rider waited in vain for an order and then eased his motorcycle off its stand. By the time he had started it, Yukichi was already striding down the pathway that led to the road, and his bodyguards jostling each other to keep up with him. Two hundred yards in the hot sunshine and he arrived in a small clearing with barely enough room for a vehicle to turn round. His driver sat up, with an alacrity that suggested he had been on the point of dozing off, and quickly handed over the map case as commanded.

Yukichi spread it on the bonnet and checked the spot where the body had been found. As he had expected, it was in reasonable striking distance of Matupi. So, it was almost certain that the four survivors had re-entered the jungle and were still capable of carrying out their mission. He turned away from the map with a gesture that indicated it could be refolded and replaced in the case, and looked thoughtfully towards the truncated summit of the volcano which showed above the trees. He felt the controlled exultation of a man who has found the key to his problem. He believed he knew what the raiders were trying to do. A plan was beginning to take shape in his mind.

Twenty yards into the jungle, Joe heard the sound of the vehicle starting up and rose to his feet. He pressed forward and peered through a screen of pandanus leaves just as the armoured car was leaving the clearing. The dust began to settle. The clearing was empty. Joe waited till the sound of the vehicles had died away and the noises of the jungle returned to normal. He listened particularly for the sharp, ticking alarm calls of a bird, that would tell him that there were still men hidden nearby. Satisfied, he retreated into the bush to the place where Hudson, Carter and Sula were waiting.

'Jap-pan 'e go. Planti kar too much.'

Carter shot a worried look at Hudson. 'Do you reckon they've found something?'

Hudson shrugged. 'We'd better find out.' He nodded at Joe and they started to move forward warily. They reached a clearing and they circled the trees and started down the path to the beach. Suddenly Joe stopped and flung out his arm in a 'go to earth' gesture. They plunged into the undergrowth. Carter controlled his breathing and eased off his safety-catch. Seconds passed and then came an unfamiliar wheezing, creaking noise accompanied by the sound of human grumbling. Carter peered through the grass and saw a plump Japanese pushing a heavy motorbike, the underpart of its engine clogged with sand. He was muttering under his breath, and it required no linguistic skill to detect the string of imprecations that were falling on every mechanical part of the machine that had failed him. There was something comically sad about the little man and his enormous, cumbersome bike. Something that made it impossible to hate him. He was an enemy, that was all.

When bike and rider were swallowed up by the undergrowth,

Joe gave the signal that it was safe to continue. They hugged the edge of the path and suddenly saw a wedge of sky and blue sea before them. Joe went forward again. Carter sank to one knee and faced the way they had come, his Mills gun at the ready. He glanced at Sula and she smiled conspiratorially. Hudson noticed the exchange of looks and kept his eyes on the path.

Joe returned and they tried to read the expression on his face. He told them that the beach was clear. Hudson hurried forward with Carter close behind him. They reached the last barrier of undergrowth and crawled until they could poke their heads through the leaves and look out onto the beach. Their eyes moved to the same place and their faces fell. The dug-outs were not moored against the rock.

Carter looked along the beach and thought he recognized the canoe he had come ashore in. There was no sign of the dinghy, which was not surprising. The natives would be hardly likely to run the risk of becoming implicated with the invaders by leaving the explosives attached to their canoes. Perhaps they had been cut free and sunk beside the rock to await collection. Carter swiftly shared his thoughts with Hudson. It was agreed that Joe should go forward to investigate by seeming to be making his way to one of the fishing towers that stood off shore. These untidy erections of saplings were lit by burning brands at night, and men waited with spear and bow and arrow for fish to be attracted by the light.

Joe left his gun and moved down the beach. The first thing he noticed was that the yellow tide had spread to cover most of the shoreward end of the bay. Instead of isolated patches there was one large stain like a scum of paint. He had never seen anything like it before. He looked up at Matupi and wrinkled his nose. The old volcano must have stomach pains to be passing that yellow shit into the sea. He glanced along the deserted beach and then waded into the sea. The water was warm. Too warm to have been heated by the sun. The heat must be coming from the volcano. When he lowered his head to water level he could see the faintest mist of fumes hovering above the surface on the Matupi side of the bay. He moved towards the rocks with the yellow paste swilling against his thighs. It was impossible to see the bottom now.

At least the yellow stain would have made it difficult for the Japs to find the explosive. He wondered uneasily how it would have responded to lying on the bottom for twenty-four hours. Would the water and the increasing heat affect it? Something stirred in the yellow tide beside him and he moved away quickly. It was a dying water-snake. It lunged at him with sluggish malice and then sank slowly in the water leaving a crust of small bubbles on the yellow surface.

Joe reached the rock and began to circle it, feeling carefully with his toes. He touched nothing but sand and stones. He looked around him at the other rocks. Had he come to the right one? There was no other rock with a flat surface of stone just above water level. He looked towards the shore, wondering how many unseen eyes were watching him, wondering what he was doing among the rocks. It would be best if he provided an answer. He came upon a dying catfish and caught it by the tail, taking care to avoid the poisonous spines. Its whiskers drooped dejectedly as it barely found the strength to twitch in his grasp. Another water-snake came to hand and he grabbed it and moved amongst the rocks.

From the top of the beach, Hudson and Carter watched anxiously.

'He hasn't found them—?' Carter asked.

'Maybe he's playing it clever,' said Hudson. 'He's not going to start jumping up and down and waving his arms.'

They waited as Joe reappeared from among the rocks and started to wade back towards the shore with his 'catch'.

Joe walked up the beach noting the tyre marks made by the motorbike and the footprints of Japanese soldiers. There were no indications that large numbers of the enemy had been there. He entered the jungle and, on an impulse, turned away from the position where he had left the others. A sixth sense told him that he was being watched.

He transferred both fish to his left hand and started to move up the path leading to the clearing. There was a slight bend in the path, and when he had passed it he threw the fish into the bush and ran as hard as he could for twenty yards before diving behind the trunk of a redwood which grew almost across the path. He drew his bush knife and sank to his haunches, prepared to spring. Seconds passed and the strain of concentration was physically painful. He listened intently for the slightest sound that would tell him someone was coming, a twig snapping or the noise of grass brushing together in a way that could not be caused by the wind. His eyes searched the canopy of foliage above his head for any sign of a bird quietly slipping away as someone approached. His nostrils sifted the thousand junge scents of blossom and decay for the alien smell of man.

Then there was a sharp prick beneath his ear. A firm pressure against his throat that did not diminish as he slowly turned his head. He saw the gleam of a knife blade and tilted his chin. His expression relaxed and a grin widened his mouth.

'Papa!'

The man who had glided up behind Joe was an adumbration of his son. A little over five and a half feet in height, his body had the appearance of a skeleton over which a skin slightly too small for it had been stretched. His ribs were a counting-frame, and there were pockets of recessed flesh behind his collar bones. His arms could have passed through a girl's bracelet up to the shoulder and his legs were scarcely thicker at the thigh than at the calf. A twist of cloth round his waist was carried forward to cover his genitals. When he grinned he revealed four betel-stained teeth.

Father and son embraced, and the old man replaced his knife in the waistband of his loin-cloth.

'I did not teach you very well, my son,' he chuckled. 'Surely you can hear an old man's bones creaking?'

Joe hung his head in shame. 'You move like a spirit, papa.'

'I will soon be one,' said the old man matter-of-factly. 'Is it true that you hid in the swamp?'

'Yes, papa. I never wish to see it again. We left one of the *tabaudas* there.'

The old man shook his head. 'It is a bad place. Put-put.'

He broke off and placed one hand on top of the other with the fingers spread to show that the crocodiles were so abundant that they had to lie on top of each other.

Joe nodded and his father continued. 'I have been awaiting

your return.' There was a note of relief in his voice.

'We have come for the explosives, papa.'

The old man laid a claw-like hand on his son's arm. 'The sago bags. I have them safely.'

Joe smiled. 'I thought you would have, papa.'

'The Japs ran through the jungle like litters of wild pig. They searched the shore but never the canoes. When night came we brought the bags ashore. The bladder boats are hidden as well.'

'You have done well, papa. Come, I will take you to the *tabaudas*. They will wish to salute you.'

He led his father back down the path, explaining that carriers would be needed as soon as night fell.

Hudson and the others were waiting anxiously, wondering why Joe had not returned. The old man ran forward when he saw Hudson and eagerly shook his hand.

'Master 'e talk 'e come back long one fella day, nau 'e come back finis!'

'Baka!' Hudson returned the handshake with interest. 'Why you come dis ples?'

The old man explained that he had supplied carriers to his son, but they had returned in a panic saying that the Japs were coming and that everyone would be killed. They had refused to go back and it was only with great difficulty and his personal *purri-purri* (magic) that he had persuaded them to bring the explosives ashore and hide them. He went on to say that although he was the *luluai*, or headman, of his tribe, the Japs had appointed his *tultul*, or second-in-command, in his place because of his widely expressed pro-Japanese feelings. The tribe was now divided into two, the older element siding with their traditional chief, the younger with the *tultul*. With every day that passed it was becoming more difficult to make the people remain loyal to the old regime.

Hudson did not find this difficult to believe. He remembered the amazement of the natives on New Ireland when white men who would not accept a box of matches from a *kanaka* unless it was offered on a tray suddenly ran like startled bandicoots at the first hint of a Jap invasion. Respect was replaced by contempt overnight. The Japs were the masters now.

Carter was worried. The risk of betrayal was even greater than he had imagined. All the more reason why they would have to carry out the mission this coming night.

Hudson was clearly of the same opinion. 'Yu kisim tenpela carriers one-time?' he asked the old man.

Baka nodded vehemently and took Hudson's hand. 'Ah! Long time me no lookim eye belong massa. You friend belong me true.'

'Joe's father is a great chief,' said Hudson to Carter. 'He helped me when I was trading here in the old days. There aren't too many left like him now.' He turned to the old man. 'White fella half you hide cargo?'

Baka grinned wickedly and beckoned with an arm like a praying mantis.

'Come, massa.'

He turned and began to move through the jungle at the pace of a fast walk. It made Carter breathless to keep up with him, yet the old man never broke into a run. He seemed to flit from tree to tree like some dark moth which could outdistance pursuit without ever appearing to be consciously exerting itself.

Eventually the ground began to rise and they came to a place where a patch of clinker showed itself through the undergrowth. Carter estimated that they were approaching the volcano and that the stony residue wass left over from some previous eruption. Strange rock formations began to appear like modern statues abandoned in an overgrown greenhouse and among them was a narrow gorge, its mouth choked by prickly vine. This plant was known to the natives as 'hold 'im fas' and could shred flesh almost to the bone with its sharp, clinging claws.

Baka paused by the gorge and looked around at his followers. There was a mischievous expression on his face. It was as if he were playing a game of hunt the thimble and challenging them to make a guess.

Carter gazed at the hanging creepers and the dark, gloomy rocks. Perhaps there was a cave nearby. He waited for the old man to continue, but Baka stood his ground and reached out for one of the creepers that hung down like a bell rope. He gestured Joe to do the same and the two men pulled in unison. The prickly vine stirred and then lifted into the air revealing that it was no more than a camouflage for what lay beneath. The narrow stone walls of the gorge were piled almost to the brim with square bale-like shapes tightly bound with sago palm leaves. Baka and Joe released their creepers and the 'hold 'im fas' dropped back into place. There was nothing to indicate what it concealed.

'You're a genius, Baka,' said Hudson.

Carter could only nod in agreement.

The old man half-inclined his head in a gesture of modesty that was obviously not heartfelt.

'Carrier come on time,' he said.

Hudson turned to Carter. 'OK. You and Joe might as well get on your way. You'll probably have to make a lot of detours and the more notice you can give Green the better. We'll stick to the same rendezvous spot—the bottom of the middle scar that appears to overlook the airfield. Both the tracks that go up from the south-west meet there.'

'So you've decided,' said Carter, lowering his voice and moving to the shelter of the rocks.

Hudson followed him. 'Decided?'

'That you want to keep Sula with you rather than Joe. Those bundles looked pretty heavy to me. I hope she can carry a hundred pounds if something goes wrong.'

Carter felt foolish as soon as he had finished speaking. He knew that his words must have sounded petulant and childish. He would have been hard-pressed to explain why he had said them.

Hudson looked uncomfortable. 'It was the original plan,' he said.

Carter shrugged his shoulders without saying anything.

'Why do you want her with you?' continued Hudson. 'Are you getting fond of her?'

Carter had not expected such a blunt question.

'No,' he said. 'Not especially.' He saw Hudson looking at him levelly. 'Well—yes. Yes, I guess I am.'

Hudson looked round to make sure that Sula was not in ear-shot.

'Since you seem to be in some doubt, let me tell you what I think,' he said. 'I think you *are* fond of the girl. And I think she's fond of you. That could be bad for both of you. If one of you gets captured or wounded the other may have to make a tough decision. Easier if there are no emotional feelings.'

Carter nodded uncomfortably. 'I suppose you're right,' he said.

Hudson's expression relaxed. 'I take your point about Joe and the loads. He's not as pretty as Sula but he's got broader shoulders.'

'Well—' began Carter.

Hudson patted his arm. 'This isn't the time for an argument, son. We've been through a lot already and there's more to come. Take Sula, but remember what I said.'

Before Carter could say anything, he had turned on his heel and walked across to the others. He spoke a few words and Sula came up to Carter. She looked into his face as if knowing that they had been talking about her.

'Is everything all right?'

Carter bent to pick up his pack. 'Fine,' he said, trying to clear any trace of uncertainty out of his voice. 'Just fine.'

The two roads that led to the airfield had been closed to all unauthorized traffic and roadblocks set up. Four light tanks were stationed round the perimeter wire and the sandbag walls enclosing the anti-aircraft guns had been lowered so that the guns could be brought to bear on the lower slopes of Matupi. Machine gun positions had been allocated so that every approach to the strip could be covered by interlocking fields of fire. Beside the control tower, two trucks waited with engines running. Each contained twenty-five marines in full combat uniform, wearing steel helmets and carrying sub-machine guns. Other detachments of marines armed with flame-throwers had infiltrated the dried-up river bed which lay between the airstrip and the south face of Matupi. They squatted in the shade with a wireless channel permanently open to the control tower. On the runway, the two Mitsubishi Betty bombers waited with their entourage of Zeke fighters. The crews of the two bombers were lined up beside their machines, standing at ease and waiting.

On the roof of the control tower, an anxious Yukichi swept the side of the volcano with his binoculars. He could see nothing but a thick carpet of green pitted by vertical depressions and giving way to fields of wasted lava on the upper slopes. There was no sudden transition but a series of spurs and re-entrants that formed an irregular pattern of green and black.

The wireless set crackled into life and the signaller looked up.

'He is approaching the road block.'

Yukichi's pulse quickened. 'Inform all units.'

The signaller talked fast into his mouthpiece and within seconds the engines of the Zekes began to roar to life. The propellers spun into a shimmering haze. Yukichi watched the first two taxi down the runway and turned his attention to the approach road.

'He has left the road block.'

Two motorcycles with sidecars appeared round the bend. On each sidecar was mounted a 7.7mm machine gun with a traverse that could cover both sides of the road. In the event of attack the motorcycles would accelerate up the road so that the enemy could be engaged on two fronts and their fire power split. Behind the motorcycles was a light truck with a machine gun mounted on the roof of the driver's cab and two rows of marines sitting back to back and covering each side of the road. Behind them came Admiral Yamamoto's vehicle, with two bodyguards sitting fore and aft of the figure in the familiar white uniform. There was wire mesh across the windscreen and along both sides to prevent a bomb or grenade from being lobbed inside. Rearing forward from the bonnet at an angle of forty-five degrees was a sharpened bar of metal which would meet any wire stretched across the road before it decapitated the driver. Last in the procession was a heavy-duty truck on the back of which had been mounted a 37mm gun. It was an impressive cavalcade which would have made even the most determined enemy reconsider the chances of a successful attack.

Yukichi looked across the blackened stretches of *kunai* grass that flanked the road. Some of them were still smoking. He had ordered them burnt in case they offered shelter to a determined attacker prepared to die in an assassination attempt. He had also had the road surface and drainage culverts examined for mines. Every sensible precaution, it seemed to him, had been taken.

Below the tower, the guard of honour came to attention and the Japanese flag swirled proudly. The first two Zekes were in the air and fanning out to circle the airfield. The anti-aircraft guns were spinning on their turntables, the gunners checking their elevations. Yukichi wiped beads of sweat from his forehead. It was not only the heat that made his shirt cling to him. Again he swept his binoculars over Matupi. Nothing.

The procession came to a halt and a cloud of red dust drifted against the white dress trousers as they descended from the vehicle stationed precisely in front of the guard of honour. The guard presented arms and two buglers blew a shrill, undulating call that startled a hornbill out of a bread-fruit tree a hundred yards away. Salutes were exchanged and the hearts of the guard of honour swelled with pride as the four rows of medal ribbons made a perfunctory sortie along each line. The inspection over, the buglers sounded a farewell call and Yamamoto's personal pilot saluted smartly and led the way through the sandbag-buttressed control building towards the runway.

Yukichi watched Matupi and waited. Yamamoto's plane was fifty feet from the control tower. The small stocky figure in the conspicuous white admiral's uniform would be clearly visible to anyone on the side of the volcano. A rifle with telescopic sights, a good eye and steady hands—that was all that was needed. Yukichi began to count the paces between the building and the plane. One-two-three. The figure moved at a steady, unforced pace as if unaware that there was anything to fear.

From the window of the second Betty bomber Admiral Matomi Ugaki, Yamamoto's chief of staff, looked down, his face drawn with worry. He knew the danger that threatened his leader and each one of them. His gaze rose unwillingly to the louring face of the volcano and he wished himself airborne.

Yukichi looked down expectantly, waiting for something to happen. The figure in white paused to exchange a few words with the crew and then mounted the steps of the plane with a smart salute. The hatch folded shut. As the Zekes roared overhead, the two Mitsubishi Betties taxied out into the centre of the runway and Yamamoto's plane gathered speed and slowly lifted into the air, tilting over to the right of the volcano and setting course for the Solomon Sea and Bougainville. Four Zekes closed in protectively and the second Betty took off and collected the two remaining Zekes.

Yukichi watched the planes until they were specks in the sky and then looked back to the volcano. From the expression on his face it was difficult to know what he was thinking.

18

Carter knelt in the *kunai* grass and listened to the Japs calling to each other. They seemed to be everywhere. All around him. This was the third patrol they had come across since leaving Hudson. Why were they so active around the airfield? Surely they were not expecting an airborne invasion? It seemed incredible but what other reason could there be for the numbers of men moving around the foot of the volcano? Troop manoeuvres? A possibility. Generals liked testing their defences by getting their own men to attack them. Perhaps something more serious. One of Baka's dissidents might have learned of the latest plans and tipped off the Japs. It was also possible that the Japs refused to believe that the raiding party had perished in the swamps and were taking no chances. On reflection, the last alternative seemed the most likely.

A hawk dipped low overhead and then sheered away in alarm leaving the Paradise Birdwing that had first attracted its attention to dither amongst the grasses. Carter looked around for Sula. This was a bad place to hide. The leeches were thick on the ground and waving their heads in the air like cobras as they scented blood. He already had a gorging black bracelet on each ankle. The mosquitoes were so thick that you could run your fingers across them in the air. There was also a biting insect so small that its presence could only be detected by the ever-spreading profusion of painful red welts on any portion of exposed flesh.

Carter tried to calculate how far they still had to go to the prison camp and whether they would get there before nightfall. Whatever happened, there was going to be precious little time to alert Green. Poor bastard—he had it worse than any of them. Their suffering could be measured in hours but he had been enduring a living death for over a year. Would he still have the strength to trek up the volcano, where even Joe acknowledged that the going was 'hard too much'?

A plane flew overhead and cut back the revs as it prepared to land. Carter could see nothing but heard the changing engine note. The airfield was over to the left lying in almost perpetual shadow at the foot of the volcano. They had decided to take to the grass to save time but had soon been pushed off the narrow pathway by the Japanese. After circling the first group who had made their presence known by suddenly opening up with a wireless set just as Sula was coming round the bend of the track towards them, they had nearly run into a second patrol. These men were avoided only by good luck. The leading Jap of the file had been looking over his shoulder so that Sula saw him before he saw her; by the time he turned round, Sula had dived into the grass. Now they proceeded with extreme caution. Sula went ahead for fifty yards whilst Carter remained in cover with the weapons. If it was safe to go forward, Sula came back for him. The stop-go, stop-go was tedious and exhausting. Waiting gave aches and pains time to grow and muscles began to seize up. The throbbing in the forearm had now spread to the whole arm and created a hard, aching swelling beneath the armpit. Carter was worried. Bit by bit his strength was ebbing away. The sole of his boot had now separated from the welt and was only attached at the heel. Attempts to bind it with lengths of creeper foundered after a few hundred yards' walking.

There was a rustling in the grass and Sula reappeared. She said nothing but picked up her weapon and beckoned him to follow. The Japs had either stopped calling or moved on. There was only the sibilant hiss of the grass-ends rubbing together in the slight breeze. Sula led the way for a dozen yards until they came to a shallow drainage ditch with a cracked, sun-baked bottom patterned like a crocodile's back. She stepped down and extended the fingers of her right hand three times to say that they should leave fifteen yards between them.

Carter let her draw ahead and watched her slim body weave through the undergrowth. With her grass skirt melting into the sun-bleached *kunai* she appeared naked. For some reason he thought of Hudson and felt puzzled and ashamed that he had so nearly provoked an argument before their parting. Why had he sought to make an issue of Sula? Had he been revealing some innate jealousy of Hudson as a leader? Or did he see him as a threat to his relationship with Sula? What relationship? He had not even embraced the girl. Yet strange how just to touch her, or feel her touch him, made his nerve-ends tingle, gave him more excitement than he had known making love to every other woman in his life. Perhaps it was because there was no pressure on them. They were not cast in the roles of man and woman and expected to perform towards each other in a certain way; their relationship had grown despite their sex and not because of it.

They kept walking along the ditch and giant grasshoppers sprang from the *kunai* like flying mousetraps. The sun was sinking and the grass-tops borrowed a flamingo pink from the paintbox of reds that suffused the western sky. It was as if they were witnessing a distant battle or Matupi had already erupted and set fire to the heavens.

Carter came to a place where the ditch crossed open ground and found that there was no sign of Sula. He knelt and she appeared from the grass.

'See!' Her pointing arm brushed his cheek as she sank down beside him.

'Ahead there is the road that passes the airfield. The ditch runs beneath it. Once we have crossed the road we will find the river that flows past the prison camp.' She smiled encouragingly and her breast touched his shoulder. 'We can follow the river. It will be easier among the trees.' She paused for a second to see if he had any questions and then rose lightly to her feet. She tilted her head coquettishly and extended a hand. 'Come.'

Carter took the hand and allowed himself to be pulled upright. They might be going for a stroll in the park rather than on a mission with more chance of death than of success. This was one of the girl's special qualities. She made the worst aspects of life seem not only bearable but almost enjoyable.

In another five minutes they came to the road. It ran on a causeway across what had originally been a swamp. To cross it was to come into full view of the surrounding countryside. As they watched, a truck full of soldiers went past, travelling towards the volcano. They were wearing packs with rolled-up groundsheets strapped to them. Carter looked at Sula and frowned. She jabbed a finger along the ditch indicating that it would take them safely beneath the road.

She was wrong. When they approached the culvert it was to find that wooden stakes laced with barbed wire had been driven into the ground across the opening to seal it. The stakes were freshly cut which was disturbing. It seemed that the Japs were always one step ahead. Sula started to move towards the barricade and Carter stopped her. He had noticed a thin wire leading away into the foliage along the side of the road. It was either an alarm signal or a booby-trap. He pointed out what he had seen and waved his hand from side to side in a 'no go' signal.

Sula hesitated and looked up uneasily towards the road before facing him with a question mark in her eyes.

Carter nodded.

Sula waited and listened. A nervous tremble ran through the grass as if orchestrating her fears. The sound died away and there was silence. She climbed the bank and started to walk across the road. She glanced towards the airfield and her heart leapt towards her mouth. Two hundred yards away a coil of barbed wire was stretched across the road to form a temporary road block. A Jap soldier with his rifle slung across his shoulder was watching her. She kept walking and waited for the challenge. Beyond the roadblock she was vaguely conscious of a lorry approaching. Her feet met the bank on the far side and she slithered down it and ran to the end of the culvert. In her panic she nearly seized the barbed wire. She whistled twice and eventually Carter's face appeared as if seen down a gun barrel. She waved her arms across her face and Carter acknowledged with a thumbs-up signal.

Sula drew back into the grass and waited. Now they were in trouble. On separate sides of the road and with no chance of Carter getting across without being seen. Would it be best to wait for nightfall or withdraw along the road until they were out of view of the roadblock? While she pondered, it occurred to her that the truck had not passed. She listened and heard an engine braying its discontent. Stooping low she moved along the bank towards the roadblock. When she judged that she was fifty yards away, she wormed up the bank and tilted her head back so that she could look down the road with the minimum risk of being seen. The barbed wire had disappeared and with it all vestiges of roadblock. The truck that had picked up the men and barbed wire was reversing down the road looking for somewhere to turn. Sula experienced a wave of relief and pressed her head down against the bank. When she looked up again the truck was vanishing in a cloud of dust.

On the far side of the road, Carter waited anxiously and fought off the leeches. He felt something drop down the back of his shirt and writhed in distaste. Of all the creatures in the jungle he loathed leeches the most. The thought of sharing his blood with these vile black worms made him sick. Yet when one dropped to the ground, bloated, he could not bring himself to stamp on it—that somehow compounded the waste. His blood was precious even if it now resided in objects that made his stomach turn.

He heard the long whistle and scrambled up the bank, a Mills gun in each hand. He crossed the road without looking to the right or left. After the claustrophobic jungle it seemed strange to burst suddenly into the open for a few seconds.

He leapt down the bank and arrived beside Sula, heart pounding. The ditch ran straight for another hundred yards before meeting a swathe of jungle that followed the line of the river. Ahead and to the left was the mountain behind which lay the prison camp. Carter had only seen it from the far side. He estimated the camp to be about a mile away. With any luck they would reach it before nightfall.

Sula glided ahead and Carter followed until they came to the bank of the river. The water level was as low as when Carter had first seen it but this time there were no rumbles of distant thunder from the hills. They waited and listened for several minutes but the only sound and movement came from screeching swallows diving to snatch up insects that hung in swarms over the shallow pools. Carter tapped his watch. Sula nodded and led the way across the river bed, skipping nimbly from rock to rock.

Carter waited for her to reach the far side unchallenged and then followed with the weapons, choosing a less adventurous route.

It was when he was nearly at the far bank that he experienced a sharp twinge of pain. A pain that filled his mind with an awful premonition. He hauled himself up by way of a tangled mass of roots and quickly sought the shelter of a grove of palms. Nothing he had ever imagined had prepared him for the fear he was now experiencing. The numbness in his arm seemed to have spread to the finger of both hands as he pulled open the front of his trousers. He paused and then looked down. A shock of horror as strong as could have been passed by an electric current seared through him. He had known what he was going to see from the moment of the first sharp, razor nick. A leech had attached itself to the rounded dome of his penis.

His first impulse was to pluck it off. Then he realized that this would not only be excruciatingly painful but increase the risk of infection to a certainty. He felt like crying out in rage, fear and frustration. In these terrible forests of perpetual twilight there was no limit to the degradations heaped upon the human spirit. What was happening to him was an obscenity.

Sula came inquiringly to his side. She looked from his agonized face to his shielding hand and tried to draw it away. Carter shook her off. The hand returned, this time with steel in it.

Carter did not resist. Like a child he allowed her to look upon his wound whilst he turned his head in shame. Almost before he realized what was happening she had dropped to her knees before him. She took his penis in her fingers and put her mouth about it. His first reaction was to draw away but she thrust out a restraining hand and gripped him tightly by the thigh. Her lips shut off the leech from the air and after a few seconds it released its hold. The moment that she felt it separate, Sula twisted her head and voided her mouth into the grass.

By the time he had stopped trembling, Sula was on her feet. He tried to blurt out some words but she silenced him with a shake of the head, and pointed towards a spot where the mountains dipped towards the *kunai*.

'Less than a mile.'

She smiled and began to pick her way along the river bank.

19

The figure in the white admiral's uniform gazed thoughtfully out of the window of the bomber. 1730 hours and the south coast of Bougainville Island was looming up ahead. Kahili Airstrip was a matter of minutes away. Previous visits to front-line military bases had bred a superficial familiarity with the route. From Kahili it would be a short drive to Buin, where a submarine chaser was waiting to start an inspection of naval units under the command of Admiral Tanaka. After that, back to the Truk Islands, a thousand miles to the north, where the flagship *Musashi* was anchored. The two bombers and their escort began their descent to two thousand feet so that they could take full advantage of their camouflage against the shadowy green of the jungle.

Four miles to the south, sixteen P-38 Lockheed Lightnings were on the last leg of their flight from Henderson Field. They had flown 410 miles at a height of thirty feet above the waves, their wings and bellies weighed down by two supplementary fuel tanks with a total capacity of 475 gallons. The pilots searched the skies ahead of them anxiously and checked their watches. Their interception point was thirty miles west of the Kahili strip and they were flying as low as they dared to avoid being spotted by any Jap planes or ships patrolling in the area. Visibility was good with flurries of high cloud above twenty thousand feet and the west coast of the island of Bougainville showed up clearly with thick jungle vegetation crowding down to the water's edge.

'Eleven o'clock!' An excited voice broke radio silence and all eyes scanned the horizon.

A V-formation of planes was approaching along the coast from the north-west—two Betty bombers with an escort of what seemed like six Zekes. The bombers were flying almost wing-tip to wing-tip with two fighters on each side and two above and a little behind. Their height was two thousand feet. Immediately four of the Lightnings jettisoned their long-range belly tanks and started to climb towards the bombers. The remaining twelve climbed more steeply to give high level protection. For the passengers in the two bombers the first warning of attack was given when the P-38s were a mile from their target. Anyone not strapped to his seat was flung across the aircraft as the Betties spun sideways and streaked towards the safety of the jungle. The escorting Zekes sprayed out to meet their challengers and head off pursuit. The first P-38 screeched down at over 400mph and the ugly yammer of 22mm cannon and 13mm machine guns vied with the scream of 2,000hp engines. The leading Betty side-slipped to safety and continued its dive towards the tree-tops. As it levelled out, its green and brown markings seemed to melt into the jungle, and the pursuing P-38 was forced to take evasive action as three Zekes closed in. Turning sharply, the pilot saw a fourth Zeke in his sights and pressed the button. Cannon shells ripped and chewed through the fuselage and the plane shuddered and slowly turned over on its back. It started to go down in a gentle curve. Now, the first Betty could be seen as a shadow flying almost at tree-top height. Two P-38s broke through the cover of the outnumbered Zekes and went after it. With a landscape of uneven green flickering beneath its undercarriage the bomber desperately veered from side to side to throw off its pursuers. A thin column of smoke began to trail like black cotton from one of its wings.

Up at seven thousand feet two more P-38s saw their chance and howled down to hurl lead hate at the second bomber. Half the tail-plane was shot to pieces. The Betty lurched sideways and slid towards the ocean like a loose slate down a steep roof. It hit the water, performed a couple of clumsy ducks and drakes, and then broke up in a cloud of spray.

Over the jungle, the first Betty hedge-hopped desperately, slipping, skidding and bunting its rudder in an attempt to reach the fighter cover that was screaming off the strip at Kahili like a swarm of avenging hornets. A P-38 sat on its tail and a long burst ignited the starboard engine. Orange flames began to kick round the cowling and black smoke streamed from the wing-tip. The bomber began to shudder and lose speed. Flame ran the length of the wing and enveloped the fuselage. It tried to climb and then slumped so that the trail of black smoke kinked like a painted eyebrow. Another burst and the plane fell out of the sky. Its undamaged wing hit a tree and splintered into matchwood. The blazing plane bounced twice, cleared a flaming trail through the jungle and exploded. Seen by the farthest flung of the P-38s, a dense column of thick black smoke began to billow into the air.

20

Hudson squatted by a rock and watched the last of the bales being brought out of the ravine. All the carriers had one thing in common: they were afraid. They muttered amongst themselves and looked suspiciously at Hudson and their loads. Hudson could sympathize with them. The weight was double what they had expected to carry and the going was sure to be tough. Only the provision of salt and stick tobacco—one third now, two-thirds when the job was done—in undreamed quantities had clinched a grudging acceptance.

Hudson felt that he needed a smoke himself. His nerves were tight as piano wire. The near altercation with Carter had not helped. They had enough on their plates without any additional tensions. He wondered what had got into the boy. Something to do with being young, he supposed.

One of the carriers tore down a large leaf and rolled it between his hands until it was a malleable wand. He folded back the end and continued to wind it tightly until he had made a small, thick mat. This he placed on his head. He sank to one knee, then two of his comrades lifted a bale and placed it on the mat. With arms outstretched he slowly rose, the veins at his temples bulging. He juggled his load to achieve the right balancing point and waited, his head low in his shoulders.

The carriers were a motley collection, mostly young but with one barrel-chested fifty-year-old whose feet splayed like a penguin's. He was bald and his head had a large dent in it where someone had apparently struck him with an axe. He scorned a mat and picked up his load and put it on his head without assistance.

Baka appeared across the clearing and Hudson repeated his thanks for the provision of the carriers. Baka took his hand and squeezed it warmly.

'Me savvy, Massa Hudson. Talk belong 'im 'e straight.'

Hudson blushed beneath his tan. 'I hope so,' he said, mainly to himself.

Not for the first time he wondered how many of Baka's people would survive if they succeeded in making Matupi erupt. Yet these same people were carrying what might be the instruments of their own destruction. It was their gardens that would be overrun with lava, their houses that would be burned to ash.

He returned the pressure on Baka's hand. 'Behind me come back. Me no can loosim you, fella.'

He turned away quickly and gave the signal to move out. He did not feel happy in his skin. Joe embraced his father and started to lead the way from the clearing. The old man waited until the last carrier had gone and then looked round carefully to see if they had left any traces that they had been there. Afterwards, he returned to his village.

Carter looked towards the prison camp and his heart fell. The swathe of cleared vegetation around the perimeter wire had been widened and the clump of rattan had disappeared. That meant that it was going to be impossible to signal to Green that they had arrived. It also meant that there was going to be less cover when they approached the wire.

Sula lay beside Carter in the elephant grass and read his expression. 'Problem?'

'Yes. There was a clump of rattan over there. We were going to break two stems across each other so that Green knew we were here. Now it's gone.'

'Maybe we will be able to see him?'

'Maybe.' Carter looked towards the high barbed-wire fences and wrinkled his nostrils. The stench of human excrement and decay was stomach-turning. It had an almost physical quality and, mixed with the heavy scents of jungle flowers, could have been packaged as an emetic. It was not difficult to understand why the Japs had their guard-house outside the perimeter wire.

Carter was lying at the opposite corner to the one by which he had first approached the camp and his field of visibility was limited. Such figures as he could see in the European compound were pitifully thin and dressed in rags. It disturbed him to watch a woman with a baby in her arms walk to the wire and point out some object in a tree. She cocked her head and held the baby to her cheek with arm extended so that he could see where she was looking. When she turned, she stumbled and nearly fell. The baby began to cry. Carter noticed the woman's dress; it had once been an elegant cocktail frock with a pleated collar. Perhaps she had packed a few things and been unable to resist taking it. It was torn to the waist with the hem coming unstitched and covered with mud.

A man stood against the wall of one of the thatched huts and scratched. That was all he did. His left thigh, his stomach, his right shoulder. Whether he suffered from a physical affliction or a mental one it was impossible to say. Whatever the ailment, it was unsettling to watch the hands that could never remain still.

As Carter continued to watch he began to realize that it was the fact that these people were white that he found most disconcerting. He had been long enough in the East to become inured to the sight of emaciated, diseased people dressed in rags. But they were not white. They were part of the landscape. You took their plight for granted. But to see white people in the same pitiful condition, that brought the tragedy home to roost: the unquestioning acceptance of the suffering of underprivileged races because it had always been there.

He leaned forward and tried to see what was happening in the rest of the camp. There was no movement in the Chinese compound and the entrance to the Indian compound was padlocked. What might have been the covered heads of sitting Indian women were just visible through the wire. Some of the huts had their entrances boarded up with red planks. No doubt an outbreak of some contagious disease had been isolated there. Carter thought uneasily of cholera. Was that why there seemed to be so few people about? He had better take a closer look.

Telling Sula to remain where she was, he began to crawl just inside the lush vegetation that abutted on the open strip of ground round the camp. The sun had now disappeared behind

233

the trees and the tree frogs were beginning to croak. Their raucous rasp ran up and down a scale, each note supplied—usually in sequence—by a different frog. Something slithered away through the grass to his right, and he breathed a sharp, itchy pollen that seemed to dig needles into the inside of his nostrils. It was unbearably hot and humid—he wondered if a storm was in the offing. To take in mouthfuls of suffocating air was like swallowing something that had substance. Sweat lathered his forehead and stung his myriad cuts. The few moist scabs on his elbows were scuffed off after he had advanced a dozen feet. Something dropped into his hair and he left it to get out by itself—to raise a hand was to invite a sting.

Moving to the very edge of the grass he peered through the remaining stalks almost at root level. He was opposite the Chinese compound and could see into one of the low thatched huts. There were no beds and people lay stretched out on the floor like bundles of rags. A cooking pot simmered on a meagre fire but there was no smell of food to waft the twenty yards to where Carter lay. Only the omnipresent stench of excrement. It was a miracle that anybody could survive for long in this climate and in these conditions. Sooner or later an epidemic would undoubtedly sweep through the camp.

As he watched, a woman emerged from the hut. She was old, her face severely lined, and dressed in a tunic which would have been loose even if she had not been starving. She took tiny, faltering footsteps and steadied herself against the side of the hut before bending down. Something began to agitate the foot of the cane wall. The woman pulled a string and a rat was revealed, dangling and making an inverted arch in an attempt to climb up its own body to the string. Whether the rat had been freshly trapped or kept alive, Carter could not tell. The old woman picked up a stick and tried to kill the rat, but she was very weak and she could not hit the rat hard enough. It squealed and scrabbled in the dust while the old woman panted. In the end she held it, still dancing on the string, and dropped it into the pot. It shrieked and then was silent.

A small child appeared in the doorway and clung unsteadily to the post. Mucus descended from each nostril onto his swollen belly. He looked towards the pot and then clambered over the threshold, turning his back and extending a leg warily as he let himself down. When he began to walk it was obvious that he had rickets. His legs were bowed and his shoulders stooped. He looked into the pot for a long time and then up at the woman. Who was she? His mother? His grandmother? The child's expression was one common to many children. Puzzlement. The old woman said something to him in Chinese and then led him back to the hut. He paused at the doorway and looked back wistfully towards the pot.

Carter shook with helpless anger and compassion. Sometimes he had asked himself what he was fighting for. Whatever it was, it must be a world in which no human beings were reduced to eating rats.

He crawled on, trying to forget the expression on the face of the child as it looked towards the pot. A new smell assailed his nostrils. A chemical smell. A harsh odour strong enough to assert itself amongst the all-pervading stench of excrement. It came from the Indian compound. A smell not unlike creosote. Carter peered through the screen of grass to the barred huts and realized what it must be. Disinfectant. His earlier suspicions must have been right. The confirmation brought him no comfort. People had already started to die. How many huts were sealed? He looked carefully. One, two, three. Had the disease spread beyond the Indian lines? What if Green was dead? The thought was numbing. The whole success of their mission depended on Green; he was the only one who knew the whereabouts of the cave that led into the volcano; without him, all their efforts would be for nothing.

Carter forced his way through the scratching, itching, needling grass. The lump under his arm felt like a petanque ball. Where were the women he thought he had glimpsed in the Indian compound? He came level with a second line of huts and saw a circle of saried women sitting with heads bent round something obscured by a piece of material. They were wailing softly, and it took little imagination to guess what lay hidden from his eyes. A corpse. Even from where he lay he could hear the communal buzz of flies celebrating their own private mass.

A few more yards on his naked elbows and he was able to spy upon the guard-house. Despite the surrounding palms, the corrugated-iron roof caught the last rays of sun. It was no surprise that a square tent had appeared next to it, the sides rolled up to a height of three feet from the ground. This at least would afford some cooler sleeping accommodation for the guards. Whether the arrival of the second structure meant that there were more men stationed at the camp, it was impossible to say. Two pairs of putteed legs could be glimpsed below the tent flap. A third man lounged on a palliasse. The wooden floor was raised from the ground to protect the occupants from snakes and other creatures that might crawl across them. A battered truck with a red rising sun emblem on the door was also in evidence. Carter tried to count the bed rolls. There must be about a dozen of them.

He was about to risk leaning out from the foliage to see if he could find the whereabouts of the missing guards when he heard a footfall. He froze motionless and listened to the sound of someone coming nearer. The footsteps paused in front of him and he heard an exclamation of boredom and weariness. Then a small snatch of melody hummed tunelessly. Carter remembered the dancing guard of his last visit and wondered if it was the same man. Seconds turned into minutes and then there was the creak of leather boots as the guard moved on.

Carter rediscovered the luxury of unfettered movement and killed two mosquitoes that were drawing blood from his eyelid. The fact that the Japs bothered to patrol during the day surprised him; from his observation, none of the inmates would have had the strength even to try an escape. He was about to turn back when he heard the sound of a lorry approaching; its engine was groaning as if carrying a heavy load. It stopped abruptly and there was the sound of two doors slamming almost simultaneously followed by a tailboard dropping and a chain rattling. Carter wriggled forward as he heard impatient orders being shouted out in Japanese.

A truck full of ragged, skeletal men had stopped outside the guard-house. Mainly Europeans and Chinese but also a handful of Indians, some wearing turbans. Their eyes, red with fatigue and buried in their sockets, glowed through the masks of grey dust that covered their faces and the upper part of their bodies. Their ghost-like appearance was matched by their pitiful thinness. When he first saw them packed together in the back of the truck he thought they looked like a bundle of kindling.

Carter realized that he was looking at a work party and eagerly scanned the faces for sight of Green. He was not there. The guards had emerged from the tent and were shouting at the men and pulling them down from the truck. They were manacled at the wrist and joined together by a long chain. Any hesitation or enforced clumsiness was met by a blow from the hand or foot. The prisoners offered no resistance. Their spirit had long since been beaten out of them. Their physical condition, apart from the emaciation, was appalling. Tropical ulcers proliferated and some of the men were shivering uncontrollably from malarial fever.

Carter looked at the condition of the prisoners and longed to break cover and start wreaking retribution with his Mills gun. The guards were animals. Filthy, brutal and sadistic, they must represent the dregs of the Japanese army, selected for duty at the prison camp because no other unit would have them.

One man, an Indian, was now left in the truck. He was lying on the floor and it was clear that he had suffered an accident. His body was covered with earth with patches of raw flesh showing through. He clutched his ribs and his teeth showed white in pain. Carter remembered the Chinaman who escaped saying that the Indians were used for digging the tunnels. It looked as if this man had been caught in a roof fall. His comrades tried to climb back into the truck to help him but were beaten back by the Japs. They screamed at the Indian and rattled the chain but he lay where he was and shook his head. He was clearly in urgent need of a doctor. This fact did not weigh heavily on the Japs. Two of them took hold of the chain and yanked it viciously so that the injured man crashed to the ground with a piercing shriek of pain. Incapable of movement, he lay on his back and received two vicious kicks to the side of the head.

Carter closed his eyes. What he was watching made him feel sick. An aching lump of misery filled his stomach. The condition of the Indian seemed to incense the Japs. It was as if they accused him of injuring himself to provoke them—as if the very act of being in pain and showing it was reprehensible and demanded punishment. Carter looked again. The Indian lay still and the Japs had turned their backs on him. Not one of the guards had shaved. Their boots were dirty and down at heel and their uniforms stained. In a strange way, their wild eyes and unkemptness made them look like their prisoners, as masters come to resemble their dogs.

The chain was withdrawn and the manacles unlocked one by one and tossed into the back of the lorry. The Indian flinched as the last whip-end of the chain struck his face. He was still alive. The camp gates had been opened and the released men went through, feeling their raw, festering wrists. Some looked back. Many did not. What had just happened was not a novelty. It might be them tomorrow.

Four Japs accompanied the men into the camp. Three remained behind. One secured the tailboard of the lorry. One looped the chain around his bent arm. One fetched a rifle with a fixed bayonet from the corrugated-iron hut. The Indian did not move.

The prisoners were now separating into their different compounds, out of view of the lorry. The three guards watched them and the man with the chain swung it backwards and forwards and then up and into the truck. Then they turned to the Indian. The man with the rifle advanced and without pausing calmly drove the bayonet into the man's stomach. The steel went on disappearing like a hypodermic needle. The Indian's mouth jumped open wide and he let out a long, strangulated groan. His back arched and his hands clasped round the bayonet. The muscles in his wasted arms tensed. Then he fell backwards and lay like an insect pinned out on a setting board. The Jap withdrew his bayonet and lunged again, this time for the chest. His long, yellow teeth were bared in a grim smile of pleasure. It was obvious that he enjoyed what he was doing. The steel blade sank in until the sight of the rifle was pressed against the man's flesh. The Jap placed his foot on his victim's chest and grunted with the effort. There was an ugly grating noise as it scraped against bone. A small spout of blood sprung from the unplugged wound

238

and then subsided instantly.

The other two Japs watched without a flicker of emotion passing across their shiny faces. Carter felt that what he was watching must be an everyday occurrence. Anyone too sick or exhausted to work would be put to death without mercy.

Was that what had happened to Green? While he wondered and worried, the two Japs lifted the Indian's corpse and carried it, head lolling obscenely, to the small truck. It was tossed into the back. The Jap who had committed the murder made an attempt at cleaning his bayonet on a leaf and crossed to the corrugated-iron hut. Fastened to the wall was a machine-like, old-fashioned pencil sharpener. He started to turn the handle and a loud wailing noise reverberated through the camp.

Carter's horror changed to puzzlement as he watched the other two Japs enter the hut. They emerged carrying map boards with sheets of paper attached. The siren must be the signal for the evening roll-call. Now perhaps he would be able to catch a glimpse of Green.

Carter retreated into the undergrowth and started to crawl back the way he had come. What he had witnessed had given him a new sense of purpose that put fresh life into flagging muscles. The itching, chafing discomfort that afflicted every inch of his flesh was no longer in the forefront of his mind. He wanted only to find Green and somehow get him to Matupi so that terrible retribution could come rolling down the mountain in rivers of fire.

As he crawled he could hear the Japs hectoring and the sound of the prisoners' voices as they emerged from the huts. Babies cried, women soothed. Perhaps disturbed by the commotion and fleeing from the camp, two rats ran through the grass ahead of him. The sky was darkening fast and a sharp squeal above made him look up to see a flying fox heading for its roosting place. Crickets began to throb a counterpoint to the music of the frogs and a small bat wheeled, swooped and scurried through the air making high-pitched squeaking noises. There was no shortage of insects for it to eat as Carter's stinging face could testify.

Sula was waiting where he had left her. She searched his grim face for news but said nothing. Carter moved carefully to the edge of the cover and checked for sentry movement before peering across the gap to the European compound. Three ranks of men were lined up untidily in the middle of the huts. It was impossible to see them clearly because of the fading light and the intervening huts. A Japanese voice carried across the open space. It was talking urgently and bombastically. When a pause came in the tumble of words a second voice could be heard, slow and halting. Carter surmised that it belonged to an interpreter. He listened hard but could make out nothing that was being said. Carter cursed the Japs for holding the roll-call in the middle of the lines. He was becoming increasingly worried that Green was dead. The uncertainty nagged at him like a toothache. He must find the answer, so that he could decide what to do next. He strained his ears as a snatch of English drifted across the wire. An Australian voice was saying something about digging tunnels. The voice was raised and contentious but almost immediately submerged in a gabble of Japanese. It did not resurface. Shortly afterwards, the Japs could be glimpsed withdrawing down the centre aisle between the huts, and the prisoners broke ranks. Fires were lit and unappetizing cooking smells achieved an unequal balance with the other odours of the camp. In the space of what seemed like minutes tropical night had fallen and it was only possible to see the outline of men as they squatted or sat around the fires. There was little or no conversation. These men were clinging to life and it demanded all their single-mindedness and purpose.

Carter waited impatiently. He dared not approach the wire while there were still so many inmates about. Any overt response to his presence would alert the guards and that would be the end of their mission. He turned to Sula and pointed toward the guardroom. He had drawn her a map of the camp and agreed a range of bird-call signals that she would use to alert him of sentry movements. She nodded and touched his arm with her fingertips before willowing away. He wondered why she was able to survive half-naked in the jungle with so little discomfort. Perhaps because of the uncomplicated attitude she had revealed with the leech incident. She lived with the jungle. He lived in spite of it. She accepted the hardships and knew how to turn them to advantage. She had shown him how to tap a thorny creeper and extract a pint of pure, cool water. He saw every plant and creature as engaged in a pitiless war of attrition with himself as the enemy.

The mosquitoes attacked in droves and the fires died down. Men came to the wire to relieve themselves and then retired to their huts. There were brief flurries of words and then silence punctuated by creaks, coughs and moans of weariness and pain as men sought sleep that always came hardest when it was most needed. Overhead, hunting owls barked to each other. The moon was obscured by cloud. Carter listened for the long, single birdnote that would tell him that Sula had the guards under observation and it was safe to move. Finally it came.

He started through the grass to the spot he had preselected for his attempt on the wires. There was a shallow depression in the ground which, experience told him, would afford enough cover from someone not standing within a few yards of him. With his Mills gun held between both hands, and his heart hammering, he emerged from the undergrowth and began to crawl across the open space. The stubble of grass over which he dragged himself was like the upturned nails on a fakir's bed. His knuckles and forearms were ripped until he could feel them slippery with blood. He reached the wire and rested, listening to every sound. Not to be enclosed by the jungle had become a strange sensation, a kind of exposure akin, he supposed, to that felt by a hermit crab as it moved between shells.

He lay on his back and removed the wire-expanding devices. One of them had become buckled in a fall and it was a struggle to erect it. Sweat dripped off him as he gritted his teeth and forced his knife round. It slipped out of the socket and his hand was badly gashed against the barbed wire. A sharp ping hummed away into the night. He waited anxiously and then tried again. This time the metal rods opened and the wires strained apart. When the lowest was resting on the ground, he pressed himself flat and wriggled forward. The stench of urine and excrement was almost insupportable at grass level. He was grateful when a puff of wind wafted smoke into his face from one of the dying fires. His uniform snagged twice but he freed it and reached the inside of the camp to listen again. Still nothing except wheezes, creaks and occasional snores from the huts.

He was about to move forward when he saw a figure amongst the huts. He froze but the figure came towards him, not in a straight line but weaving slightly from side to side. He was not a Jap but the presence of anyone in the open was not to be welcomed. Carter held out his gun in an intimidating gesture and recognized the scratching man he had seen when first looking into the camp. He was muttering and talking urgently to himself, obviously mentally disturbed. He looked down at Carter and one of his hands clawed at an upper arm before darting on impulse to the back of his head. His head craned forward and he made an uneasy noise at the back of his throat. His eyes were wide and feverish.

Carter scrambled quickly to his feet and grabbed the man's arm. The skin was rough and lumpy.

'Where's Harry Green?' he hissed. 'Harry Green. Take me to him!'

The man shook free, obviously alarmed. He began to jabber incoherently. From the direction of the guardroom came two sharply defined bird-calls—the signal that something was happening. Carter seized the man and dragged him towards the shelter of the huts. The man began to call out in fear, and Carter thrust a hand over his mouth. Two skinny hands closed on his wrist and terrified eyes opened wide. A shale of loose skin showed itself at the edge of the man's thinning hair. Carter did not like touching him.

'I am looking for Harry Green,' he whispered. 'Harry Green!' He repeated the words as if talking to a child and fought to keep his voice calm. 'You know him?'

The man moved his head up and down and made acquiescing noises through Carter's hand.

'Will you take me to him?'

The man nodded again. He seemed to be calmer. Carter removed his hand and immediately the man opened his mouth to shout. Carter shoved his hand forward again, catching the mouth while it was still open. He pressed hard until the cane wall creaked. Behind came three bird-calls, the signal that a sentry was on the prowl. Carter felt desperate. He brought his mouth to the man's ear.

'The Japs are coming. If they find me here they will kill us both.' He paused to let the words sink in. 'You must take me to Harry Green—now!'

The man's eyes swivelled to look over Carter's shoulder. Carter turned to see a thin pencil of light at the far end of the camp. It showed briefly and was then blotted out by the huts. The sight seemed to make up the man's mind. He nodded and gestured to one side. Carter slowly released the pressure of his hand. If the man tried to cry out again he would have to kill him.

The man muttered something and shivered. Then he took Carter's hand in a grip like wet sandpaper and pulled him along the wall to the end of the hut. They were facing open ground when the moon came out. What had been almost total darkness was transformed into a shadowland of black and silver. The area to the wire and beyond was lit as if by a searchlight. Carter followed the tugging pressure on his hand and waited for the challenge. They crossed an open space between two rows of huts and then paused in the shadow of a doorway. Boards creaked as someone turned in his sleep. The man entered the hut, pulling Carter after him. The walls stopped a foot below the roof and the moonlight streamed in.

Two dozen men lay on the floor, most of them without any covering. Some were curled up in foetal positions with their hands between their legs. Others stretched out as if at the other end of life, corpses on an undertaker's table. They were packed shoulder to shoulder with scarcely room to turn. The hut buzzed with flies and mosquitoes and the stench of rotting, unwashed flesh was stomach-turning.

Carter let himself be led between the rows of men and searched for Green. There was one man at the end with his back to them who looked promising. Carter hurried forward, relief beginning to flood back in place of doubt. The pressure on his arm was released and the mentally disturbed man hobbled to the side of the sleeping figure. He bent down and shook his shoulder. After a pause, the man grunted and turned round. Carter's face fell. It was not Green.

In fear and desperation Carter dropped to his knees. 'I'm looking for Harry Green.'

The man shook his head. 'He ain't here any more.'

21

'Not here?' Carter felt as if he had received a violent kick in the stomach.

'The Japs took him away yesterday. They caught him stealing rice.' The man shook his head and squinted at Carter. He spoke with an American accent. 'Who the hell are you anyway?'

'It doesn't matter,' said Carter. 'Forget you saw me. Where did they take him?'

'To the pit,' said the American.

'To the pit?'

'In the jungle, near here.' He jerked a skinny arm over his shoulder. 'There's a track. That's where they execute people.'

Carter's heart fell. 'So he's dead?'

'If he's lucky.'

'What do you mean?'

'They don't always kill people right away. Not if they steal things. The Japs are kinda scrupulous. They don't like thieves.'

The acid irony in the American's voice was etched as deep as the lines in his face. He saw something and tugged Carter's arm. 'Get down!'

Carter dropped to one knee and turned his head. Through the chink in the ill-matched cane wall could be seen the bright glare of an approaching torch. The deranged man began to babble in alarm. He was moving towards the doorway before anybody could stop him. Carter pressed himself into the line of bodies and lay still, his heart thumping. With a quick movement, the man he had been talking to leaned across to pull a tattered blanket over his legs. He turned his body so that he was facing the doorway and lay eyeball to eyeball with Carter, the Mills gun concealed between them.

Carter heard the deranged man's voice leaving the hut and the immediate challenge. There was a guttural explosion of Japanese and the sound of a blow, followed by a yelp of pain. The agitated mumble quickly receded into the distance. Then there was a short silence and the creak of a board as a rubber-soled boot trod on it. Carter could feel the Jap's presence in the doorway, surveying the interior of the hut. A beam of light travelled up the far side and then splashed over him as it returned down the second row of bodies. He held his breath. The floorboard creaked again and then the light withdrew. No word was spoken.

Carter lay in silence and felt tell-tale signs of movement across his thighs and belly. The hut must abound in vermin. Minutes passed and then his companion raised himself on one elbow and looked around. He held his finger to his lips and rose to move stealthily to the doorway. When he returned he lay down and spoke in a low voice.

'They've gone. What do you want Harry for?'

Carter had been dreading the question and its implications. 'It's too long a story to tell now. I've got to get going.'

'I'll come with you.' The words tumbled out in a flash.

'No chance. I'm sorry, but you could balls up the whole operation.'

'Listen, buster. I'm a fellow American. I was shot down over the jungle. Are you going to leave me here to die?' There was the pressure of claw-like fingers on Carter's arm. 'That's what it amounts to. They're going to start making us dig tunnels in the rock. They've killed nearly all the Indians.'

The man's voice was rising dangerously high. His neighbour stirred in his sleep and told him to shut up.

'I'm sorry,' said Carter. 'I can't take you with me.'

'You selfish bastard. I saved your life just now. Is this your—'

There was a sharp crack as the butt of Carter's gun ended further argument. Jerked from a few inches away it connected flush with the side of the man's jaw and knocked him senseless. The man was right about saving his life, but one life wasn't enough.

Carter waited for any reaction to the noise and moved swiftly to the doorway. The moon was about to disappear behind a bank of cloud. He calculated that he had about thirty seconds to reach the wire before it reappeared. Listening carefully for any unusual sound he scanned the surrounding huts, hoping desperately that the deranged man had been dissuaded from any further roaming. The moon dimmed and was soon extinguished. Behind him he could hear the American pilot begin to groan as he came round. It was time to go.

Carter sprinted for the wire, keeping as low as he could, and sprawled full-length before it like a pinch-hitter stealing a base. He listened again, then quickly changed his position and wriggled under the wire. Out with the knife and the extending rods were released as the moon reappeared. He held them against the Mills gun and crawled back across the agonizing stubble of severed stalks to the temporary safety of the undergrowth. He felt physically and mentally exhausted. The news about Green had dealt a body-blow. What the hell were they going to do now? He gave the bird-call signal for Sula to return and began to fold the wire expanders prior to replacing them in his pocket. How were they going to position the explosives on Matupi, short of tipping them over the edge of the crater?

Sula appeared through the undergrowth. The look of anticipation on her face quickly turned to one of disappointment when she saw that he was alone. He beckoned to her to follow and they retired into the bush. Once confident that they were out of earshot of the camp, he turned and faced her.

'Green wasn't there. There's a strong chance that he's been executed. Have you heard of a place called the pit?'

Sula shook her head. 'There are places like that everywhere.' Her voice faltered. 'You remember my father?'

'Yes,' said Carter. 'I'm sorry.' With so many deaths it was easy to forget one. Not excusable, but easy. 'Apparently there's a track over by the corner of the camp. We'd better take a look and see if we can find it.'

She nodded and started to pick her way through the dark forest. Carter blundered behind her wondering whether she had a different kind of eyes to the rest of humanity. She ducked and weaved past creepers and obstructing branches while he diverted them with his head. She walked on a carpet, he on a mattress of seared twigs that exploded like shots with every step he took.

Around them, unseen creatures rustled and slithered away into the protective darkness. After a quarter of an hour, the jungle lightened on either side and he looked up to see a corridor of stars far above his head. The ground was soft and pitted. He risked shining his flashlight quickly at ground level and saw the unmistakable prints of heavy-duty tyres. They had come to the track.

Now the going was easy, their path illuminated by clumps of glow-worms and clouds of fireflies that danced in the air like miniature firework displays.

Suddenly Sula paused and sniffed. Carter strained his nostrils. There was always a sweet smell of decay in the jungle but on this occasion the air was larded with a stronger, more bitter odour. The smell of death. Carter steeled himself and pressed forward warily. Nothing seen at the prison camp had suggested that a Japanese execution ground would be a place for the squeamish.

After they had walked along the track for two hundred yards, a faint glow showed ahead. This grew in intensity as they approached until a single lantern could be seen hanging among the trees. The smell there was overpowering.

Sula moved forward stealthily, gliding from tree to tree. Carter followed her, a hard knot of tension building up behind his ribs. When they were within twenty yards of the lantern Sula stopped and motioned towards the ground. Carter sank down on one knee and listened. At first he thought he was listening to a human being moaning in pain. Then he realized that the sound was a low, tuneless dirge not unlike a monk's incantation. It came from a single throat within a stone's throw of them. Carter started to crawl forward.

The lantern illuminated a small clearing, the ground muddy and churned by turning lorries. At one side was a crude shelter of palm leaves supported by a framework of saplings. In the centre of the clearing hung a man. He was trussed with his knees against his chest and his wrists bound round his shins. He was suspended by his ankles, his head lolling down, a splash of blood at the temple. The rope from which he hung was looped over two horizontal poles lashed to facing uprights. The ends of the two poles overlapped slightly so that it required only a slight movement from the man to work himself free from one pole and impose all his weight on the other. The poles were already bent dramatically and it was clear that one alone would not support him. If he dropped it would be into the mouth of the pit above which he was now dangling. The man's face was unrecognizable under a mask of flies. At first glance he appeared to be dead but as Carter watched in horror he shook his head to rid himself of the tormenting insects and the rope slipped another half-inch towards the end of the pole.

From the pit came a noise like a submerged beehive. A throbbing, reverberating hum. The stench of rotting flesh made the senses swoon with revulsion. To and from the maw streamed a moving column of insects, spiralling up like an incipient tornado or spilling over its edge as if sucked into a black drain. They in turn attracted bats and small owls so that the air was full of squeaks and screeches and the beating of a myriad of wings. Disjointed shapes fluttered and swirled like cinders over a bonfire.

To Carter, the scene was like an engraving of purgatory. The horror he felt was tinged with fear and awe. He did not know that he was watching a refinement of the *ana-tsurushi*—the hanging-in-the-pit—a method of torture employed by the Japs to make sixteenth-century Christian martyrs recant their faith.

Carter shrank back as another figure came into the light. A Jap soldier with a rifle slung over his shoulder. For a moment the long bayonet bisected the light of the lamp. It was the Jap who was making the noise. A kind of desiccated humming that might have borrowed its burden from the noise the insects were making. He was circling the pit and singing to himself. Suddenly his leg jerked forward and he gave a little dancing skip. Carter remembered. This was the guard who had been patrolling the wire on his first visit. On that occasion, Carter had felt a certain sympathy for the man. Now he viewed him as a creature from a different world.

Carter looked back to the hanging man and understood the cruel reason for the wound on his temple. A vein had been severed to provide some outlet for the blood, and to prevent the victim finding release in unconsciousness and too easy a death.

He winced as the man twisted slightly on the rope and the light glistened on the black coils of flies around his nostrils, eyes and mouth. The Jap was talking to the man now. Talking and singing snatches of a tuneless melody. His movements were unsteady and disjointed, and it dawned on Carter that he was drunk. As if to confirm the fact, the Jap bent down and rose with an earthenware vessel that he raised to his mouth and swilled greedily. So greedily that he lost his balance, staggered backwards and nearly dropped his rifle. . . . This act of clumsiness made him furious and he shouted at the figure on the rope as if blaming him. A groan was the trussed man's only reply. This seemed to act as a further goad. The Jap seized his rifle in the port position and passed it threateningly below the man's face.

Carter looked about him desperately. Were there any more Japs in the neighbourhood? By the time they had checked, the man under torture would be dead. Even now the Jap was reaching towards the support poles with the tip of his bayonet. Carter put down his Mills gun silently and slid out his knife. The Jap jabbed at one of the poles and missed. Carter came up behind him fast, but the Jap heard his footfall and started to swing round. He had half-turned when Carter caught him round the head and pulled him backwards. He bit Carter's arm but was held tight against his chest, still clinging to the rifle. The knife went into the side underneath the right arm and glanced off a rib. The Jap gasped in pain and surprise and then bit even deeper. Another blow to the chest struck his breastbone. He dropped his rifle and kicked his legs in the air in a desperate attempt to break Carter's grasp. He was a small man but the knowledge that he was fighting for his life made him writhe and wriggle like a pinned snake. He parried a third blow with his forearm and dug back viciously with his elbow to the pit of Carter's stomach.

Carter dared not loosen his grip around the man's head in case he started screaming. His teeth were almost meeting through Carter's flesh. Carter struck again, and this time the blade went home without striking bone. The Jap's struggles became a series of weak fluttering spasms and then ceased altogether. Carter felt the teeth relax their grip and slowly began to lower the dead weight of the Jap towards the ground. The fight that the little man had put up amazed him—but it was not over. As Carter released his grip on the knife the Jap seized it, plucked it out of his body and hacked backwards at Carter's testicles. Carter had time to half-turn his hip in self-defence and the force of the blow spent itself against the metal rods in his thigh pocket. The Jap sprawled backwards under the force of the thrust, and before he could move again, Sula had driven his bayonet into his heart. His mouth jerked open but Carter saw the danger and dived to smother the cry with his body. He pressed down with all his weight and slid his hands under his chest to meet around the Jap's throat. Then he squeezed, forcing his fingers deep into the windpipe. There was no tremor or movement but he did not release his grip until he was certain that the man was dead. He rolled to one side and rose unsteadily to his feet, breathless but at the same time loathe to take in any of the contaminated air that pervaded the clearing. At his feet, the Jap's teeth were a snarl that defied even death. Carter looked down at him with hate yet, at the same time, grudging admiration. Nobody could equal the Japs for sadism. Few came near equalling them for raw courage.

Carter's need for air was so great and the stench so nauseating that he took a few steps into the jungle and grabbed a handful of humus to hold before his face whilst he breathed. As he recovered he listened for any sound that might indicate that the struggle had been overheard. The throbbing of insects had been replaced by an eerie silence but now it began to build up again. The ratchety croak of a tree frog rattled out from a nearby cedar and distant cousins in the swamps fluted and belched. The sounds of a jungle night returned to normal. From the direction of the prison camp there was no noise.

Carter moved swiftly to the side of the pit and shone his torch in the man's face. One eye opened and blinked beneath its covering of flies. Carter twisted his head and recognized Green, his face a ghastly swollen grey in the faint glow of the torch.

'Harry,' he called softly. 'We've come for you. Hang on.'

There was a mild explosion from the suspended figure. 'I don't have much fucking alternative, do I?' The rope edged to within a hair's-breadth of the end of one of the poles.

Sula called softly and drew Carter's attention to a long pole leaning against the thatched shelter. They ran towards it and brought it back to the edge of the pit. The stench of death clung to it like a skin. Carter gestured Sula to the opposite side of the pit, near one of the uprights, and raised the heavy pole to his shoulder. Taking a deep breath and steadying his nerves, he began to edge it forward. When he reached the stretched triangle of rope, he slowly inched the pole through the middle. The balance began to shift as the pole reached out farther and the tip suddenly began to drop bringing the wood dangerously close to the rope.

Carter shifted his stance and felt the sweat dripping off his forehead. Sula clung to the upright and stretched out her hand. Her finger-tips brushed the end of the pole and then she began to guide it towards her side. It was nearly over her shoulder when Green flinched and the rope slipped the end of one of the transversals and snapped away from the other end with a noise like a bow being fired. Carter clung on desperately but Sula's end of the pole was torn from her grasp and bounded on the edge of the pit. Green cried out in terror and swung against the side. For a second it seemed that he was to drop but the end of the pole came to a rest two inches away from disaster. Sula dropped to her knees and bent down to grab the rope. Whilst she clung on, Carter slowly lowered his end of the pole to the ground. It was now lying across the hole with Green dangling against one wall. Carter ran round the pit to Sula and together they hauled Green to safety. Sula produced her knife and moved to cut his bonds.

'No!' Carter seized her wrist. 'Untie him.'

Sula looked puzzled. 'Why?'

'Because we're going to need the rope.'

Green groaned. 'Thank God you got here.'

He snorted violently and a blow-fly reluctantly emerged from a nostril. Sula wiped his face and then set to picking apart the knots that had cut deep into his flesh. When she released his legs, Green cried out in pain as he tried to straighten them.

Carter massaged the ankles hard. 'You'll be OK once we get the circulation moving.'

He spoke with a confidence he did not feel. Green might, in

fact, be crippled. If he was, there was no chance that they would be able to carry him up the side of Matupi in the space of three hours. He began to manipulate Green's legs as Sula started on his wrists.

'How long have you been like that, Harry?'

'Since this evening. It's the second time you've saved my life today.' He broke off to clear his nostrils and spit noisily. 'They had me down in the jail. Interrogation. They'd have killed me. Then some colonel strides in—nasty little one-eyed bastard—and they all start panicking. I didn't understand much but enough to know that a party had been put ashore. They forgot about me after that. Chucked me in a cell till they brought me back here.' He groaned again and closed his eyes. 'Bloody head's like a sockful of crickets.'

'How did you get in trouble?' asked Carter.

'Some might call it stealing,' said Green, his eyes still closed. 'I knew I had to build myself up a bit to be any good to you. I needed some extra grub so I took a few risks when I was working in the docks. Slashing open rice bags, that kind of thing. In the end I helped myself to a guard's dinner.' He grimaced with pain as he tried to move his freshly released arms. 'He took a poor view of it. "Sabotaging the Japanese war effort." That's how it was translated to me.'

Carter pulled the rope away from Green's body.

'Don't worry, Harry. With any luck you're soon going to be doing a lot more sabotaging. Now, can you get your shorts off by yourself?'

'My shorts? Why?' Green's voice was incredulous.

'You're going to change clothes with the Nip.'

He did not wait for a reply but started stripping the uniform from the dead Jap. The open mouth still grinned up at him although the corpse was beginning to stiffen.

'I'm not going to wear that filthy little sod's uniform.' Green suddenly sounded very British.

Carter did not pause to argue. 'Give me your shorts.'

Green hesitated and Carter nodded to Sula. Green's shorts were down to his ankles before he could deliver another protest. Carter pulled off the Jap's boots and looked at Green's bare feet.

The boots were going to be a tight fit but everything else seemed all right. Green did not have the physique of a football player, even when he wasn't half-starved.

Carter pulled the shorts onto the Jap and tied them round his waist. Playing-dresser to a corpse was not an experience he would ever want to repeat. Even though the man was now dead the memory of his ferocity prompted wary respect. Carter would not have been totally surprised if a limp hand had suddenly stiffened and lunged for his throat. Carter smeared grime on the body and folded the knees to the chest.

Green was sitting up now and watching him in subdued amazement.

'What are you doing?'

Carter started tying the wrists to the shins. The Jap's head was lolling against his shoulder like that of a sleeping baby.

'I'm trying to save a few hundred lives.'

He called to Sula and told her to keep watch up the track. There was no certainty that another guard might not arrive to relieve his comrade.

Green waited until Sula had gone and then started to pull on the trousers that had rested modestly on his lap whilst she was present.

'Where's Andrew Hudson?'

'Waiting for us on Matupi, I hope.'

'Thank God. I thought they might have got him. Damn beautiful girl you've found there. Great asset.'

Carter had to smile. 'I'm glad you can still notice things like that. Try to stand up.'

Green collapsed immediately.

'Legs?'

'Legs and head. It's like a snowstorm when I move.'

'It'll get better. I'll walk you around in a moment.'

Carter took a loop from one of the Jap's ankles and let it out to the length by which Green had been hanging. He then secured the rope round both ankles. The Jap was now folded up in a foetal position exactly as Green had been, his head almost resting on his knees. Carter smeared more dirt on his back and stood up. This was the moment he had been dreading. Ever since coming to the pit he had avoided looking into it. The dense cloud of flies was enough. The carpet of beetles that crunched underfoot at its edge. The awful choking stench.

Taking the torch and trying to form a seal at the back of his throat, he approached the pit and looked down. Twenty feet below the ground seemed to be trembling. A persistent undulation like the sea. Carter saw that he was looking at a moving pall of maggots. They danced and jiggled in a stew of decomposing bodies that stretched from wall to wall. With a shock of recognition, Carter saw the handsome, wasted face of the Indian half-submerged in a mulch of human detritus.

Carter turned away, gagging. He crossed to the Jap and lifted him up by the loop of rope sprouting from his ankles. He dragged him forward, head bumping along the ground, to the edge of the pit and hoisted him up with one hand underneath the bent knees. Summoning up all his strength, he heaved him head downward, into the centre of the pit. There was a sound like the breaking of egg shells and when Carter shone his torch downwards, the Jap's head and shoulders were half-buried between two other corpses. Obscene, gaseous bubbles broke the surface, and the smell that welled up made his stomach bolt for his mouth. Carter checked that the tell-tale rope trailing away from the ankles was clearly visible and turned away.

Green was struggling with his boots, unable to bend forward. Carter helped him and was heartened to see that his body did appear to have more flesh on it than at the time of the first visit. Perhaps the fattening programme had been marginally successful. He finished tying the laces and made the bird-call whistle for Sula to return. Green rose unsteadily to his feet while Carter retrieved his knife and found the Jap's cap and rifle. He handed over the cap.

'I'll carry the rifle for a while.'

Green looked down at himself with repugnance. 'I can feel the vermin crawling all over me already.'

Carter clapped him on the shoulder. 'That's the least of your worries. Try walking.'

Green took a few unsteady paces and started to rub his arms. 'I'll be all right after a couple of miles.'

Carter grinned. 'OK.'

When Sula returned they replaced the pole and took a last look round. Carter found the jar that the Jap had been drinking from and sniffed it. It was clearly some local rot-gut either bought or stolen from the natives. Carter poured it away behind a tree and left the empty jar clearly visible near the shelter.

'Right,' he said. 'Matupi.'

They had taken a dozen steps through the jungle when Green stopped and supported himself with his arm against a tree. Carter closed with him anxiously.

'What's that smell?' said Green.

Carter felt relieved. 'Air,' he said.

22

Hudson squatted in the darkness and listened to the rain splashing off the leaves. It had started at about nine. A continuous, heavy, tropical downpour turning the pathways into rivulets. That was nearly two hours ago. Carter and Sula were almost an hour late. And Green? Even if they had succeeded in getting him out of the prison camp, it was difficult to imagine worse conditions for a wasted fifty-year-old to travel in. Even the normally sure-footed carriers had been slipping and sliding on the steep glass-like slopes. Sometimes the water coming down had been over their ankles.

The carriers were cold and beginning to grumble. Twice it had been necessary to hide from Jap patrols and the disruption of their normal walking rhythm plus their struggling with the heavy loads had begun to sap their strength. They were also frightened. Frightened of the Japs who they knew would show them no mercy if they were caught carrying loads for the enemy. Frightened also of the mountain. To them, Matupi was a holy place and the volcano a god who sometimes spoke out angrily to the human lice that nested in his hair.

Every generation had passed on stories of eruptions to the next. Every movement of the mountain was monitored and interpreted. Joe had reported that the rain was Matupi's tears because the white men were coming to harm him. Such superstition was powerful and irrefutable; Hudson did not know how long he could fight against it. It was useless talking about the evil done by the Japs and the necessity of overthrowing them. Before the Japs there had been the Australians, and before them the Germans. They were *tabauda*—masters—but Matupi was the king. He never varied his position against the skyline. His whims were far more terrifying than anything perpetrated by the Germans or the Japs.

The rain continued to drum down. Hudson shivered as the cold and fever racked his body. Why were the Japs out in such force? Were they still looking for them? If not, they had certainly stepped up their activities since the first visit to the prison camp when there had been no evidence of inland patrolling. Hudson considered his best course of action. It was very possible that Carter and Sula were either dead or captured. A hundred things could have gone wrong on the way to and at the prison camp. He would give them until midnight and then plant the explosive at a point of his own choosing near the summit, set the fuses and retire.

'*Tabauda.*'

Joe appeared at his side to say that one of the carriers who had injured his leg in a fall was complaining and demanding to return to his village. He was a bad influence on the others and Joe thought that they ought to let him go. He, Joe, could carry the load. Hudson disagreed. If they let one go, then the others would want to go. There was also the danger that another fall or a desertion would force them to jettison a load—a tenth of their explosive potential. Detonating the full thousand pounds might be vital if they were unable to find the tunnel.

Hudson gave his decision and explained the reasons for it. He also described the action to be taken if the second party did not arrive by midnight. Joe received his orders without comment and withdrew into the glistening foliage. Minutes passed and the rain did not slacken in intensity. The sound of it trickling down the mountainside became a subdued roar as sun-baked fissures turned into streams and then cataracts. Hudson pricked up his ears as he heard the rumble of a small landslide caused where the sudden rains had undermined a stretch of mountainside and uprooted a few trees. He hoped it was not a path that they were due to take. He hoped also that the carriers would not be reading their own interpretations into the sound: the mountain is angry and is telling us to return.

Hudson's clothes stuck uncomfortably to his smarting skin, and the cold rain awoke old wounds and memories. It was the rain that had brought on the fever from which Marjory had died.

He wondered why he had stayed on after that. He had never intended to; just long enough to sell up and then it was going to be back to Aussie. But no purchaser had appeared immediately and so he had thrown himself into the store, to give himself an outlet for his grief and make the business a more valuable asset. As the months passed, the wound had begun to heal; by the time he bought the plantation he knew that he was not going to leave after all. He lived alone, but it was a life that suited him. Until the Japs came.

The triple screech of a cockatoo snapped Hudson back to the present. 'Kwi-kwi-kwi!' The sound came again and Joe materialized at his side, his eyes agleam with hope. Hudson jerked his head forward; Joe listened for a second and then glided into the shadows. A worrying length of time passed and the dark shapes of bushes and creepers swayed and shimmied before the buffeting of the rain. It was impossible to hear any movement further than a few feet away. A Jap patrol could arrive on top of them without being detected. Suddenly, the foliage parted and Joe's glistening body appeared, followed by Carter.

Hudson waited and then gripped Carter's hand.

'What happened? Where are the others?'

'Prepare yourself for a shock,' said Carter.

He whistled softly and Sula appeared, guiding a Jap soldier who had difficulty in keeping his footing. Hudson peered forward incredulously and was amazed to recognize Green beneath the forage cap.

Green seemed unaware that his appearance might be considered unusual. He stretched out a tired hand and sank gratefully onto the muddy ground.

'Sorry to hold you up, Andrew. Bit out of training.'

'I thought you'd signed on for the Emperor,' said Hudson. 'Don't apologize. It's bloody marvellous that you got here at all.'

'You don't know how marvellous,' said Carter. He began to give a quick run-down of the events at the prison camp.

Green lay on the ground, impervious to all that was being said. The rain beat down and a small rivulet of water was forced to divert itself round his body. His eyes were closed but there was a determined set to his jaw and the corners of his mouth were turned up.

The two Jap soldiers approached the clearing and flashed their torches.

'Where is he?' asked the first.

'He is crazy,' said the second. 'You wait. He will probably come leaping out on us.'

He started waving his torch round the trees and calling out.

'Show yourself, Soryu. Don't be a fool.'

The first man shone his torch towards the pit and up at the empty poles.

'The old thief didn't last long.'

He pinched his nostrils and advanced to look down into the pit. The body lay hunched up in the writhing slime like an embryo tipped out of an eggshell. The rope trailed from its ankles. 'Agh!'

The first Jap cried out in fear as his comrade gripped his arms and pretended to thrust him forward. 'You slug! I thought you were Soryu.'

'Soryu would probably have pushed you in. Where is the stupid fool?'

'Turn off your torch.'

'Why?'

'Do as I say and you will see.'

The torch was turned off and a faint glow of phosphorescent light hung below the mouth of the pit.

'That is the beetles.'

'No. It is a chemical reaction. All bodies are made of chemicals.'

The second Jap switched on his torch. He did not want to get involved in a scientific conversation. He hawked up the contents of his throat and spat.

'This place smells like all the arseholes in the world.'

The first Jap agreed with him and shone his torch. An exclamation of discovery came from the back of his throat. He hurried towards one of the trees surrounding the clearing and picked up an earthenware jar. He sniffed it and grimaced.

'Jungle juice.'

The second Jap took the empty jar, sniffed and shook it towards the back of his hand. A few drops sprinkled down and turned the skin cold. He sniffed again and recognized the fermented juice of mashed paw-paw, which had been mixed with sugar and distilled in an oil-drum still. The practice was illegal but much indulged in by Japanese soldiers who preferred insensibility to boredom.

The second Jap held up the jar and shone his torch into it. The recent presence of liquid could be detected to a line just below the rim. He whistled through his teeth.

'If he drank all this he may be gone for days.'

'For ever,' said his companion.

Hudson watched the carriers forming up with their loads, and for the first time he felt a genuine sense of excitement. Suddenly it was within their grasp: what had first seemed like a scheme conceived by optimism out of insanity now had a real chance of succeeding. All that was necessary was for Green to find the tunnel. That, and something that had been conspicuously lacking in the operation so far—luck.

The first evidence of a change of fortune came when it stopped raining: Matupi had dried her tears. Hudson resisted drawing any allusions before the eyes of the carriers. That would only make them suspicious and cause them to ponder how the *tabauda* was manipulating the truth to serve his own ends. Best keep to a motivation that was easily understood and unfailingly successful. Three times the normal rate for the job. He knew that it was sheer human greed that kept the carriers placing one foot precariously in front of the other.

Sula rolled the cloak of bark that she had prepared for herself and dusted the water from her breasts. The simple ingenuousness of the act caught Hudson's eye and enchanted him. She was a beautiful girl, and he was not so ancient that he did not appreciate it. He smiled as he remembered what the New Guinea old-timers said: 'There are two types of Islanders. Those who sleep with native girls—and liars.'

Carter watched the carriers lifting the explosives onto their heads. Thin shafts of moonlight had been quick to break through the lowering clouds. There was a danger that the carriers would start taking their loads for granted and forget that they were carrying something so potent that it could blow them to powder. Maybe it was because the menace of the white bags was concealed beneath a packaging of palm leaves. It looked like any other load that could be dropped with comparative impunity. Joe wove amongst the carriers like a sheepdog. A sharp word here, the condition of a load checked there, a word of encouragement where it was needed. These were his people and he felt doubly responsible for them. Any failure would reflect on him both as a man and as the son of a chief.

Green's eyes probed the darkness. Now that the sky was opening he could look up to the summit and down towards the airfield. He could remember it when it was a peacetime strip with a few ancient Lockheeds taking care of the inter-island traffic and a crowd of gawping natives round the door of the terminal. The local matrons had decided that flowers and shrubs should be planted outside the entrance to enhance the image of the tin-pot town to newcomers.

Green took a breath of the cold air and shivered. His legs were turning to jelly—he only hoped that they would not suddenly collapse under him. There was nothing he could do about it: strength was ebbing out of them as if he were running in a race. There came a time when there seemed to be nothing between you and the ground.

'OK?' There was an edge of worry in Carter's murmured question that he could understand.

'Fine. We have to follow this track round towards the back of the mountain. We split off to the right when we get our first glimpse of the scree.' *If* we get it, he thought to himself as he spoke. How many years had it been since he was last up here? Certainly a year before the Jap invasion. And he had never seen the volcano at night—except out of a pub window. He smiled to himself. That was the spirit. You had to look on the bright side. If he could just lead them to the tunnel he would be satisfied. There had been talk about getting away on a submarine after the explosion, but he had not really listened. Whether the Japs believed he was dead or not, there was no point in struggling back to the camp. But a submarine? That was like waking from a drugged sleep to find that not only was it Christmas Day but someone had filled your stocking with gold bars.

'We'll lead the way,' said Carter. 'Tug my shirt when you want to rest.'

Carter and Green moved at the head of the convoy with Joe in attendance, in case it was necessary to scout ahead. Then came the ten carriers and Hudson behind. If any bearer wanted to desert he had to go past Hudson or Carter or dive into the bush. Sula stayed two hundred yards in the rear in case the Japs came up fast. The pace of the convoy had been slow even before Green arrived.

The path began to veer to the right. Green was relieved to look up and see a distant patch of scree where the jungle began to lose its fingerhold on the clinker-strewn slopes of the volcano. A few yards ahead a well-used path plunged over the lip and down the mountainside. Green congratulated himself. So far so good.

As they approached the intersection there was a discontented murmur from the carriers. One of them began to hobble and said that he could not go on. It was the man with the stoved-in head. Carter stepped forward and learned that the man was saying that his village lay down the track and that he had a lame foot and could not go on. Other carriers said that they wished to go no further. Carter looked and could see where the village lay by some pinpoints of light on a distant ridge. There was a fierce argument conducted in whispers. Hudson stepped in to settle the matter by offering a slight increase in the reward already promised, mingled with threats of what he would persuade Baka to do to any man who reneged. Joe looked at the ringleader as if he would like to kill him, but the man's look of surly resentment as he took up his load offered no guarantee of his future reliability. Carter could understand the look of strain that now permanently inhabited Hudson's face. They were sitting on a powder keg in more ways than one.

After a few hundred yards the path was blocked by the remains of a recent landslide. A giant mole-hole of glistening earth from which rose tree roots projected. The carriers immediately began to murmur and Hudson cursed under his breath. Not only would it be difficult to cross this obstacle but their tracks would be clearly visible to any Jap patrol.

Joe wasted no time but waded into the soft earth and began to pick his way round and over obstacles. The carriers watched apprehensively until he was swallowed up by the darkness. After a few minutes had passed there was a crashing noise like a sapling falling in the forest and a patter of earth and debris dying away down the slope. Hudson looked at Carter without saying anything and then at his watch. They were behind schedule and falling further behind with every second.

Four minutes later, Joe returned. 'Behind time 'e good fella.'

'It gets better,' said Hudson.

'I've heard that before,' said Carter.

Hudson detailed Carter and Green to accompany Joe and began to chivvy the carriers. Green was sandwiched between Carter and Joe and received help from each as he panted over the obstacles, sometimes up to the waist in wet earth.

'Are you OK?' asked Carter as he sprawled across the trunk of a fallen redwood.

Green nodded grimly. 'You need my friend Errol Flynn for this number. On the evidence of the films I've seen he's stood up a bit better than I have.'

'You're doing great,' said Carter.

'Dawn Patrol,' said Green.

'What?' Carter sank down behind the tree, pulling Green with him.

Green looked at him in astonishment. 'It was one of his films. Came out to Rabaul just before the Japs. I thought he was a better actor when he was in New Guinea.'

'Save your breath,' urged Carter.

'He was a damn good tennis player, though,' mused Green. 'Mind you, you had to be if you turned up on court in a pair of white jodphurs.'

Carter pressed his finger to his lips. 'The Japs, Harry!'

'Sorry.' Green remained silent for a few seconds and then leaned forward urgently as Carter started to move. 'Did I tell you about the time I knocked him down?'

'So help me, I'll knock you down if you don't shut up,' said Carter.

He moved on before Green could speak.

Behind the carriers, Hudson watched anxiously, as the men struggled to keep a foothold. He felt a buried branch stir beneath his feet and with it a tremor ran through the newly stirred earth. It would need no more than a misplaced foot to start the slide off again. If Matupi generated a full-scale tremor then the whole party might be swept away.

Ahead of him a load went down and rolled a few feet down the hillside before coming to a rest against a spray of half-buried foliage, where it perched precariously. Hudson held his breath. It only needed a wet branch to penetrate one of the bags and they would be jostling each other in a line before their Maker.

He told the other porters to go on and started down the hillside with the boy who had dropped the load. It took him only a couple of steps to know that the going was treacherous. Earth began to drain away beneath his feet with the pull of a powerful tide. The boy cried out in fear and tried to scramble back up the mountain, which made matters worse. Hudson stood what firm ground there was beneath his feet and spoke with a calm he did not feel.

By bending his knees into the slope he could exert enough leverage to maintain his position. He called to the boy to do the same and slowly the slide became a trickle that could be heard pitter-pattering away against the jungle hundreds of feet below. Still leaning in, he began to edge downwards, inch by difficult inch. The earth started moving again but this time it stopped when he did. Encouraged by what he saw, the boy began to descend until he was level with Hudson. Together they approached the load from opposite sides and began to sidestep back up the slope, dragging it between them. Once, Hudson felt his foothold begin to sag alarmingly but after a quick shuffle he found firmer ground. Eventually they regained their original position and the carrier was able to lift his load and scramble on his way.

Hudson heard something and turned in alarm. It was Sula who had caught up with them. She was wearing the bark cloak that she had fashioned to keep off the rain and her normally springy hair was bedraggled and clinging close to her gleaming face. The fine design of her bone structure was even more evident. She looked into his face anxiously. On an impulse he took her hand and squeezed it.

'It's all right,' he whispered. 'Everything under control.'

She smiled, showing her white teeth, and returned the pressure on his hand before going back down the track. Hudson looked after her for a few seconds before starting to scramble through the roots. Just a few years younger and he might be offering Carter some competition.

Now the going became tough enough to silence even Green. He who had spoken continuously with what men took to be the babblings due to a bout of malarial fever could only groan and wheeze under Carter's worried eye as the mountain reared up before them like a wall. The further round the side of the volcano they went, the thicker became the vegetation. Bush knives were needed on even established paths. At this altitude mosquitoes ceased to be a problem but leeches thrived. The thighs of the porters were covered in them, looking like weal marks in the darkness.

'How much further?' asked Carter.

Green stopped and lent against his rifle as if it was a shepherd's crook. He seemed at the last extremities of exhaustion.

'Why? Are you getting tired?' he asked.

Carter controlled himself. 'Just thinking about you,' he said.

'I'm fine,' said Green. 'Getting my second wind.'

His thin body was racked by a violent spasm of coughing and for a second Carter thought he was going to fall. Then he pulled himself erect and took a firm grip on his rifle just below the muzzle.

'Right-o. Let's push on. We've got a way to go yet. There should be a zig-zag path up here on the right. Any chance of a spot of light on the subject? I remember there used to be a rather oddly shaped rock opposite it.'

'Wait for the moon,' said Carter. He could not help being sceptical of Green. Even if Joe had been leading the way he would have been worried. The idea that an old Limey who had once come up here looking for butterflies should be able to find his way around at night was too much to swallow.

'Ah, I think this is it.' Green parted some grass by the side of the road. 'That torch please.'

The three words were uttered with an unexpected firmness that did not brook refusal. Carter shone his torch and saw to his amazement that there *was* a curiously shaped boulder lunging out of the undergrowth.

'I have a remarkable visual memory,' said Green. 'Don't like to sound conceited, but it's true. If you drove me anywhere in a car I should always find my way back.' He crossed the path and started peering into the undergrowth. 'Here it is. It gets a bit hairy from now on.'

Green did not exaggerate. The path went straight up the side of the mountain and was no more than a series of vertical stepping-stones. It was necessary to bring the knee up to chest level at each step. Carter offered to take Green's rifle, but he refused, saying that he was using it as a staff. Carter wondered how he could keep going. The climb must be pulling the sinews out of their sockets. Perhaps working in the docks had kept him in some kind of physical condition despite the starvation rations.

A large boulder jutted out from the mountain and Carter stood on its edge and looked up. Just visible by the fitful light of the moon was the rim of the volcano. He felt a start of excitement—they really were almost there! After all that they had been through it did not seem possible that there could actually be an end to this purgatory.

Behind, the carriers toiled on, their knotted muscles glistening and their eyes wide with concentration and fear. A misplaced step here could cost them their lives no matter what load they were carrying.

On the path, Hudson waited and worried. The moonlight was a two-edged weapon. It made it easier for them to see—and be seen. Looking towards the summit he could pick out places where the vegetation was beginning to be divided by outcrops of volcanic rock and shale which afforded less cover than they had enjoyed so far. The tunnel had to be close.

There was also the noise. Fourteen people and ten heavy loads could not travel silently under these conditions. If the Japs had ventured this high they would surely hear them.

Carter had climbed ahead when Green called softly up to him. 'Hold on. I think it's around here somewhere.'

They were entering a strange region where a grey-green moss covered every surface like an all-reaching shroud. It hung down from trees and creepers and made footholds difficult to judge. What seemed like solid ground could turn out to be a crevice between two rocks covered by the treacherous lichen. The risk of a fatal error by the carriers was now quadrupled.

Carter called a halt and waited for Green to find his bearings. He looked hopefully at Joe, who shook his head. Apart from the moss, this scoop of vegetation on a steep mountainside had no easily identifiable feature to render it different from any other spot they had paused at. Green obviously thought differently. He scrambled up to Carter's side and looked down to where he had been standing.

'This is definitely it,' he said. 'I can see the Birdwing as if it was yesterday.'

'You said it was a Grass Yellow when you first talked to us,' said Carter.

Green looked annoyed. 'Are you sure?'

'Positive,' said Carter. He could not resist adding, 'I have a remarkable verbal memory.'

If the shaft struck home, Green showed no sign of it. He started to ease himself down the way he had come. Carter followed, giving assistance where he could. On the rocks, the carriers put down their loads and waited in grudging silence.

'It's very annoying,' said Green as if he had misplaced a collar stud. 'I know it's around here.' He moved into the waist-high vegetation and prodded at the lichen-hung mountainside with his bayonet. There was the unmistakable sound of steel meeting rock. Carter scrambled down from the rock and moved to Green's side. He was becoming exasperated.

'There must be a million places on the mountain that look exactly like this.'

He struck contemptuously at the moss and suddenly felt his fist travelling through space. Thrown off balance, he stepped forward and the ground disappeared beneath his feet. For what seemed like an eternity he hung in space and then met a hard, unyielding surface that drove his knees towards his face and sent him sprawling backwards with the wind temporarily knocked out of him. He felt about him gingerly in the pitch darkness and looked up to see Green's face silhouetted against the grey sky.

'Well done, old chap,' said Green. 'You've found it.'

23

Carter nursed an aching elbow that felt as if it had been struck by lightning and fumbled for his torch. The most eerie thing about the darkness was that it was warm. The inside of caves in his experience had always been cool. Not only cool but actually cold and clammy. There was no scent of moisture in this air—it could have come rolling in enveloping waves from a freshly opened oven. He pressed the button and a dim circle of light revealed that he had fallen onto a table of rain-spattered rock that sloped down to a narrow opening like the mouth of a funnel. The rock rose steeply above his head, and water was still dripping from the recent storm. Where it had formed small pools on the cave floor, the surface was steaming as the heat evaporated it. A sudden shape invaded the air, and a bat with a wingspan like an eagle swooped down and under the rock, delivering an admonishing squeak.

Carter looked at the tunnel. He had been expecting something much larger. A hole the size of a subway tunnel into which an army might march. He picked himself up and went forward to shine the torch under the rock overhang. The tunnel opened up on the other side but was still not high enough for a man to walk upright. What was noticeable was the smell that prickled his nostrils. The acrid smell of sulphur wrapped in a simoom.

'Are you all right? You came rather a cropper.'

Carter detected a slight edge of triumph in Green's remark but swallowed his irritation. The success of the operation was the important thing. He could not afford to be distracted.

'I'm fine.'

He started to shine his torch at footholds in the rock.

'Tell Hudson we've found it and get the boys to start lowering the stuff down.'

'Right-o.'

Green's head disappeared and Carter considered making a preliminary sortie into the tunnel. He decided against it in the light of the previous consequences of private initiatives. Better to wait for the others.

After a few minutes he began to wonder where the others were. Impatiently, he climbed to the mouth of the cave and found Hudson and Joe involved in a bitter dispute with the carriers. All of them were refusing to go any further. In particular, the man with the cleft head was gesticulating so that his belly wobbled like the folds of a concertina. He kept pointing to his foot and turning the sole upwards as if to indicate that he was carrying a thorn. The other carriers looked warily at the mouth of the cave as if expecting a demon to emerge from it.

Joe was determined that his fellow tribesmen should carry the explosives into the tunnel and fulfil their contract. The carriers were adamant that they would not. The spirits of the mountain would strike them down if they entered Matupi's belly. Just to walk on his skin was to invite trouble.

Hudson was certain that it was the man with the cleft head who was causing all the trouble. A self-appointed spokesman, he did most of the talking while the others merely nodded. Now that the loads were outside the cave they could do without him. The longer they stood here, the greater the risk of the Japs stumbling across them. To be caught a few yards from triumph would be tragic.

Hudson took off his pack and removed enough salt and tobacco for one man. He gave it to the trouble-maker, thanked him for his efforts and, expressing the wish that his leg would soon be perfectly recovered, sent him on his way. The man departed almost unwillingly, as if suspicious that he was being forced to miss out on something. His followers looked at each other for a new spokesman and then, when none was forthcoming, followed Joe's lead and started moving the explosives to the lip of the cave.

Ropes of liana were cut and several men scrambled down into the cave to receive the loads as they were lowered. Carter watched the bulky shapes coming down towards him and thought back to the transfer operation from submarine to tossing dinghy. Had that really been only two days before? Jerry Johnson had been very much alive then. It was a pity that he could not be here to see this moment. Perhaps the moment existed because of him and the sacrifice he had made in the swamps.

Yukichi pulled his waterproof cloak tighter around his shoulders and listened to the spasmodic drip, drip, drip of rain dropping from leaves. The gap between each sound was becoming longer. The heavy rain had stopped over an hour ago and bright moonlight fragmented through the undergrowth. Yukichi was beginning to face up to the fact that he had been wrong. The raiding party had not been planning to assassinate Yamamoto when he took off from the airfield. Perhaps they were not even on the mountain. It was conceivable that they had perished in the swamp. The man whose body they had recovered might have been struggling on by himself after having left his dead comrades. All the planning and deployment of men and materials had been for nothing. Well, not for nothing. The first objective of the operation had been achieved. Yamamoto was alive and safe.

Yukichi yawned. He had now been on the mountain since the Admiral's plane took off. There was no point in waiting in ambush any longer. He would order all units to return to base and place patrolling activities on a pre-alarm footing.

Yukichi looked across the trees to the prospect of distant mountain rising above banks of serene white cloud. He half-closed his eyes and could see the prospect of his homeland in northern Honshu. The forests of pine and sugi, of oaks, maples and keaki. Those scars on the hillside could have concealed a Buddhist temple or the graceful tower of a pagoda. He looked again at the banks of cloud and made up a poem that he would send with his next letter to his wife.

> Now beneath the moon
> Clouds pass like pillow
> I wish my head on one
> My face next to yours

Then there was a tug on the string attached to his ankle. Someone was approaching down the track.

24

After they had crawled beneath the overhang they had to drag the explosives down the passage. The going was hard, and the claustrophobic conditions terrified the carriers. The walls of igneous rock were pitted and calloused, and coated in places with a muddy brown deposit. Carter surmised that the shaft must represent the site of an ancient lateral eruption which had branched off from the central cone by means of this radial dyke. The rocks up which they had climbed to reach the cave opening could have been spewed out at the same time.

'How far in do we want to go?'

Carter's voice echoed before him down the dark corridor. He was still speaking in a hushed whisper, although there was no need for it. No need other than that imposed by the atmosphere of the place. It encouraged sepulchral whispers, like the inside of a church.

'We might as well go the whole hog,' said Hudson. 'The nearer we can get to the middle, the better.'

Another bat squeaked overhead, the shadow of its wing-tips brushing the walls of the corridor. Green shuddered. 'Probably a bloody vampire,' he said.

'A horseshoe bat,' said Hudson. 'You're safe if you're not an insect. There must be a cave around here.'

'I can't believe we've really done it,' said Carter.

'We haven't,' said Hudson. 'Not until we've set the fuses.'

'How about a song?' said Green. 'What do you fancy? Yankee Doodle Dandy, Waltzing Matilda or Rule Britannia?'

'You're incredible, Harry,' said Carter admiringly. 'When I first saw you this evening I thought you were dead.'

'It's my indomitable spirit,' said Green. 'Stood me in good stead in my battle with Flynn. Did I ever tell you about that? It was after the tennis club dance—'

'Do us a favour, Harry,' said Hudson. 'Save the reminiscences for later.' He shone his torch forward. 'Looks as if it's opening out ahead. We'll take a look.'

He motioned to Carter to come with him and adjusted his torch so that it shone on maximum beam. The roof soon lifted above their heads and they came to a cavernous chamber carved by escaping volcanic matter. The floor was deep in foul-smelling bat droppings and bright red eyes glinted down from the ceiling where nursing mothers hung with their young folded in their wing membranes. Carter felt a pang of guilt at the fate in store for them.

It was difficult to be certain, but from the air that was available it seemed that another sill might go off from high in the roof of the chamber. In the corner of the cavern was a floor opening and a drop of about ten feet into another stage of the shaft. The acrid smell was more intense and there was a noise like the magnified beat of a human heart: a rhythmic pumping noise from the bowels of the earth that was both awe-inspiring and frightening.

Hudson turned off his torch and a faint glow was visible at the mouth of the lower tunnel. Carter could see his serious face weighing up the alternatives and trying to come to a decision. To place the explosive in the chamber or press on further towards the heart of the volcano. He turned to Carter.

'Bring the others up. I'm going to take a look.'

Carter returned to the rest of the party and told them about the cavern. The carriers were huddled together, trembling with fear despite the heat, and it was obvious that they could not be expected to go much further. They kept darting longing glances towards the tunnel entrance, and only the presence of Joe's broad frame blocking the way dissuaded them from making a bolt for it, even at the risk of leaving behind their reward.

Sula's breasts glistened enticingly as she leant forward beneath the low roof. She had folded her bark cloak and returned it to her *bilum*, which she carried native-fashion with the string handle round her forehead like a bandeau and the bag on her back.

The last load had been manhandled into the chamber when

the light of Hudson's torch could be seen wavering along the lower shaft. His face appeared above floor level and he shook his head.

'It's amazing. There's a lake of boiling basalt. I can't see the far side of it.'

He appeared more excited than Carter could ever remember. His reaction was one of an explorer not a soldier.

'Should we get the stuff down there?' asked Carter. Unspoken but implicit were the words 'or is it too dangerous?'

Hudson considered for a moment.

'Yes. The first fifty or so feet are difficult but after that we're in the central cone. It's—' he struggled to find the right word, 'fantastic!'

Hudson pulled himself up and addressed the sullen carriers. Their reaction was the opposite of his enthusiasm. More argument followed and they were finally promised categorically that they could return to their village after the next barrier had been passed. Grudgingly, they prepared to carry their loads.

The entrance to the lower shaft was narrow and tortuous, like the bend in an attic staircase. It took two men to manoeuvre each load round, and one pulling and one pushing and lifting to move it down the undulating corridor. The heat was suffocating and the floor littered with small boulders, some fused into the rock, others free-moving with sharp, rasping edges that threatened the bags as they bumped and ground over the floor.

Carter tried to help Joe, who was carrying the load abandoned by the deserting bearer, and was soon reminded that his mauled arm was becoming useless. The pain had subsided to a throbbing ache but the power that could be generated was minimal. He could feel the ache beginning to spread across his shoulder.

Arms aching, eyes watering, legs and sides scraped by rocks, the carriers emerged from the tunnel like corks from a bottle. Carter followed and rubbed his eyes. The sight that met them was truly amazing. Below a shore of strangely shaped, petrified lava was a smooth-sided basin dropping to a lake of molten matter, hissing and steaming like the surface of a witch's cauldron. The regular pulse beat already heard was now much louder, and sent an angry ripple churning through the mass of basalt in fusion. The heat was like that felt when standing near an open blast furnace. It was difficult not to see an analogy between the two and imagine that at any moment a blazing river of lava would be tapped to pour all over them. The angry splutters and spoutings spoke of a restless potency eager to overspill the banks and wreak havoc and destruction. The salamander who could live in fire might be roaming beneath the surface impatiently flicking with its tail to hurl molten matter towards the invisible ceiling. The torch beam could find no limits to the great space that formed the hollow central cone of Matupi. The jagged teeth of rock stretched away on both sides. The throbbing mass of lava buckled and broke into infinity.

Carter felt diminished and terrified. A small human presence seemed an anachronism here, the attempt to interfere with one of Nature's most awe-inspiring mysteries, an impertinence. They were literally dwarfed by what lay before them. He could understand the carriers who shrank back against the outer wall, their palms pressed flat against it and a look of open-mouthed wonder on their faces that almost bypassed fear. He thought back to all the signs: the tremors, the boiled fish, the sulphur stream, the yellow tide. It was impossible to believe that they had not been right. Matupi was primed for an eruption.

Hudson held up a hand as a shield against the heat and looked about him. The side of the volcano nearest the town and the airfield would be the natural choice for the siting of the explosive but it might not be the most easily breached. Probably better to concentrate the force of the explosion at a spot where a previous eruption had occurred: in and around the tunnel they had entered by.

Hudson confirmed his reflections with Carter and issued orders to the carriers. Sensing that deliverance was at hand the men worked at a pace little short of frantic. The loads were tucked contiguously under the rock that loomed forward to form the roof of the vast chamber, knitting into the twisting convolutions as if they were a part of them. The palm-leaf covering was beginning to curl and turn brown with the intense heat. The stench of sulphur coated the inside of the mouth. It was no longer possible to swallow.

Carter opened up his pack and took out the detonators. He prayed that neither sea nor march had penetrated the container and that the heat would not affect the timing mechanism. The detonators had been tested beyond the most demanding natural conditions but they little approximated the pressures found here in the molten heat of the volcano.

Carter began to place the detonators while Sula and Hudson parcelled out the salt and tobacco. The carriers clustered round, revealing that untapped reserves of stamina still remained as they argued and complained about the apportionment of their fee.

Carter hesitated. He was still not happy about the detonators. They were hot between his fingers, so hot that they seemed to melt. It would be best to test one under the worst conditions available. As near to the side of the lava lake as he could get.

Green appeared beside him, his face awash with sweat. 'Warm enough for you?'

'Just about.'

Carter continued to fiddle with the detonator.

'Reminds me of the night of the dance,' said Green. 'When I knocked out Errol Flynn. He was a different man when he was drunk.'

'Aren't we all,' said Carter.

Totally preoccupied with the detonator, he left Green behind and began to edge towards the insufferable heat of the crucible. He walked until his feet were roasting through the soles of his boots and his eyebrows were singed against his forehead. Ten feet from the brink he bent down and prepared to release the detonator.

Two powerful flashlights shone down as if an electric light had been switched on. Joe spun round with his Mills gun rising to his hip and there was a brief yammer of automatic fire. Joe fell backwards with blood spouting from his body like liquid from a ruptured carton. His hands scrabbled against the rock and lay still. Instantaneously, Jap voices shouted that no one should move. They echoed away into a silence broken only by the frenzied pulsing of the lava lake.

Yukichi stood behind one of the searchlights and quickly

assessed the scene. The dead black with the gun, the girl on her knees with the gun beside her, the two whites. The cowering black carriers in the background he was less interested in.

Yukichi advanced and saw that one of the whites was wearing a Japanese uniform. No doubt stripped from the men he had murdered in the swamps. Yukichi felt a wave of anger sweep over him as he thought of the lives that had been lost. The terrorists would surely suffer for their actions. Beheading was too good for such scum. The two men looked at him with exhausted eyes that seemed scarcely large enough to contain all the bitterness they felt. He was surprised how old they seemed. Perhaps it was the strong light on their haggard, pitted faces. He turned to the girl. She looked up towards the light with undisguised loathing. So— that was it. At last he had the four of them. And just when he had been about to call off the search patrol. How fortunate that the talkative carrier had strolled into their hands carrying his bag of salt and his tobacco. Hardly any inducement had been needed to make him tell them why he was breaking the curfew and where he had come from. In fact, he had been almost happy to lead them back to the cave entrance.

Yukichi kicked the gun away from the girl's grasp and it clattered across the rocks. A couple of words and one of the flashlights veered towards the loads. He approached them and spoke again. A Jap soldier stepped forward and swung a bush-knife. There was a gasp of alarm from the carriers.

'No!'

Yukichi stayed the descending blade and tore back the leaf covering. Under a mess of string like a complicated cat's-cradle were packed shiny transparent bags that seemed to contain a white powder. Yukichi was puzzled for a moment. Then he found the first detonator. He looked around at the combined bulk of the square bundles and whistled through his teeth. It was incredible. Incredible but true. The bags contained explosives, and the terrorists had been intending to detonate an explosion inside the volcano. They had been trying to start an eruption that would bring a tidal wave of lava down on Rabaul.

Yukichi could not help feeling a certain grudging admiration. It was a scheme that showed a bravura imagination in both conception and execution. And it had come within an ace of being implemented. If he had called off the ambush five minutes earlier. . . .

A high-flung spatter of lava warned Yukichi against complacency. The volcano was in a highly volatile condition. Perhaps the Australians had accumulated specialist information during their time at Rabaul and knew when it was likely to erupt. It was probably this knowledge that had led to the formation of the plan. If the lava started to expand over the lip of the subcrater as it was threatening to do then the explosive would go off without the need of detonators.

Yukichi quickly came to terms with the full extent of the danger. The volcano might erupt of its own accord at any moment. An expert opinion would be needed but this would take time. Almost certainly somebody would have to be brought from Japan. In the meantime, the presence of the explosive anywhere in the vicinity of Matupi constituted an enormous threat. The capture of the four terrorists did not signal the end of the danger. Far from it.

Yukichi began to shout orders and soon the angry growl of Matupi was silenced by the shrill voices of the Japs. More had emerged from the tunnel and, moving like imps in the confused brilliance of the flashlights, they began to pressure the carriers once again to take up their loads and drag them from the chamber.

Sula and Hudson were forced to lie on the hot rock. So, too, was Carter. When the flashlight first came on he had been stooping by the lava lake forty feet away from the others. In the space of a second he had dived behind some rocks and had lain there, hearing the burst of automatic fire that had killed Joe, the sound of his body falling and the clatter of his weapon hitting the rock. It was unbearably hot but he knew he dare not move. With every Jap voice he anticipated discovery but no one had come near him. The heat of the lava was enough to drive anyone back and *the Japs were only looking for four invaders*. They did not know that Green had been taken from the prison camp. As far as they were concerned he was one of the three men believed to have survived the swamp. He involuntarily changed places with Carter.

To the Japs, Carter did not exist.

As Carter lay in agony he knew that this was their only hope. At all costs he must avoid capture. But how much pain could he endure? His feet were facing towards the lava lake and he could smell the rubber soles of his boots melting. Inside them his feet were literally baking. The rocks on which he lay were like the hot plates of an oven, lifting the skin from his body. At every point where his flesh touched rock it was blistering. The hairs inside his nostrils were singed, and to breathe the dry, sulphur-laden air was to inflict terrible pain on himself. Why not put himself out of this misery? Stand up and fire a burst into the explosive so that the whole lot went up. Mission accomplished and an end to the agony. But something inside him rebelled against this. He was not a Jap. While there was life there was some kind of hope. Even if he took his own life he could not sentence the others to death. He ground his teeth together and fought the desire to scream.

Suddenly, as one of the flashlights went out, he heard footsteps approaching the point where he lay. His fingers brushed against the hot metal of his weapon and then lay still. The footsteps had stopped. Was a smiling Jap looking down at him, his finger curling contentedly round the trigger of his automatic? There was a slight expulsion of air as somebody stooped to retrieve something and the footsteps moved away again. One of the Japs had been ordered to pick up Sula's Mills gun.

After what seemed to Carter's tortured body to be like an eternity, the number of voices in the chamber began to diminish and he could hear the muffled sounds of movement back up the tunnel. The artificial light began to drain away and then disappeared altogether. There was silence save for the rhythmic pumping of the lava, seeming if anything to have increased in urgency and pace.

Carter counted off ten unbearable seconds and then jerked his roasted flesh away from the crucible. He ran a dozen unsteady steps and nearly sprawled over the body of Joe. The huge man looked majestic in death. With the flickering light from the dancing lava playing on his gleaming black chest he was like a marble statue resting on its tomb in a subterranean cathedral. The inside of the volcano was a Valhalla worthy of Joe.

Carter pressed his torch and found that it did not work. He cursed and looked about him. All the equipment and arms had been taken, including the explosives and detonators. The detonators—Carter was reminded that he had been testing one when the Japs arrived. Should he bother to retrieve it? He hesitated and then turned to face the lava. He might possibly need it, if it had not melted away to nothing. Taking a deep breath he ran back and snatched up the detonator in his blistered fingers. It was too hot to hold and he threw it behind him, feeling his hair scorch as the close-range glare of the molten lava threatened to blind him. The heat lanced deep into his eye sockets. If he breathed in he would burn out his lungs.

He found the detonator and tried to cool it by spitting on it but it was impossible to summon up any saliva—the inside of his mouth was a dry gourd. He gathered up the detonator and pressed it into one of his pockets. Now, somehow, he must find his way out in the dark. He must not lose touch with the others. He was their only hope and they, his.

When they came out into the open air and from the cave, Hudson saw that there were about twenty Japs. All heavily armed and wearing helmets. A force of marines, by the look of them. Showing his teeth in a mocking leer was the carrier who had been sent home and who was obviously responsible for their discovery. Hudson felt physically sick. He should never have let the man go. He was a trouble-maker and there had always been the chance that he would blunder into a Jap patrol. It seemed so obvious now. Sula emerged and the man strutted towards her as if eager to show her that his limp had magically disappeared. Sula let him get near and then lashed out with a kick to his testicles. It was a blow of such uncontrolled ferocity that the man was nearly lifted off the ground. The pitch of his screech was shattering as he collapsed motionless in a heap with his knees drawn up before his chest. The Japs chattered angrily and one of them kicked Sula's feet from beneath her. Before she could move, an automatic was pressed against her temple and she, Hudson and Green were manacled.

Yukichi hurried to the wireless operator and told him that he wished to speak urgently with General Koji.

25

General Koji tapped his spectacles back up his nose and frowned.

'You heard what Admiral Yamamoto said, Namura. More attention must be paid to the condition of the prisoners. We must consider increasing their rations.'

Colonel Namura shifted uneasily. The skin in his eye-less socket was bunched together like a knot.

'At the expense of our own men?'

Koji said nothing.

Namura took advantage of the silence to continue, 'I am a combat officer, General. For a man in my position to be responsible for prisoners and internees, it is—' he broke off, trying to find the right word, 'demeaning.'

'Nevertheless it must be done. And done efficiently. The discipline at the camp leaves a lot to be desired. This soldier who has disappeared—'

'A mad man, General,' interrupted Namura. 'Nothing he did would surprise me. Twice he has gone absent without leave in the past. He probably has a still in the jungle. That is another problem. The quality of the men placed at my disposal. All units that are asked to supply men for duty at the camp take the opportunity to purge themselves of their most degenerate elements.'

'I am not interested in excuses. I am interested in action,' snapped Koji. 'You must instil in these men your own tenacity and sense of duty. You have never failed in the field. Give me no cause for complaint now. When the prisoners are brought here to work in the tunnels they will require diligent supervision.'

'I am used to commanding soldiers, not coolies,' said Namura proudly.

General Koji sighed. Like Yukichi and every other officer in the Imperial Army he found it difficult not to sympathize with

Namura's attitude. To him, too, the internees were a nuisance and the prisoners an execration. The thought that men in full possession of their faculties could lay down their arms and surrender was painful to him. Such creatures were so craven as to have forfeited all right to be treated like human beings. To have to associate with them was to be spiritually tainted. Nevertheless, for the glory of Nippon, it must be done.

There was a discreet tap at the door and Koji's personal signaller appeared.

'I have Major Yukichi on the wireless, sir. He wishes to speak to you urgently.'

Koji stood up and beckoned Namura to follow him.

'Is there any word from Bougainville?'

The signaller shook his head as he stood aside and held open the door. 'No, sir.'

Koji frowned. 'Strange. We will contact them after I have spoken to Yukichi.'

He strode down the musty corridor and into the small room banked to the ceiling with powerful transmitters. The signaller's pad and headphones lay on a small table surrounded by code books. Koji sat at the table and reached for the headphones. Namura and the signaller stood behind him.

'Samurai One. This is Shogun speaking.'

Yukichi's voice was clearly audible through the static. He spoke slowly and calmly, accentuating each word.

'Samurai One to Shogun. I have intercepted an enemy party. One killed and three captured. Also large quantity of unfamiliar high explosive carried by ten bearers. Enemy were in process of placing explosive inside crater of Matupi—'

There were exclamations of amazement from the three men in the room. For the moment all rank had disappeared.

'—I believe that volcano is about to erupt. Repeat, about to erupt. If explosive ignites the outcome could be catastrophic. Have you understood me so far? Over.'

Koji swallowed. 'Message understood.' He thought quickly. 'Suggest you take every precaution and move explosive to nearest road. We will organize lorries to transport it to barge for disposal at sea. Report your position and where you estimate you will reach road.'

He stood up and shoved the headphones into the hands of the signaller who started to take down map references.

Koji spun round on Namura.

'If the volcano erupts, there is a grave danger to the tunnel system. Fall in all available men—including the prisoners—and set them to filling sandbags and blocking the entrances. Can we find a barge? There's a supply convoy standing off tonight, isn't there?'

'Yes, sir,' said Namura. 'Nearly all the barges are unloading materials, but there is one in for servicing that I think we can use.'

'Check that,' said Koji. 'If it's out of action we'll have to take a barge off the convoy detail.'

'What about the airfield?' asked Namura.

'Red Alert. Everything standing by to take off. We'll have only a few minutes if Matupi erupts.'

The signaller turned round towards Koji. 'Have you anything more to say to Major Yukichi, sir?'

Koji leaned towards the mouthpiece.

'Shogun to Samurai One. Well done. Return to base immediately with prisoners. Over.'

There was a pause, and then the same calm, ordered voice came back over the airways. 'Samurai One to Shogun. Message understood and will be acted on. Out.'

Yukichi rose from his knees beside the wireless set and took a deep breath before beginning to issue orders. Away from the suffocating heat of the interior the air seemed positively cool. Calling over his lieutenant he told him unemotionally that he and fifteen men were going to be responsible for conducting the carriers and explosives to the road. He indicated the rendezvous point on the map and suggested a route that avoided the landslide. His lieutenant asked him what was to be done with the carriers at the other end. Yukichi told him that when there was no further use for them they were to be taken to the centre of the nearest village that could be reached by road and shot. This would provide both a divertissement for the inhabitants and a warning. The lieutenant nodded and saluted. He folded his map, returned it to his case and began to issue his own orders.

Yukichi called up his most trusted sergeant and told him to select the five best men in the party. A length of chain was procured and threaded through the manacled hands of Hudson, Green and Sula, fastening them together in a cumbersome line. As soon as it was secured, a blow from a rifle butt urged Hudson forward.

On the slab of rock, the treacherous carrier rose unsteadily to his feet and was promptly thrust towards the nearest load. The first word of crutch-grasping protest was rewarded with the flat of a rifle stock against the side of his jaw and a stream of Japanese that left no doubt as to its meaning. He hurried towards a load before the rifle could be raised again.

From behind the screen of moss that hung down over the entrance of the cave, Carter watched the scene with mounting dismay. The escape from the heart of the volcano in the dark had been horrendous. Crawling over obstacles, never certain if he was taking the right route or diverging into a labyrinth of tunnels from which there would be no escape. Picking a way through foul-smelling excrement alive with tiny worms, while nursing bats squeaked overhead and others brushed against him in the darkness. Never being able to see anything until the grey circle of light at the end of the first tunnel. And now that he had escaped, Hudson, Sula and Green were being led away in chains and he could not follow them because the carriers were still loading up.

The Japs were dividing into two parties, that was obvious. The moon was now shining brightly and he could see that seven men were accompanying his comrades, the rest staying with the explosives. He looked sideways and saw that the moss curtain extended along the side of the mountain. Perhaps if he edged along behind it he could bypass the slower moving carriers. Once they joined a track he would never be able to get past them.

The rock was still wet and he sank to his blistered knees and pressed his mouth to the rainwater that had gathered in a shallow depression. His split lips stung but there was a relief in being able to swallow again and feel his tongue change back into an organ, as opposed to a dried-out loofah that someone had tried to thrust down his throat. He rose and, wiping the slippery bat shit from his boots, climbed across the rock to the side of the mountain. He was holding his gun in his fast-weakening right hand and it was because of this that he let it swing clumsily to strike against the rock. There was a loud clanging noise and he froze, listening for sounds of discovery. Fortunately, the Japs were too busy shouting at the bearers and chattering to each other to hear him.

He waited a few seconds and pressed on until the damp moss was brushing against his face. Hoping that no eyes were turned towards the mountain he continued to edge along until human noises began to fade and there was a gap in the moss. Looking down in the moonlight he could see a steep descent to where the path ought to be, picking its way through grass-strewn clinker and the occasional outcrop of heat-blasted rock. He lowered himself and tested the clinker with his foot. It seemed to have welded into a solid mass. Slowly, he began to make his way down, pre-selecting each objective on the route and gauging the number of steps and footholds needed to reach it. Pain and exhaustion were taking their toll but if he kept moving, he told himself, he would not have time to feel them.

Apart from starting one minor landslide, he reached the path without mishap. He was now further round the mountain than he had been when they branched off so it was necessary to retrace his steps. He moved carefully, prepared to dart into the undergrowth at the slightest warning, and after about fifty yards heard signs of someone descending to his left. A torch flashed and a Jap voice cursed as there was a slight fall of stones. Carter ducked down the edge of the path and saw the first two marines emerge. Then came Hudson, followed by Sula and Green. The chain that joined them rattled and glinted in the moonlight. Green was staggering, and it looked as if his legs would give out at any moment. One of the Japs was an officer, recognizable at night by the fact that he wore a cap instead of a helmet and carried a large pistol. He pushed forward along the path to station himself behind Sula and spoke succinctly and urgently. The party began to move forward at a smart pace that jerked Green along like a reluctant beast of burden.

Carter let them get twenty yards ahead and followed with a sense of mounting despair and confusion sweeping over him. The same desperation that he had felt when alone in the sea and seeing the dinghy drifting away from him. What could he do? He was blindly following Hudson and the others. What could he achieve against seven heavily armed Japanese marines? He might account for one or two but the others would take cover and flush him out in no time. Manacled and chained together as they were, his companions had no chance of fleeing into the bush. They would probably be cut down instantly by the Japs if the party came under fire. There was no chance of getting ahead of them and trying an ambush. Anyway, he knew that the idea was implausible even as he thought about it. He would have to continue tagging along like an abandoned dog.

A quarter of a mile down the path, the Japs suddenly stopped and went for cover. Lights were approaching. Challenges were made and replied to in Japanese and there was an excited gabble of greeting. Another patrol had arrived. Carter could hear the chain rattling as the prisoners were dragged forward to be shown off. There was the sound of blows and a cry of pain that he recognized as coming from Green.

Another patrol—and a large one by the sound of it: that made his position as a rescuer even more derisory. He was powerless by himself. Torches flashed again and men started to move towards him. Carter barely had time to take cover before gaitered boots went swishing past, presumably going to reinforce the party accompanying the explosives. He counted ten pairs of feet. If that were half the patrol then there were now seventeen men guarding the prisoners. The situation was hopeless.

Clinging to the mountainside below the path, Carter looked about him. There was a large gap in the clouds and the moon shone down, throwing a ghostly grey light over the tight folds of jungle and the razor-back ridges that gained in height as they stretched away to become part of the distant mountains. Paths ran along some of the ridges and zig-zagged up their sides through patches of cultivated land hacked from the dense undergrowth. Clinging to the topmost sides of the ridges were clusters of huts positioned to give the best vantage point against attack by neighbouring villages.

Carter orientated himself in relation to Rabaul, invisible round the side of the mountain, and realized that he was looking down at the village from which the carriers had come. Joe's village. In one of those huts was Baka, unaware that his son was dead. Baka was Hudson's friend. He had hidden the explosives and found them carriers. Now he was their only chance. Could he be persuaded to mount a rescue party? A lot would depend on his attitude to his son's death. Would he be eager for revenge or would his mood turn to bitterness and recrimination against those who had put Joe's life in peril? There was only one way to find out. Even as he thought, Carter was calculating the distance to the village and the best route to take. He knew it meant abandoning the others but he also knew that he was serving no useful purpose tagging along behind them. What he was going to do if he did recruit some men from Baka he had no idea. All he knew was that he had to try something.

The far side of the valley leading to the ridge showed a path dropping steeply that must eventually ascend towards his position. The actual course of the path could not be seen because of the convex swelling of the mountainside and the vegetation. Down to the right was a ragged line running through the grass. This might indicate the course of the path. Carter did not waste time but lunged down the mountainside, immediately encountering a prickly vine that nearly took his eye out. The hooked thorn tore through his flesh like fish hooks. He knew that he was making a noise but hoped that the Japs would think that it came from a cassowary or a litter of wild pigs. There was no time for stealthy movement. Blisters rubbed off against the rocks and he began to wonder if he had a square inch of skin left on his body.

Carter paused to look back and could see isolated pinpoints of light on the mountainside. Thankfully, they seemed to be moving horizontally. The carriers had only just got down the staircase of giant rocks. He struggled on and fell into the path, a deep furrow almost overgrown with grass and turned into a canal by the torrential rain. The descent was so slippery and precipitous that Carter could not keep his feet and was constantly forced to cling to the razor-sharp grass to stay upright. His hands were wet with blood and his injured arm ached unbearably with a pain that ricocheted through the whole of the right side of his body. When he reached the bottom he slipped and fell ten feet to land in a narrow stream swollen with the water that had run down from the mountains.

Now began the ascent and the agony of driving exhausted limbs beyond the pain barrier. Waves of dizziness and nausea clouded his eyes half-closed by insect bites. Sometimes he reeled sideways, unable to stand up without support. After five minutes' climbing, he was above the dense thicket of trees that crowded in around the stream and could see across to Matupi and the route he had taken. He wiped the lather of sweat from his forehead and looked below the looming black outline of the volcano. What he saw filled him with new fear. A file of light was descending the mountainside and coming towards him. He saw the light bob and waver as the men holding them hesitated before selecting a foothold. Then they came on, dropping relentlessly. Had the Japs seen him? Impossible. They must be planning a punitive expedition against the carriers' village. The Japs he had met on the mountain path had seemed voluble and excited, eager for action.

Carter turned and desperately resumed his scramble up the ridge. Now he had another incentive to reach the village—to warn the inhabitants. He stumbled and fell awkwardly, jarring his injured arm. The pain was like an electric current being passed through his body. To breathe was to have a saw drawn across his lungs. He dragged himself up, gasping with pain and exhaustion, and watched his knee rise towards his face as he sought the next slippery foothold. Looking back he could see nothing because the vegetation had closed in about him. For fifteen minutes he hardly raised his head, trying to preserve a dogged rhythm that would keep one foot rising in front of the other. When he looked up it was to find himself in a grove of bamboos, their leaves rustling in the slight breeze. The path took a long diagonal turn along the side of the ridge and he was able to straighten and rub his aching back as he walked. Ahead of him he could see the top of the ridge silhouetted against the sky and he estimated that the village must be above him.

He glanced up into the trees and started back. A man was looking down at him. A man hunched up on an untidy throne of stakes and twigs like a shored-up bird's nest. The man did not move but leant forward showing all his teeth in a wide, mocking grin. He was withered and wasted and his skin was pocked with hundreds of small worm-holes like an old piece of furniture. His eyes were deep black holes and he had no nose, only a scrap of material thrust like a wedge into the nasal orifice. His flesh was hollow parchment, ruckled and split by time. One hand leaned forward across a knee, the bony finger pointing admonishingly.

Carter looked round the grove and saw that the trees were full of such men, each propped in a sitting position on an untidy scaffold, each long since dead. The bodies had been preserved, probably by smoking. The grove must be some kind of burial ground. How eerie they looked with their rows of white teeth grinning in the moonlight! Carter shivered. If he had need of omens, this was not the place to find them.

Fear drove his aching feet forward, and he heard a dog barking as he came round a bend where the path rose steeply. He must be near the village. Soon he saw a glimpse of thatch amongst the palms and a rattan fence interwoven with spiky palm leaves. More dogs started to bark. He started towards a hut and was met by a wild-eyed man grasping a spear that he was clearly prepared to throw. The man crouched at the doorway of his hut and jerked back his arm threateningly. Carter decided that it was advisable to stop in his tracks.

'Chief Place?' he said trying to introduce a question mark into his voice.

'Luluai?' He pointed over his shoulder. 'Japan 'e come. *Raus!*'

The last words were more successfully interpreted than the first. The native looked in the direction Carter had pointed and lowered his spear. He listened for a moment and could obviously hear something beyond the range of Carter's ears. He stared once more into the American's face, clearly puzzled by the sudden arrival of an exhausted white man in the middle of the night, and pointed further up the hillside. The barking of dogs now sounded from a different side of the village and Carter guessed that the Japs had taken a short cut through the burial ground. They must know the village from their patrolling activities. He ran across open ground slippery with rain and heard the first shots without knowing if they were aimed at him. A semi-circle of huts loomed up behind an ornamental stockade and he hurdled it as men, women and children began to spill into the open. The first man he blundered into was Baka clutching a bow and long arrows.

'Japan 'e come!' he repeated.

The old man seized his arm in a grip of steel. 'Joe?'

Carter shook his head, loath to hear the words come from his mouth.

Baka did not relinquish his hand but tightened his grip.

'I done savvy.'

Carter saw the ash daubed on the man's face. It was a sign of mourning. How had he known that his son was dead? Two long bursts of automatic fire crashed through the flimsy walls of the huts as if the Japs were firing with the aim of killing anyone inside them. Sago fronds splintered into chaff and a child screamed. Carter's first instinct was to return the fire but he re-strained himself. At the moment, the Japs did not know that he existed. They soon would if a Mills gun opened up. The clearing was full of shouting people and a woman went down squealing, her hands clasping her thigh. Carter saw the blood pumping through her fingers. Baka was calling to men as they ran past but total panic prevailed. Carter knew that if he stayed where he was he would be dead. He ran hard for the far side of the village, Baka after him. A man in front of them was hit and spun over and over like a rabbit picked off in full flight. Carter veered away and threw himself down behind a hut as a hail of bullets sprayed the air above his head. He turned and saw that Baka and two warriors were lying beside him. Beneath the hut, a pig calmly continued to nose amongst the human excrement which formed the mainstay of its diet.

Carter sniffed smoke and heard the crackle of flames. They had to keep moving. He wriggled backwards to where the ground began to fall away and had just slid behind a huge ficus-tree when he saw his first Jap. The man was moving quietly up the slope, his weapon at the ready. He was clearly waiting for anyone who ran from the huts. Carter heard Baka moving beside him and saw the chief drawing back his bow. There was a twang and a thump and the Jap placed his hand against his neck as if stung by an insect. If he still possessed a sense of touch at that moment he must have felt the shaft of the arrow that had transfixed his neck. His fingers were still at his neck as his knees buckled and he slumped forward, legs twitching. After a few seconds the legs stopped. More huts were burning and a fresh breeze fanned smoke down the hillside. Flames roared skywards and turned walls of interwoven sago palm into blazing banners. The Japs were moving through the village shooting and bayoneting anyone that moved. They intended that their reprisal should be complete. The word would spread through the whole peninsula that the wrath of Nippon once aroused was awesome in its savagery.

Carter hesitated. Two more Japs were approaching up the hillside. He shrank back behind the tree, not certain if he had been seen. There was a warning call and a cry of discovery. The body of the dead Jap had been found. Immediately, bullets started kicking up earth around the ficus-tree. The Japs had reacted astutely, firing blind at the point where they reckoned the arrow had come from. Carter huddled behind the tree with Baka and the two warriors knowing that he had split seconds to come to a decision. If he used his weapon he would give himself away. If he did not, he would die. The Japs had stopped firing. One of them was probably crawling out amongst the trees. There was a great whoosh and a hut collapsed in a cloud of sparks. Burning timbers started to roll down the hill. At the same instant, half a dozen terrified women and children ran from the burning village and were silhouetted against the flames.

Carter saw a chance that the Jap's attention would be diverted and ran straight ahead of him, trying to keep the ficus-tree between himself and recognition. There was a cane fence surrounding a garden and he dropped his shoulder and went through it as if it were a paper hoop. It was only then that bullets whistled round his head and he heard someone cry out. He did not stop. Cassava and sweet potato crunched under foot and he slithered and slipped in the soft cultivated earth. Then there was another wall and he went through that to feel nothing beneath his feet. The ground opened up and he fell, pitching forward with a force that jerked his gun from his grasp. He rolled over several times and came to rest, with all the wind knocked out of him, in the middle of a thicket of *pit-pit*—ten foot high canegrass normally growing so thick as to form a solid wall. The force of Carter's fall had thrust him into it like a knife blade.

His head whirling, Carter clawed his way to a kneeling position and out of the *pit-pit* to find that he had plunged over the far side of the ridge. The fence he had crashed through marked the border of the village gardens. Above his head a red glow lit up the sky and he could still hear the crackling flames and the screams of the dying. Baka scrambled down beside him with another man who retrieved his weapon. There was no sign of the other warrior.

They lay still for a few moments and then, when there were no sounds of pursuit, Baka led the way round the *pit-pit* and down into the shelter of the thick jungle.

Carter followed, scarcely able to stand upright. He had come for help and was left escaping with an old man and a warrior who was scarcely more than a youth. The night was half-over and everything they had so nearly achieved lay in ruins.

26

Hudson sprawled disconsolately in the back of the lorry, his shoulders against the driver's cab. Green lay at his feet, breathing irregularly and occasionally twitching convulsively. He was nearer death than life and the pendulum was not going to swing back. Sula sat proudly erect against the side of the lorry. The scowl of haughty defiance she had worn since their capture was still there.

Now they were going through the dock area devastated by American bombing. No fixed installation remained standing; gutted warehouses were all that could be seen, cranes twisted beyond recognition to look like fire-scorched trees, heaps of rubble, some of it still smoking. But this did not mean that the port was out of action. Everywhere he looked, Hudson could see groups of men toiling at their appointed tasks. Some were man-handling a lorry that had been burned out in an earlier raid and was half-blocking an approach road to the wharves. Others were working on the wharves themselves, unloading the flat-bottomed barges packed to the gunwales with ammunition cases and gasoline cans, and loading the contents onto lorries that waited with their engines revving. Mobile cranes bumped over the quays. The operation was geared to speed and instant disposal in the event of an air-raid.

Hudson looked and saw to his amazement that some of the wharves were made from the hulls of bombed vessels that had been towed to the side of the dock and filled in with cement. As he watched, a Jap emerged from the below-deck area, which could clearly be used as a shelter at time of air attack. Hudson was forced to pay grudging respect to Japanese ingenuity and tenacity. He looked out to sea but could only detect the pinpoint red lights of the barges which would not be visible from the air. The ships they were plying to were obviously dispersed outside the harbour to minimize the risk of air attack.

The lorry slowed down to allow one of the laden trucks to pull out. Hudson looked past the barrel of the sub-machine gun that rested almost against his temple and saw something in the water that puzzled him. At first he thought it was a submerged submarine being towed by a barge but then he realized that the long cigar shape, its outline barely breaking the water, must itself be a submersible barge that could be used for transporting gasoline or oil without being spotted from the air. A few minutes first-hand observation was making it clear how the Japs were able to outwit all the Americans' long-range attempts to prevent them from building up supplies of men, arms and provisions. And, once entrenched, how difficult it would be to budge the Japanese. To remove a limpet from a rock was hard enough, but to remove a limpet from *inside* a rock . . .

The lorry started up again and Hudson looked at the scene of devastation and frenetic activity about him and thought back to the town he had known. Orderly lines of red-and-green-roofed bungalows with wide verandahs set behind avenues of shady trees. Each street named after a different species of tree: Yara Avenue lined with tall casuarina trees, Mango Avenue with its rows of mangoes, and Malaguna Avenue with its line of huge rain-trees planted in the middle of the wide road. Well-kept lawns, pathways of white coral, hedges of coleus, croton, hibiscus and frangipani. Bright colours dozing under a tropical sun.

Now the colours were grey dust and brown mud. Most of the bungalows had been swept away and the trees blasted down to their roots. The sleepy tropical town had been bombed flat.

The lorry left the harbour area and, with its escort vehicle, passed through a road block, then entered the road that curved between the narrow strip of coconut palms abutting on the sea and the cliff face. At every tunnel entrance they passed, gangs of men were feverishly filling sandbags and building walls across the openings. Hudson saw the precautions that were being taken and smiled wryly to himself. The Japs had not lost any time.

Ahead, a torch waved them down. The lorry slowed to a halt.

The Jap guard standing up in the opening beside the driver pressed the muzzle of his sub-machine gun into Hudson's neck. If anything happened, Hudson knew that he was going to be the first to die. In his present mood of self-accusing bitterness the thought did not distress him much. Almost contemptuously he twisted his hand to knock the barrel aside and peer through the opening in the back of the cab. To his amazement, he saw that the stern of the barge was emerging from one of the tunnels. It rested on a trolley of rough-hewn logs, which in turn glided on a pair of rails which sloped down through the palms towards the sea. The short, stubby funnel emerged, barely clearing the tunnel roof, and then the prow, pushed by three sweating Japs, their faces glistening in the moonlight. A wire hawser was attached to the prow and this stretched tight as the barge began to slide backward. Hudson could hear the sound of a winch creaking as it jerked towards the sea.

So, the barges were kept inside the tunnels as well. This explained why the most diligent air reconnaissance around the area of the bay had never shown where they were moored. Hudson cursed himself again. What a prize had been within their grasp.

The hawser went slack as the barge entered the water, and the lorry started to move forward. As it gathered speed, Hudson glanced at the men who were filling sandbags outside the next tunnel entrance. They were skinny, emaciated Europeans working under the surveillance of Jap guards. They must have been brought from the camp. The Japs were clearly treating the possible eruption of Matupi as an emergency. Poor bastards. Some of the prisoners could hardly lift a bag.

Hudson caught Sula's eye and tried to smile. Her face remained sullen. Her eyes glistened with tears. What was she thinking of? Joe? Carter? The failure of the mission? All three perhaps.

A gap opened up in the palms and Hudson could see across the bay to the outline of Matupi. Dawn was less than a couple of hours away and already a faint grey light was beginning to diffuse the horizon. What had happened to Carter? Had he managed to get out of the volcano? Had the Japs got him? He prayed that somehow Carter would escape, that some human life would be salvaged from the operation. There was no hope for the rest of them.

The six lorries were lined up in a clearing from which stone had once been quarried. The jungle finished abruptly on the semi-circular rim, and the ground was patterned with tyre marks. Some of the Japs were smoking when the first bearers arrived but they conscientiously ground out their cigarettes and nervously straightened their forage caps on their heads. Nobody knew what the explosive was, which gave the imagination much to feed on. Two light tanks were parked strategically and discreetly across the other side of the clearing where it opened onto the track which led to the road.

When the carriers had assembled it was confirmed that there were indeed ten loads of explosive. Yukichi's lieutenant responded to the Captain in charge of the convoy and it was agreed that the loads should be allocated two in a truck and a gap of three hundred yards left between each vehicle. The route taken to the embarkation point had been signposted and would avoid passing close to the airfield for security reasons. Each vehicle would carry two armed guards and would not proceed faster then ten miles per hour. The three-hundred-yard gap between vehicles would be shortened at the risk of a court martial. The carriers would travel in the sixth lorry. Yukichi's lieutenant armed himself with details of the circuitous route and started to give orders for the explosives to be loaded onto the lorries.

Behind a screen of foliage at the top of the quarry, Carter looked down on the scene with an increasing sense of helplessness. He, Baka and the warrior whose name was Tukis had worked their way round from the burning village and had at last caught up with the train of carriers and their guards as they wended their way down the mountain. After an hour's talking, they were now powerless to do anything. Worse, the prize was being driven away from them. A familiar sense of emptiness and futility began to close in.

Exhausted as they were, almost to the point of death, it was difficult to maintain hope in the face of constant setbacks. At a rough estimate there were forty Japs below, not including the crews of the two tanks, whose presence made any thought of attack risible. Once again Carter wondered whether to put a bullet into one of the loads and produce the biggest quarry in the whole of New Guinea. Again, some strange, atavistic feeling decided him against it. He had fought so long to stay alive.

Below, the tailboard was raised on the first lorry and the driver eased forward, as if carrying a load of egg-shells. An officer watched it pass out of the quarry and down the track, then he dropped his arm for the second lorry to follow. The minutes passed with Carter waiting for something—anything!—to happen that would give him a lead. One of the tanks had left after the second lorry but its companion remained, the stubby 37mm gun pointing banefully towards Carter's position as if daring him to move. With one load of explosives left, three armed Japs started shepherding the carriers towards the final truck. There were some murmurs of protest and suddenly one man broke from the groups and raced for the side of the quarry. He climbed like a spider, and for a moment Carter thought that he was going to escape. Then a stitchwork of bullets climbed faster and he fell backwards, landing heavily in an untidy heap. One of the Japs walked towards him and fired again. The other carriers climbed into the back of the lorry.

The last explosives truck received the signal and began to pull out. The carriers were made to lie down in the bottom of their truck in case any of them still had an appetite for escape. The guards climbed in. Seconds ticked away and the tank still watched and waited. The carriers' truck pulled away and started to bump over the ruts. It slowed down at the entrance to the quarry and the officer climbed in. The tank jerked forward. Soon the quarry was empty and the drone of the vehicles had died away.

Carter stood up and started to follow Baka down to the shot man. A widening pool of blood was spreading out beneath his back and some of the bullets had passed through his body. Flies were already abundantly in evidence. Despite the wounds, a tremble of life still passed through the man's limbs. One eye stared wide and uncomprehending. Baka dropped to his knees and spoke urgently into the man's ear. At first there was no reply. Then the lips started to move, but soundlessly. Baka spoke again in a tone that was almost hectoring. The eye closed in a wince. Another pause. Then a mumble of words.

Baka listened till the man was silent and placed a hand on his shoulder as if in thanks and benediction. Then he turned to Carter and explained in halting English that the lorries were going to the sea. He picked up a stick and drew a rough map on the ground. Carter saw Matupi, the airfield and the bays. Baka jabbed at a spot to mark their position and then pointed to the side of the main bay beneath the volcano.

''E go dis fella side.'

Carter looked at the map. They must be going to dump the explosives out at sea. Unless they were planning to take them somewhere by water. Either way, the embarkation point would remain the same. It did not seem far by Baka's rough map, but they had no vehicle.

Baka started to draw again with his stick. Long lines, forming three sides of a rectangle from where they were to the sea.

'Car 'e go dis road,' he said, tracing the route with his stick to emphasize how long it was. 'Long time too much. 'E go, 'e go, 'e go, 'e go!' He sat up and pointed to the hill opposite. 'Good fella road. Mupela likum wara small time.'

The chief was saying that they could soon be at the sea if they took the path over the hill. Carter looked at the shot carrier. There were flies clustered over his eyes and mouth. He was dead. Carter turned away and dragged himself to his feet. Perhaps the carrier was the lucky one.

Hudson walked down the tunnel, marvelling at its length. They must have covered almost four hundred yards already and passed half a dozen intersections with other tunnels that could accommodate an automobile. There were subdued lights strung along the roof at thirty foot intervals and a thick concertina tube that must pump air into the interior. One of the side tunnels had contained a row of strangely assorted beds, doubtless looted from the houses in the town. In the beds were sick and wounded men being tended by uniformed Japanese nurses. Part of the tunnel system was obviously used as a hospital. Another tunnel running diagonally across the one they were in had contained forty-eight inch rubber pipes stinking of gas and fuel oil which rainbowed in splashes across the rough stone floor. It seemed as if the Japs were also storing fuel in the tunnel.

They passed another tunnel where extractor fans roared and, in the foreground, men worked with welding equipment on a damaged anti-aircraft gun. As far as the eye could see there were machanics renovating and assembling equipment. It was an impressive sight, not unlike a production line in a modern factory.

Hudson looked at the major who was accompanying them and read the expression in the man's eyes as he glanced about him and looked back. Pride. 'This citadel will not be easily taken,' said the glance. 'We have wrought much here and we will not give in easily.'

Another hundred yards down the slightly sloping tunnel and they came to a brightly lit open space in which several tunnels converged. Looking back, Hudson could see that all but one of them contained rails like the ones on which the barge had been moving. Presumably they were used to transport goods and material into the centre of the tunnel network. On one side of the open space was a shelf of rock with a guard-rail in front of it. Behind the rail were three doors, one with two armed marines on guard outside it. They snapped to attention as Yukichi approached, the sound of their boots echoing down the long corridors. Yukichi ordered the accompanying guards to hold the prisoners, tapped on the door and slid it open when a voice told him to enter. The door slid shut behind him.

Hudson looked at Sula. Her chin still lifted proudly. Green shivered uncontrollably so that the chain rattled, but it was due to fever and exhaustion, not fear. Hudson moved to support him but one of the guards jabbed him away roughly with the muzzle of his rifle.

Then the door opened and Yukichi reappeared. He said something to the guards and they thrust their prisoners forward.

Hudson blinked as he entered the room. His eyes were still not accustomed to the bright light after the semi-darkness of the tunnels. An officer wearing general's insignia, spectacles and a small moustache rose to his feet.

'Lieutenant-General Koji,' he said in almost perfect English. 'Commander of the Imperial 17th Army. We have been expecting you.' He turned towards a figure sitting beside the desk. 'Allow me to present Admiral Yamamoto.'

27

Hudson looked down at the short, stocky figure in confusion. He felt like a hunter who enters a cave in pursuit of a bear cub and finds himself face to face with its father.

Yamamoto looked up at him, his sensitive, aesthetic face a mask of sadness. He was wearing his white uniform with epaulettes, four rows of medal ribbons and white shoes. He carried his white-topped hat on his lap. In this position he seemed withdrawn, almost deferential, not the most feared and famous admiral in the Pacific. When he spoke it was with a faint trace of an American accent.

'I am sad,' he said. 'Yesterday, I lost nine friends, but my life was saved—by you.' He smiled a bitter smile. 'Can you tell me a greater irony?'

Hudson said nothing. He was trying to put a jigsaw together in his mind. Yamamoto saw that he was confused and continued.

'When your presence on the island was discovered it was thought that you had found out about my visit to the garrison. General Koji here believed you had been put ashore to assassinate me.'

So that was it, thought Hudson. That explained the patrols, their implacable determination to hunt them down.

'Nobody could understand what you were doing in the area of Matupi. It was heavily defended yet not a place I was likely to visit. Then Major Yukichi, the tenacious Major Yukichi,' Yamamota smiled at the man of whom he was speaking, 'had an idea. The airfield. As I boarded the plane I would be vulnerable, exposed; an easy target for a marksman aiming from the side of the volcano. He estimated that you would be waiting for me when I left for my next destination. I am told that my white uniform does make me very distinctive.'

'There are other reasons for your distinction,' said Hudson. His tone was uncomplimentary.

Yamamoto continued calmly. 'I will finish my story. I think you will find it interesting. Believing that you intended to kill me at the moment that I boarded the plane it was decided to set a trap for you. Units took up ambush positions on the side of Matupi and around the airfield. They waited to intercept you or to pounce at the moment you opened fire and revealed your position.' He paused dramatically. 'It was my double who drove to the airport and boarded the plane with my senior staff.'

Yamamoto's voice trembled and he looked at Koji.

Koji spoke like a man reading a funeral address. 'We have recently learned that the plane that would have been carrying Admiral Yamamoto was shot down by American fighters. Up to now, there is no news of any survivors.'

Green groaned and shook his head.

'You see why I speak of irony,' said Yamamoto sadly. 'You would have been delighted to kill me but you have ended up saving my life. Now it appears likely that you had no inkling that I was at Rabaul. You were here solely to make your incredible assault on Matupi.' He waved a hand. 'Speaking as one soldier to another, I must congratulate you.'

'I wish I could find a reason to congratulate you,' said Hudson coldly.

There was an angry murmur from Koji which Yamamoto silenced with a gesture. His voice lost none of its measured calm.

'I can understand your attitude and I know what causes it,' he said. 'However, I have only one statement to make about my decision to attack Pearl Harbor: when a man is choking the life out of you, you drive your knee into his testicles.'

Yamamoto rose to his feet and put on his hat. He looked very sure of his convictions. General Koji rose with him.

'And now I will go to my room and do some work until it is time for my plane to leave.' Yamamoto turned to Yukichi. 'Have you any more news?'

'The explosive should be nearly at the dockside now, sir. I will check on the wireless and let you know. After that, another half-hour and it will be outside the harbour. As soon as we receive word that it has been sunk we will leave for the airfield. I calculate that you should be able to take off by dawn.'

Yamamoto nodded. 'A sample of the explosive is being kept for analysis?'

'Yes, sir.'

'And the vulcanologist?'

'We have two arriving at fourteen hundred hours tomorrow.'

'Good. I think one of them had better stay here.'

'Yes, sir.'

Yamamoto turned to the three prisoners. 'It is most unlikely that we will ever meet again. I salute you.'

His hand snapped to his forehead and he went out.

Barefoot and nearer dead than alive, Carter slipped, slithered and fell down the last twenty feet to the beach. An untidy snaggle of driftwood had been trapped amongst the rocks and shifted in a tangled mass as the sea rushed through it. Carter took up a position behind it and looked down the narrow strip of beach. Fifty yards ahead a makeshift pontoon jetty stretched out to sea with a concrete bunker behind it. A strip of jungle had been cleared to make a track and a turning area. Some battered oil-drums were in evidence.

Carter guessed that the area had once been used as a fuel dump, probably before the tunnel network had been developed. The beach was tucked away from the main dock complex which also supported the fuel-dump theory. A barge was moored against the jetty, rolling slightly on the swell. There were lights moving on the jetty and Carter strained his eyes to see how many men were there. It looked like three, most likely the crew of the barge waiting for the lorries.

They did not have long to wait. As Baka and Tukis crept to his side the sidelights of the first lorry could be glimpsed approaching slowly down the track. Again, Carter felt a sense of stomach-gnawing desperation. What in God's name was he going to do? The presence of Baka and Tukis, willing as they had proved, hardly changed the odds against a successful attack. He was as helpless as a kitten watching a bull mastiff lapping up its bread and milk. Would he finally be reduced to detonating the explosives with a bullet? What other alternative was there? It was no good waiting for something to happen that would turn the odds magically in his favour. Nothing was going to happen. If there was any luck on this miserable island it rested solidly on the side of the Japs.

The lights swung round and faced inland as the lorry prepared to reverse towards the jetty. Get off your arse and make something happen, Carter told himself. He made a sign to Baka and Tukis and ducked back towards the boulders at the rear of the beach. A colony of tiny crabs scattered like flies. The sharp stones took lumps out of Carter's bare, blistered feet, but he no longer noticed pain. He knew he would go on until he was walking on stumps. Roots grew out of the undermined cliff and clawed at his face as he approached the jetty. Now he could make out the truncated smokestack and the wheelhouse amidships.

A pinpoint of light showed that somebody was smoking at the wheel. That meant four men, or maybe still only three. Two men were walking down the jetty towards the lorry. From where he crouched Carter could not see what was happening but he heard the tailboard going down and soon two figures reappeared, carrying one of the familiar loads. The palm-leaf covering had now fallen away and the shiny bags glinted in the moonlight. The sky lightened in the east and the moon was a luminous ball hanging against a backdrop of white steel.

The lorry revved noisily, simultaneous with the sound of the tailboard slamming, and the driver ground his gears in his eagerness to get away. On the jetty, the two men walked carefully as the pontoon structure undulated between them.

Carter hesitated. Were there any guards left on shore? Was there a chance of seizing the barge and one of the loads before the second lorry arrived? He started forward and then shrank back immediately. Another vehicle was approaching but it was not a lorry. The lights were set much closer together and the engine note was different. It was the first tank which had overtaken the second lorry. Carter stumbled back beneath the roots and foliage that hung down from the cliff like a screen. He looked towards the barge, his heart hammering. The men had just lifted the first load aboard. Nine more to come. The minutes ticked away and he was achieving nothing. *What could he do?*

General Koji moved round his desk and advanced towards Hudson. His face was angry.

'Your tone towards Admiral Yamamoto was impertinent and unbefitting an officer.'

Hudson said nothing. He knew that there was no point in trading insults. Anything he said would only make things worse for all of them.

Koji glared at him and turned to Yukichi. 'These are the three survivors?'

'Yes, sir. There was also the man who died in the swamp, and we killed a man in the volcano, as I reported over the wireless. These are the other three.'

Koji curled his lip contemptuously. 'Two old men and a black woman. It does not say much for the Allied resources at this time.'

Hudson smiled. 'If two old men and a black woman could get so far, perhaps it doesn't say much for Jap defences.'

Koji's brow knitted. 'You appreciate that I would be quite justified in treating you like spies and having you executed.'

'You viewpoint comes as no surprise to me,' said Hudson calmly.

Koji turned back towards his desk. 'Your chances of survival depend on the amount of co-operation that you give us.'

Hudson said nothing. He did not believe that he would set foot outside the tunnels alive unless it was to be taken for execution. Every coast-watcher that had been captured had been beheaded, usually after torture. He knew how the Japs would behave. They would slap you round the face, then give you hope and a cigarette then slap you round the face again. No matter what happened you always ended up the same way. Dead.

'There are many questions that intrigue us,' continued Koji. 'How did you know about the condition of the volcano?'

Hudson looked at Green out of the corner of his eye. The old man flinched and his mouth hitched a defiant quarter of an inch.

His senses were still functioning. Hudson chose a corner of the room and stared at it without speaking.

'How did you bring the explosives to the island?' Koji's voice droned on. 'Who were your contacts amongst the natives? Were you working with your so-called coast-watchers? What were your plans for withdrawal?' He broke off for a few seconds. 'It is no good avoiding my eyes. Believe me, my questions will receive answers. There is no doubt of it.'

The last six words were spoken with a chilling intensity.

Green started to cough and Hudson looked at Sula. She flared her nostrils and looked deep into his eyes. Her expression said, 'Do not weaken. I will stand by you, always.'

Koji turned to Yukichi. 'Where is Colonel Namura?'

'He is sealing the tunnels, sir.'

'Ask him to come immediately.'

Yukichi bowed stiffly and went out.

General Koji sat behind his desk and pushed his spectacles up on his nose. This chore completed, his fingers descended slowly to his moustache, which he pulled thoughtfully. His eyes passed from Hudson to Sula to Green and back again. One of the guards standing against the wall quickly scratched the end of his nose. He, too, was included in Koji's scrutiny and did not relish seeing the cold, snake eyes rolling over him looking for signs of fear and weakness. Koji knew that with men of a certain calibre silence was more effective than threats and bluster. The imagination could furnish better images of terror than he could describe. That was, until the real pain came.

The door opened and Namura came in, the sides of his cap dark with sweat where it rested against the temples. His empty socket gaped intimidatingly. Yukichi was behind him. Both men saluted.

Koji turned towards Hudson and spoke with a certain complacency. 'Your prisoners, Colonel.'

Namura turned his eye on Hudson. Then Sula. Then Green. Green's head had fallen on his chest, his chin tucked in close to his body. The expression on Namura's face changed. He advanced to Green, seized his chin and twisted it into the light.

'This man was in the prison camp!'

'What?' Koji jerked to his feet.

Yukichi stepped forward. 'Are you sure?

'Positive.'

'When did you last see him?'

Namura hesitated. 'Yesterday. Yes, yesterday. He was at the jail for interrogation.'

Koji, Yukichi and Namura looked at each other. It was almost possible to hear their minds working. Sifting, resifting the facts. Making sure that what they were forced to believe was actually true.

'Then there is another man still at large?'

Nobody said anything. Hudson looked at their faces and started to laugh. Koji slapped him hard across the face. 'Silence!'

Yukichi spoke urgently. 'I am going to check that the explosives are all right. May I recommend that Admiral Yamamoto does not move from here until I return?'

'Agreed,' said Koji. 'I will inform all units and issue a Red Alert.'

Yukichi saluted and ran from the room.

Koji turned to Namura and spoke grimly. 'I am handing over the prisoners for questioning, Colonel. 'You will find out everything they know—and swiftly!'

The air-raid siren coincided with the arrival of the last lorry. At first Carter thought it was an alarm signal in some way connected with him. Then, within seconds, he heard the drone of the Liberators and saw the flashes from the anti-aircraft gun emplacements ranging round the twin horns of the harbour. There was the crackle of exploding shells and puffs of smoke hung in the clear sky, small and concentrated at first then drifting away like blobs of cloud. Now he could see the planes, flying in a diamond pattern, spread out in clusters of five. Searchlights raked the sky but the planes were already as visible as a flight of geese. The first sticks of bombs fell and there was a vicious crump, crump, like heavy blows sinking in to the pit of a stomach. Now the sky was suddenly full of cotton wool and spurts of flame. A Liberator was hit and caught fire immediately, as if made of tissue paper. It screamed down, leaving a trail of smoke, and exploded on impact with the sea.

Carter pressed his hands against his ears. There was no escape from the relentless hammer of pounding guns, the hollow rocket burst of shells, the shrill whistle of falling bombs and the dull thud of the explosions that shook the whole of the wharf area. One thing was certain. The bombers were coming nearer. Their bomb run was from one end of the docks to the other. On the jetty, men were scattering for the shelter of the concrete bunker. The last load of explosives lay alone and isolated beside the barge. Two of the crew leapt aboard. The third was in the wheelhouse. The last man dived inside the bunker. Inland there was the scream of engines as the two tanks and the lorry dispersed into the jungle.

Suddenly the barge was defenceless. The realization dawned on Carter as a bomb fell five hundred yards from the beach, sending balks of timber flailing a hundred feet into the air. He tugged Baka by the arm and started to run down the beach towards the jetty without waiting to see if he was being followed. The noise was ear-shattering. At any second he thought that something in the flashing, exploding night must hit him. He clawed himself up onto the jetty and started to run. Behind him he heard a thump, thump of bare feet that told him he was not alone.

A stick of bombs fell in the sea a hundred yards away, and a fountain of water soared as high as a church steeple. The blast knocked him sideways, and the spray fell in a hissing shower. Beneath him, the pontoons slapped the water and the jetty reared like a bucking horse, making it impossible to stand upright.

Carter pulled himself up as the buffet of the first wave died away. He saw that the last load was being edged towards the side of the jetty. Every wave-induced tremor that undulated through the floating structure was jogging it nearer to the sea. As he ran forward, a Jap jumped onto the jetty and moved towards the stern line. He looked up in surprise as he saw the figure running towards him. Another bomb screeched down with a sound like a glass cutter being wielded across an endless pane. The Jap sank to his knees and protected his head with his hands. The bomb exploded in the jungle, bringing a hail of debris clattering down on the wooden planks. Carter shouldered the bale back into the middle of the jetty as the Jap rose to his feet. For a moment, comprehension and a new fear dawned on his face, then Carter clubbed him into a heap with a blow from the Mills gun and kept running for the wheelhouse.

A second Jap appeared looking over the side and had time to call out before Carter hit him. He fell back clutching his head. Carter ran along the jetty until he was level with the wheelhouse. He saw a man reaching to unhook an automatic and fired a short burst through the glass. The glass shattered and the man slid from view, leaving the automatic swinging gently where his finger had brushed against it.

Carter leapt aboard and saw that the man in the wheelhouse was dead. He turned and nearly fell over the man on deck who was having his throat cut by Tukis. Baka had already dealt with the man by the stern line.

Another bomb fell further along the coast. Carter looked back anxiously down the jetty. There was no sign of movement from the blockhouse. The barge was throbbing and the motor running. How the hell did you drive it? It could not be too complicated. He called to Baka and Tukis to cast off the lines and bring the dead Japs and the explosives aboard. He tried to breathe normally and looked at the dials, gauges and levers with increasing desperation. A quick glance told him that everybody was aboard. Then he turned a lever to the left. The noise of the engine increased but there was no indication that power was being transmitted to the propeller. Then the nose of the barge started to swing round towards the shore. He could feel Baka's and Tukis's eyes on him. Unless he did something fast the barge would drift gently onto the beach.

'*Tabauda!*' Tukis plucked at Carter's arm and pointed along the shore.

Along the coast the headlights of two vehicles could be seen approaching the jetty.

*   *   *

Yukichi cursed his driver and told him to go faster. He knew that he was being unreasonable but he needed to shout at someone. The driver made a token gesture of hunching over the wheel and checking in the mirror to see that the accompanying truck was keeping up with them. He could not go any faster without losing it and in these conditions excessive speed was madness. Already they had nearly driven into a bomb crater in the centre of the town.

Above their heads, the aerial battle was still going on. The Zekes and Zeros waiting on call from Matupi to erupt had been quickly launched into the air and were trying to smash through the fighter cover of the F–6F Hellcats and get at the Liberators. The airfield itself was getting heavy bombing.

Yukichi wondered why the Americans had changed the pattern of their attacks and were coming in just before dawn. Perhaps they hoped for an element of surprise as well as the advantage in accuracy that the light would give them. Maybe they were trying to get the barges as they returned to the tunnels. Whatever the reason, they were taking a big risk. Without cloud cover the cumbersome Liberators were sitting-ducks for the veteran crews of the anti-aircraft guns and any fighter that could get past the Hellcats. As he watched, two pin-point lines of tracer intersected on the tail of a bomber and flames started to pour from it. Slowly but inexorably the nose dipped and the plane dived towards the sea, leaving a trail of black smoke. Yukichi's view was interrupted by a clump of trees. When he next looked there was only a scatter of burning wreckage on the surface of the water.

The vehicle bumped over a pot-hole and Yukichi's head hit the roof. He swore at his driver and the road, and strained his eyes into the darkness. They must be nearly there now. The headlights picked up a lorry pulled into the side of the road. Yukichi swore again as his driver had to slow down and edge round the obstacle in four-wheel drive, the vehicle side-slipping crazily in the soft earth. Now he could see the concrete bunker ahead and figures emerging from it. The driver found the road again and within seconds Yukichi was jumping out and running towards the jetty.

It was empty. The outline of the barge could just be seen pulling away from the shore. Yukichi turned to the men who had come from the bunker. They told him that they had nearly finished loading the barge when the raid started. They had taken cover, they admitted slightly shamefacedly. The barge captain must have taken the decision to proceed with his instructions and dump the explosives out at sea without further delay. Yukichi nodded. The man had made the right decision. If the barge was hit, the further away from shore that happened, the better. The man had shown courage and initiative. Yukichi would see that he was recommended for a decoration when he returned. *If* he returned. The danger was not over yet. Nevertheless, Yukichi felt relieved as he turned away from the jetty. Now he could concentrate on finding the missing raider.

28

Hudson sat in the cell and waited. It was dark but he could see light through the grill in the door and hear the sounds of feet and orders being shouted. The Japs seemed to have a lot on their plates at the moment. They had taken his watch but he calculated that it was half an hour since they had been thrown into the cell. Green appeared to be in a coma. Sula was sitting with her back to a wall and her long legs drawn up almost to her breasts. A hand rested against Green's temple as if she were caressing a pet. They were still manacled and chained to each other. The air in the cell smelt foul but it was probably just the stench of their bodies.

Hudson looked at his two companions and thought of the conditions they now found themselves in. Waiting for torture and certain death. He closed his eyes. If only he hadn't let that carrier go.

It was Green who broke the silence. His voice was faint but perfectly under control. 'Andrew?'

'I'm here,' said Hudson.

'There's something that's been worrying me.'

Hudson looked at Sula. Her eyes met his and she shook her head gently. 'What is it, Harry?'

'I didn't tell you the truth about Errol Flynn.'

'It doesn't matter, Harry.'

There were probably a hundred old-timers in the Islands who had Errol Flynn stories. Few of them had even met him.

'I didn't knock him out. Damn fellow hit me with a bottle before I could get my guard up.'

'Don't worry, Harry,' said Hudson. He laid a hand on Green's shoulder. 'When I tell it, you knocked him cold. With a classic straight left to the point of the jaw.'

Green made a contented noise at the back of his throat as if savouring the image. 'I could have done too if he'd fought like a gentleman.' There was a pause. 'Andrew?' The voice was fainter.

'Yes, Harry?'

'Do you remember why I wanted to get out of the camp?'

'Something about a hundred thousand quid, wasn't it?' Hudson waited for another confession.

'Yes. Chap who'd made a strike up at Edie Creek. He hid his cache when he came out here to see his brother. The Japs got him the same time they got me. When he was dying he drew me a map.' Green raised his hands and tapped the breast pocket of his tattered Jap tunic. 'Help yourself.'

'You want me to look about it for you?'

Green made a wheezing noise. 'You're very diplomatic for an Australian, Andrew. I'm not going to have any use for it. Take it!'

Hudson saw that there was no point in arguing and managed to retrieve a ruckled piece of paper which he thrust into one of his own pockets.

'Thanks, Harry. Remember, I'm just holding it for you.'

'See that our girl friend gets a cut.' He lowered his voice to a whisper. 'And Will, when you see him. He was a good boy.' He fell silent and then sighed. 'Do you remember the old days, Andrew? When the only Jap we knew was Jap River-fever. Do you remember the cure? A handful of quinine tablets and a bottle of whisky. It was a toss-up which killed you—the fever or the scotch.'

He started a laugh which ended in a violent spasm of coughing.

'Don't talk,' urged Hudson. 'Save your strength.'

'We didn't do badly, did we?' said Green, contentedly.

'You did great,' said Hudson.

'The Japs may have this place but they'll never win. They haven't got it in them, you know.' Green's accent became very British. 'They're like monkeys climbing up a tree. The higher they get, the more you see their arses.'

The cell door crashed open as if an eavesdropper had heard the last remark. Framed in it was the squat menace of Namura with a guard behind him. His eye-less socket was a black hole in his face. He looked from Hudson to the recumbent Green. Green's mouth was open as it had been so often during his life but his eyes were closed.

'He's dead,' said Hudson.

If Namura understood he gave no sign of it. His hard eye fell on Sula and a finger advanced in a beckoning gesture. The guard stepped forward and unlocked the padlock on the chain. Sula was pulled to her feet and the padlock relocked. She turned to Hudson and for the first time her composure began to weaken. Now she was face to face with the reality.

'The girl doesn't know anything,' said Hudson.

Namura paused in the act of leaving the cell and glanced sharply at the guard. Instantly, a boot thudded into Hudson's kidneys, causing him to cry out in pain. Sula was thrust from the cell as she tried to protest and the door slammed shut. Now Hudson was alone in the darkness and chained to Green's corpse. He groaned as the waves of nausea-bringing pain flowed through his body and tried to keep his brain functioning clearly. It was not easy.

Carter spun the wheel to port and felt the barge respond. He enjoyed an unaccustomed sensation that he dimly connected with elation. It was always good to find that one possessed a new skill. Never more so than when the only alternative was death.

His first relief after feeling the barge move through the water had been the lack of pursuing shots from the jetty. He took this to mean that the Japs had assumed that it was the captain taking the vessel out to sea, not a self-preserving reluctance on their part to risk improving the deep-water facilities of Simpson harbour by detonating the explosives with a stray bullet.

Carter looked towards the main dock area. A second wave of bombers was coming in, and puffs of smoke and fountains of spray showed the path the bombs were taking. As far as he could see there were no barges still at the wharves and only one gutted lorry, propped on its end against a pile of rubble and burning brightly. The barges seemed to be taking shelter in the lee of the cliffs. As he watched, a Hellcat came in low over the water and started strafing one of them. A Zero came sweeping down on its tail, and the F6F pilot pulled back his stick and climbed for safety.

Carter peered through the shattered window of the wheelhouse uneasily. A stray bomb was one thing. He had not reckoned on being singled out for a personal attack by one of his own side. The pilot could well get the surprise of his foreshortened life. Along the shore the anti-aircraft gun emplacements were blazing away and Carter could see the men and the patterns on the camouflage netting illuminated in the flash every time they fired. Out to sea, there were other flashes as Jap ships opened up at the attackers. Beside him, Baka and Tukis cowered, scared to the point of numbness. Nothing in their most haunted dreams could ever have prepared them for what was going on about them.

The prow of the barge struck something. When Carter looked down at the wreckage floating in the water he saw a seat with a man strapped in it. He was burnt and dead. There were two other bodies wearing flying helmets and a piece of fuselage with a saucy painting of a Vargas-type bathing cutie on it. The name scrawled in bold italic letters beneath it was invisible below the waves. This was the remains of a downed Liberator. There were no survivors.

Carter left the corpses of his fellow Americans behind and felt the desire to strike back rekindled in his veins. Without the raid he would still be pinned down on the beach. Now he had a weapon. A weapon with a destructive force hardly less than the combined weight of all the bombs now falling on Rabaul. How was he going to deliver it? He looked towards the cliff face which hid the main entrances to the caves and felt his top pocket. He still had the detonator he had been about to test in the volcano. He pulled it out and examined it. As far as he could see it was in perfect condition. He could take the barge in close, set the detonator, lash the wheel and jump overboard with Baka and Tukis. The barge would run up on the narrow beach and with any luck bring half the cliff down. But how much damage would that cause in relation to the tunnels? And what about Sula, Hudson and Green? Was he going to abandon them?

He thought of Sula and the possibility of never seeing her again. Not a possibility—it was a near certainty, dammit! His eyes were drawn to the cliffs again. She must be in there somewhere. They must all be.

As he looked he saw a bright red light flashing from the cliffs just above sea level. And then another, slightly to starboard. The lights were obviously signals. But to whom? Then he saw one of the barges near the beach give a quick answering flash. It threw up a small stern wave and steered in on the light.

Carter was puzzled. Surely the skipper was not going to run his craft up on the beach and abandon it. For a few seconds it seemed that this must be what was happening. The barge nosed in against the shore, its prow almost touching the steeply shelving beach. Then, as Carter watched in amazement, the barge started to move slowly up the beach like some prehistoric reptile emerging from the sea. He looked again and realized what must be happening. The light was being flashed from inside one of the tunnels and was invisible from the air. It was a guide light for the skipper and a signal that the tunnel team were ready to receive his craft. The barges were winched up the beach and berthed in the tunnels. The red light Carter had been watching went out and another started flashing beside it. Another barge flashed and move in.

Carter was impressed. Inside the cliff the barges would be perfectly protected yet accessible to the docks. They could pop in and out like mice from the wainscotting. Inside the cliffs. The words repeated themselves in his brain, and the fingers of his injured arm gripped the wheel with a vigour born of new-found excitement. Was it possible? Could this floating bomb become a Trojan horse that the Japs winched into their stronghold? He began to steer towards the cliffs almost oblivious to the hell that was still breaking out all about him.

Oblivion did not last long. Alerted by the warning shriek of a 1700 hp engine hurtling out of the sky, Carter looked to port and saw a TBF-1 Avenger swooping in low towards him. A trail of machine-gun bullets accelerated towards him and a silver cigar dropped from the plane's belly. A torpedo. As the Avenger zipped overhead Carter spun the wheel and flung Baka and Tukis across the wheelhouse. The bales of explosives slewed across the deck and slammed against the side with a nerve-jarring thud. The stubby little craft keeled over at such an angle that it shipped water. The bales tumbled down and nearly vanished over the side.

Carter clung to the wheel and saw the seascape blur past. At any second he expected to feel himself being torn apart by the force of a gigantic explosion. The vessel began to right itself on its new course and he scanned the water anxiously. Gliding serenely towards him as if drawn by a magnet was a silver shape trailing a long line of bubbles. It was so close as to be recognizable but not avoidable. The prow was still coming round and as Carter braced himself, the torpedo missed it by a foot and continued towards the shore. He began to breathe a sigh of relief cut short when another menacing shape swooped towards him—a Zeke fighter. His instinctive reaction was to duck. Then he realized that there was no need. The Zeke was on his side.

The Zeke swept overhead in pursuit of the climbing Avenger and tracer started carving up the sky. The torpedo exploded harmlessly against a wharf. Carter brought the vessel round and resumed his course towards the cliffs. Two barges were moving up the beach simultaneously and another light beckoned. Carter looked about him. On the starboard side of the wheelhouse hung a signal lantern. What was he waiting for? There was only one other barge visible that was still at sea. Calling to Tukis to hold the wheel steady, Carter switched on the lamp. It glowed red, illuminating Baka's worried, perplexed face. Carter switched off the lamp and began to explain what he was going to try to do. He told the two men that there was no obligation to come with him. They could be dropped off to swim ashore. Baka looked at Tukis and both men shook their heads saying that they would stay with him. Tukis admitted that his decision was helped by the fact that he could not swim.

The shore was now two hundred yards away. Carter could see the palms hanging over the water and the dark shadow that was the mouth of the tunnel. The red light kept blinking. Two figures were waiting knee-deep in the water and there was a dark shape between them. Seen from afar they looked as if they were shaking a carpet. Carter surmised that the shape must be a platform or trolley on which the barge would be winched into the tunnel. He hoped that the men would be so conditioned by what was to them an everyday task that they would not pay too much attention to the crew of the barge they were berthing. Looking back, he saw that the bales were scattered all over the open hold. He told Baka and Tukis to place them together near the funnel and below the level of the gunwales.

The air attack appeared to have finished, as far as the docks were concerned, although the anti-aircraft guns around the airfield were still hammering away. A few fires burnt among the wharves and there was a dense column of smoke rising from the hillside above the town where a Liberator had come down. Men were calling to each other and flashing torches among the bomb craters. Searchlights combed the sky as if neurotically searching for actors to people a stage. The smell of burning men and machines drifted across the water. People were crying, dying or making the best of being alive.

Less than a hundred yards now. Eighty, fifty. Baka and Tukis crouched at his feet, clasping their bush knives. Carter could see the faces of the Japs clearly now. One of them wore a cap pulled low over his eyes. The other had a white handkerchief knotted round his head. Their hands came up to receive the prow of the barge. Carter cut power, sensing that he had left it too late. There was an angry shout from the shore which bore out his impression. The barge crunched against something and scraped to a halt. Palm fronds were brushing against the side of the wheelhouse. Carter trembled with tension and excitement. A grunt from the unseen Japs against the hull and the the sound of something cranking against the prow. Carter shrank back into the shadows, his heart ticking like a bomb. There was another shout. Discovery? He stooped towards the Mills gun that lay at his feet. Then there was a cranking noise and the sound of a hawser stretched tight. The barge trembled, lurched and began its journey up the beach.

The Trojan horse was on the move.

29

Yukichi paced impatiently as he watched the gang of men filling in the bomb crater. From where he was standing he could see the cliffs. It would be quicker to walk there than wait. Quicker but to no avail. Admiral Yamamoto would have to take this road to the airport. The crater would have to be filled in before he could move. Yukichi looked out to sea towards the east. Now dawn was breaking. The first fingers of pearly light were reaching over the horizon. Soon the sun would be up, showing itself gloriously as the emblem that adorned the national flag, reanimating in each son of Nippon that looked upon it a sense of faith in his country's unquenchable destiny.

Yukichi filled his lungs with the scents of honourable battle and turned away from the men repairing the damage to the road. He walked along a line of splintered tree stumps and past bungalows smashed almost out of recognition by bombs and looting. A dog ran past him with something in its mouth. Yukichi watched it disappear into one of the houses. No matter what the Americans threw at them they would never retake Rabaul. They could dig a crater six feet deep with their bombs and never harm the tunnels.

Yukichi came to an intersection and looked up towards what remained of the corrugated-iron building. The events of the last forty-eight hours had driven all thoughts of the House of Contentment and Love from his mind. Now the problem had been resolved by an American bomb. Except for one wall which abutted on the hillside and part of a steeply shelving floor there was nothing left, save a heap of twisted metal like crumpled silver foil from a pre-war cigarette packet. Saraps of scorched clothing flapped grotesquely amongst the rubble and an ambulance truck was taking away the bodies. Other men picked through the smoking ruins looking for surviviors. There must be some because there was the sound of a muffled voice from somewhere in the rubble.

Yukichi turned on his heel and started walking back the way he had come. The girls in the brothel should have been housed in the tunnels. Although indispensable to the welfare of the troops, they had not been considered worthy of sharing their accommodation. So they had died. Yukichi felt sympathy with them and anger against the flawed moral code that had consigned them to their deaths. At a propitious moment he would raise the matter with the General. With more tunnels in the process of being dug it should not be too difficult to find a discreet corner for the next batch that would surely arrive. If they travelled with the troops and serviced their physical needs, they should at least be entitled to live with them in the same degree of safety.

Yukichi noticed that fresh earth spattered the road and crossed to find a deep hole in one of the overgrown lawns. Projecting from it was the tail fin of an enormous thousand-pound bomb that had not exploded. Either the firing mechanism had failed or the bomb was on a delayed-action time-fuse. The Americans had dropped several delayed-action bombs in recent weeks and taken a heavy toll of men brought in to clear up damage. Yukichi turned his back and hurried away. It would be a disaster if the bomb went off when the Admiral was passing. He would have the street sealed off for twenty-four hours.

Yukichi had reached the end of the road and was in sight of his vehicle when the bomb went off. The blast hurled him forwards. He felt as if a battering ram had smashed his backbone and thrust the pieces into his rib cage. His ears sang and his nose was bleeding. Earth half-covered his body and spattered down like rain on the surrounding foliage. He tried to pull himself to his knees and then fell forward on his face.

Carter heard the explosion as the barge shuddered awkwardly across the road, but he hardly noticed it. He had more immediate problems on his mind. Shrinking back into the shadow of the wheelhouse he looked down to see a group of men parting as the barge approached the tunnel entrance. They were holding sand-bags. Carter saw the emaciated bodies in tattered shorts, and recognized faces he had seen at the prison camp. What were they doing here? His question was soon answered. As the barge entered the tunnel, its funnel nearly scraping the roof, the men stepped forwards and started laying lines of sandbags across the entrance behind it. They were making a wall three sandbags thick, presumably to keep out the lava if Matupi erupted. Two guards supervised, rifles slung over their shoulders. They carried canes which they were quick to wield if a bag was misplaced or not positioned fast enough.

Carter swivelled round to look in front of him. Two men operated the winch which was set in the side of the tunnel, with the hawser taking a couple of turns round a movable capstan set in a slot in the middle of two rails. Other slots receded into the tunnel suggesting that the capstan could be moved to accommodate more than one barge. At the moment, there were no barges ahead. The two men at the winch were not armed. The barge rocked on its trolley and came to rest with its prow nudging against the capstan. The tunnel sloped slightly into the interior so that the capstan acted as a buffer. Take it away and unhook the hawser and the barge would only need a slight push to glide into the interior of the mountain.

Carter thought fast. Baka and Tukis could take care of the two men on the winch. That left the two guards for him. He whispered to Baka and Tukis and dropped to his hands and knees to crawl from the wheelhouse. Now he was in the narrow gangway and moving past the smokestack to the open hold. He looked down at his Mills gun and prayed that it would not choose this moment to jam. The mouth of the cave was just beyond the stern and he could hear the hectoring whine of the Japs and the swishing of their canes. When he arrived at the stern he would be right above them. He eased off the safety-catch and crept past the bales of shiny death to take up a position beside the rudder mechanism. Looking forward he could see Baka waiting for the signal beside the wheelhouse. He extended an upraised thumb and rose to his feet.

The first Jap had his arm raised in the act of striking a prisoner and Carter shot him through the head from point-blank range. His head jerked back and blood pumped from the wound as the cane dropped and his knees buckled. The second Jap ducked and turned and a short burst clipped the sandbags before setting the back of his uniform smouldering. Flames leap-frogged the bullet holes to be put out by falling sand as he crumpled up beneath the punctured bags. The prisoners cowered, thunderstruck, unable to come to terms with what was happening. Carter vaulted from the barge to find himself face to face with the man he had knocked out in the prison hut.

'Christ,' said the man. The expression on his face suggested that even the appearance of the real article could not have prompted a stronger reaction.

Carter snatched off one of the guards caps and shoved it on the head of the smallest man present.

'Pick up that rifle and look as if you're guarding us,' he hissed. 'The rest of you keep working and listen.'

Sula lay naked on the table, her body spreadeagled and leather straps cutting into her wrists and ankles. Above her, a bright light shone down from a low ceiling. The dimensions of the room would have been claustrophobic in any circumstances. Carved out of the rock it was like a tomb. The room smelt of blood and urine and an indefinable essence which can only be distilled from pain and fear.

Namura stood near the door. He felt ill at ease although he did not show it. To be present at an interrogation was something he abhorred. Not because he had any repugnance for bloodshed but because he believed that it was beneath his dignity. However, General Koji had ordered him to attend, and the order of a commanding officer must be obeyed. He dabbed at the sweat that had been running into his eye-less socket and nodded at the interrogator to continue.

The interrogator was a toad-like man with thick lips and nails bitten down to the quick. He spoke slowly.

'I am going to repeat a simple question. Where were you

meeting the submarine?'

Sula closed her eyes tight. 'I know nothing about a submarine.'

Namura shifted impatiently, and the interrogator rightly interpreted this as a sign that his slowness in getting information was meeting with disapproval. He decided to change his approach. Perhaps humiliation would be the answer. He showed his yellow teeth in the mockery of a smile and moved closer to the table so that his thigh brushed against one of Sula's spreadeagled legs.

'You have two choices. I can be gentle with you . . .'

He let his words tail away and raised his hand in the air before letting it fall on Sula's breasts. He massaged them slowly and then, inch by inch, lowered his finger-tips so that they trailed across her belly and fell between her legs. The guard craned forward to get a better view. Sula jerked her head from the table and spat in the interrogator's face.

There was a moment's pause and then a sharp crack as his fist came down to shatter her nose. Blood splashed against the wall and the back of Sula's head hit the table with stunning force.

The interrogator's voice took on a chilling edge of harshness.

' . . . or I can be very hard.'

Sula fought to breathe. Blood was flowing into her mouth. She was suffocating.

Namura stepped forward and spoke in Japanese.

'We have no time for subtlety or finesse. You are a woman and we will find the simplest way to cut the truth out of you.'

He nodded briskly to the interrogator who translated his words and then turned to the guard. He held out his hand.

'Give me your bayonet.'

General Koji sat in his office and looked at his watch. Yukichi ought to have been back by now. There had been no word since his report that the barge had picked up the explosives and put out to sea. Perhaps the wireless room was too busy with messages relating to the bombing raid. First reports suggested that the Americans had paid heavily for their temerity. Seven bombers and three fighters had been shot down. Three bombers so badly damaged that it was highly doubtful if they could ever have returned to base. In return, three Zeros and a Zeke had been lost and considerable damage done to the runway at the airfield, making it difficult for the returning planes to land. The harbour area had received its usual battering but with minimal damage to installation, materials and personnel: two mobile cranes and an ammunition truck destroyed, one barge and a submersible barge—thankfully empty—damaged. Thirteen men dead, forty-five injured.

Koji looked at the telephone on his desk, anticipating that at any moment it would ring and he would hear Yamamoto's voice patiently asking why it was still impossible to leave for the airfield. He knew that the Admiral mourned the loss of his friends and aides, and wished to finish his tour and start reorganizing his staff with the least possible delay.

Koji stood up and walked to the door. He would visit the wireless room himself and see what was happening. He was eager for the latest details of how his brave soldiers had repelled the enemy, as well as news of Yukichi. The two guards outside the room came to attention and he saluted as he started to move across the open space towards the communication centre. A familiar whirring noise made him look to his right and he saw one of the battery-driven floats approaching with two soldiers on board. Koji frowned. It was laid down in brigade regulations that the floats would only be used for towing materials. Ordinary soldiers were expected to walk in the tunnels.

General Koji looked round for an officer or NCO. It was not his place to reprimand private soldiers. The two soldiers saw the General standing in the middle of the open space and stopped the float immediately. They jumped from it as if it were white hot and stood with heads bowed. Koji asked their names and what they thought they were doing. They told him that they had been on guard duty and were returning their weapons to the armoury. Koji told the men to complete their business and then report to their sergeant. They were to inform him that they had been riding on a float without good cause and ask for punishment. The men saluted and hurried the last few yards towards the armoury.

Koji went on his way and entered the communications centre, telling the men not to stand up but get on with what they were doing. He asked for the latest details of the raid and learned that a Zeke had been badly damaged when landing and the pilot killed. Planes could take off from the airfield but they would need another hour to get it fully operational. The corrected figure for enemy losses was now six bombers and three fighters destroyed.

Maintenance units were working flat out in the middle of the town to repair the main road which had been straddled by bombs and rendered impassable. Trucks trying to seek a diversion had become bogged down and there was now a traffic jam. Only track vehicles could get through. There was no word from Yukichi. Did the General wish to contact him by wireless? Koji considered and declined. Yukichi must be held up by the road-works. He would be back within the hour and by that time the airfield would be fully operational and Yamamoto could take off in safety. There was no need to cluck over his adjutant like a broody hen. Yukichi had proved that he was shrewd, resourceful and more than capable of looking after himself.

General Koji left the communications centre and climbed the stairs to his office. He paused outside the room he had placed at Yamamoto's disposal and listened. There was no sound. For a second he thought of knocking and giving the Admiral the latest news. Then he decided against it. Yamamoto would be working, planning, perhaps even getting some much-needed sleep. It would be best to leave him alone. In truth, Koji confessed to himself, he was grateful to find reasons for not appearing before the Admiral. He was too much in awe of him to ever feel completely at ease in his presence. General Koji entered his office and slid the door shut behind him. The two guards stood at ease and looked across the open space towards the abandoned float standing at the mouth of one of the tunnels.

Hudson sat in the darkness and instinctively glanced at the wrist where his watch should have been. How long since they had taken Sula away? Twenty minutes? Half an hour? He strained his ears for sounds he did not want to hear. There was little the girl could tell them even if she wanted to.

He got up to move to the door and found himself checked by the chain that attached him to Green's corpse. Not without repugnance, he half carried the body to a spot beside the door and laid it down gently. Poor old Greeny. Looking at that wasted body it was impossible to believe that the man had been capable of driving himself up the side of Matupi. A life that had been feckless and ill-disciplined for most of its length had suddenly concentrated itself wonderfully at the end. War had thrown down the ultimate challenge and Harry Green had accepted it gloriously. Hudson thrust his fingers into his breast pocket and retrieved the crumpled piece of paper that Green had given him. He unfolded it and held it up to the grill. By the faint light he could make out a map reference and two maps drawn to different scales. One showing an area of Edie Creek and the other, larger scale, indicating exactly where the cache was buried in relation to a building. The drawing was done with the shaky hand of a dying man. The writing was almost indecipherable. It seemed genuine enough but who was ever going to benefit from it? Certainly not the poor devil who had originally worked the claim. Or Harry Green. On reflection, it seemed like a very unlucky piece of paper to be stuck with. The guard's face loomed up at the grill and Hudson dropped his manacled hands. The guard scowled at him and turned away. Hudson stayed where he was, his nostrils straining for any breath of fresh air that penetrated the tunnels from the outside world, his ears listening to every sound.

The four Japs left the armoury and started to walk up one of the tunnels used for berthing the barges. They each carried a submachine gun and were going to relieve the crew of one of the anti-aircraft guns positioned on top of the cliffs. None of them was sorry to be leaving the stifling atmosphere of the tunnels. There was always a breeze on the cliffs and they would be able to light a fire and smoke out the lice which infested their uniforms. As they walked, a party of prisoners approached, accompanied by two guards. Some of the men carried spades. The Japs did not pay much attention. They certainly did not recognize the stooped figure in jungle green concealing a Mills gun in the centre rank. To the Japs these were just prisoners being marched to extend the tunnels. They would not be passing this way often.

The prisoners stumbled along in ragged columns and pressed in against the wall to let the Japs past. They waited humbly, spades on shoulders. The first Jap turned his head to speak to a comrade and saw the warning signal ignite in the man's eyes. He spun round and received the cutting edge of the spade in his neck like an axe blow. The other three Japs were engulfed before they could call out. A flurry of arms dragged them down and the life was choked or beaten out of them. Their weapons were reallocated and their bodies dragged on down the tunnel and thrown behind some ammunition boxes piled in a hawn-out alcove. There was the sound of heavy, nervous breathing as men looked at each other knowing that the die had been irrevocably cast. Then the untidy columns formed up again and the men in the Jap uniforms pulled their caps low over their faces and held tight to the slings of their rifles, aware that they might have to use them at any moment. The other weapons stayed with the men in the centre column. Now they had four automatics, including Carter's Mills gun.

Ahead, some light splashed into the corridor and there was the grinding noise of a machine. Carter urged his men to close up and keep marching. So far they had been walking in semi-darkness and the men in the centre rank with the weapons could be easily concealed.

The light came from a workshop area in which a man with a protective mask worked at a motorized lathe. A shower of sparks spilled across the stone floor. Other men were working at benches or overhauling a plane engine which was suspended on a pulley from the ceiling. None of the mechanics gave the prisoners more than a glance as they passed on their way towards the interior.

Carter looked ahead anxiously. Every step was taking them closer to trouble and further away from the explosive. What ever happened, somebody had to get back to that. Where the hell were the others? With tunnels going off to left and right it would take hours to find them. And it was impossible to march around with forty men, two of them dressed up as Japanese guards and failing miserably to look the part, if seen in anything stronger than candlelight, for more than a few minutes without arousing suspicion. He had bitten off more than he could chew and even forty men were not going to be able to help him digest it.

Ahead, the tunnel levelled out and opened up. A glare of bright lights stabbed through the gloom. Carter was wondering what to do when he heard the scream. Long and rising and piercing new layers of pain as it went on. Carter was running before the scream had entered its dying fall. He knew the voice as if it were his own. Sula. Somebody was tearing her apart.

Carter burst into an open space and saw two Jap marines staring at his ragged, bare-foot body in amazement. The scream started again and he was running before they had unslung their weapons. Up another corridor, past a blaze of lights. One of the marines came to his senses and dropped on one knee to take aim. He threw up his automatic and a burst of bullets from the tunnel mouth cut him down and sent him pitching forward with his face hanging over the ledge. The second guard swung round to return the fire and went down in a heap as bullets pock-marked the wall behind him. Men began to flood into the open space.

Carter found himself outside a door with the scream filling his ears. There was a madness in him that could have kicked down a brick wall. His boot lashed out and the door burst open with a noise like a clap of thunder.

He glimpsed Sula pegged out on a table and three Japs, one of them almost on top of her.

Namura's eye-less socket was nearest the door. Before him he saw the guard's look of horror as he fought to unsling his rifle. Namura started to spin round, grabbing for his pistol. Carter shot him through the head and opened up on the guard, who jerked backwards as if pulled by a rope as the Mills gun stitched a line of waistcoat buttons down his belly. Then he slid to the floor, leaving a red trail on the wall. Now there was

just the interrogator standing pertrified with the bloody bayonet in his hand. Carter shot him through the heart and he fell
backwards on top of the guard. The air was full of smoke and
cordite.

Carter stepped over Namura's corpse and advanced to the
table. Sula's face was a mask of blood and her nose swollen
across her face like a hump-back bridge. There was more blood
between her thighs. She started to cry again but this time in
unbelieving joy at seeing him. He drew his knife and slashed
through the bonds at her wrists and ankles. He could see what
she had endured from the depth of the weals.

'Can you move?'

She threw her legs from the table and cried out as she put her
weight on them. Blood was running down to her knees. She
closed her eyes momentarily and gripped his arm, her face con-
tracted in pain. Then she stopped and snatched up the guard's
rifle. She said nothing but looked into his eyes and nodded, her
once beautiful face devoid of expression except in the resolute set
of its jaw.

From outside came the hammer of automatic fire and a volley
of shouts and screams. Carter watched Sula take two steps and
moved quickly to the door with her at his elbow.

'Where are the others?'

He slid back the door and peered out at floor level. He could
see men firing from the mouths of the tunnels. The air was thick
with smoke. In the confined atmosphere of the tunnels the noise
was deafening.

Sula's eyes roamed the corridor. She was clearly confused.

'I think—' She pointed uncertainly away from the central
junction.

Carter rose to his feet.

'You wait here.'

He started in the direction she had pointed. Sula came after
him.

Hudson heard the sound of shots and craned his head to see out
of the grill. His heart suddenly started pumping at twice it's

normal rate. Who was doing the shooting? It was beyond belief that somebody could be coming to rescue them. Some Japs must have gone crazy and embarked on a programme of group hara-kari. Then there was the sound of more shots and of a small battle breaking out. Hudson began to believe in the impossible.

Outside the cell his guard was clearly of two minds: uncertain whether to search out the action or stay with his prisoner. He ran a little way down the tunnel and then returned. The sight of Hudson's staring face infuriated him and he jabbed his bayonet through the grill.

'Better pack it in while you've got the chance, mate,' said Hudson.

The Jap screamed a volley of indecipherable threats and withdrew his bayonet.

There was the sound of more firing. Then a voice shouting his name. At first he thought he must be dreaming. Then he heard it clearly. 'Hudson! Hudson!' It was Carter's voice.

He threw himself at the grill and started to call out, 'Over here! Over here!'

The Jap turned and drove his bayonet straight at Hudson's face. It was diverted by one of the bars of the grill and narrowly missed his cheek as he started backwards. He tripped over the chain and fell. The Jap opened fire and bullets creased the air above his head. Carter was still shouting. Desperately he scrambled for the corner of the cell farthest from the door and nearest the wall of the tunnel. The bayonet swung round with him until the bars of the grill stopped it from moving any further. Bullets chewed chunks out of the soft pumice stone. Hudson dragged Green's corpse behind him and pressed himself flat against the wall. The Jap fired again but the bullet thumped harmlessly into the wall. Hudson was within the angle of safety. The Jap would have to come into the cell to get him.

There was a burst of fire from the tunnel and the bayonet tilted up crazily towards the ceiling and eventually slid from sight. The cell door slid open and Carter and Sula crashed in.

'What took you so long?' said Hudson.

Carter said nothing but sucked in a mouthful of air. He looked down at Green's body.

Hudson shook his head. 'He's dead,' he said.

The menacing chatter of a Nambu 92 machine gun cut short any thought of obsequies. Hudson rattled the chain.

'The guard has a key.'

Sula was at the door keeping watch. She started to drag the body into the cell and searched through the pockets, tossing the key to Carter. He went to catch it and suddenly found that his right arm would not move. The key dropped to the ground. Hudson snatched it up and grabbed the padlock.

'Is that arm bad?'

'It's not good,' said Carter.

Hudson unhooked the padlock and hurled it across the cell. His manacled hands tore at the chain.

'Right! Show me the way out of here.'

Carter gripped his Mills gun with his left hand and moved for the door. He paused and looked over his shoulder at the others.

'OK. Follow me.'

General Koji had heard the opening burst of fire with the same sense of astonishment as Hudson. It sounded so close as to be right outside his door. His first reaction was for the safety of Yamamoto. Drawing his revolver he had run for the door and tried to pull it open. As more shots sounded, he found the door difficult to budge. The reason was soon obvious. As the door slid open a few inches the body of one of his guards was revealed slumped against it. Koji squinted through the gap and saw that the mouth of the tunnel opposite was full of men. Ragged men, whom he recognized as part of Colonel Namura's work force. They must have overpowered their guards and seized their weapons. Another burst of fire sprayed the front of the offices and he scrambled back to his desk and snatched up the telephone. It was dead.

The situation was desperate. At any second the men might burst through the door—or worse—through that of Yamamoto's room a few yards away. Koji dashed back to the door determined to give his life to hold off the insurgents until reinforcements arrived. He was taking aim with his pistol when he glimpsed the sling of the dead guard's sub-machine gun an arm's length away. Lying flat on the floor and using the corpse as a shield he stretched out an arm and plucked at the air until his fingers close round the sling and he could pull the weapon to him. Scrambling to his knees he squinted down the barrel and felt for the safety-catch. It was not where he expected it to be. After a moment's surprise he realized that the model must have changed since he last fired it. He examined the weapon and quickly discovered what modifications had been made.

From the mouth of the tunnel opposite, three men made a rush towards him. He aimed at their knees and fired a long burst, wavering the muzzle slightly as if shaking drops of water from it. The first man pitched forward, losing his weapon, and the man to his right tried to pick it up. He, too, went down. The third man lost his nerve and ran for the shelter of the nearest tunnel. There was a belated burst of covering fire that splintered the door above Koji's head and then silence. Koji risked a quick glance towards the tunnel mouth and saw only the two bodies of the men he had shot. He had won a temporary respite. But how temporary? And what had happened to Yamamoto? There was another sign of movement in the tunnel mouth and he fired a discouraging burst. If he could just keep them at bay for a few more seconds, reinforcements must arrive.

Yamamoto was sleeping when the shooting started. It was his habit to take short, restorative cat-naps whenever a suitable occasion presented itself. In this way he found that the hours which other men devoted to sleeping could be more profitably employed. Quickly identifying the noise of automatic fire he swung his legs from the low bed and moved towards the door. He had taken two steps when a sharp pain stung him just below the left collarbone. His hand instinctively moved to the spot, and he was surprised to feel something damp and see a patch of red spreading out from beneath his fingers and staining his white uniform. He realized with a shock that he had been hit by a bullet. A neat, round hole was visible in one of the door panels.

The pain was not as great as his sense of surprise. Had his life

334

been spared one day only to be taken the next? It occurred to him that he was unarmed, apart from his ceremonial sword which lay on a small table. He drew it with difficulty and looked down at the shining steel. The act was a symbolic one. The thought of defending himself in a physical sense did not enter his mind. He was thinking of a poem he had written a few days before:

> I am still the sword
> of my Emperor
> I will not be sheathed
> Until I die

The blood has now spread to his medal ribbons and he crossed the room and lay on the bed. Looking up, the ceiling was bathed in grey light and he remembered how, when he was a child, the icy wind blew across the Sea of Japan from Russia and the snows came. Even in October the snow had fallen to a depth of twelve or fourteen feet in the village and the small thatched house had been buried until spring. Planks had been propped on poles underneath the eaves and these kept the snow away to form passages by which the people of the village could move from house to house, burrowing through tunnels dug at the street corners. Yamamoto had lain on the *tatami* with a blanket over him and gazed through the oiled-paper window at the imprisoning walls of snow that cut him off from the outside world. Now it was almost the same. He could even feel the cold, creeping into his bones. He closed his eyes. The noise of battle seemed a long way away.

When Carter emerged from Hudson's cell it took him seconds to realize that the odds were stacking against them. The sound of automatic fire was drowned by the heavy death-rattle of the Nambu machine gun which was spraying the open space as one might hose down a yard. He guessed that the prisoners had been held up at the junction of the tunnel—those of them that were left. It was only a question of time before they were overrun. Somehow, Carter knew, they had to get back across the brightly-lit intersection. And fast.

A party of Japs ran out of a side tunnel and Carter pressed back against the wall. Fortunately, the Japs were only interested in the area the shots were converging on. They started firing indiscriminately. It was clear that panic reigned and the Japs had no idea what was happening. If they had known what they were up against they would have been on their feet and charging. Parties of defenders were opening up from several different tunnels and this probably confused them as to the real strength of the enemy.

Carter waved the others back and then ducked into a side tunnel, piled to the ceiling with giant spools of signal wire. He looked about him quickly but there was nothing else. No convenient box of hand grenades. Hudson plucked at his arm and pointed ahead with his manacled wrists.

At the intersection of the tunnel with another of the main arterial tunnels was the square black bulk of one of the battery floats. Carter ran towards it and threw himself down against the wall. The noise of the machine guns was now deafening. He extended his head into the main tunnel and saw that the two-man team were tucked in against the wall with the gun mounted on three speedily-arranged sand-bags to stop the tripod sliding to the floor. They were pouring lead into the open space. A dozen Japs armed with carbines and sub-machine guns were edging down the opposite wall, clearly about to attack.

Carter turned to the float. There was room for four people on the narrow driving platform. The steel shields on each side were intended more as protection for the battery than for anyone riding on the float. Carter fitted his last magazine and looked at the others. Their faces were tense. Time was running out. They had to take any chance that presented itself. He ran forward and jumped onto the float. There was a driving wheel, a hand brake and an upright lever for engaging the power. Sula arrived at his left side and rested her rifle on the battery. Hudson was on the right of the platform. Carter took off the brake with his left hand and tried to press the lever. His arm let him down again. Hudson thrust forward with his manacled hands and there was a low whirring noise, virtually indistinguishable amid the rattle of gunfire. It sounded as if there was still somebody firing from the barge tunnel. The float began to glide forward and close the distance to the unsuspecting Japs. Carter held his Mills gun in his left hand and tried to take steady aim at the machine gun team.

The float was now building speed as Hudson hunched himself on the platform and pressed his shoulder against the lever. Carter squinted down the wavering barrel and pressed the trigger. The machine-gunner jerked forward and the barrel of his weapon slewed up towards the ceiling, still firing bullets. The second man rolled aside and found himself directly in the path of the float. He twisted again and one of the protective shields caught him a glancing blow on the head, which stretched him out senseless. The float charged on down the corridor. Sula shot two Japs at point-blank range before clubbing down a third who sprang before she could take aim. Carter was firing behind him now with Hudson desperately trying to steer with his manacled hands.

The float burst into the open space. There was a blaze of lights and the acrid smell of smoke. Bullets ricocheted off the steel plating, and the float lurched as it bounced over the outstretched arm of one of the dead men who had tried to rush the offices. Carter turned to see the choice of two tunnels and nearly struck a second float before swinging the wheel over and skimming through the litter of broken glass and spent cartridge cases into welcome darkness.

The scene around them was one of appalling human destruction. Those not dead or dying and still able to move were retreating up the tunnel, shooting out the lights as they went. Carter weaved through the pathetic remnants of men who had had nearly everything taken from them and were giving away what remained. They tried to run as the float went past and then relapsed into a stumbling walk as they cursed their wasted limbs.

Carter steered the float into the alcove where they had hidden the bodies of the Japs, and led the others towards the tunnel mouth, praying that they would not be met by Japs flooding in. He saw the silhouette of the barge against the lightening sky, and the sight gave him the strength to drive his exhausted legs forward. All he needed was a couple of minutes. Behind them was a violent glare of light and heat and a volley of terrifying screams. Carter turned to see that, fifty yards back, the tunnel was a mass of flames. The Japs were using a flame-thrower. Anybody in its path was being turned into a human torch.

Carter reached the barge and was met by Baka and Tukis, who told him that lorries were disgorging men outside the nearest tunnel entrance. Desperately he called on the two men to help him over the side of the barge, then urged Sula and Hudson to remove the capstan. He tossed his weapon into the barge and jumped to claw at the gunwale with his good arm. Baka and Tukis pushed him upwards. He landed in a heap on top of the explosives.

Beneath him Carter could feel the barge trembling and Hudson calling for help with the capstan. The obscene roar of the flame-thrower sounded again and the screams of burning men seemed only a few yards away. Carter fumbled in his pocket and withdrew the detonator between two fingertips. Unable to use his right arm, he immediately dropped it between the bales. Shots started to screech off the hull. His face pressed against the bags, Carter forced his arm between the loads and stretched out the fingers desperately. There was a warning shout from below. The barge was beginning to slide forward. Carter pulled out the detonator and pressed the minimum setting. He could feel the barge moving. He thrust the thin tube beneath the rough twine and rolled over the side as the barge gathered speed. He fell clumsily and lay half-stunned as bullets spattered around him and the terrible heat of the flame-thrower scorched his cheeks. Then the firing stopped and there were shouts of warning and alarm to join the screams of pain.

Carter did not wait but drove for the tunnel entrance with every ounce of strength left in his body. Baka and Tukis had fled. Hudson and Sula were in front of him and he could already see the palms and smell fresh air. He dived over the sandbags and glimpsed a row of trucks a hundred yards down the road. There were shouts and then a machine gun opened up. With Sula and Hudson by his side he raced across the road and into the coconut palms.

Koji emerged from Yamamoto's room with tears in his eyes. He looked around desperately and saw a medical orderly kneeling by one of the guards. He started to call to him and then looked up. There was a strange noise approaching down one of the tunnels. A shaking, shuddering grating roar, it sounded like a tank out of control. Koji glimpsed a shower of sparks and realized what it was, seconds before the prow of the barge burst into the open area with its smokestack scraping the tunnel roof. The trolley disintegrated, and the barge spun round, slithering broadside against the ledge, to stop with a thunderous crash. There was a pause in which the dust began to settle and men began to scramble to their feet. Then the barge exploded.

As seen from the outside, the explosion lifted the cliffs five feet into the air and then dropped them in an untidy heap. A column of orange and yellow flame burst from the ground, as if a gas jet had been turned up. The tunnel exits spewed forth men, machines and matter. Trees that stood in the way were blasted into pieces. A mushroom cloud of thick black smoke climbed high into the sky and layers of cliff collapsed into the road, burying men and trucks, and spilling rocks almost to the water's edge. Long after the first explosion, the ground shook as subterranean fuel and ammunition dumps were ignited by the intense heat. No subsequent noise compared with that of the first bang, a full-blooded clout to the eardrums that left the hearer dizzy and giddy, the inhabitant of a twilight world where all the senses were turned down to the wattage of flickering candles.

Carter lay on his face in the sand and felt the hurricane roar over his head. He could sense the palms straining before the blast, their trunks bending to within an inch of snapping, their roots desperately clinging to the ground. He could hear the avalanche of stone crashing down on the road, the splash of rocks dropping like mortar shells into the sea. With every second he expected to be engulfed or smashed to pieces. There seemed to be no end to the enormous weight of earth that had been belched into the air. It was only when the roar had become a rumble and the rumble a trickle that he opened his eyes and looked around. Palms were torn out of the ground, the road had disappeared. The cliffs were now a scree wreathed in thick clouds of red dust. Flames danced above the turned earth.

Carter rose unsteadily to his feet, his ears ringing. He gazed about him through the blasted palms and suddenly remembered the two Japs who had guided his barge onto the trolley. There was no sign of them. He took half a dozen painful steps and leaned against a palm. The trunk was the same colour as the sand and the sky and the sea. Everything was grey. He closed his eyes and opened them to see movement in the trees ahead. He dropped to his knees and felt a wave of dizziness and nausea sweep over him. Then he started to crawl for cover and toppled over on his side. With a start of fear he realized that his strength had given out. This was it. He could not go any further.

'Will! Good God, boy, are you all right?' Hudson's voice sounded against his ear. The manacled hands were gripping his shoulder.

'We've found the canoe. Come on.'

Carter allowed himself to be hauled to his feet and accepted Hudson's support through the palms. He started to look about him.

'Baka and the other guy,' he asked. 'Did they—?'

'They're OK. I told them to beat it.'

Carter felt relieved. Before him was the sea. Thousands of ivory-white fragments of coral lay like an unending carpet along the water's edge. The canoe straddled them. It was a dug-out with an outrigger and three paddles.

Sula had been collecting palm fronds for shade and coconuts for food. She dropped two nuts into the bottom of the boat and ran up the beach to throw her arms around him. For a few seconds he could feel her heart beating against his.

Hudson moved on towards the canoe and started pushing it into the water. There was hardly a ripple to disturb the surface.

Carter looked down at Sula and stroked the back of her head. Out to sea, the sun was starting to rise. The grey mist lifted from his eyes and his head cleared. With a growing sense of amazement he put his good arm around Sula and started to move towards the canoe. They were actually going to make it.

Yukichi leaned the barrel of his pistol against the palm and tried to hold it steady. The pain in his back was excruciating but he fought to maintain control of his senses. The tall man was holding the prow of the canoe. The girl was climbing into it. Now came the man he wanted more than either of the others. The man whose existence he had only learned of a few hours before. The man who had outwitted him until this, the very last turn of the cards. Yukichi closed one eye and squinted down the barrel. A fresh wave of pain broke over him but he conquered it. The sight wavered over the centre of his target. Yukichi's finger tightened. At that instant, the first rays of sun broke over the horizon and the picture before Yukichi's eyes disappeared into a dazzle of orange. His pressure on the trigger slackened. It was no good. He would have to run forward and fire from point-blank range. He grit his teeth and lowered his pistol to waist level so that he could hold it steady between two hands. Now he was ready. He would die with honour.

Carter looked at what had once been the cliffs. Fires were still burning but the eerie silence was now broken by the calls of men who could be glimpsed clambering over the rubble. Soon they would start moving away the earth, and the cycle of human activity would start all over again. He took a step towards the canoe and gazed up at Matupi. The eastern face of the volcano was painted a soft pink by the first rays of the sun. It looked almost benign in the early morning light. He turned back to the canoe. Sula sat in the prow. Their eyes met and she smiled up at him from her broken face.

'*Banzai*!'

Sula spun round, rifle in hands, as a Jap staggered from the palms with a pistol in his outstretched arms. She fired as Yukichi pulled the trigger.

30

The PT-boat had been searching for survivors from the two Liberators that came down after the big raid on Rabaul. After twenty-four hours of diligent sweeping that took it within sight of the coast of New Britain, it had found nothing and the sea was getting rough. The captain was about to return to base when Seaman Pervis, the youngest and newest member of the crew, swallowed his nerves and shouted that he saw something on the starboard bow. Older hands followed his pointing arm and saw what might have been a scrap of wreckage or driftwood lifting above the waves. Closer inspection showed that it was a dug-out canoe with outrigger containing two half-naked bodies lying side by side under a crude shelter of palm fronds and articles of clothing. They looked like corpses laid out on a funeral pyre. It was only when the noise of the engines came deafeningly close that they began to show signs of still being alive. The canoe was held steady with boat hooks and a party scrambled over the side to recover the bodies.

Pervis, who came from Burwell, Nebraska, and had always wanted to go to sea, was fascinated. This was the first rescue operation he had taken part in. He watched the swollen, sun-blistered bodies come over the side and winced.

'Jeeze!' he whispered. 'Are they going to live?'

'Sure,' said his confidant, Angstrom, who had been on the boat for three months and knew everything. 'They're in great shape compared to some of the guys we've fished out.'

'But his arm. It's hanging like a piece of string.'

'He'll be playing with himself in a few weeks,' said Angstrom. 'The human body is very resilient. Tenacious. You know what I mean? I've seen guys—air crew mostly—you wouldn't have given a plugged nickle for their chances. Burnt, covered in oil, their faces just smears, some of them.'

Pervis shuddered as he was expected to do.

'And they lived?'

'Shit,' said Angstrom. 'Some of them lived.' He stepped aside as Hudson's bush jacket was thrown onto the deck from the canoe.

'What do we want this shitty thing for?' he asked. 'The guy's never going to wear it again.'

A rating scrambled over the side and the men with the boat hooks released their hold. The engines of the PT-boat fluffed the water and the empty canoe started to drift away.

Angstrom continued to look down at Hudson's jacket disapprovingly. He hooked his toe under the torn, bloodstained cloth and flicked it into the ocean. The map to half a million dollars worth of gold was still in the breast pocket as it skipped jauntily on the long, white wake and then disappeared beneath the waves.

In the tiny cabin, Carter lay on a bunk and looked at the rivets a few inches above his head. The captain had visited them and Carter had seen his jaw tighten as he looked down at his arm. Their wounds had received routine attention and the captain had informed them that he had radioed his base with news of the rescue. He would try and get them back as quickly as possible.

Carter had drunk water until he expected to see it running out of his wounds. His stomach ached, his arm throbbed and he felt an intense bitterness. In the cramped surroundings he remembered the waiting to go ashore from the submarine. He thought of Sula coming through the mist to pick him up. He tried to swallow his misery. Now she was dead. Lying on the beach beside the Jap. Dead, along with so many other people. Johnson and Joe, the innocent women and children of Baka's village, the inmates of the prison camp whom they had set out to protect and ended up by sacrificing. And what had they achieved? Human beings had suffered and died but Matupi had not erupted. Carter turned his head and saw that Hudson was watching him.

He groaned. 'What a fucking mess we've made of everything.'

'You mean Sula.'

'Everything.'

Hudson shook his head.

'Yeah. We survived.' Carter's voice was weak but he forced himself to speak. 'If we'd stayed at Moresby we'd have survived and so would've a lot of other people.'

Hudson pulled himself onto an elbow and drank some water.

'Listen, boy.' His voice was uneven but he spoke with a passion that Carter had never heard from him before. 'Maybe we could have done it different or done it better but what we did was right. If you believe in something you have to fight for it. You can't just sit back and wait for the other guy to see reason. I have a stake in this country and only death is going to take it away from me—not the Japs.'

His head fell back against the pillow.

Carter listened to the creaking whirr of the fan.

'I know what you mean, but—?

He slowly spread the fingers of his left hand as he tried to find the words.

Hudson turned his head again. 'You don't think we achieved anything? You know who was in that tunnel network when it went up?'

Carter did not have time to answer before Pervis appeared in the doorway of the stifling cabin. He held a packet of Camels with two cigarettes protruding. After a closer look at the swollen, cracked lips, he tapped the cigarettes back into the packet.

'Hi,' he said uneasily. 'I don't know what outfit you guys are from but we just got some news that might interest you. 339 Squadron out of Guadalcanal have shot down Yamamoto. The little bastard's dead.'

He waited for sounds of pleasure and approval. There was a silence punctuated by a short, bitter laugh from the older man.

'Thanks,' said the man who he had heard the captain say was going to lose his arm.

Pervis was nonplussed. He shifted uncomfortably for a moment and then picked up a jug.

'I'll get you some more water,' he said.

There was no reply so he went out.

Carter stared at the ceiling and thought about Yamamoto. It was difficult to single out a response to the news of one more death, no matter how important the individual. His flesh would still rot, his wife weep, his children ask why he did not come home. He lay still for several minutes and then stretched out a hand towards Hudson and rested it on his arm. A lot of thoughts had been building up inside him and despite the pain and the fatigue he felt he had to make the effort to say them.

'I'm trying to see it straight, Andrew. I don't believe that every Jap wanted this war any more than we did. War corrupts you, it distorts your thinking. Your talents are frittered away on things that mean nothing. Look at what the Japs achieved in those tunnels, at what we did to get to that volcano.' He paused for breath and moistened his lips. 'Isn't it sick and sad that men's greatest feats of courage and invention happen when they're destroying each other? If this fucking stupid war does nothing else it ought to make people see that.'

The last few words could barely be heard above the mounting roar of the engines.

Hudson placed a hand on top of Carter's.

'It ought to, son. Do you believe it ever will?'

Postscript

A war historian with an appetite for statistics has recorded that 20,959 tons of bombs were dropped on Rabaul by Allied aircraft and 388 tons of projectiles fired at it from naval vessels. Despite this relentless bombardment, Rabaul was never successfully reinvaded once the Japanese had installed themselves after their invasion of 23 January 1942. It was bypassed by General MacArthur's island-hopping strategy and it was not until 6 September 1945, in the post-Hiroshima and Nagasaki era, that the then commander, Lieutenant-General Hitoshi Imamura, surrendered his 57,368 men to General Sturdee of the Australian Army on board H.M.S. *Glory* off Rabaul.

Not all the tunnel network was destroyed. A few tunnels are still penetrable. There are even the rusted hulks of barges that the Japs used to bring their supplies ashore. Other equipment rusts and rots. It may be that there are tunnels which hold secrets so far undiscovered. The Japanese naval radio station, hidden in a tunnel only a few hundred yards from the main street of the town, escaped attention for more than twenty years after the end of the war.

Although an eruption was recorded in 1969, Matupi has not seriously erupted since 1937. However, another Papua New Guinea volcano, Mount Lamington, exploded on 21 January 1951 with the destructive force of an atomic bomb, devastating 68 square miles and killing nearly 3,000 people with a 'burning cloud' of fragmented lava. A Volcano Observatory now exists at Rabaul and regular soundings of Matupi are taken so that advance warning may be given before it next erupts.

Lieutenant John F. Kennedy, later to become President of the United States of America, commanded PT-boat 109 in the South Pacific. When his ship was wrecked on a reef, Lieutenant

Kennedy was saved from the Japs by loyal natives and Coast-watcher Reg Evans operating from Kolombangara in the Solomon Islands.

General Douglas MacArthur was fifty-five years old and retired from the US Army when, in 1935, he agreed to undertake the reorganization of the Philippines Army, to all intents and purposes a dead-end job.

When the Japanese attacked the Philippines in December 1941, he led a spirited but unsuccessful resistance which culminated in his being ordered to Australia to become Supreme Commander of Allied Forces of all services in the South-West Pacific. In this post he proved himself to be one of the greatest logistic commanders the world has known and a man whose flamboyant egotism ensured that his enemies were not only numbered among the armies he fought against.

After victory in the Pacific, MacArthur became a much respected Supreme Commander in occupied Japan and, in 1950, when he was seventy years old, a brilliant but controversial commander of the UN forces in Korea. He was recalled by President Truman in 1951.

Errol Flynn arrived on a yacht from Australia in 1926. He spent seven years in New Guinea as a cadet patrol officer, planter, labour recruiter and gold prospector. None of the careers he embraced ever yielded him anything. Most of the ladies he embraced yielded him everything. Jealous husbands queued to aim punches at him but there is no recorded evidence of his ever having been bested in a fight. Harry Green's recollection of being laid out by a bottle was unusual. Flynn normally needed only his fists. He left suddenly in the direction of Hong Kong—and, of course, eventually Hollywood—leaving a number of broken hearts and jaws and an even larger number of debts. Shortly after his departure, the owner of a local hotel where Flynn had been staying opened a trunk that the future movie star had left behind. It was full of the hotel's sheets and towels.

As recorded by the Americans and Japanese, the death of Admiral Yamamoto poses many interesting questions, few of which have been satisfactorily answered.

When his plane was shot down in the Bougainville jungle,

none of the rescue parties sent to the spot were able to penetrate the thick jungle before a Japanese lieutenant on a routine patrol in the area was led to the wreckage by a native. He was apparently qualified to identify a charred body that had been thrown from the plane as that of Yamamoto. The body was taken by carrier and boat to the town of Buin. There, a shallow grave was hastily dug on the top of a nearby mountain and the body placed in it and covered with bundles of palm leaves and branches. Gasoline was poured on and ignited, and the resulting ashes were taken to Japan by destroyer.

It was not until a month after the arrival of the ashes that a Japanese radio broadcast announced that 'Admiral Yamamoto, while directing general strategy in the front line in April of this year, engaged in combat with the enemy and met gallant death in a war plane.' The announcer then choked and burst into tears. The announcement on Radio Tokyo caused a great deal of speculation in the United States. The *New York Times* commented: 'This indicates that he had not been killed outright but died later from his injuries.' The mystery remained because there had been no major activity in the Pacific during April. There were rumours that Yamamoto had committed suicide.

It may seem amazing that the American press, being armed with all the details of Yamamoto's death, should have had need of conjecture. But they did not have all the details. The American forces were strangely reticent about revealing just how their most hated military rival had died. Despite the morale-boosting possibilities of the coup against Yamamoto's plane, news of the exploit was suppressed until *after the war*.

Today, the reasons given seem singularly unconvincing. The first was that details of the raid would have alerted the Japs to the fact that their code had been broken. Since three of the Zekes escorting Yamamoto's bomber survived the American attack, it must be assumed that they were in a position to give first-hand information of their battle with a force numerically twice the size of their own which had suddenly loomed up from the Solomon Sea. What further information did the Americans need to provide to make the Japs suspicious? How could saying nothing lull Jap suspicions?

The second reason, produced belatedly, for not informing a revenge-hungry American public that Yamamoto had been shot down was that the brother of one of the pilots taking part in the raid was held as a Japanese prisoner of war and there was a fear of reprisals. This risk could have been obviated simply by mentioning neither the unit nor the pilots responsible for the attack in any bulletin that was released.

The attitude of both the Japanese and the Americans to Yamamoto's death does invite conjecture. Was it in fact his body that was identified amidst the burnt out wreckage in the Bougainville jungle? Perhaps it does not matter. Admiral Yamamoto did die in April 1943, and with his death Japan lost the one military strategist capable of steering her from defeat. The details of his death pale into significance beside this fact. Whether in the Bougainville jungle or the tunnels of Rabaul, Yamamoto remained dead.

All Futura Books are available at your bookshop or newsagent, or can be ordered from the following address:
Futura Books, Cash Sales Department,
P.O. Box 11, Falmouth, Cornwall.

Please send cheque or postal order (no currency), and allow 25p for postage and packing for the first book plus 10p per copy for each additional book ordered up to a maximum charge of £1.05 in U.K.

Customers in Eire and B.F.P.O. please allow 25p for postage and packing for the first book plus 10p per copy for the next eight books, thereafter 5p per book.

Overseas customers please allow 40p for postage and packing for the first book and 12p per copy for each additional book.